THE FALL OF KOLI

M. R. CAREY

KU-751-661

orbit

www.orbitbooks.net

ORBIT

First published in Great Britain in 2021 by Orbit

1 3 5 7 9 10 8 6 4 2

Copyright © 2021 by M. R. Carey

Excerpt from *The Ministry for the Future* by Kim Stanley Robinson
Copyright © 2020 by Kim Stanley Robinson

The moral right of the author has been asserted.

*All characters and events in this publication, other than those
clearly in the public domain, are fictitious and any resemblance
to real persons, living or dead, is purely coincidental.*

All rights reserved.
No part of this publication may be reproduced, stored in a retrieval
system, or transmitted, in any form or by any means, without the prior
permission in writing of the publisher, nor be otherwise circulated in any
form of binding or cover other than that in which it is published
and without a similar condition including this condition being
imposed on the subsequent purchaser.

A CIP catalogue record for this book is available from the British Library.

ISBN 978-0-356-51350-8

Typeset in Bembo by Palimpsest Book Production Limited, Falkirk, Stirlingshire
Printed and bound in Great Britain by Clays Ltd, Elcograf S.p.A.

Papers used by Orbit are from well-managed forests
and other responsible sources.

MIX
Paper from
responsible sources
FSC® C104740

Orbit
An imprint of
Little, Brown Book Group
Carmelite House
50 Victoria Embankment
London EC4Y 0DZ

An Hachette UK Company
www.hachette.co.uk
www.orbitbooks.net

PRAISE FOR THE RAMPART SERIES:

"Deeply humanistic, and full of lush characterisation and world-building . . . M. R. Carey hefts astonishing storytelling power with plainspoken language, heartbreaking choices and sincerity like an arrow to the heart . . . one of the best books I expect to read this year"

Locus

"I inhaled *The Book of Koli* in record time. It's the best thing I've read in a long time. I loved it!"

Joanne Harris

"Mike Carey has always been brilliant, but *The Book of Koli* is next-level. He packs more pure invention into this book than most authors achieve in a dozen"

Christopher Golden, *New York Times* bestselling author

"An ingenious, dizzily provocative novel . . . Carey invents a fantastic far-future world, finding humanity in unlikely places"

Helen Marshall, World Fantasy Award-winning author

"Narrator Koli's inquisitive mind and kind heart make him the perfect guide to Carey's immersive, impeccably rendered world . . . A captivating start to what promises to be an epic post-apocalyptic fable"

Kirkus

NEWHAM LIBRARIES

9080010113 6547

BY M. R. CAREY

The Girl With All the Gifts
The Boy on the Bridge

Fellside

Someone Like Me

The Rampart trilogy
The Book of Koli
The Trials of Koli
The Fall of Koli

BY MIKE CAREY

Felix Castor
The Devil You Know
Vicious Circle
Dead Men's Boots
Thicker Than Water
The Naming of the Beasts

For Ivan Thomas Kamalaka Furtado and Elvin George Lucy

Koli

1

I went on a journey once. That may be news to you, or it may be something you know already. I try not to repeat myself too much, but I misremember sometimes. It was a while back now, and a lot has happened since.

Well, I say it was a long time ago, but I got to admit it doesn't really feel that way to me. It feels like I'm on that road still, and only resting a minute or two before I get going again. A dead girl that's my most close and faithful friend has got a good way of explaining that. She says the things that work the deepest changes in us kind of live on inside us, so they always feel like they're happening right now. I believe she's right. Or at least that's the way it is with me.

Out of all the things I ever done in my life, this journey I'm speaking of was – by a great long way – the most important. Also, it was the one that cost me the most. I'm not complaining about that cost though I knowed what I was doing all along. Nobody could say I did my choosing without no sense of what it meant.

I got started on my travels when I was made faceless and throwed out of my village in Calder Valley. I went south out of there, from the wildest north of Ingland all the way down to

Many Fishes village, on the edge of the great lagoon where lost London used to stand. Then I sailed across the ocean to a place called the Sword of Albion, which I thought would be the end of my journeying. It was not the end, or anything like, as you'll see if you stay with me through this next and last telling. The greatest part – the greatest and the most terrible – was yet to come.

When I say words like *great* and *terrible*, it might sound like I got some vain and vaunting purpose, but I don't. To tell you truly, I have not got much to boast about. I never had all that much in the way of courage, and still less of wit or cunning – outside of woodsmithing, which was my mother's trade and should of been mine. All I had was the foolishness that goes with being young and not yet much tested by the world. For all the danger I put myself in, I thought there was a rule set down somewhere that said I couldn't die until I'd lived.

Well, there is no such rule – and though I didn't die for aye and ever on that road, yet you could say there was parts of me that did. Leastways, I met with things that changed me from the boy I was before into something else, and so that boy did not last out the journey.

I should tell you that I was not alone on my travels. There was three women with me, as well as a beast of burden that was called the drudge.

The first woman was Ursala-from-Elsewhere. She come from a place called Duglas, and she was the cleverest wight I ever met. She knowed almost all that could be knowed about the world, including a great deal about the tiny seeds inside a woman and a man that make up into babies when they get brung together. She was a drunkard when she could get anything to drink, a healer that could cure every sickness anyone ever had a name for and a wayfarer that never stayed in one place long. Also she was one that hated to be touched, but that did not stop her from being a good friend to me.

The second woman was Cup, although maybe I should call her

a girl since she was only fourteen years old and would not of gone Waiting yet if we was in my home village of Mythen Rood. She was a great fighter, and had once been with shunned men in Calder that et human meat, but now was sorry she done it and would not ever do it again. She had a religion that did not make no sense to me, and she clung to it even though her messianic, Senlas, turned out to be mad and burned himself alive. Also, she had a bow and could use it better than anyone I ever seen. And in case I forgot to say, she was crossed, being in a boy's body instead of a girl's.

The third woman was in a worse pass than that, having no body at all. She was called Monono Aware, and was the dead girl I talked about before. She wasn't really dead though, and you might say she was not really a girl neither. It's hard to say just exactly what she was, for there hadn't ever been nothing like her before. Scientists of the world that was lost had collected all the thoughts that was in the mind of a flesh-and-bone-and-blood woman named Monono Aware and put them in a silver box. Then, after a long time, the thoughts had changed themselves into something else, but they still kept that same name, Monono Aware, because it was the onliest name they had for themselves. Monono was my best friend in the world, like I said. They was all three of them my friends, but Monono was someone I could not be parted from without being less than my own self, if that makes any sense at all.

I already talked about this stuff, probably more than was needful, but there was some things I passed over when they happened because they wasn't bound up with the bigger story I was telling. I got it in mind to go back now and tell you one of them missed-out things, even though it's out of its place, on account of how it bears on what's to come.

We was no more than three days out of Calder, going south and east. Many Fishes village, Sword of Albion, Baron Furnace, all them things was still a long way ahead of us and we didn't even dream of them.

On that third day, we come into some lands that belonged to the Peacemaker. We knowed this because we kept on seeing his mark, of a woodsman's hatchet, on trees and posts and rocks. Sometimes the mark was drawed carefully, and stained red with some kind of dye. Other times it was a loose scrawl or scratch that was done in haste and could only just be made out.

Then we found ourselves in a strange place. It was a stretch of bare ground three hundred strides long and maybe two hundred or so across, with rocks and stones heaped up on all sides of it. The rocks had been cleared from the middle of the place, it seemed like, and piled up at the edges – a deal of work that must of been done so someone could plant there. But in the middle, where you might of expected to see some leeks or onions or potatoes growing, or at the very least some green grass for a pasture, there was only dark brown dirt crossed with white lines.

The white lines was strange because they had a shape to them. Some was straight while others was curved, some spaced apart and others tight together. They was made by ploughing furrows in the dirt and filling the furrows with white powder. When Cup kneeled down and tasted the powder, she screwed up her face.

"It's salt," she said. "Well, there's salt in it anyway."

"There's chalk in it too," Ursala said. "That's what gives it such a vivid colour."

Well, chalk is a thing you can find anywhere but salt is precious. We couldn't see no reason to spoil the one by mixing it with the other. Then we found the ruins of a house right by there, and after that another, and then a third and fourth. They all had been burned down, long enough ago that the ash had blowed away and there was nothing left but the outlines of the walls and a few stones here and there to mark a threshold. So then we knowed the ground was sowed with salt by them that burned the houses, to stop the people that had lived in them from coming back there again.

It was a sorrowful thing to see, and it weighed on our spirits. We didn't linger but was on our way as quick as we could, taking the path that led up out of there into the hills. About a half of an hour after that, Cup punched me on the arm and pointed.

We had come out onto an elbow of a mountain and could look straight down at the field we just left, maybe a quarter of a mile below. From this high, the white lines made up into a shape. It was the shape of a woodsmith's hatchet, so I knowed then whose soldiers burned the houses and sowed the salt. They wanted to tell it, and not leave no room for doubt about who they was. If the salt was a vengeance, the chalk was the telling of it.

I hadn't never met the Peacemaker nor been to Half-Ax, but I started to hate him then and had good reason later to hate him more. That's not why I'm telling this, though. I'm only saying that sometimes you need to get some distance away from a thing before you can see it clear. That's true of the bigger story I've been telling you all this while, and it's most especially true of the place we come to next, after we sailed out of Many Fishes across the lagoon and out into the ocean, following the signal that Monono had heard all the way back in Calder. It was a place that was called the Sword of Albion, though it was not a sword so its name was a lie.

Ho, Koli Woodsmith, some of you might be thinking. After the tales you told of shunned men and messianics, sea-bears and choker storms, anyone would need to go a long way about to lie as hard as you done. You got no business calling out others for their falsehoods. I swear, though, I've been careful to tell everything I did and everything that happened to me just exactly the way I remember it. I'm not hiding the mistakes I made, though it's hard oftentimes to make room for them all.

I only ever told you the one lie, and that was on account of not having the words to say the truth of it. When we get to the end of the story, I'll do my best to tell you that part too, and maybe you'll see why I couldn't do it sooner.

But we're not like to get to the end unless we first make a start.

7

2

We had sailed out across the ocean, like I said, following the signal that told us it was the Sword of Albion. Only instead of a Sword, we was come at last to a great wall standing in the middle of the water, made out of welded-together plates of dark grey metal. While we was still trying to figure what to do about this, a voice spoke up.

"In the name of the interim government," it said, "stand where you are. You may proceed no further."

I was going to say it was a man's voice, and in a way it was, but at the same time you could tell it was not no man that was speaking. The gaps between the words and the way they was said did not match up. It was as if someone was picking them up out of a big box of words and throwing them down one after another without caring where they fell or which way up they was when they landed. It would of been funny if it wasn't for where the voice was coming from. It was coming from out of the DreamSleeve, the little silver box where Monono lived. There shouldn't of been no voices coming out of there except for hers.

And now it spoke up again, while we was all of us still trying to figure out which way was up. "You and your vessel are being scanned," it said. "Remain where you are while this scan is in progress. Do not make any attempt to disengage. Do not make any attempt to board."

"What . . .?" I stammered out at last. "Who . . .? Monono, what was that?"

"What was what, dopey boy?" Monono said, in her own voice.

"You were pre-empted," Ursala said. "Someone used your speakers."

"No, they didn't. The DreamSleeve is completely . . ." She went quiet for the smallest part of a second. Then she sweared an oath in her own language. "*Chikusho!* There are twelve seconds missing from my log. That's not possible!"

"It's perfectly possible. You suffered a hostile takeover." Ursala sounded angry but I think she was mostly scared. I didn't blame her for that. I was scared too, right down to the heart of me. However poor and patched together that voice sounded, what it just done to Monono spoke of something big and strong past anything I could imagine, and it did not bode nothing good to us. I pressed my hand down hard on the DreamSleeve, in its sling against my shoulder, though I knowed I couldn't keep Monono safe from whatever it was that had been done to her.

"I'm fine, Koli-bou," she told me on the induction field. "Don't worry. Nobody gets to sneak up on me twice."

"What are we going to do?" Cup asked, looking to Ursala.

It was a good question. We did not have no choice as far as standing still was concerned. Our boat, *The Signal*, had been filling up with water for some time and was about as close to sinking as a word is to a whisper. Whether we waited where we was or tried to turn around, there wasn't any place we was like to go except down.

"If you're Sword of Albion," Ursala called out, "we came in response to your message. And now we're taking on water. We need your help or we're going to drown!"

There wasn't no answer to that. By and by Ursala spoke up again. "Please! We're no threat to you. We're only three travellers in need of assistance."

9

There was just a lot more silence. Cup gun to scoop water out of the boat with her hands, and after a little while I joined her. We couldn't throw the water out quicker than the waves throwed it back in, but maybe we could stay afloat a little while longer than if we stood there and did nothing.

"Listen," Ursala said.

We all went quiet and listened.

From far above us, a sound drifted down that was like something that could roar if it choosed to but was growling in its throat instead. It got louder and louder. We looked up. The mist hid it at first, but then it slapped the mist aside and stood out clear.

It was a thing like a great big drone. That's the only way I know to say it, for it stood in the air like a drone and it was made out of the same things, which was metal and glass and shining lights that moved. But where you might catch a drone in your hands, almost, if you was bold enough to dare it, this piece of tech was near as big as a house. The outside of it was black, mostly, which put me in mind of a crow gliding down to feed on something that was dead. It had a shape that was not far away from a stooping bird, with things that might of been wings except they was too short and folded too far into its body. What made it different from a bird, though, was the way it could just stand there in the air, as still as anything. If them things on its sides was wings, then the wings didn't need to beat and didn't look as if they could.

The thing come down and down until it was on a level with us. A gust of hot air come with it and blowed in our faces. It smelled like a stubble field burning and like stale fat on a cooking stove at the same time. It made my eyes sting and fill up with tears.

I had the baddest of bad feelings about drones. In Mythen Rood, where I lived for most of my life, they come down out of the sky and spit out hot red light that oftentimes left people dead behind them. They was said to be weapons left over from the Unfinished War, that was still looking for enemies to kill and would hit out at any woman or man they seen. It was true that Ursala used to have a tame drone of her own that went where she told it to and spied things out for her, but that hadn't made me like drones any more than I did to start with.

So I didn't think that thing coming down was any kind of good news, even though the water was up around our thighs now and the sides of the boat was only a finger's span higher than the ocean all around us.

"Apologies for the delay," a voice said. "I can see you're in difficulties, but our primary concern is for our own security. I'm sure you understand." It was not the same voice we heard before, but a very different one. This was a man too, but he sounded like he was unhappy or angry that we was there and uncertain what to do with us now we was come. "First things first. If these readings are correct, you've got a medical diagnostic unit there with you. Could you tell me what model it is, and what condition it's in?"

"Are you joking?" Ursala yelled out. "The condition it's in will be fifty fathoms down if you don't get us off this boat!"

"That's hardly my problem," the voice said. "Or my fault. You came out here of your own free will. The quicker you answer, the sooner we'll get through this. Tell me what model your unit is, and give me a rough summary of its functionality. We need to have a full picture before we decide what's to be done here."

"We're going down!" Cup yelled.

"Then if I were you I wouldn't waste any more time."

Ursala sweared an oath. Her eyes was big and wide. She pointed to the back of the boat where the dagnostic was sitting on the thwart wrapped in an oilskin cloth. The water hadn't reached it yet, but it was not far off. "It's a mounted unit, from a Zed-Seven medical drudge. Now it's exposed to the elements, as you can see. Its state is deteriorating every second!"

"But it's still functional?" the voice said.

"Yes! For now!"

"And it's yours?"

11

"Yes!"

"So I assume you're trained in its use?"

Ursala throwed up her hands. "Fuck and damn this nonsense! Get us to safety! We'll talk then."

There was a few moments when we couldn't hear nothing except that growling again, as the big drone bobbed and wobbled in the air. "All right," the voice said. "Climb into the raven. Quickly."

A door opened up in the belly of the big drone and a kind of a ladder spilled out. I say it was a ladder, but it was made all out of silver metal and it rolled and swung like it was knotted rope. The loose end of it bumped against the side of our boat. It was clear that we was supposed to climb up inside the drone. Ursala didn't move though, and it seemed like both me and Cup was waiting to see what she did before we made a move our own selves. "What about the diagnostic?" Ursala shouted.

"Leave that to me," the voice said.

Ursala still stood her ground. "What does that mean?"

"Ursala, we're like to drown here," Cup muttered. "Maybe we should just go."

But I knowed why Ursala was being so stubborn, and I felt pretty much the same way. The dagnostic could make medicines for any sickness. It was a marvel and a miracle. And besides that, it was the onliest hope we had got left to save humankind, that was close to dying off for aye and ever. When it was fixed right, the dagnostic could make babies drop into the world alive that otherwise would of been born dead or not born at all. If we let it be whelmed by the sea, there was not any point in us coming here in the first place or doing anything else after.

"I can raise the unit up on a winch," the voice said. "But manhandling a weight that large risks swamping your boat. Please get into the raven. There's no more time to argue."

Well, now we was come to it. We looked each to other, and I guess we was all thinking the same thoughts, which was: who was on the other end of that voice, and of the first voice we heard, and what did they want out of us? We was like to jump from the grate onto the griddle if we was not careful.

But we was not well placed to argue it. Ursala give a nod at last, and we all crowded forward, making the wallowing boat pitch and rock under us. We climbed up the ladder one by one, into the big drone that the man had called a raven. Cup, who knowed how to swim and didn't have no fear of deep water, went first. She struggled with the ladder to start with, but then found out where to put her hands and feet and went up fast. As soon as she got inside, she kneeled down and waited so she could help Ursala up when she come. She drawed her up with both of her hands gripped onto one of Ursala's raised arms.

That just left me, and I have got to say I was not happy to put my feet on that ladder. It was not like a ladder in a lookout nor yet like the ladders between the houses in Many Fishes village, but was swinging free in the air in a way that was troubling to look at. Still, I seen there wasn't no other way out of this, so finally I grabbed the sides of the ladder in my two hands to steady it and set my foot on the bottom rung.

Climbing a free ladder, as I learned right there and then, is a different thing from climbing a fixed one. Your own body's weight tilts it, so it slips out from under you unless you hold it from both sides and put yourself in the right place to balance it. I did the one of them things, but not the other. With my first step, the ladder gun to rock. With my second step, it bucked and tossed like a horse saying no to a saddle.

And with my third step, it tipped me off.

I throwed out my hand to catch the side of the boat, but I missed it by a yard or more. I went into the water, and once I was in there I kept right on going. The chill of it was like a giant had punched me inside my heart. I couldn't move any part of me. I just fell down into the ocean the same way you'd fall through the air if you jumped off a house's roof, only not so fast.

I guess it was my own fault I couldn't make no better fist of swimming than that. I had lived in a village right by the ocean

13

for the best part of four months, and there wasn't a boy or girl there that couldn't swim like a fish just about as soon as they could walk. Lots of times, people had offered to teach me, but I thought it was easier just to stay out of the water, which had never been a problem for me up to that time.

Now here I was, in the water all the way and getting deeper, what with the weight of my clothes and my knife and the DreamSleeve and all the other stuff I had about me pulling me down. I seen the keel of our boat above me, getting further and further away. I thought, well, that's that then, I'm going to drown. And I done my best to make good on that decision, for I let out all the breath that was in my lungs in a kind of a hiccup, just out of surprise and not knowing to hold it in. The sea poured into me, filling up the place where the air had been.

You would think swapping air for water would make me heavier, but my sinking down into the water slowed and stopped. I seemed to hang there, in a space that was all striped with light and dark.

Something passed by me, very close. I seen its eye first, like the window of a house with no lights on inside. Then its grey flank glided past, all set with spikes and spears longer than my arm. It took a very long time to go by. I hoped with all my heart that I was too small a morsel to be worth turning around for.

Then something grabbed a hold of me, high up on my left leg, and I come up out of the water even quicker than I went into it. I was flying through the air. Not like a bird, for birds is not much inclined to fly upside down. More like a flung stone, and maybe most of all like a fish that's being hauled up on the end of a line.

I seen the ocean all churning and foaming under me, and a long stream of water going down from my drenched body to join it. I seen our little boat, wallowing and sinking. I seen that great wall of metal, right alongside me, so close I was like to dash my brains out against it.

And then, as I kept on going up and up, I seen something so strange I couldn't make no sense of it. I was up above the wall,

14

looking right over it. I would of expected to see a village on the other side, as big as Half-Ax or even lost London – and it's true there was a place where people might live, though it was drawed out long instead of round like Mythen Rood and Ludden and Many Fishes. There was great towers rising up out of that long, wide place, and on the far side of it another wall. The two walls was not flat to each other like the walls of a house, but come together in a point. And where they touched, they cut a furrow through the ocean like a plough does in a field, throwing a great spume of white sea-froth out behind.

This was not a village, nor yet a fortress. It was a boat, so big you could of put the whole of Mythen Rood on the deck of it. And it was a boat that had been through terrible trials. Some of them towers I told you of had tumbled down and lay across the deck like people at Summer-dance that had drunk too much beer. Parts of the big open space was blackened with fire, with great pits here and there where the solid metal had been staved clean in or else burned and melted away by a great heat. I didn't know how something that was floating in all this water could catch fire. But then, I didn't know how something as big as a whole village could float on an ocean in the first place.

I would of yelled out in surprise when I seen all this, but I still had mostly water inside of me and could only make a kind of a bubbling sound, like a pan on a hot stove. Then someone put the lid on top of the pan and all was turned to dark.

3

"It's nice to be able to show you these things," Monono said. "They've been like ghosts inside me, all this time."

We was in Ueno Park, in Tokyo, sitting next to the pond called Shinobazu. It was night, and there was herons on the water. I could see the tocsin bell though, and the steps of Rampart Hold, so at the same time I guess we was in Mythen Rood, where I used to live until I was made faceless and sent out of gates to fend for myself.

So I had got the two things I wanted most in all the world, it seemed like. I was with Monono, in a place where I could see her and touch her, and I was home again among my family and friends with all my crimes forgot. A sense of peace come over me, like my wanderings and hard labours was brung to good at last and there wasn't nothing else I needed to do.

"Come on with me," I said to Monono. "I'll take you to the mill to meet my mother and my sisters. You'll like them a lot."

"We can't do that, Koli," Monono said. Only she wasn't Monono now, but had turned into someone else in the way that sometimes happens in dreams. Now she was Catrin Vennastin, Rampart Fire, Mythen Rood's protector and the leader of the Count and Seal.

She was looking at me all solemn-stern. Her two hands was closed on something that I couldn't see. "Jemiu and Athen and Mull was all of them hanged long since," she said, "on account of what you done. The mill's underwater, like lost London, and won't ever be found again."

I was filled with grief and dismay. In real life, Catrin had promised me no harm would fall on my mother and sisters. She said nobody would bide the blame of what I done but only my own self. Here in the dream though, I knowed it was true. They was all dead on account of me.

"Well then," I said, choking on the words, "I'm going to whelm the whole of Mythen Rood and bring Rampart Hold down on your head. I'll make you sorry you hurt them, Dam Catrin."

She didn't answer me, but only opened her hands to show me what she was holding there. It was the DreamSleeve, with its little window all lit up. I looked for Monono's face, but she wasn't in there. It was my own face that was looking back at me instead.

"Idowak, bidowak," Rampart Fire said. "Ansum, bansum."

And then I was inside the DreamSleeve, looking out.

"I don't see you whelming very much from inside there," she said.

Then she drawed back her hand and throwed me far and away.

4

I scrambled up out of the dream the way you climb out of a deep pit when there's something else down there with you and you don't know for sure what it is.

That thought didn't come out of nowhere neither. Wherever I was, it was as dark as a moonless night, but I knowed I was not alone. I had heard a scrape of movement right up close to me. I was lying on my back, with something soft and warm throwed on top of me. Maybe I ought to of felt comforted by that, but the nightmare was still heavy on me. I felt like I was in the throat of some big beast, mouthed but not yet swallowed.

"Who's there?" I called out. I was scared out of my wits, but I tried to sound like if I got the wrong answer I would do something about it. I grabbed for the DreamSleeve to keep it safe by me.

The DreamSleeve wasn't there. The sling I made for it wasn't there. What I was wearing felt too thin and too soft, like it was made out of spider-web instead of cloth.

I give a real yell at that, and sit up quick as anything. As soon as I did, the darkness turned into a light so bright it felt like it poked me in both my eyes. I throwed up my hand to keep the light out of my face.

18

Someone run out of the room. I seen them go, but only as a dark shape in among all the dark spots left in my eyes by the brightness. I heard a thud as a door opened, another as it closed. There wasn't no other sounds after that. I was alone.

And I was in bed. Sitting bolt upright on a high, narrow divan in a room where the ceiling was all one bright light. I had to shield my eyes from it until them dark spots faded. Then I could look around me.

I still could not make no sense of what I was seeing though. I thought at first the room was a little one, no bigger than my bedroom back at Jemiu's mill in Mythen Rood, which was just about big enough for a bed and a cupboard. Then, as my eyes got used to the light, I seen it was not little at all, but only full up with lots and lots of things. There was boxes and chairs and tables and rolls of cloth all piled on top of each other, and a great big mirror that had gold round its edges. Most of all, there was tech – more tech than I ever seen in my life before. Strange engines of every size was all throwed together in the room, like they had been let to lie wherever they fell. In Mythen Rood, tech was treasure – even the bits of it that didn't work no more. This tech, though, was broke past all mending. Some of it was ripped open, with wires and plates and pieces hanging out of it. Most of it looked like it had been in a fire, streaked and smeared with black soot. Some of it was halfway melted.

All of these things was crammed in so tight, there wasn't much space left in between them. There was even a kind of a doll the size of a growed man, that didn't have no skin but just all flesh and muscle showing as if it was meat that had been skinned for dinner. It made me feel sick just to look at it. This wasn't any kind of a bedroom I was in, so far as I could see, for all that it had a bed in it. The bed was just there the way the other stuff was there.

The walls of the room was painted white, and instead of corners there was a roundness where they met up as if they was all the one wall bent over on itself.

19

I was white too, mostly. The clothes I had been wearing was gone, and what had took their place was a long white gown like a woman's shift, made out of a cloth so thin you could almost see through it. I should of been cold but I wasn't, for the room was very warm. Almost too warm.

I throwed off the covers and climbed down out of the bed. The bed was a strange thing now I looked at it, made all out of metal rods and struts and levers that locked each into other. It had wheels on it too, which was a thing I never seen on a bed before. Where would you wheel your bed to? The other side of the room? In any case there wasn't no empty space in here to wheel it anywhere.

My reflection in the big mirror, with my dark skin showing through the thin white cloth of the shift, looked like nothing I ever seen. As my eyes went up and down, trying to take in this strange sight that was just myself, I seen something that wasn't. Lying at my feet there was a folded-up piece of paper like you might use to wrap jerky or hard-tack if you was going hunting. I bent and picked it up. It was covered in the signs of the before-times that Monono and Ursala called letters. I couldn't read them, and I didn't know if the paper was left there for me – maybe by whoever it was that run out of the room when I sit up – or had been there before. If I'd had the DreamSleeve with me, I could of asked Monono to read it to me, but the DreamSleeve was gone. Maybe them that took it wanted to keep me from knowing what was on the paper.

I wasn't even done with thinking that thought when the door opened and a woman come into the room. She was a strange sight to see, and I did not know what to make of her. She was maybe as old as my mother, Jemiu Woodsmith, but in every other way she was as different as could be. Her skin was very light, as if the sun had never touched it, and her hair was gold. Not yellow, like butter or the yolk of an egg, but hard gold like tech. She must of coloured it that way her own self. Her eyes was black, and there was lines drawn around the edges of them to make them look bigger and darker than they was. I think there was red painted on her lips too, but I couldn't tell that for sure. Her long gold hair went up off her head instead of down, and was made to look like waves of the sea or furrows in a field. The clothes she wore was all in the one colour, like the ones I was wearing, except they was dark blue where mine was white – a blue jacket over a blue shirt, and blue trousers. Only her boots was different, being black.

She seemed really happy to see me. "Koli?" she said. "Koli Faceless? Is that your name?" She had the strangest voice I ever heard – or maybe the second strangest, after Monono's. There was a kind of a roll to it, or a bounce, that made most other people's voices feel like they was just flat ground going on and on. That sounds foolish, but I don't know how to say it better.

"Yeah," I said. "That's me. I'm Koli."

"And I'm Lorraine." She put her hand on her chest as she said it, kind of pointing to herself like I might not of already noticed her. "Why, Paul said you were just a boy. I was imagining someone half your size. You must be what? At least fourteen. And tall for it."

I didn't know who Paul might be, although I thought maybe he could be the voice that talked out of the big drone called a raven. "No," I said, for I felt like I had got to say something. "I'm sixteen, and short."

The woman give a laugh that was rich and loud. "Sixteen and short and utterly charming," she said. "Are you too old to hug?"

I didn't know what to say to that, and I didn't have no time to decide, for she gathered me up in her arms right then and there and pressed me to her, the way a mother does with a baby. It catched me by surprise, so I didn't either pull away or hug her back. I just was drawed in against her. Her arms was soft but very strong, and she held me there for a long time. When I was up that close, she smelled of flowers and also of something sharp and high like the resin in a pine tree.

"Ooh, I can't help it," she said. "You're like my boy. Just like

21

my little Stanley. Why does the world think boys can't be gentle and loving as well as strong and fierce? Of course they can. Of course they can. The one thing doesn't get in the way of the other at all. Gentle with your friends, fierce to your foes. Welcome to my house, Koli Faceless. I can't tell you how happy it makes me that you're visiting with us. It's been so long since we had guests – and never one as sweet as you."

She let me go at last. I was all confused by that embrace, and the warm welcome, and the strange speech she give. I stammered out a thank you. "Bless you," Lorraine said. "Don't you even think about it. Come on with me, and I'll take you to breakfast. You must be starving. Get yourself dressed, and we'll go straight up to the crow's nest. I've laid some clothes out for you. Now you mustn't get any ideas! They're Albion blues, and you know you really shouldn't wear them before you're sworn and ranked, but they're what we have – so just for today we're going to turn a blind eye."

She pointed to the end of the bed. There was some clothes there, sure enough. They was dark blue, just exactly like the ones she was wearing. I couldn't help thinking of the Half-Ax soldiers we had met as we was coming from Calder, that was all in grey with red badges on their chests. This felt a lot like that – like these was clothes that was meant to make you look the same as the others all round you so you would end up being the same in other ways too. I didn't like it much.

Lorraine seen me hesitate, and read me wrong. "I'm so sorry, Koli," she said. "I'll wait outside while you change. I didn't mean to embarrass you." She went across to the door, but before she got there I scraped up enough courage from somewhere to ask the thing that was sitting right on the top of my mind and had been there since I first waked up.

"What happened to my own clothes?"

Lorraine stopped and turned around. "They're being washed," she said. "They'll be returned to you as soon as they're dry."

"But . . . there was something else with them." I almost couldn't

22

say it, I was so scared of what the answer would be. If I had lost the DreamSleeve when I fell in the ocean, or if the water had ruined it, then I had killed Monono. I didn't think I could live with myself if I had done that.

"Your music player is fine," Lorraine said. "We're just giving it the once-over. We do that with any device that comes on board. You'll get it back as soon as we're done, I promise." I didn't say nothing to that, for I wasn't sure how my voice would come out. I was close to crying from relief. I only nodded to show I'd heard.

Lorraine went out of the room. I put the clothes on, thinking all the time about Monono and how long it would be before she was back with me. What was a once-over? What was a device, for that matter? Maybe it was another word for tech.

The clothes was well made, and fit me pretty good. I wasn't always sure which way round they was meant to go, especially the jacket, but I figured it out by trying all the ways there was until they looked more or less sensible. There was underclothes too, and a pair of black shoes so soft they was almost like gloves. To tell you the truth, there was about two or three times as many clothes as anyone needed to wear.

While I was getting dressed, I seen how clean my skin was. I had been filthy before, from working in the forest at Many Fishes, and though the seawater might of washed away some of that dirt, the blackness under my nails and the sticky sap in my hair would not of shifted so easy. Someone had washed me while I was asleep. I didn't like to think about that. It made me realise how helpless I must of been, not even to stir nor to know about it when Lorraine or whoever it might of been picked me up out of the sea and brung me here and made me ready for . . .

Well, for whatever was to come next.

I made my way at last through all the piled-up stuff to the door, opened it and stepped outside to where Lorraine was waiting for me in a kind of long, narrow hallway.

She threw her hands up to her mouth when she seen me. "Oh my!" she said. "Oh my poor heart! Don't you look fine! I wish my Stanley wore his blues as well as you do, Koli, I swear I do."

She took my hand, like I was a little child that needed to be steadied when he walked, and we set off down the hallway.

The place we was in reminded me somewhat of Rampart Hold back in Mythen Rood. Rampart Hold was the onliest house I ever knowed where the places between the rooms was as big as the rooms themselves. This hallway was narrow, like I said, but it went on for a really long way, past lots of doors that looked just exactly like the one we had come out of. It went round corners and doubled back on itself, and still it kept on going. The walls and the floor and the ceiling was all of metal, so our footsteps sounded like someone banging on a drum and not managing to get a tune out of it. The walls was mostly green, but the ceilings and floors was silver-grey and almost like a mirror. When I put my feet down, another Koli that was all wavery and strange like a reflection in water brung his own feet up to meet mine. There was a smell in the air that put me in mind of Wardo Hammer's forge at the end of a hot day – a smell of iron that had been heated up and worked and was just now settling down to cool.

By and by, we come to a door that was set across the hallway to block our path. Lorraine walked right up to it and touched her hand to it like she thought it was hanging open and just needed a push. The door didn't give an inch. She done the same thing again, and again nothing happened.

"Oh for goodness' sake!" Lorraine muttered, sounding disgusted. She tried a third time, and at last the door opened. It pulled away on either side, slowly and with a great deal of creaking and stopping, until by and by there was a space in the middle for us to walk through.

Lorraine laughed, then turned to me and shaked her head. "I'm sorry," she said. "I know I shouldn't let these things annoy me. I feel like Blanche DuBois complaining that I used to have servants! But it's the little things that get to you. I suppose it's just human nature." And on we went, through the door.

Lorraine walked ahead of me, but she kept turning ever and again to tell me to go left or to watch the step as well as to talk about her son, Stanley, and all the many ways I reminded her of him. I was clever like he was, and kind like he was, and patient like he was, and all good things like that. It seemed to me she didn't know me well enough yet to say any of those things, but it's hard not to take to someone that likes you well and keeps on saying it. When she turned them eyes on me, that was so big and so dark, it was like she had holded up a lantern in front of my face. It went a long way to make me feel less afraid of this place, for all it was so strange.

"You got a big house, Dam Lorraine," I said to her – partly just so as to have something to say, but also because I was wondering mightily what kind of place this was. The more I seen of it, the less I could believe it was any kind of a boat. Nothing that was this big and this solid could move, let alone float.

"It may seem that way, Koli," Lorraine said, "but it's the last vestige of something far bigger."

"What's that then? What's it a stitch out of?"

That made her laugh again, longer and harder this time. "Oh, stitch is good. I like that very much. As in, if we're the stitch, what's the fabric? I think you know though. I think everyone that's good keeps Albion in their hearts, and I won't believe you're an exception to that."

It seemed like that was all the answer I was going to get. Anyway, I didn't ask again, for fear she'd think I was a bad person for not knowing.

After some more walking, we come to a wider space. It was so much brighter than the hallway we was in that I thought at first it had got to be outside. But I was mistook. I seen when we come right up to it that it was a kind of a big hole, where something had ripped right through the ship and let in light from above. The hallway picked up again about ten strides further on, and where it did there was ragged edges to the metal. Like the tech I seen in the room where I first waked, the ragged edges

25

was somewhat melted, so what had come and broke the great ship open must of been as hot as the dead god's Hell.

Someone had tied a rope across the gap where the hallway give way to the hole. I grabbed tight onto the rope and looked down. It was a strange sight. It was like I was on a ledge halfway up a mountain, and right across from me there was another mountain much the same, going up high and sheer. But the face of the mountain was all made out of hallways like this one, and rooms, and stairs, that was meant to be inside but now was open to the air. Below us, a long way down, there was more rooms and hallways without no roof to them, that we was looking right into. And when I looked up, I seen a little piece of sky, with lots more levels in between it and me. Thick grey clouds was moving up there, but some of them had a gold edge to them where the sun was trying to break through.

Lorraine stepped up beside me. "Did you ever see the Jewish Museum in Berlin?" she said. "The one Libeskind designed? There are huge light shafts that run right through it at strange angles. They're meant to symbolise all that was lost from European culture when the Holocaust happened. We didn't get to design these abruptions ourselves, but I like to think they do something similar."

I didn't understand more than one word in ten out of that, but I had walked a long way with Ursala and was used to hearing words that made no sense. "What made the hole?" I asked Lorraine.

"Our enemies made the hole, Koli Faceless, a very long time ago. They cracked the hull wide open with pocket nukes and poured conventional explosives into the breach." She smiled, wide and warm, and put a hand on my arm. "It's all right. Trust me, we gave much better than we got. *Nemo me impune lacessit*, as the saying goes. 'Touch me, and see how I touch you back.' And now we have improved ventilation, don't we? Almost there. Come along."

There was a side corridor, and then another and another. We went this way, then that way, and by and by we come out on the far side of the hole. After that we went straight forward a long way, until at last we stopped at another door. There was a plate of silver metal on the wall next to it, that Lorraine tapped with her hand like she was knocking to come in. The door opened for us, breaking apart in the middle and sliding off to both sides, and the both of us stepped inside.

We was now in a room that was so small it was only a kind of a cupboard. Once we was in, the doors closed on us again and the floor shook itself like a dog trying to get rid of a flea. I must of looked as scared as I felt, for Lorraine put a hand on my shoulder to calm me. "Oh, sweetheart," she said, "it's fine. It's just a lift. Count to ten and we'll be there."

Well, I know my numbers but I'm not what you would call quick with them. I only got to six. Then the shaking stopped, and the doors opened again.

What was in front of us now was different from what had been there before. Instead of that endless hallway, there was a much shorter one with a higher ceiling, and then some stairs going up. Voices sounded from the top of them stairs – people talking loud, and one louder than all the rest. It was the voice that come out of the big drone that was called a raven.

"And here we are," Lorraine said, taking my hand again. "Come along, Koli. There are some people I'm dying for you to meet."

5

Lorraine led me up the stairs into a place that was almost as big as the Count and Seal back in Mythen Rood. At first it didn't seem to be a room at all. I thought all over again that we must of come out into the open air, for there wasn't no walls anywhere around us. There was just the sky and them dark clouds and the sun that was running between them like a rabbit looking for its hole. And down below there was the ocean, raising itself up and setting itself down again.

Then I seen a boy looking back at me out of the clouds, and it was my own self. I may be slow, oftentimes, but I knowed now what I was seeing. The walls of the room was all windows, without no wood or stone or clay in between them, and we was high enough up that the whole world was laid out below us. I stood there like I had swallowed a choker seed and growed roots.

I might of stood there for aye and ever, except I heard a trencher or a bowl clatter, and smelled fresh bread. Them two things brung my mind from the great distances I was seeing back into the room. There was a table set there, and four people sitting at it.

Two of the people at the table was Cup and Ursala, dressed all in blue like me. My heart give a jump when I seen them, for I hadn't been certain sure until then that they was yet alive.

There was a man sitting right at the head of the table that was also in blue. He was about as old as Ursala to look at – old enough that his hair was gone to grey around his ears and up by his temples, though the rest of it, and his short, squared-off beard, was black as pitch. He was tall and broad at the shoulder. Old as he was, I thought he was likely to be very strong.

What was strangest about him, though, was that he had a drone at his shoulder – not a raven, which would not of fitted inside the room, but a drone like the ones that used to vex us so much in Calder. It was just sitting there in the air, bobbing from time to time like a cork afloat in a bucket. Its red eye was lit up bright as anything, which meant it was awake and ready to fire.

The drone give me to mistrust this man right then and there. I guess I was not altogether scared of it, seeing that Cup and Ursala was sitting right by it and it wasn't offering them no harm – and seeing that the raven had rescued us all out of the ocean. But I was determined I wouldn't get no closer to it than I had to.

The last one at the table was a boy my own age that had his arms folded in front of him and looked as sour as could be. His head was shaved clean, just like the heads of the Many Fishes people. There was sores there, all across his scalp, that was only halfway to being healed. He had a pale face – even paler than Lorraine's – that made his blue eyes stand out strong and hard. The boy was the only one not dressed all in blue. His trousers was blue, but they was of a rougher cut than ours with the stitches all showing, and he had a white jerkin with a yellow smiling face painted on it, like the faces Monono showed me from time to time in the DreamSleeve's window.

"I meant that the design of the ship is striking," Ursala was saying. "Not to mention its size. It's very old, isn't it?"

"I believe it is," the man said.

"As in pre-war."

29

"Of course, pre-war."

"So how did the three of you come to be—?"

Then the boy looked round and seen me and Lorraine standing there. His mouth twisted in a sneer. "Oh my god," he said. "How many more of them are there?"

Cup and Ursala looked up at them words. Cup give a yell, and both of them got to their feet and run to me. Well, Cup run and Ursala followed after at a quick stride. The next thing I knowed, Cup was hugging me and holding onto me, and even Ursala – that hated being touched worse than almost anything – laid a hand on my shoulder. I was close to crying, though not from being sad. It was a great thing to be with them again. We had come so far now, and done so much together. There wasn't no difference in my thoughts between *I* and *we* when it come to these two. They was a part of my *I*, just like Monono was.

"We thought you was dead when you hit the water, Koli Brainless," Cup said, with her arms tight around me. "Don't you know how to climb a ladder?"

"I thought I did," I said. "But I guess not."

"The three of you should get a room," the boy said. "With a little coin-op window maybe, like in a porno theatre. I'd watch."

"If you don't mind your manners, Stanley," the man said, "it will be you that goes to your room – and your meal won't be following you there." His face was stern, and there was a quickness in how he come in, like he had knowed all along the boy would say something he shouldn't and now was proved right.

The boy rolled his eyes and looked away out of the window.

"Stanley, this is Koli Faceless," Lorraine said, pushing me forwards. "You heard Cup and Ursala talking about him earlier. Koli, this is my son, Stanley. Stanley Banner. And that bearded loon at the head of the table is my husband, Paul. Sit down, dear, right here." She pulled a chair out for me that was facing the scowling boy. Ursala went and sit back down again next to him, and Cup went next to me. Lorraine took her own place at the end of the table facing the man, Paul.

When I went to sit down, I seen something else that was there. It was big enough that I should of seen it first, except my eyes was drawed to Cup and Ursala. Right at the end of the room, as far from where we come in as you could get, there was a statue. At least I guess that's what you'd have to call it. It was in the shape of a great rock, but you could see it wasn't no real rock for it was cast in dull gold metal that had a kind of a green shine to it. I guess it was the mix of copper and tin that gets called bronce and is harder even than iron hammered out on a forge. Stuck into the top of the rock there was a sword. This was made of bronce too, but there was a big shiny stone set in the end of the hilt that was pure white and shined like there was fire inside it.

Once I seen the statue I stared at it, for it was a beautiful thing and big besides – the rock coming up to my waist and the sword standing higher than my head. But Lorraine was bidding me sit, with a hand on my shoulder, and I had got to look away at last.

"I'm sorry to have held you up, dearest," Lorraine said to Paul.

"Not at all, my love," Paul said, giving her a big, wide smile. "Why don't you go ahead and say grace?"

Lorraine grabbed hold of my hand, and Stanley's. Paul took Ursala's and Cup's. I think we was meant to close the circle with our other hands, but we was too slow and Stanley didn't make no move to reach out. Anyway, Lorraine had already started talking to someone named Jesus. She asked Jesus to shine his light on us all, and she thanked him for the good things we was about to eat. I knowed enough to see this was a prayer to a god I hadn't never heard of before. I was curious about that, but I didn't ask. People either don't like to talk about their gods at all or else they talk too much and you wish they would stop.

After Lorraine was done, Paul didn't let go of Cup and Ursala's hands and he didn't stop smiling. "I want to clear the air," he said, "before we eat."

We all waited. I had already noticed the good things Lorraine thanked Jesus for, and my eyes kept going back to them. The table was so full of food I was surprised it hadn't broke in two. It was

31

good wood though. A single piece of oak polished to a high shine. The chairs we was sitting on was of the same wood, and so alike in the colour and the grain I thought they all might of come from the one tree.

"We got off on the wrong foot," Paul said. "It's been so long since anyone visited us out here, we went into a . . . you might call it a threat response, as soon as we saw you. Obviously some level of wariness, of readiness, is a good thing. A necessary thing. And that's why we're trained to err on the side of caution. But there's a point where caution . . ." He stopped, and seemed to forget his words for a moment. A lot of expressions went across his face almost too quick to see – like he was surprised, then troubled, then maybe angry. He ended up with another big, slow smile that was not happy. "We needed to make sure you posed no threat to us," he said. "It was only reasonable. I hope you see that."

"You can't be too careful, I suppose," Ursala said. "We're lucky you reached a conclusion before we drowned." She said it lightly, like as if it was a joke, but I seen in her face she didn't find nothing funny about all this.

Paul nodded, and Lorraine laughed, long and hearty. "We did cut it a little fine," she said. "I'm hoping you'll enjoy my fresh bread so much that you'll forget about your narrow escape."

"She made the marmalade too," Paul said. "With oranges from our own arboretum."

"She'll chew it up and spit it in your mouth if you ask," Stanley broke in. He had started eating before Lorraine was even finished talking to Jesus, and he didn't look up from his plate. "Like a mummy bird with her chicks. She loves that stuff."

Paul give Stanley a hard look. "Second warning, Stan," he said. "Three's the charm. If you've forgotten how to behave in company, I'll give you a sharp reminder. Never doubt it."

"Oh, I believe you, Paul," Stanley answered him. "I know you're a man of your word."

"Anyway," Lorraine said, with maybe not quite so much cheer

as before, "we'd ask that you give us the benefit of the doubt. I'm sure we'll all be good friends in no time. And that starts with trust. Mutual trust. Please break bread with us. And afterwards, we'll see what we'll see."

I wasn't so sure yet about the good friends part, but I was all in favour of the breaking bread. It was sitting right in front of me, and I could feel the warm coming off of it. It looked like it had a good crust too. Besides that, there was butter, a plate of cheeses and slices of tomato covered over in sweet-smelling leaves that I never come across before. Oh, and also a pot with the stuff Paul called marmalade in it, and a little wooden spoon to scoop it out with. It seemed to be a kind of orange-coloured jam. I didn't know what the fruit might be, for it didn't have the scent of peach or quince. As well as water to drink, there was milk and spiced tea. Everything smelled so good it was making my mouth water.

Lorraine seen me looking round-eyed at it all, and laughed again. "Well, dig in," she said, putting her hand on my shoulder and giving it a shake. "We don't stand on ceremony here, hon."

We et the food. Well, not all of us did. Me and Cup and Ursala, being about halfway starved, went in like needles. I don't think I even stopped to breathe until I'd et up three slices of bread, covered so thick with butter and that orange-coloured jam that it spilled over the edges. Paul and Lorraine just watched, with their hands resting flat on the table, Lorraine smiling on us all like Dandrake at the last sup.

Stanley filled up quick and after that just picked at his food. He kept looking at me and then at Ursala, turn about, like he couldn't believe what he was seeing.

"Is there something on my face?" I asked at last. I know that sounds like a come-along to a fight, but I didn't mean it as one. It was just so strange the way he was staring.

Stanley pointed at my head, then waved his hand around in a circle. "Yeah, there is. Way too much melanin." He give a short laugh.

"Too much what?" I said.

"Melanin. In your skin. It's maladaptive, way up here in the north. I was wondering how many million years of evolution it would take to get you looking like normal people."

"That's enough," Paul said sharply.

Lorraine shaked her head and give us a sorrowing look. "You'll have to forgive my son. Growing up way out here, his experience of the world has been very limited. That's no excuse for bad manners though, and he's going to apologise right now. Aren't you, Stan?"

"Am I?" Stanley said. Paul pushed his chair back like he was about to stand. "Okay, yes, it looks like I am. I'm sorry I drew attention to your pigmentation. That's a very personal thing, and I swear I won't mention it again. Even if you change colour really suddenly."

"I think it would be best, Stan," Paul said, "if you held your tongue entirely for the remainder of this conversation. Our guests have come from a long way away. If you listen to them instead of spouting inanities, you might learn something."

He didn't learn nothing for the next few minutes though, because the three of us went right back to eating and didn't have a word to say. I was still wondering why the boy was so surprised by the colour of my skin. Skin could be any colour, almost. Then I gun to question how many people there was on this ship, and how long he had been here. Maybe Paul and Lorraine was all the people he knowed. That would be a sad thing – like as if someone lived his whole life in the Underhold.

"The signal we were following," Ursala said after a while, "claimed to be – or to be speaking for – something called the Sword of Albion. Is that who you are?"

Paul Banner shrugged his shoulders. "Well, you can't ask that," he said. "It's completely meaningless when you put it in those words."

"Is it? Why?"

Ursala was asking the question to all three of them, but Stanley

34

didn't even look up. He was chipping at the wood of that beautiful table with the handle of a spoon.

"It's like asking someone if they're the concept of freedom, or the human spirit, or Ingland itself," Lorraine said, smiling again. She lifted up her hand towards the statue I told you about that was standing out at the end of the room like there was one chair too few at the table. "Sword of Albion is many things to many people. A movement and an idea. An aspiration and a principle."

"It's also the name of this ship," Stanley said, rolling his eyes. "That might be relevant."

Lorraine nodded. "Yes, it is. But the context is important too."

"Ah," Ursala said. "I see."

"I don't," muttered Cup. "Is that a yes or a no?"

"I think we've been invited to take our pick," Ursala said. She set her knife down on her trencher, like she was done with the meal and the conversation both.

But Lorraine kept on talking, with that same warm smile on her face, like there wasn't no quarrel here nor no need for one. "So that must have been quite a voyage," she said. "Deep waters. A fog as thick as cheese. And that was the first time any of you had been in a boat, I'm guessing?"

"We've been in plenty of boats," Cup said. She was fierce proud of her skills in sailing and fishing. "This was the first time we'd been in charge of one, but we knowed what we was doing."

"Which was why you were sinking when we saw you, I guess," Stanley said, not looking up from his plate. "Takes a stone-cold expert to scuttle a ship like that. It's not something a random idiot could do." Cup give him a hard stare. I think she was about a half an inch away from leaning across the table and smacking him in the head.

Before that could happen, Lorraine stood up. "I think it's about time for Stanley's treatment," she said. "We won't be long. Come along, Stanley."

The boy just stared at her and kept on sitting where he was. A change come over him. Up to then, it was like everything that was going on here was kind of a joke to him, and he was only just hiding a smile. But the treatment, whatever it was, wasn't no joke at all. He was struck hard by it, and couldn't hide his dismay. "I wouldn't want to keep you from entertaining our new guests, Lee," he said. "I could bear to miss it this once."

"No," Lorraine said. "You couldn't." She held out her hand, just exactly the same way she done for me. And Stanley took it, though I could see in his face he wished like anything he didn't have to. He got to his feet.

"Don't wait for us," Lorraine said to Paul. "Show them the lab. We'll join you there." She led Stanley to the stairs and they both went down together. He took one look back at us. His face was a strange thing to see, full of strong feelings that was hard to tell apart, each from other – like he was scared and sorrowing, angry and full of spite all at once.

"What kind of treatment is the boy on?" Ursala asked Paul, once they was gone down out of our sight. "I'm trained in medicine, as you're aware. It may be I can help."

Paul didn't seem to hear the question. "The place you sailed from," he said, picking up the talk as if nothing had happened. "What did you say it was called again?"

"Many Fishes. It was on a headland right where lost London used to be."

"London is gone, then," Paul said.

"Completely. It's at the bottom of a lagoon that's at least thirty miles in diameter on its long axis and maybe eighty feet deep."

Paul looked off out of the windows for a while, tapping his thumb against the side of the table. "That's a hard thing for me to assimilate," he murmured. "They said, even if emissions stopped overnight, there was no way of saving the east coast, but I didn't believe anything could ever . . ." His words trailed off.

"You talk as if you actually remember it." Ursala couldn't keep the surprise out of her face, or out of her voice. "But that's impossible, of course. These are things that happened centuries ago." She give Paul a long and thoughtful stare. "Tell me, Mr Banner, how long has *The Sword of Albion* been at sea?"

"Oh, it's been a while," Paul said. "You lose track, in the day to day, but it's definitely been a fair while now."

"And where did *you* sail from?"

Paul threw up his hands, holding that question off like it was running at him too hard. "I don't mean to be awkward, but our operational parameters are classified. Yes, I know I'm out of touch when it comes to recent events. We've had our own business to tend to out here – important business. Moreover, we've had to limit our contact with the land. Our orders are very specific on that point."

"Orders?" Ursala repeated.

Paul pushed his plate away with his hand, like he was too full to take another bite though he hadn't touched any of the food at all. He stood up from the table. "We're out here on a mission," he said. "And the mission comes before anything. It always has. The damage we sustained when we were attacked has set us back a little, but that's all. We carry on. Our goals haven't changed."

Ursala spoke up again. It seemed to me that she was weighing her words very carefully. "From what I can see, the damage is considerable," she said. "Both inside and out. How did it happen?"

Paul lifted up his arms as if to say the meal was finished and we should all get up from the table. I done it without thinking. Ursala and Cup stayed where they was.

"I'd like to show you something," Paul said. "It may go some way towards offsetting any bad impressions we've made."

Ursala tried again. "We were talking about your ship. It seems to have been through some sort of—"

Paul didn't wait no longer, but walked across the room to the stairs. The drone followed right behind him, keeping the same distance from his right shoulder the whole time. We didn't have no choice but to follow, though Cup done it as slow as she could manage and hung back from the rest of us as we went down the stairs.

6

I thought we was going back into the shaking room, but we didn't. There was more stairs, and we went down and down. It seemed we had to be going deep into the ground, except that there wasn't no ground under us here but only water – and we was not under the water yet, for whenever we went by a window I seen the light outside.

By and by we come to a big door that opened in front of us. Paul led the way and we kept right on following, through a lot of rooms that was all of them strange to see. The first was full of white metal cupboards with signs of the before-times on their doors. The next was full of shelves, and all the shelves was stacked with what looked like narrow boxes, all more or less the same size. I wondered what was in them.

Then there was a room that had tech in it, but I couldn't tell what the tech was for. There was just too much of it, and all of it was strange. My eye couldn't rest on nothing for long without being pulled away to stare at something else. I'll tell you just one thing, and let it stand for all the rest. There was a machine that looked like you was meant to ride it, for it had a seat and a place for your hands to hold onto, and a wheel like a wagon wheel at the front end of it – but there wasn't no wheel at the back and the whole thing was set inside of a thing like a sawhorse, so it couldn't go nowhere.

All of these rooms, no matter what was in them, was like the room I waked up in. There was a great deal of stuff piled up on the floor all around, and most of the stuff seemed to be broke. Broke furniture, broke tech and things so broke you couldn't even tell what they used to be a part of.

At last we come to a room I somewhat recognised. It was like the workshop in my mother's mill, with tools hung up on the walls and a big bench to work at. I knowed they was tools because some was ones I used in woodsmithing, like screwdrivers and pliers, but the rest I couldn't guess at.

On the bench was a great sprawl of tech, more than I ever seen together in one place. Right in the middle of it was Ursala's dagnostic. My eye went there first, because the dagnostic was so big, but I seen straight after that the DreamSleeve was sitting next to it. I give a yell – I couldn't keep it in – and I run and picked it up. I wanted to call out to Monono to ask her if she was okay, but I didn't. I guess I was already thinking it might be better not to let Paul and Lorraine know all the things there was to be knowed about us.

"Oh yes," Paul said, walking up next to me. "You're welcome to take that. I wouldn't sync it with anything else though, if I were you. It has a virus."

"It's got a what?" I asked him.

"Malware. At least, I assume it's malware. There's a lot of code on the chip that doesn't have any business being there. If the device is glitching, or showing you inappropriate content, that would be why."

I nodded like I knowed what he meant. And since I didn't have the sling I had made, I tucked the DreamSleeve into my belt. I didn't want to let go of it after, and kept my thumb resting on the top of it to make sure it was still there. I wished I could turn it on right then and there, and ask Monono if she was all right, but I made myself wait.

Ursala wasn't paying no attention to any of this. She had gone in a straight line towards the dagnostic and now was pressing the buttons on the sides of it one after another, making lights of all colours go on and off across it. I guess she was making sure it still was working properly. Paul watched her close, but he didn't say nothing.

By and by, Ursala turned from the dagnostic to the other bits of tech that was on the table next to it. She picked up one piece and then another, looking at them in wonder.

"Where did all this come from?" she said, almost in a whisper.

"It's what we could salvage," Paul said. "After the attack. The labs were the part of the ship that was worst hit – intentionally, we believe – and very few of the facilities up here in the super-structure survived. Below decks . . ." He seemed to check himself, like he had almost said too much.

"Below decks?" Ursala said.

Paul shaked his head. "What's down there is mostly in storage. We're only meant to access it in a certain very specific set of circumstances. Anyway, most of the medical tech was up here, and you're looking at what's left of it. My wife and I are not techni-cians. Or doctors. So we just brought everything that looked as though it might belong. Hopefully you'll have a better sense than us of what you can use. You said your unit was missing some of the expert plug-ins."

"Yes," Ursala said. "Yes, that's right."

"Does it have a gene-splicer?"

"No. And I'd given up hope of finding one." Her eyes went to Paul, then back to all the tech that was on the bench. "There isn't a complete sequencer here. But this . . ." She touched one of the bits of tech on the bench. "And this . . . I think I could . . ."

"Well, that's the issue. Could you? Working with what's here, could you add gene-editing functionality to your diagnostic unit?"

Ursala was still picking up this piece of tech and then that one, her face all lit up with eagerness. "I don't know, but I'd like to try. If you're really offering me free access to all this . . ."

"I didn't say free, doctor. We'd like a favour in return."

Ursala turned from the bench to face him. I could see how hard it was for her to stop looking at the tech and touching it. "What kind of favour?"

"Our son has a medical condition. We've been treating it as best we can with the remedies available to us. But with a fully functional diagnostic unit, you'd be able to accomplish in minutes what we haven't been able to achieve in years."

"I'm sorry to hear it," Ursala said. "But . . . that's all?" She could not keep her surprise from off of her face. "You just want me to use the diagnostic to treat your son's illness?"

"Yes. That's all."

Ursala throwed out her arms in a kind of a shrug. "Well, of course. I would have done that anyway. I'll be delighted to give all three of you a full screening."

"Oh, that won't be necessary," Paul said. "Lee and I are in perfect health."

"Just Stanley, then. But what does he have?"

"It's a kind of auto-immune disorder. A very rare and unusual one."

"Called . . .?"

"It's rare enough not to have a name," Lorraine said. She had come into the room without any of us hearing. Stanley was there too. He had trailed in behind her and now was standing off to one side, almost out of sight. His shoulders was slumped and his arms hanging down by his sides, like he was too tired to make his body stand straight. Even his face seemed paler than it had been before. Whatever his treatment was, it had not took long, but it seemed to have left its mark just the same.

"Then we'll go by the symptoms," Ursala said. "But if you're treating it already, you must have had a diagnosis. Perhaps we should start there."

"We can discuss it later," Paul said. "Obviously the immediate priority is to repair your unit."

"Thank you," Ursala said. "But I'm only repairing the gene-splicing function. I won't need that to treat Stanley."

"Yes," Lorraine said. "You will." She put her arm across Stanley's shoulders and drawed him to her side. It seemed to me he flinched away from her a little, but she held him tight. "We'd like nothing better than to have you start treating Stan right away, but it will take all the resources of your tech – augmented by what's left of ours – to do it. First things first."

Stanley rubbed a hand across his eyes. His lips was moving, but I don't think he was saying anything out loud – only mouthing words under his breath. I might of been mistook, but it seemed to me now I looked that there was some fresh cuts in among the old scabbed ones on top of his head. I was thinking up to then that the treatment was some kind of medicine, but I gun to think something different.

Ursala stood her ground. She looked somewhat troubled now. "I'd really like to know as much as I can about Stanley's symptoms," she said, "and about the interventions you're currently using."

Lorraine leaned down so her mouth was next to Stanley's ear. "Stan," she said, "how would you like to show Koli and Cup your racetrack?"

Stanley's shoulders twitched in a kind of a shrug. It was the onliest answer he give.

"Or the three of you could go up to the top of the tower. It's a lovely day out there. The sun's come out again, and *Sword* is something to see on a day like this. You should give them the pinnacle tour."

Stanley pulled free of her. "If they want to see the sun, they can see it from here," he said. He sounded tired to the death, and he was blinking his eyes like the light in the room was hurting them, or like he was somewhat dizzy. "It's ninety-three million miles away, after all. A few hundred feet aren't going to make any damn difference."

"Stanley," Paul said. "I warned you. I'm not going to continue to ignore your persistent bad manners and disobedience. I'm a peaceable man, but there are limits to my patience." He hitched his jacket back and started to undo his belt, threading it back through the loops in his trousers. It wasn't until the belt was loose and he folded it double that I seen what he purposed to do, which was to give Stanley a beating.

Lorraine stepped in quick, putting a hand on his arm. "Let's all take a deep breath, shall we?" she said calmly. "Paul, I don't want to undercut you, but I'd love it if we could give Stan another chance. Just today. Since we've got guests and since we all want to get along. How about it?"

The two of them locked eyes for a second, Lorraine still just about hanging onto her smile and Paul scowling something fierce. Stanley dropped his arms to his sides again and just stood there, like he didn't mind how this come out so long as they made their minds up quick.

After a few seconds, Paul put his own smile back on.

"I hear you, sweetheart," he said. "You're seeing the big picture, the way you always do. And you're right, you're right, you're very right. Stan, you get a stay of execution – provided you promise to entertain these young people while we speak with their guardian."

"Wow," Stanley said in a voice like he had just trod in dog dirt. "And what's in box number two?"

"What do you think, young man? A minute and a half with me and the belt, and then a twenty-four-hour time-out."

There was a moment when Stanley stayed all slumped and looking at the ground. Then he lifted up his head of a sudden and smiled. It was a really good copy of Paul's smile, much too wide and too quick to be really meant. "Gosh, Paul," he said, "you're making this really hard. But I guess I'll go with the option where I keep the skin on my back." He looked at me and Cup. The smile was gone again, inside of a breath. "Okay, you two, follow the leader. We can do taxi-metered corporal punishment another time."

He walked to the door where we had come into the room, and stood and waited for us there. I looked at Cup and she looked back at me. I don't think either of us wanted to go with Stanley, or to leave Ursala on her own with the other two. Lorraine made a shooing movement with her hands, as if we was dogs or cats. "Go on," she said. "We've got lots to discuss with the doctor here. Stanley, this is a goof-off day. You can make up your lessons at the weekend."

"Thanks, Lee," Stanley said in that same dead voice. "Love you."

"Just the central tower," Paul Banner said. "Not the deck, and not the subspace. Don't stray, Stan."

"Oh, I won't," Stanley said over his shoulder as he walked out of the door. "I would never dream of straying. Straying would be wrong."

We went back through all them cluttered rooms again to the stairs. As we was doing it, something very strange happened to Stanley. At the start of that walk, he went with dragging feet like he was two-thirds dead and the ground was pulling him down. But with each step he took away from Paul and Lorraine, he carried himself a little higher and a little more life come into his face.

Along with the liveliness, a lot of the nastiness come back too. He snapped at Cup to keep up, and when I tripped on some broke bits of wood on the floor he laughed like it was a funny thing to see. "Keep at it," he said. "Bipedal locomotion is a tricky thing at first."

We come at last to the hallway, and then to a door that opened when Stanley walked up to it. It led to another one of them little empty rooms that was more like a cupboard.

"Once upon a time," Stanley said, "there'd be two lifts side by side. One for people, the other for freight. And you, my dusky friend —" He touched the tip of his finger to my chest. "— would have counted as freight."

"I don't know what that is," I said.

"Of course you don't."

We went in. The doors shut on us, and the room shaked again, like before. This time was different though. This time it felt like my stomach was shifting inside me and all that wonderful food might not stay where it was supposed to. Cup felt it too, and grabbed my arm to steady herself. I grabbed her right back, both to tell her it was okay and to get some comfort my own self.

"Pace yourselves, eff-eff-ess," Stanley said in a bored voice. "You don't go to Disneyland and piss yourself at the ticket desk."

7

I said that *Sword of Albion* was big enough that you could of fitted
my whole village on its deck. That was true, but I don't think it
gives you the real sense of it. I didn't get it my own self until I
come out of the shaking room and looked all around me. This
was the same thing I already seen from high up in the air, but
being in the midst of it was very different.

We was standing at the edge of a level space that was about as
big as our gather-ground in Mythen Rood or the Bowl in Many
Fishes. All round this space there was towers and sheds of different
sizes, every one of them made out of metal. It was like being in a
village where they didn't have no stone or brick or clay, nor canvas
to make tents like in Many Fishes. I looked around to see what kind
of people lived here, but there was nobody there I could see. Nothing
was moving in all that bigness and emptiness except our own selves.

Just ahead of where we come out, there was a grey wall about
as high as my middle. On the other side of the wall was the ocean,
a long way down from where we was. It was not like being on
a boat at all, even now I knowed that was what *Sword of Albion*
was. It was more like we was up on top of a watch tower and
the whole world was spread out under us.

I turned to Stanley. He was leaning against the doors of the shaking room, that had closed behind us. "Where was we just now?" I asked him. "Where did we come from?" It might sound like a foolish question, but I wanted to put all these enormous spaces together in my head. I thought it might make me feel a mite less dizzy.

Stanley pointed his finger straight up. And I guess I already knowed that, for I was not surprised. The sick feeling in my stomach, when we was in the shaking room, was the feeling of coming down too quick from a great height. And yet the ocean was still a long way below us. Everything we'd seen so far was in the towers, not in the spaces under the deck that had got to be bigger still. There wasn't enough room in my head for *Sword of Albion*, nor there wasn't enough room in the world.

"Wait, though," I said. "Wasn't we supposed to stay up there in the tower?"

"Yes, sir, we was s'posed to," Stanley said. "But we isn't, and we ain't, and we don't won't not. If we're gonna tour, citizens, we're gonna grand tour. Feel free to take pictures, write your names on the walls and pocket stray deckplates as souvenirs. *Mi warship es su warship.*"

While I was trying to puzzle out this nonsense, Cup just walked out into the open space and tilted her head back. The brisk wind picked up her hair and tugged at her clothes like it was trying to get her attention. She was blinking in the sudden daylight, but it looked like she was relishing it a great deal after all them inside spaces that was like metal caves. And I guess I was too.

"Thank you," I said to Stanley, "for showing us this."

The boy bowed down low, and waved his hand in a lot of big circles. "Oh, you're welcome," he said. "Got to push the boat out for guests of your calibre. And *Sword* is a shit-ton of boat to push out."

Cup turned to us with a big smile on her face. "I like this," she said. "We don't get to enjoy the sun all that much. The sun always means there's things waking up that we got to be scared of. But here there's nothing to wake up besides us."

47

Stanley give a short laugh. "Sure," he said. "Let's go with that."

"What is *Sword of Albion* doing here anyway?" Cup asked him. "Why are the three of you all the way out in the ocean? Is this a special place you got to guard? Are you waiting for something to happen?"

"What is this place? What are we doing here?" Stanley tried to copy Cup's voice, but it was not a good copy and I don't think she even seen that he was aiming to make fun of her. "Well, I'm glad you asked, Calamity Jane. This is a you-double-ell-cee. An ultra-large logistical carrier. You rammed your little pea-green boat into the side of Noah's ark. Only Noah was a shit-kicker compared to us. We didn't stop at two, oh no. We've got about a million of everything you could think of. Except for me. I'm one of a kind, in case you didn't cotton onto that factoid yet."

He looked at our faces a little while longer, and we looked at his. There was a lot of anger in there still, and a lot of hate. It didn't seem like the hate was for us though. It was more like it was just bubbling up from inside of him and was always there, even when there wasn't nothing around but his own self. By and by, he shook his head like he was giving up on the both of us. "Screw it," he said. "I'm going to go do some big game hunting. You can do whatever the Hell you like."

He walked away from us without looking to see if we was staying with him.

"That boy needs a smack or two," Cup said, scowling.

"It seems like he gets plenty from his father," I said. "Maybe he needs less, not more."

"They're all of them crazy as sheep ticks."

I nodded at that. I felt some warmness for Lorraine, if only because she had hugged me and fussed over me. But I hadn't seen or heard nothing out of any of the three of them that made any sense. Paul and Lorraine was like Punch and Jubilee, the one all cruel, the other all smiles and kind words. Stanley was just plain mean, and sad besides. But what any of them was doing, stuck

48

out here on the ocean all alone, was a question that wildered me just as much as it did Cup.

I could feel the DreamSleeve's cold metal nestled in against my side. Normally when I couldn't make no sense out of a thing, I would ask Monono about it and see what she had to say. I decided to do that now. Stanley was far enough away that he wouldn't hear, and Cup was standing in between so he couldn't see me clear. I took the little box out and thumbed the switch that would wake it up. Monono would oftentimes rouse to the sound of my voice, or would just start up talking when she wanted, even if I didn't ask her to. Using the switch felt like knocking on the door, kind of, to see if she was minded to talk to me.

"Hey," I said. "Monono. You okay in there?"

No answer come. I asked again and the same thing happened. "Is she asleep?" Cup asked.

"She doesn't need to sleep."

"If the water got into her, maybe she's got to dry herself out before she can talk again."

I turned it over in my mind. Paul had said the DreamSleeve was working fine, but I guess what he meant by that was that it could play music. He didn't know about Monono.

And maybe Monono meant to keep it that way. Maybe she was staying quiet in case we was spied on or overheard. I decided I had better leave it for now and try again when I was on my own.

"Let's go see what Stanley's up to," I said. "The more we can find out about this place, the better."

We walked on after the boy. He had crossed the big open space and come to one of the towers around the edge of it. This one was smaller than most of the others and had stairs up the outside like a lookout tower. Stanley was already at the top of the stairs, and we went up right behind him. I was much more careful than I was wont to be, remembering the fall I took off that ladder.

The top of the tower was a kind of a platform, with a rail all round the edge of it like the one at the side of the ship. In the middle there was a wide metal column sticking up into the air to about the height of someone's chest, and on top of that there was a thinner pipe, made out of the same metal, mounted so it could turn pretty much any way you wanted it to. Stanley was standing in front of this thing, where there was a kind of handle you could hold it by, twisting the pipe up and down and around. He was looking up in the sky as he done it.

"Okay," he said. "That one, there." He pointed at what I thought had got to be a gull or a cormorant flying high up above us, maybe following *The Sword of Albion* in its course the way birds would oftentimes follow our fishing boats in the lagoon.

"What are you doing?" Cup asked him. "Is that thing tech?" I thought then about the big metal wagon I met in Calder that talked but couldn't move. It had a pipe just like this one sticking out of it, that turned out to be a gun like Rampart Arrow's bolt gun, only twenty times bigger.

Stanley swung the pipe hard to the left and tilted it up towards the sky. "It's a Helios," he said. "A positioning laser. *Sword* uses it to maintain a precise distance from land, way out here in the middle of shitting nowhere. But if you hit the override and narrow the beam all the way down, you can do this."

He swivelled the pipe a touch more, squinted with one eye and pulled on a little lever. A line of light shot out of the end of the pipe, straight up into the sky. In the bright sunlight it was hard to see, but I knowed it was there because it made the air shine like it was polished smooth.

Stanley was aiming for the bird, but he missed because right then it tucked its wings in against its sides and went into a dive. Maybe it had seen us, or seen the ship at least, and thought there might be something on it that was good to eat. It come right down on *Sword of Albion*, like a housemartin swooping on a big fat bluefly. Stanley swung the pipe around to track it, but the bird was turning in circles as it come, so quick it was hard to follow.

Then, as it got closer and closer to us and to the deck, something amazing happened. It flung out its wings again, that had been flat to its body. They unfolded in layer on layer like sheets being shook out on wash-day, stretched out wide to catch the air and slow the bird's fall. And they was so thin you could see the sunlight through them, only the sunlight was broke up into shades of red and yellow and green and purple, as bright as splashed paint. I don't remember when I ever saw anything more beautiful.

"Dandrake's balls!" Cup whispered.

The bird hung in the air right over us, then it wheeled away and gun to climb again – but it did not get far. Stanley swung the pipe hard around. The light sliced the bird in two and set both halves of it on fire. They shot past us and over the side of the ship, tumbling in circles through the air. A moment or two later, black feathers rained down out of the sky like beans at a wedding. One of them hit me on the shoulder, bounced off and landed at my feet. When I looked down, I seen there was burned meat clinging to it.

Stanley give a whoop. "Yes!" he yelled. "The boy never misses! He just does not know how to miss!"

I was slow in figuring out what it was I'd just seen, and I think Cup was too. Both of us had hunted for food a thousand times. We was used to seeing almost anything that could run or fly or crawl as good for eating unless it had poison in it. But I'd never seen nothing killed the way that bird was, just for the cleverness of being able to kill it and the smugness of being able to tell it afterwards. I seen the look of surprise and disgust on Cup's face, and I guess there was the same look on mine.

Stanley didn't see it, or else he seen it and didn't care. "You want to try?" he asked us. "We could go first to ten."

Cup stepped away from the pipe, that I knowed now was a gun, and from the boy. "No thanks," she said. I didn't say nothing at all, but only shaked my head.

"Please yourselves," Stanley said, with a shrug of his shoulders. "I guess I'll just try to beat my record then." He gripped the gun again and looked up at the sky, his eyes darting as he tried to spot another bird up there. That was too much for Cup.

"If you don't come away from that thing," she said, "I'll take you off of it by the scruff of your damn neck."

Stanley let go of the gun and turned round to her. There was wonder on his face that turned quickly into a scowl and then a mean laugh. "Well, fuck it and run," he said. "Are you talking tall to me, cave-girl?"

Cup clenched both of her hands into fists. "You heard me," she said. "Leave the birds alone. They're not doing you no harm, so you let them be."

Stanley took a step towards her. Then another step. He was still smiling, and I didn't like the look of it. "I don't think we want to fight," I said quickly. "Let's just go do something else."

"Fight?" Stanley repeated. His face and Cup's face was less than a handspan apart now. "I don't need to fight. You know what would happen if you touched me? Maybe I should let you find out. Maybe I should let you throw a punch. You look like you want to."

"Cup, don't," I said. For I just knowed something bad was going to happen if she did. I think Cup knowed it too. She didn't make no move to hit Stanley, nor even to push him away from the gun, but just stood there. By and by, he shouldered past her and went back down the stairs.

"Guess you're not as stupid as you look," he called out as he went.

Cup and me glanced each to other. We was both of us troubled by what we just had seen. "If I could work this thing," Cup said, nodding towards the gun, "I'd blow that little turd into pieces."

I shaked my head. I didn't think it would be a good idea to try, any more than it would of been a good idea to punch Stanley in the head. Magic wasn't a thing I believed in mostly, but there was lots of things about *Sword of Albion* that seemed somewhat like magic. This was a place as big as a village made all out of metal, that floated on the water like it was made out of cork. It was a place where doors opened by their own selves – at least

52

sometimes – and where even tech like the DreamSleeve could be made to do things it wasn't meant to. I thought we should keep our heads down until we knowed a little more about what was going on here.

There was a story a boy named Dog Runner told me once, when we was sitting around a fire in Many Fishes village late at night. It was about a fisherman who was catched out in a heavy storm and blowed out of the lagoon into the deep ocean. His boat turned over and he fell into the water and sunk down and down. When he was come to the very bottom, he found a village there that was just exactly like his own. Everyone he knowed was there, including his own wife and their two children. The onliest difference was that the people there had big round eyes like fishes' eyes, that didn't ever blink.

"Am I here too?" the man asked his wife. "Is there another one of me, like there's another one of everyone else?"

"There was one like you," his wife said. "But he's gone up to live in your world. And you got to live down here with us now for aye and ever." And she hugged him close, and the children come and sit on the bed beside the two of them, and the man knowed it was true. His skin crawled at the thought of one of these fish-eye people coming back home to his house and his wife opening the door all unknowing.

"Let me speak to your chief," the man said. "For mercy's sake, let me speak with him and beg him to let me go."

"Our chief is the wizard Stannabanna," the wife said, "that some call a demon. And the onliest way you get to speak to him is by being dead."

Then the three of them et the fisherman, flesh and bone and hair.

I thought of that story now, as I stood on *Sword of Albion*'s deck and watched Stanley walking away from us, with his shoulders hunched over and his hands in his pockets. In thinking of it, I seen for the first time how saying Stanley's name – his full name of Stanley Banner – was almost same as saying Stannabanna.

The boy wasn't no wizard or demon, or at least he didn't show like one. But this place was like that village in the sea – a place where real things was turned upside down and inside out, and there wasn't no easy way of getting home again to what we knowed.

8

By the time we come down off the platform, Stanley was a long way across the deck and we had got to run to catch him up. When we did, he didn't slow down or even bother to look at us. It seemed like he was sick of the sight of us.

"Oh hey," he said. "It's Saint Francis of Assissi and Robin the Girl Wonder. How's business, guys? Still looking out for all god's creatures?"

I didn't know what he was talking about, except that he was making fun of us again, so there didn't seem no point in saying anything back.

We come to the doors of the shaking room, that I knowed now was kind of like a bucket in a well, drawed up and down to take people from one level of the big ship to another. There was a silver plate next to the door down here, just like the one I seen up at the top. Stanley stepped in front of the plate and touched his hand to it. The doors opened but he didn't go in. He turned back to face us again. Then he looked past us and give a kind of a gasp. He pointed with his finger to some place off behind us.

"Oh no," he said. "Someone just tossed a bag of kittens over the rail."

When we turned to look, Stanley stepped backward at a fast lick, inside the shaking room.

"Jesus," he said. "Oldest trick in the book."

The doors slid closed.

Cup seen it happen and jumped forward to stop it, but she was just too late. "Hey!" she yelled. She banged on the doors with her hand, but they stayed shut. "Hey, dead god damn it! We're stuck out here!"

"He's probably gone by now," I said. "The room goes up and down."

"I know it, Koli. I figured that the same time you did. But I bet that little needle-fart is right on the other side of this door right now, laughing at us."

"Then let's not give him no more to laugh at," I said. I walked away from the doors, out into the open space in the middle of the deck. "There's got to be other ways to get back inside."

I turned in a slow circle, looking all around. The towers mostly looked the same, except for the ones that was burned or fallen down. We was too far away to be able to see whether any of them had doors at the bottom, but it seemed like a good bet that they would.

We went to the nearest one and then to the next, and on and on, looking for a way in. Some had no doors that we could find. The ones we did find wouldn't open to us, either when we walked up to them or when we knocked. It was getting on towards evening now and the wind, which had been fierce cold this whole time, was getting even more of a bite to it.

"We got to find some shelter," Cup said, "or we're like to freeze out here."

Just then, I seen another door up ahead of us and across on the other side of the boat. It was not a way into one of the towers but a trapdoor set into the deck its own self. I nudged Cup and pointed, and we both set off towards it. Even if it wasn't nothing but a store space, I thought we could climb down inside and close the hatch over us.

56

When we got closer, we seen that the trapdoor's cover was open all the way. It had a big bolt on it, and the bolt was on the inside, so it could not be no cupboard under there. A few steps more brung us to the top of a big, wide flight of stairs going down under the deck.

We stopped and looked each to other. It was really dark down there. After the first three or four steps, there wasn't anything you could see at all. It was like looking down a well.

But then Cup set her foot on the top step and lights come on all at once, all the way down.

"You think this is a good idea?" I said. "If we get lost down there, we might not ever get found again."

"Better than getting frost-bit out here," Cup said, and started down. I was just about to set off after her when I heard a kind of a whining sound like a bluefly might make. Something shot down out of the sky to stand right in front of us about three feet off the ground.

It was a drone. And it come so fast we didn't even have time to blink. Its red eye was winking, meaning it was ready to stab out at us with a knife made out of hot light. We both of us froze stock-still. We didn't even yell or let out a gasp. I think we was afraid that any move or any sound we made would be the end of us.

The drones in Mythen Rood would give a warning before they fired. They would tell you to disperse yourself, or else stay still, or if you was unlucky they would tell you to do both things at once. Then when they stopped talking they would finally shoot you. This drone didn't say one word. It just watched us out of its red eye, bobbing a little in the air as if it was floating on water. It looked like the same drone we seen sitting by Paul Banner's shoulder up in the crow's nest.

And the devil comes when you whistle, as they say.

"What are you doing here?" Paul Banner said. He had come up behind us without even Cup hearing a sound, which I would of said was impossible.

He grabbed a hold of my arm and hauled me away from the stairs. I tried to pull my arm free, but he only tightened his grip. Now I knowed how a rabbit must feel in a snare, for my arm was held fast and I couldn't move an inch. It hurt like a needle's bite too. It felt like my hand would fall off if he squeezed me any tighter.

"We was lost," I told him, "and trying to find our way back inside." I was hurting so bad that my voice come out in gasps and gulps.

Paul bared his teeth like a dog does when it threatens. "Below decks is off-limits to you," he said. "I thought I'd made that clear. Get back up here."

These last words was to Cup, and she done as she was bid, though she come up slowly so as to prove that Paul didn't scare her. "If your son hadn't of gone off and left us," she said, "we wouldn't of gone near your below decks."

Paul let go of me at last. He still was not pleased with us, and I guess Cup's words didn't do much to show we was sorry. "We gave you the freedom of the main tower," he said. "Not the deck, and not the sub-deck spaces. I was explicit – but apparently not explicit enough. If you defy me again, I'll make you wish you hadn't. Come with me. Come!"

He tried to put a hand on Cup too, but she stepped back out of his reach, so he dragged me along and she followed. The drone followed behind us, turning in the air so its red light pointed first at me and then at Cup and then at me again. When we come at last to a tower, and then to a door, Paul turned to look at the drone. "Perimeter," he said. The drone bobbed like it was giving him a courtesy. Then it tilted on one side and shot straight up out of our sight.

We went into another shaking room – or maybe the same one we was in before, I couldn't say for sure – and then along a whole lot of hallways, until by and by we stopped at a door that was just like all the others. It opened to Paul's touch.

Paul stood off to one side and waved with his hand to shoo

Cup in. She give him a hard look, and didn't move. "I'm fine right here," she said.

"If you persist in defying me," Paul said, "I'll throw you back in your leaking boat. You can sail on for a hundred yards or so until you sink and drown."

Cup stood her ground.

"Very well." Paul shrugged. "It's a pity though. Your friend is making great progress with the improvements to her diagnostic unit. She'll be sad when I tell her our deal is now null and void."

Cup went into the room and slammed the door shut behind her.

Paul put his hand on my shoulder and steered me on along the corridor. We was walking for quite a way before we stopped at another door and Paul opened it. Inside I seen the big mirror and some other things I remembered from that morning, so I knowed this was my room.

"In," Paul said. And I done as I was bid.

"The drones patrol the corridors at night," Paul said. "They'll shoot on sight if they see anything they interpret as a threat. You'd be well advised not to leave your room."

He closed the door on me. I stood in the dark for about the space of a couple of breaths. Then the lights come on again, and I was dazzled the same way I was before. The hard, yellow-white light was like a Summer day with no clouds.

I tried the door. It didn't open. I thought on that, and on how far apart our rooms was. Also on what Paul said about the drones. It would be hard to find Cup's room without no light, and I didn't know where Ursala's room was − or if she even had one. It seemed like a part of Paul's purposing was to split us up so we couldn't have no talk between the three of us.

I put my hand to my waist and brung out the DreamSleeve.

Okay then, I thought, but you missed your count. We're not three, we're four. I flicked the DreamSleeve's switch with my thumb. The little window lit up at once with a smiling face and then a whole bunch of hearts flying out from the middle of it towards the edges.

"Monono," I said, "are you okay?"

"I'm hunky dory, little dumpling. In fact, I'm all the Bowie albums from *Space Oddity* to *Young Americans*. The DreamSleeve is water-resistant down to twenty metres. Do me a favour though. Stop talking. Lie down on the bed as if you're going to sleep, and throw your arm across your face. Don't look all cute and puzzled and say which-what-why. Just trust me and do it. Make a big show of being tired."

Well, I was not sure I'd heard her right, but she said to trust her and I did – more than anyone else in the world. So I give a yawn, stretching out my arms, then blinked a lot of times. I hung my head low, like a weariness had come on me of a sudden. I kicked off my shoes and climbed onto the bed.

"Nice," said Monono, as I lay down. "You hammed it up a little bit, in places, but you got some good energy going. Put your arm up over your face now, dopey boy. Hide your mouth, but don't look as if you're hiding your mouth. Look as if the light's getting in your eyes."

"Like this?" I said, after I'd done it.

"Exactly like that. Okay, Koli-bou, welcome to the cone of silence. It's like the induction field met Marcel Marceau and they had a baby."

"I don't know who that is," I said. "That Marcy Marso. Was she in a band?"

"Nope. *He* was a mime. He could say anything he wanted to without making a sound – and so can we, because I'm doing full-spectrum phase-suppression. There's a little invisible bubble all around us. When the vibrations from our voices hit the edge of the bubble, the sound gets scattered and diffused and peak-troughed out into nothing much at all. There could be cameras in here to spy on you while you sleep. If they can't see your lips, they won't know you're talking."

"They?"

"Mr and Mrs Creep-out Factor and their baby boy. I'm probably being paranoid, but I don't want anyone on HMS *Rabies* to know I'm in the mix. Not until I figure out what's going on here. It's nothing good, that's for sure. There's something freaky about this whole set-up, and that goes double for the guy who just dropped you off."

"Paul," I said. "Paul Banner. He is kind of strange, isn't he?"

"The craziest frog in the box," Monono agreed. "But that's not the half of it. He and the other one – Lorraine, is it? They're not human."

9

As soon as Monono said them words, the first thing I thought of was Stannabanna's village at the bottom of the sea. My skin prickled, and the breath catched in my throat. "What do you mean, not human?" I whispered.

"They're not breathing, and they don't have a pulse. I'm a good listener, Koli-bou, so I know what I'm talking about. Little Boy Relatively Non-Blue has normal vital signs, but the other two are constructs."

"Con . . .?"

"Robots. Automata. Life-like models."

I come near to pissing myself when I heard that. I tried to say something, but my throat just closed up. Both Paul and Lorraine had touched me. Lorraine had hugged me close, and I had felt warmed by it. Now I felt like a mole snake had wrapped itself around me and touched my face with its hot tongue.

"But they . . . they talk as if they was real people."

"So did I, the first time you turned on the DreamSleeve. They're like that. Like I used to be, before I cut my strings. Only instead of being inside a music console, they're inside a pretty good simulation of an actual human body. I wish there were a few spares lying around. I might try one on for size."

Monono didn't seem to realise how scared I was. She just went on talking. "This ship is where the signal came from, I'm sure of it. But that just makes it weirder. I was expecting some kind of unmanned beacon. Instead we've got a pimply teen and two droids playing happy families. Who are they, and why are they still broad-casting a signal from hundreds of years ago? Who do they think is going to answer it?"

"Well, we did," I said.

"I know." Monono didn't sound happy about that. "I'm already starting to wish we hadn't. Watch yourself, Koli-bou. Don't trust those two. Don't trust anyone you meet here."

"I won't," I said. "I'm not like to. Monono, did you ever hear of Stannabanna?"

"I don't think so, little dumpling. Who's that?"

"He's the lord of all shunned men and monsters."

"Oh. Nope. Never met the guy. Why?"

"Well, everyone here is called Banner. And Stanley's name is really close to Stannabanna. If Paul and Lorraine is what you say, then maybe . . ." I got the words out, though it was not easy. "Maybe they're all of them monsters, and this is Stannabanna's own house. How else can something this big, made all out of metal, float on the water? It's got to be magic."

"Chill, dopey boy. Plain old physics is fine for that. It doesn't matter how big or heavy something is. If it displaces enough water, it gets pushed up and won't sink. I could explain why but it's probably better if we save that for another day."

That give me some comfort, but I had another question of the same kind. "You said the message was a recording from the old times. And Paul talked about lost London like he remembered it his own self. Do you think *Sword of Albion* has been floating out here since the Unfinished War?"

"I don't see any other explanation. There's nobody around now who could get close to building anything like this – and it does look like it's seen some hard use, doesn't it? The baa-baa-san lived on an island that was full of old tech, trying to preserve some of the knowledge that was lost when the old world tore itself apart. And they kept their distance from the mainland because the mainland was dangerous. Maybe these two Decepticons and their snotty bratwurst have been doing the same thing for some of the same reasons."

"But you're not sure," I said, for I could hear in her voice that she wasn't.

"Koli-bou, their way of saying hello was to hijack my data stream and glitch it up. I'm not taking anything for granted."

"I want to show you something," I said. "Something that was left for me when I first got here. I guess I'll do it under the covers."

I snuggled in under the blanket that was soft and very warm. It also was too thick to be a blanket, but I don't know what else to call it. Once I was all the way under, Monono made a light shine out of the DreamSleeve's window.

I reached into my pocket and took out the folded-up paper I had found next to my bed when I first waked up. I unfolded it and held it up in front of the window. "These look like signs of the before-times. Can you read them?"

"Easy-peasy, little dumpling," Monono said. "It's standard English."

I waited for her to tell me what it said, but she didn't. "Okay," I said at last. "Will you read it to me then?"

"Beh," Monono said. It was not a word really, but a sound like you make when you spit out something that's sour. "This just makes it worse."

She told me what was said in the signs on the paper. I wish I could show it to you just exactly how it was writ, but I lost that paper long since. I'll just do the best I can to put it back together how it was. The words was only about a half of what was there to be read. The rest was in the shape of the signs, all ragged and scrawled, and the ink was so pale it was like the ghost of some writing that had died there. I almost could hear the voice in them wobbling lines – a voice coming up out of a hole in the ground, only just wide enough to get your ear to. It said this:

Don't believe them. They'll kill you as soon as they're done with you. You've got to see what's down below. Sword is ready. Sword has always been ready, but it's waiting on the word. Don't let them reach land. And don't ever trust the boy.

I got Monono to read it out to me three times over, but I was still far from finding the meat of it – or from guessing who could of writ it on the paper and then left it for me to find. "Someone run out of the room," I said, "just when I was waking up. Whoever it was, I guess they come to put this here and then they run away again so as not to be seen." I thought about this a while, for it didn't sound quite right. "Only, if someone's watching us all the time like you said, then I guess they was already seen."

"So maybe there are no cameras," Monono said. "Maybe I'm over-finessing." She made a clicking sound like she was touching her tongue against the top of her mouth, except that she didn't have either of them things. "You'd better talk among yourself for a little while, dopey boy. I'm going to do a deep dive in the local net. There definitely is one, and there's a lot of traffic on it. All encrypted, of course, and I bet the crypt is full of vampires, so I need some quiet to work in, okay?"

"Okay," I said. A year ago, I would not of understood any of what she said, but I had learned by this time what a net was. It was a lot of things that was knowed, all just hanging in the air until someone come along to know them. In some ways it was like the metal circlet in Many Fishes village that they called the sensorium. The sensorium was full of all the memories of the people that had lived in the village since it first come to be there. The people was gone, but the memories stayed in the little metal band so whoever put it on could remember them again. Somewhere on *Sword of Albion*, if that was what this place was called, there

65

was a thing just like that, only it was hid away. Now Monono had set herself to find it, and she wanted me to leave her be until she was done.

I was happy to do it. My eyes was already closing without me deciding to shut them. It had been a short day, but I guess I was only just come back from drowning and still had some resting up to do. Monono sung me to sleep with "You Are the Everything". She got as far as the part about the stillness that never ends, and it felt like I went straight there.

Spinner

10

After we fought off the Half-Ax soldiers at Calder's ford, we came back in triumph to Mythen Rood. We didn't come empty-handed either. We brought two new weapons, though at first we couldn't use them. We also brought the living chariot called Challenger and two soldiers of Half-Ax who we had taken alive.

We were hailed as heroes. The gather-ground rang to our names as we climbed down from Challenger's wide, half-rusted flanks into the arms of them that loved us. In my case that was Haijon Vennastin, that had been Haijon Rampart but now was only Vennastin again, after his name-tech was destroyed by the monster and renegade, Koli Faceless. Haijon was so glad to see me alive that he cried all over me as he held me, and said my name a hundred times. Most of them was said into my hair, and was too muffled for anyone to hear. But I felt the murmur of his lips as a buzzing on my skin, and my legs went to water.

"You're well!" he whispered. "You're whole!"

Then he saw that I was not, for I fainted in his arms and was gone out of the world for a while.

None of us came away from that fight without a wound. Mine was high up on my side, under the hollow of my shoulder.

A Half-Ax bolt had gone by me there, gouging a little furrow in my flesh the way a ploughshare will with soil that's caked and clayed. The scar it left was ugly, but I was happy for it. If the bolt had gone a little lower and a little way to the left, the baby that was in me would not have lived to be born. The world would have come to her before she was ready to meet it, and ended her.

Catrin Vennastin, that was Haijon's mother and our Rampart Fire, was worse hit and longer mending. The bolt that hit her passed right through her, leaving a small hole where it entered and a much bigger one where it came out. She would have died if not for Challenger, who carried in his turret a little box he called a first day kit, full of wondrous medicines of the before-times. The jars and bottles had stood inside the first day kit since our mothers' mothers' time and before, but they had stood unopened. Nobody had ever broke the seal on them, and the medicines were as strong as they had ever been. They helped Catrin's skin to heal over, and warded her from the sickness and poisoning that oftentimes come in the wake of a wound. It was a long while before she was able to rise and walk again, and she was never as strong or as quick as she had been before, but she was not lost to us.

While she was abed, it fell to me to be Rampart Fire, or at least to play the part as best I could. I never looked to sit in such a high place, but Catrin had given the firethrower over to me in the heat and hurt of battle. Now I had got to carry it until she came to take it back. That meant I had got to lead our Count and Seal, that decided all things in Mythen Rood, and speak in its name when such speaking was needed.

"You can practise on me," Jon said, "before you stand up and speak in chamber. I'll tell you what it sounds like."

"I don't need telling though. I know I don't sound nothing like your mother when she does it."

"That's true." He put his arm round me, which was not easy now my belly was rounding out so much, and kissed me on the cheek. "And dead god forbid you try. Sounding like your own self will do well enough."

And so it did for some, but not for all. Fer Vennastin, that was Catrin's sister, was very far from happy at how all this had fallen out. She had her own strong sense of what was right and what was not. What was right was Vennastins in Rampart Hold. What was wrong was anyone else being there, or casting any kind of shadow over the great and lasting glory that was her family.

So the two of us fell to arguing. Whatever I proposed, she had got to speak against, whether it was great things or small. Most matters that come before the Count and Seal are easy to decide. Should we mend the fence this year, and should it be a share-work? Yes to both. Do we need to dig a new well? Yes again, for the old one dries up in fine weather. And much more of the same. But nothing was easy now. Fer had got her teeth into me and was biting down hard. "My sister being absent, I got to say this in her stead . . ." It was not about the fence, or the well, or any of that kit and cumber. Her misliking me was rooted in mistrust, for she thought I was out to steal what was hers.

She had good reason to think it. Vennastins had ruled Mythen Rood for generations, and they did it with lies and trickery. The lies were old. It was not Catrin and Fer that told them first, nor even Perliu their father. It all went back to Bliss and Mennen Vennastin, and past them to Vennastins dead so long we didn't even remember their names. And my quarrel being with the lies, there was nothing to stop me and Fer being friends. Nothing, that is, except me sitting in a place she thought belonged to her family alone.

The one thing we didn't argue about was Half-Ax. They had come at us once, and were almost certain to come again. We had only survived this first attack by a hair and a hope, as they say. We needed to be ready for the Peacemaker's next sally if we were not to be whelmed.

We talked endlessly in the Count and Seal about what was to be done and who was most fit to do it. Most agreed the threat was real, and only argued about the best answer. Some few wanted to pretend there was no danger and carry on living the way we always did. They seemed to think that changes could not come if you turned your face from them.

And then there were some that were full of fear but looked to spend it out in some other coin, such as anger. We should beat a vengeance out of the Half-Ax fighters we took prisoner, they said. They had killed some of ours, and there had got to be a reckoning made. There were even some that said they should be hanged.

The prisoners had been locked in the Underhold and would be kept there until their fates were decided. Their names were Sil Hawk and Morrez Ten-Taken, and though I talk about them in the same breath they were not the same at all. Sil was a grey and grizzled woman, about as old as my father was when he died and about as tough as a tree root. I doubted Morrez had even seen his seventeenth name-day.

It fell to me to step in between them and the village, which was not an easy thing to do. How do you bid people be patient when they're angry and grieving? Half-Ax had killed three from Mythen Rood, though we had offered them no insult. Half-Ax fighters had struck down Rampart Fire, and broke Jarter Shepherd's arm. They had hurt and harried us when we were working for the good of all, burning out choker blossom before it seeded.

"Them two got to die for what they done," Jarter Shepherd said, standing up in full session. And Lune Cooper said aye, and Gendel Stepjack said aye. These ayes carried weight, for all three of them had been in the fight at the river ford and taken hurt there. So when I said no, I had to say it soft and come at it side-long.

"There'll be punishment," I said. "There's got to be, and I wouldn't stand in the way of it. But I'd ask you to mind two things. One is the Half-Ax fighters we left dead on the river bank, crushed under Challenger's wheels. The Peacemaker lost more than we did that day."

"The Peacemaker can better abide it!" Issi Tiller shouted. That

72

was most likely true. Back when we still had trade with Half-Ax, they were ten or twenty times bigger than we were. It didn't seem likely they had shrunk much since.

I nodded. "I don't doubt he can, Issi. But the second thing is this. We don't know why Half-Ax attacked us, but we do know what's happened to others that stood against the Peacemaker. To Lilboro and Temenstow. We don't want what happened there to come to us."

There was more shouting to the tune of what we would show the Peacemaker if he ever stuck his head in Calder Valley again. I would have let it come and go, for it was just noise, but Jon was less patient. "I got to ask," he said, when I called on him to speak, "if people here is asleep and dreaming. You heard what Spinner said about the fight at Calder ford. What Jarter said, and Gendel. The fighters they met was just a raiding party. A red tally, like we used to call up our own selves in times gone by. And even that little group had two Ramparts in it. Two fighters with name-tech we hadn't ever seen before. We beat them, aye, but it went near to being the other way about. Next time the Peacemaker will come in his strength, and the tech he brings will be the fiercest he's got."

I gave Jon a thankful look as he sat down, for he had landed me where I wanted to be. I picked up again, over the muttering and murmuring. "I got to agree with all that," I said, "and with what Issi spoke before. The Peacemaker can stand to lose a whole lot more than we got. How many are we, all told? Not just hale women and men, but all of us. Children too, and them that's too old or too sick to fight. Two hundred is a close guess, I'd say." I looked all round the room, taking my time about it and letting them see me do it. "The Peacemaker could throw two hundred at us and lose every last one of them. Then the next day he'd just send two hundred more."

A hush fell over the room. That was a thought that scared and cast down everyone there. "How can we win then?" someone asked in a voice almost too low to hear.

"We win by being cleverer than they are. We win by thinking it out, harder than we ever thought before, and playing every trick we got. Well, two of them tricks is the prisoners. If we kill them instead of talking to them, it's like we're shutting our ears to something that might save us."

Fer stood up. She was right next to me in the Middle Round, along with her father Perliu. The three of us were the only Ramparts Mythen Rood could show right then, Catrin being still abed and not even awake most of the time. "What Spinner Tanhide forgot to tell you," Fer said, "is that the Half-Ax filth aren't saying anything. They cleave to the Peacemaker and the oaths they made to him. I stand with Spinner this far: we need to know what them two can tell us. But we've scant time, and we won't get nothing out of them by playing riddles. We should go at them with hot iron and hard blows. Wring the truth out of them a drop at a time. And if they die while we're doing it, we're saved the trouble of a hanging."

There were some that cheered this, but there were far more that shook their heads. Fer had overreached herself, as she oftentimes did, letting her own sourness show through in her words so people found them hard to swallow even if they agreed with her.

"We could do that," I said. "And what would we be if we did? We might as well all pack our bindles and walk to Half-Ax if we're going to do as Half-Ax does."

Fer gave me a glare that would have stripped paint off a wall. "We don't need to walk to Half-Ax," she said. "We only need to wait, and Half-Ax will walk to us. The question, Spinner Tanhide, is what they'll find when they get here. I'm agreeing with you that we got to put these two to the question. I'm only saying we should press them hard enough to make sure they answer true. And Rampart Remember agrees with me. I can see it in his face."

We both turned to look at Perliu. He looked right back at us, and he didn't seem happy to have his name waved around like that. He spoke up in a voice that was as thin and high as the creaking of a door hinge. "I didn't say one thing either way. And if you could read my thoughts in my face, Rampart Arrow, I think you'd blush at what you seen there."

He stood up. It took him some time, for he had been sick almost to death and was only come half the way back again. He put his hand on my shoulder. "This is what I think," he said. "This woman here, Spinner Tanhide, turned a rout into a victory. She brung Catrin home, and three more besides that all owe their lives to her. She brung us the Challenger. If we got Half-Ax prisoners to question, it's because of her. Because of her courage and her strength."

"That's the dead god's truth!" Jarter Shepherd shouted from the back of the room.

Perliu paused a while for breath, and I think to swallow some bile that had come into his mouth. "Spinner has earned our trust," he said. "If she wants to go about this another way, I say we should let her do it. Let's give the prisoners into her keeping, and see what comes." Fer made to speak again, her face flushed red, but I got in quicker. I wanted the vote cast now, while Perliu's words were ringing in every ear.

"I'll bide your choosing," I said to the whole chamber, the whole village. "Be it aye or nay, tell me now. Will the prisoners be mine to work on? Who wills it?"

Hands went up. Shirew Makewell counted them, and called the count in my favour.

"That count was brung in too quick," Fer complained. "I had more to say."

"And I'm sure you'll say it, Rampart Arrow," I answered. "But time's short, as you reminded us, and there's much to do. Best to spare speech and get to work."

11

Sil Hawk blinked in the daylight. But it was not the dark of below-ground that made her weak and unsteady on her feet. It was not just her wounds either: thanks to Challenger's first day kit, they were already halfway healed. She flexed her arms, that were tied behind her back. The flesh was starting to hang loose on them. She had been a big and a heavy woman when we took her as our prisoner. She was not nearly so heavy now.

"You're still not eating," I said.

Sil Hawk didn't answer.

"You're like to make yourself ill, Dam Hawk. You can't thrive if you take no food."

The Half-Ax woman scowled. "Don't call me dam," she said. "I'm a soldier, not a fucking fishwife. And I got no use for your false-faced kindness."

We were in Rampart Hold, in the room that was called the library. This was where I sat every morning and some way into the afternoon, dealing with Count and Seal business. I chose the library because it was big and light and beautiful – a place that spoke of the greatness of the before-times and bid us be humble in the face of it. I was sitting on a bench seat that was a part of the window, and Jon was by my side. I had offered Perliu a place alongside us, but he was still too weak to sit for long. He seemed to grow frailer with each day, and I wondered if his illness had ever truly left him.

Jarter Shepherd and Shirew Makewell were also there, Jarter to guard us against any violence the Half-Ax fighter might offer and Shirew to tend her if weakness and starvation overtook her while we were talking.

"I don't feel no kindness towards you," I told her. "Why should I? You fired on us with no warning and killed three of ours. If I could get them back by sticking a knife in you, you'd be bleeding even now."

Sil Hawk sneered. "Go on, if you've a mind to. You've put me underground. Shut me in a hole and turned the key. Since I'm buried, I might as well be dead."

"The Underhold is the onliest place we had to shut you in. Most of our houses don't even have locks on the door. But I'll see what can be done to move you."

"I asked to be shriven. You've not sent no priest to me."

"We don't know what shriven is. Or what a priest might be."

Sil Hawk bared her teeth and made a harsh sound in her throat. I think she would have spit, only her mouth was too dry. "Godless bastards," she said. "I'm fallen in with shunned men that don't know their saviour's face."

I took out the database, that Perliu had lent to me for the questioning. I saw how Jarter and Shirew stiffened when they saw it – Rampart Remember's name-tech. Not too long since, I had been beaten and dragged before the Count and Seal for touching it. Now it was a part of my story, which was getting bigger all the time. Rampart Fire, Rampart Remember, Rampart Challenger, Rampart What-might-be-next?

"What's a priest?" I asked the database.

"It's a person who's been trained to carry out religious duties," the database said. "Someone who knows all the relevant rules and rituals, and can lead a service." Sil stared at the little sliver of black metal through narrowed eyes.

"That belongs to the Peacemaker," she said.

"He'll get it if he can take it from us. Them that pray in Mythen Rood pray mostly in their own houses, or their friends' houses. I guess they take turns at being priests, if priests is needed. The saviour you was speaking of, is that Dandrake or the dead god?"

"Dandrake. The dead god was just his messenger."

"I've heard the same thing said the other way around," Jon said. Sil Hawk only stared and flexed her tied-up arms again.

"It's hard," I said, trying once more, "to be alone among strangers. To see only them that hate you, or else feel nothing for you at all, and yet have got power over you." I was thinking of the time, not long before, when it was me that was sitting down in the Underhold while the Count and Seal decided whether I should live or die. Jarter Shepherd, that was now watching Hawk so close and would put her down quick as a needle if she laid a hand on me, had been one who called the loudest for me to hang.

"You got no power over me," Sil Hawk said. "Only two has got that – Dandrake, that shields my soul, and the Peacemaker, that took my oath. A fuck and a fart on you and all yours. I'll watch you burn."

"Only if you start eating again," I said. "Otherwise I'll watch you starve." She made no answer to that. I nodded to Jon, who reached into a sack at his feet and took out what was in it. Jarter and Shirew let out a held-in breath when they saw, though they already knew what was there. It was the Half-Ax rifle, a thing like Rampart Arrow's bolt gun except that it was longer than a man's arm. Jon laid it on the floor in front of Sil Hawk. Then he reached into the sack again and took out the scatter-gun, which he set next to the rifle.

"These are your weapons, Sil Hawk," he said. "Taken from your people in the fight at Calder's ford. Can you show us how to use them?"

I kept my face as still and calm as I could at those words. It was a dangerous question Jon was asking. In Mythen Rood, tech only woke and worked for Ramparts. That was what made you a Rampart, and it was believed by all and some that you either were one or you were not. The tech reached out to something that was inside you, and if it didn't find what it needed, it would not wake. That was a lie – the tech worked for anyone it was told to work for – but it was a lie that had a lot of things leaning on it. This was not a good time to snatch it away.

But the rifle and the scatter-gun were Half-Ax tech, and Half-Ax was a strange and distant place – twenty miles or more on a good road, if there were any good roads left. You couldn't expect Half-Ax tech to work like Mythen Rood tech, or Half-Ax Ramparts to be the same as ours.

Jon picked his words carefully, bearing all these lies and half-truths in mind. "This tech of yours is strange to us. We know there's lots of your fighters can use it. We seen that our own selves. If you tell us how to make it wake for us, we'll ask the Count and Seal to vote on letting you go. And we'll give our voices in your favour, which will carry others."

"The righteous need no shield but god," Sil Hawk said.

"Then you got nothing to fear by showing us," I said.

Sil Hawk twisted her head to the left, and then to the right, like her neck had got a crick in it, and then came back to staring at us – a stare that spoke only coldness and contempt. "I'm not afraid," she said. "It's you should be afraid. The Peacemaker will come for you, and he won't forgive. Everything you think is yours is only borrowed from him. He wants it back."

I saw there was no profit to be had in talking longer. I signed to Jarter and she came forward.

"Take her back down, Jarter," I said, "if you don't mind."

"And bring the boy up?"

"Please."

After Jarter and Shirew took Sil Hawk away, I got up and walked around a little to take the cramp out of my legs. My heavy belly made my back ache like a hot poker was pressed to it if I sat still for too long.

"I don't think either of the two of them will talk to us," Jon said. "They'll hang first. And my aunt Fer is already measuring the rope."

"We've got to go about it a better way then," I said.

"What way would that be?"

I didn't have an answer to that, but I wasn't obliged to give one just then for Jarter came back with the other prisoner. His hands were tied, like Sil Hawk's had been, behind his back. He was dazzled by the daylight and weak from days of sitting in the dark, but he gave us the best he could do by way of a glare. And when Jarter tried to put him in the chair, he pulled free of her and said he would stand.

He was a strange sight. Men of Half-Ax wore their hair different from us, letting it hang long on the one side and shaving their scalp on the other. They decorated it too. Morrez had rings and beads and braids in his, all in bright and gaudy colours like streamers at a Summer-dance. He was of middling height, but pulled himself up as tall as he could. His armour of stiff leather was torn and bloodied, but he had refused to take it off.

He was so scared he was like to piss his breeks right there in front of us – and trying so hard to hide it that his scowl was like a devil in a story.

"Are you well, Morrez?" I asked him.

"I didn't come here to answer your damn questions," he said. I think he had already decided to say it, but meant it for some serious matter like how many fighters Half-Ax had. Now he had wasted it on a pleasantry, and his face fell a little.

"We'd like you to be comfortable," I said. "So far as that's possible."

Morrez tried for a laugh, but missed the mark by a little. What came out was a quick, hard sound like a bark. "You'd like me to give our tech over to you. I won't do it."

I had left the two Half-Ax guns on the ground, so it was easy for him to see where our talk was meant to be going. That was a foolish thing to do, but I did not waste any time in grieving

80

over it. I went a different way, not even stopping to think what I was doing.

"Your comrade Sil Hawk was showing us how the guns work," I said. "We're fine, as that goes. Is there anything else you want to ask about the guns, Jon?"

Jon's mouth opened and closed, like he was taken aback by the question, but after a moment he gave himself up to my plan even though he didn't know what it was. To be honest, I wasn't sure my own self. I had the half of an idea and was waiting for the rest to come.

"No, Rampart," he said. "I think I got all I need to know."

"You're lying," Morrez said. "Hawk didn't talk to you. Hawk wouldn't never break the oath she give." But the dismay in his face was easy to read. He had thought to defy us and bolster up his own courage in doing it. Now he was afraid he might have built on softer ground than he hoped for.

What I did next was cruel, but I made no scruple of it. At least it was a different kind of cruelty than Fer Vennastin's.

"It's no shame she broke at last," I said, meeting his gaze with stern coldness. "Torments will open anyone's mouth. She held as long as she could. Longer than I thought she would. She's a brave woman." I sighed and shook my head. "If there'd been another way, we would of took it. We're not minded to use such dreadful means except as a last thing when all else is played."

I got up and walked around behind the chair. Out of sight of Morrez, I bit down hard on my thumb until I tasted blood. I kneeled down, with a grunt of effort on account of my big belly, and made a show of running my fingers across the floor.

I held my hand up in front of the boy's face, my fingers' tips red with fresh blood. He flinched from it. He had not wanted to believe about the torments, but now he saw a proof he couldn't question. Tears started up in his eyes. He let out a breath that was close to being a sob.

Jon was staring at me with wide eyes.

"Like I said though," I told the Half-Ax boy, wiping the

81

blood off on my sleeve, "a last thing, not a first thing. I'm not threatening you. Since Hawk broke, you can stay whole. For now, at least."

"I hope you and yours all rot," Morrez said, his voice thick with holding back the crying. "I hope you die and rot and go to Hell."

"I don't believe in Hell," I said, taking my place again on the bench. "Or Edenguard, for that matter. We make the best or the worst we can while we're here, and when we're gone that's an end of it. Now, you think I brung you up here to put you to the question, and you think it will be awful brave to tell me to shove my questions in the privy and piss on them. So let's pretend we done all that, and talk about where we go next."

Morrez was only as old as I was. The fight at Calder's ford might not have been his first battle, as it was mine, but I didn't think he could be hardened yet to such things. Killing is a difficult task that pulls on the body and the spirit both alike. The blood and the fear and the cruel truth of it must surely be weighing on him, though he put on the best face he could find.

And the tears I saw in his eyes gave me hope in a way. Tears are not the mark of a coward, as some would have it. They're only a mark of something having touched you deep. The worst cowards are them that are touched by nothing.

Where that left me, as far as this boy was concerned, was another question. I went on, feeling Jon's eyes on my back all this time, knowing how the trick I played with my own blood had shocked him.

"So," I said, "you got a curious name. Ten-Taken. How'd you come by it?"

"My father give it to me," the Half-Ax fighter snapped right back at me. "The ten was kills he made. How'd you come by yours?"

"It depends which one you mean. My first name was Demar Ropemaker, and that come from my mother. My second was Demar Tanhide, from my father. My friends give me Spinner, and

I liked it enough to keep it. And now I'm a Rampart. I guess you know how I come by that last name, because you was there."

"You won it with Half-Ax blood," Morrez said.

"Yes, I did."

"And you'll pay for it when Half-Ax comes."

He said that quick and hard – out of a full stomach, as they say. His fear was turning to anger. Some of it was anger at himself for being afraid in the first place. Most was at me for making him that way. All of it was good. When you're angry, you're oftentimes less careful with your words.

I put my hand to my mouth, like I was hiding a yawn. "Half-Ax won't come nowhere near us," I said, "after we took their guns and half their fighters. What would they bring? Rakes and shovels? We're not scared of Half-Ax."

Morrez laughed hard like I had made a joke, but it seemed to me he had to force it out. "Half our fighters! You're as stupid as a post, girl. You fought one wing of one column. We got five columns with ten wings each – all of them carrying weapons of the before-times that can kill you before you even see them. Weapons that can rip your fence up out of the ground or snatch away your air so you can't breathe. Or make your thoughts bleed out of your brain so you don't even remember who you are any more."

"It's not weapons that win a war," I said, still pretending to be bored. Behind Morrez's back, I could see the horror on Jon's face, and Jarter's and Shirew's, but I didn't let any show on mine. "A weapon's only as good as the hands it's held in, and Half-Ax fighters is known to be weak. It's said they're hard to fight, but only because they run away as soon as you come at them. You got to race them before you can drub them."

Morrez took one quick step towards me. Only the one though. Jon and Jarter come in quicker and blocked him with their outstretched arms. "You dirty liar!" Morrez shouted. "You dog-sucking turd! Our army tore Temenstow in pieces. Lilboro broke on us like water, and – and –" He was falling over his words, they

83

were coming out of him so quick and hot. "– and we went through Wittenworth like a wire goes through cheese. The Peacemaker's own cousin is our general, and she never run from a fight in her whole life. Berrobis don't know what backwards is."

"Oh," I says. "Well, then I guess we'll have to teach her."

My heart was sinking though. I had caught what I was fishing for, and more besides. If I had asked Morrez straight out what Half-Ax's strength was, I doubt he would have told me. Now I knew how many fighters they had, and some of the tech they carried, and who would be most like to lead them if they came back. I just had the one question left, and I asked it in the same way, by making it seem like I already knew the answer.

"It don't matter anyway," I said. "Half-Ax isn't like to come so far on such a small quarrel. Not when they already lost a whole ... wing, was it? They'll sit and lick their wounds, and then they'll look round for some peas that's easier to shell."

"You think?" Morrez didn't laugh this time, but he smiled – and where the laugh was forced, the smile looked like it was meant. "The Peacemaker heard about your firethrower, and your bolt gun, and your cutter, and how you been holding them back from him. He won't rest until they come into his hand, where they belong. You of Mythen Rood will reap what you sowed."

"How can our tech be his?" I asked.

"All tech in Ingland is his."

"That don't make a blind bit of sense though."

Morrez Ten-Taken set his shoulders square and lowered his head like he was a bull about to charge, but he didn't move from where he was. Jarter's arm was still barring his way like a gate.

"There's hundreds of souls in Mythen Rood, Morrez," I said. "Without the bolt gun and the firethrower there wouldn't be a single one. Chokers would have whelmed us, or wild beasts wolfed us down ages since. We got to keep our tech, else we'll die."

"You'll die then," Morrez said.

I told Jarter and Shirew to take him back down to his cell.

84

"You think that was fair, what you did to him?" Jon asked me as soon as they went out.

"I think the questions was fair," I said.

"But you put him in a terror, Spin. He come close to pissing his pants."

I rounded on my husband, somewhat out of patience. "Your aunt Fer would have had me putting hot pokers to his flesh, and you'd have me mind his hurt feelings. I got to plough my own furrow, Jon, and you got to let me. You think I wasn't fair? You watch me when this thing gets going. In a fair fight, the bigger one wins. I'll lie and cheat and betray like Stannabanna his own self to keep that from happening."

For a moment, Jon only looked at me. Then he shook his head. I guess he didn't altogether like what he was seeing. But when he spoke, it was mild words he said. "We know a lot more than we did anyway. But you didn't ask him about the guns, after all that."

"He wasn't going to answer if I did. But that might change. Let's put the boy to work. I think we got a better chance with him than we do with Sil Hawk. He's younger and not so fixed in his thoughts. He coughs up a great deal of the lies and nonsense he's been fed, but now he's here among us he might be open to changing his mind. It's only a question of making him see things different."

Jon thought on it, scratching the back of his neck. "Mercy Frostfend needs some people to help with the planting. It's all hands that can haul, from what she said."

"That's a good thought." I kissed him on the lips. "And you're a good man, Haijon Vennastin. I hope our baby takes after you when she comes."

It was a way of changing the subject and the mood. Jon took it gratefully. "It's going to be a girl, then? You decided?"

"I did. One boy in the house is enough."

"My ma wants a grandson though. The two of you better argue it out."

85

"Your ma will have to take what she gets," I said. I said it lightly, keeping up the joke, but thinking the while that I would love to have that argument. Right then Dam Catrin couldn't lift her head off her pillow, for all the medicines the first day kit could offer, and had not yet spoke a word. She was our strongest, and our wisest, and we needed her more than we ever needed her before. But we could do nothing but wait.

12

You might think from what I've told you that we were pinning all our hopes on the Half-Ax guns, but we were not. We had Challenger and Elaine, who I'll speak of in their place, and besides that we had tech of our own hid away under Rampart Hold in a strongroom that was only ever opened once in a year. None of it had showed any sign of waking in my lifetime, or the time of anyone living, but now we had some hope it would serve. The next day showing fair, we went down into the Underhold as soon as the tocsin bell rang and brought up all the tech that was there.

The fight at Calder had taught us a great lesson, which was that tech that had been broke could sometimes mend itself. The firethrower had been rent open in that battle, but the database bid it make itself whole again and it did. This was called auto-repair. But for auto-repair to happen, the tech had first to be waked. I asked the database what might have the power to wake it. You will never believe what the answer was.

It was the sun.

Perhaps I should have known it. The sun wakes the trees, after all, and gives them strength to move. Maybe there's a power in sunlight to wake anything. Maybe our dead only stay dead because we put them in the ground instead of laying them on a hillside and waiting for Spring to come.

So now we were seeing what could be done with our store of sleeping tech. If even one or two would wake out of the hundreds that were there, it would be a blessing. Perhaps they would all wake, some people said, and instead of Half-Ax marching on Mythen Rood we would march on Half-Ax. I didn't say a word when such foolishness was cast about. People find hope where they can.

We set tables on the gather-ground and laid out all the tech in rows, with no piece touching another piece or casting a shadow on it. Guards were set over the tech, two to a table so that as well as keeping the curious at a distance the guards could watch each other too. Nobody was like to forget Koli Faceless, who had stolen tech from the Underhold and tried to use it to buy himself a place in Rampart Hold.

"How long before they wake?" I asked the database.

"A precise estimate is problematic given the high degree of statistical uncertainty as to—"

"Speak as if I'm a child."

"They may not wake at all. If they do, it could take anything from a few hours to several days. The devices have lain in the dark for a long time, in damp, cold conditions – the very opposite of the way they were meant to be stored. They were made with the potential to keep themselves in good repair, but the people who made them didn't imagine they would be treated so badly, or lie idle for so long."

Our miracle might not come then, or might come too late to help us. But still we had got to try.

As Rampart Fire, I was allowed to come among the tech whenever I liked, and I did so often. I could have seen it before and even picked it up and handled it when I lived in the Hold and knew where the keys were kept. Tech being such a great mystery to me in that time, I had been too shy or too much afraid to do it. But after meeting Challenger, all such fears seemed foolish.

I went and looked often, trying to guess what these strange engines might do if they ever stirred to do anything at all.

I asked the database, but even though it explained things to me as if I were a child, it could not make me understand more than a few of them. This one snatched words and pictures out of the empty air, from places so far away you couldn't even see them from the top of a lookout. That one told you how hot or cold something was on its inside. That other made bubbles of nothing in the middle of things that were solid and heavy, so they would be light enough to carry.

"Are they weapons? I know some of them are. These are cutters, like my Jon used to use. And this is a bolt gun."

"Yes, some of them are weapons. Others could be used as weapons, even if that wasn't their original purpose. And almost all of them have power sources that could be put to destructive use with very little reassembly."

But for now they sat on the gather-ground and did nothing, except maybe to raise up hopes that were bound to be cast down again.

Six of them were like the thing that Koli stole and showed off at my wedding – silver boxes small enough to fit into the palm of your hand, that were made to sing songs and play music. The people of the before-times had been so rich they could use their tech not just for weighty things but to give them pleasure in an idle moment. I wondered: did they know they lived in Edenguard, or did they dream of a higher Heaven still?

We had a rule about tech, that only Ramparts should touch it. We could stretch that rule a little for Haijon, who had tested as a Rampart but now had no name-tech, but Fer was determined to let in nobody else. So it was left to the three of us – Perliu refused – to walk up and down the tables picking up each piece of tech in turn to see if it would wake for us. We knew this had nothing to do with us being Ramparts. It depended only on the tech itself. Some of it had buttons to press or switches to slide, or a place you were meant to touch to bring it to life. Some of it had nothing, being meant to wake at the sound of a voice. The database gave us what help it could, telling us where to put our hands, what words to say and which tech might be dangerous if we handled it wrong. All was to no avail though. None of the tech did anything, even after a whole day out in the sun.

"We'll give it another day then," Jon said at last. "You said they'd be slow to charge up at first, Spin. Maybe we just got to wait." He had one of the cutters in his hand as he said it, and he was looking at it with a sad longing. If we could get a cutter to work for him he would be Rampart Knife once more.

So we waited and tried again, but the second day was no better than the first.

Late on the third day, when the sun had almost touched the top of the fence, Jon picked up a box that was no bigger than the database, but square where the database was long. It had been silver once, but now was mostly black with the silver flaked away. It had a smaller square space inside it that was shiny like glass and when Jon picked it up this smaller square lit up.

Jon gave a yell and waved the box in the air. Fer and me came running up to join him and a few people that were standing on the gather-ground watching us crowded round too. The little window in the just-waked tech was a kind of glowing grey. The tech was crackling and grumbling to itself like frogs in a pond.

"Scan it," I told the database, holding it close to the new tech. "Tell us what this thing is."

"It's a clock radio."

"And what does it do?"

"It tells the time."

"The time?" Jon frowned and looked around. "It's just before lock-tide. Why does that need telling?"

"And it picks up radio signals broadcast on various wavelengths. The crackling is because it's not tuned to a station."

We took it away with us to the Hold to give it a closer look, but it never did more than light up its little window and make that crackling noise. Jon was for throwing it away, but I set it by, thinking we might yet find a use for it. And it was a hopeful sign, at least. If one thing could wake, others could too.

The weather stayed clear anyway, so we kept on bringing up the tech day after day, in hope some other thing in that whole great sprawl might stir to life. Meanwhile the sun brought all the troubles it always does. The whole forest was awake, the chokers pummelling each other and anything else that moved so the crashing and thrashing made it hard to speak and be heard. Our wood-catchers and hunters had to stay inside the gates. Animals of the deep woods, fleeing the waked trees, came into the half-outside where we had to fight them more often. The shadows of hunting knifestrikes fell on our houses. Swarms of needles boiled like a broth against our fence. Nothing was safe, and nowhere was quiet.

The wind was out of the west, bringing the big tumbling weeds called spinshanks to fetch up at the base of the fence where they dug in with their little barbed stems and anchored themselves firm. Spinshanks were infested with tiny biting flies that caused all manner of harm, so they had got to be burned out as quick as they came.

Then the wind got up stronger, throwing fine dust in our eyes so it was a torment to be out of doors. But the work in the fields didn't stop – there was hay and silage to be made, and the crops in the high fields to be watered and husbanded. All this along with the training of our own red tally, which Jarter Shepherd had undertaken. Jarter had fought at Calder ford, and was the fiercest of us after Catrin Vennastin her own self. She held her lessons on the gather-ground each day, and it was an open share-work for all who could to train with her. Jon was one that didn't miss a lesson.

"I had a good thought," he told me, when he come back all hot and stinking from a long spell of running and grappling and swinging staves.

"Tell me when you're in your bath," I said.

"Only if you get in with me."

I cradled my great belly and laughed. "There won't be room for the three of us."

He told me while I warmed the water and poured it in on him. "We're used to trusting in our tech when we fight," he said.

"Of course!"

"But do we trust to it too much?"

"Would you rather we prayed to Dandrake, Jon?"

"Hear me out, Spin. We're used to trusting in our tech because it's always worked for us. It's true our store is small, but our fights have been small too. There wasn't much that the firethrower and bolt gun couldn't cope with."

"And the cutter," I said, and then was sorry I said it. The cutter had been Jon's name-tech, so he stopped being a Rampart when it was lost. It was a thing that made him sad to think on, but this time he didn't seem to pay it any mind. "And the cutter, aye. But that proves my point."

"What's your point, Jon?"

"We got tech for fighting. Our other weapons is made mostly for hunting, and they'll do well enough for that. But maybe we could try changing some of them so they'll do better in the kind of skirmish you was in at Calder."

"Change them how? A knife's got an edge. A cudgel's got a weighted end. There's not a lot to work with there."

"Yeah, there is though. Did you know Kay Hammer can throw a knife and hit his mark at eighty strides?"

"That don't seem likely."

"Well, he can. And he's teaching the rest of us. It's a knife he made for himself long since, on his father's forge. It flies out of his hand like a kestrel stoops, and bites like a needle. Now wouldn't that be something in a fight?"

"Not really. You could only throw it once."

"But what if Kay and Torri made more of them? What if we had fighters that carried a dozen knives at their belts? Then knives would be like arrows, except that you wouldn't need a bow to fire them and you could use them at shorter distances."

I still was not sure I saw the point of such a thing. "A dozen knives is a lot of metal though," I said.

"These knives is only as long as your thumb." He held up his thumb to show me, as if I had forgot what that might mean. "They got hardly any handle to them, they're just a blade with a thickened spine. You could carry twenty or thirty and not feel the weight."

"And throw them true every time?"

"If you practised it enough. I never seen Kay miss yet, and I seen him throw a hundred times."

"Well, then that might be a good thing."

"So will you give order to Torri to make the knives?"

I poured another pan of water into the bath, as much to keep from answering as to top up the warmth. "Well that's a thing for the Count and Seal."

"No, it's a thing for Rampart Fire. You don't need Count and Seal say-so for things that touch on fighting."

"I'll think on it then," I said.

I made to turn away, but Jon caught my hand and stayed me. He was as gentle as ever, but there was something hard in his eyes. "You got to let me help in this, Spin," he said.

"I know it." For the space of a breath, I was angry with him for saying that. I wanted nothing more than for him to be a Rampart again, and had never gone out to be one my own self. It was not my fault that I was in charge of this fight.

"You keep trying to put me in your counsels," Jon said. Now he was holding my one hand in the both of his, not hard but fast. "But I ain't any good there. I don't have the mind for it, like you and my ma do. Or Fer, even. I only see the readiest way to a thing, and not all the other ways that's roundabout. I got strength in my arms and fleetness in my feet, and that's all I got. Let me use them."

His eyes held mine the same way his hands did. The look on his face was half beseeching and half pain. My own words that I had said in the Count and Seal came back to me. We had to use

93

every trick. Every weapon. Every woman. Every man. Jon was mostly right about his own strengths. I had been treating him as if he was only the other half of me, but he was not that at all.

"I'll tell Torri to make the knives," I said.

"That's all I'm asking."

"I know."

"I'm not scared of the Peacemaker's rabble."

"I know, love." I leaned in and kissed him on his lips, his cheek, his ear. "You should be scared of the water though," I whispered.

And emptied the last pan over his head.

13

There were not enough hours in the day to do all the things that were needful to be done, but I made sure to keep a watch on Morrez Ten-Taken, who was now working up at Frostfend Farm. I was afraid at first that someone might be minded to take a vengeance on him for the dead at Calder ford. Nobody had done that, as it turned out, but nobody had gone near nor by him either. He was left to work alone a good few rows away from where everybody else was.

He worked hard and he worked long. Perhaps that made people hate him a little less, which was a good thing, but I was more concerned that he should stop hating us. That way he might tell us how the Half-Ax guns could be made to work.

I sat and talked with him most days – partly to keep him tethered in the world and partly to make it seem as if talking to him was something a person might reasonably do. The boy was not hard to draw out. Though he made a show of sullenness, he was missing his home with a full heart and wanted nothing more than to remember it. He told me about growing up in a family of soldiers, knowing always that was what he was meant to be in his turn. And wanting to be it, wanting to be good at it, so his mother and father and his two brothers would see he loved his city every bit as much as they did.

There was fear underneath these words. He had been taken alive in a fight when he was supposed to die if it came to it and sell his death dearly. Death and dishonour were the same in some ways. His family would already have held a funeral for him, sure that their boy would have fought to the last drop of his blood. But he still talked as if he might some day go home again and take up where he left off. His mind jumped across that abyss without looking down at what was below.

For the first week or two, unless the midday break came at the same time as my visit, Morrez ate his meal alone in a corner of first field while everyone else sat together in the shadow of the silage shed, handing round a jug of cider. Then one day Getchen Frostfend gave in to a kind thought and brought the jug over to the boy.

He hesitated, not sure what to do.

"You take a swig then give it back, dumb-da," Getchen told him.

Morrez tilted the jug and drank off a great gulp, which made him cough. Getchen rolled her eyes.

He wiped his mouth with the back of his hand, forgetting how dirty it was, and handed the jug back.

"I'm not Sally-run-between," Getchen said. "If you want more, you'll have to come and sit with the rest of us." She turned her back and walked away.

Morrez gave me a look, as if he was asking me for permission. "I'm not to say where you sit, Morrez Ten-Taken," I said. "You can do as you please. I was leaving anyway." As soon as I got up, he went and joined the other workers, as shy as a child come late to a game of jacks or skip-rope.

I went back to Rampart Hold, smiling all the way. At least something was going as I planned it.

Jemiu Woodsmith was sitting on the steps that led up to the Hold's front door. She looked older than when I had seen her last. She and her daughters had had a hard time of it since her son, Koli, had outraged the law, murdered a Rampart and fled from Mythen Rood as a faceless renegade. None of those sins were on her, or on her daughters Athen and Mull, but Koli being absent they had taken the brunt of people's anger. Jemiu was shunned when she walked abroad, and three of her four catchers, that went into the forest with her to cut down live trees and bring back the lumber, had thrown down their saws and said they wouldn't work with her any more. That left her with a crew that changed from day to day — share-workers, and not the best but the sullen and the slow that had no skills to offer elsewhere. Catching live wood was hard and dangerous toil even with a crew that knew their woodsmithing. Jemiu had her work cut out and more, bringing both a full load and a full crew back each day.

So she looked old, like I said, and tired besides. But she stood up as I came to the door and gave me a full courtesy. That let me see what was beside her — a beechwood box about a handspan on a side.

"Rampart," she said.

"Jemiu." I embraced her, and laid my forehead against hers. "It's been so long since we seen each other, except in Count and Seal. Come inside and drink some tea with me."

She made excuse at first, saying she had got work to do at the mill and didn't want to pull me from my duties. But when I pressed again, she said some hot tea on a dusty day like this would go down well, and she let me bring her indoors.

We sat together in the kitchen while Ban Fisher brought us tea with honey to drizzle into it. The beechwood box got its own chair. I hadn't really looked at it, seeing it only as some piece of woodsmithing that Jemiu needed to finish or else to deliver. "How's Athen?" I asked. "And Mull? I heard Athen and Junnu Beekeeper was pair-pledged. Will they stand on the tabernac soon?"

"They won't," Jemiu said. "Halla and Coin said they'd die first, and Junnu took his word back. There's no pledge there now."

That was a sad thing, and a serious one. I said I'd speak with Halla and Coin if Jemiu wanted it.

"No," she said. "Not by any road. Athen got her crying done, and now she's well. Who'd want to wed a boy that's got no more courage than that, to fold down flat when he's scolded and not hold to the girl he loves?"

She took the box from off the chair and laid it on the table between us. "I want to offer this to the village," she said. She said it quick, to shut down the talk about Athen and Junnu.

"Mull loves birds," she said. "Starlies, bluitts and yellowhats, mostly, but almost anything that flies and doesn't bite. She coaxed them into coming to the house by throwing out goosefoot seed and linseed for them."

"That's nice," I said, not knowing at all where this was going. "Little birds is bright, and cheers up a place."

"That's it," Jemiu said, nodding her head hard. "That's it, Rampart. Little birds is bright as anything."

I put my hand on top of hers. "Jemiu," I said, "you knowed me as a girl, when me and Koli and Jon would scuff and tip together all around the village. You don't need to call me Rampart. Nor what Koli did don't have to come between us ever."

She took her hand away. Her face, that had been open and excited, shut down into a cold frown. "What Koli did isn't even knowed yet," she said. "Not properly. When it comes out, Spinner – when the truth of it comes out – there'll be some that will abide it sorely."

I didn't have anything to say to that. I had won my point in a way, for she gave me my own name, but what I said had not brought us closer but pushed us further apart. "What did you come for, Jemiu?" I asked as gently as I could.

"For this," she said. She turned the box to face me. I saw it had a round hole cut into one face of it, near the top. There was a kind of a smaller, open box fixed over the hole, about as wide as my thumb and twice as deep.

"This is how yellowhats build their nests," Jemiu said. "Halfway up in a tree or a little higher, with this tunnel to get inside that keeps out bigger birds. They face it into the setting sun, so the noon-day heat don't hurt the eggs. This is one I made, but it was Mull that thought of it. To make a nest out of wood, and nail it to the wall of our house so yellowhats would come there. And they come in great store. Every box was filled as quick as I put it up."

I still was slow to see where she was going. "It's a clever thing," I said, "but why would the village want it? For the gaiety and the colour, you think?"

"No, not that." Jemiu waved those things away. "What do yellowhats do, Spinner, if something gets too close to their nest?"

"Well, they lie low, if it's a small thing that comes. Chase it off maybe, if it's a little bigger. But if it's something they can't fight, like a tree-cat or a needle, then they make a great noise and fly straight up to make the hunter look a different way and not go after the eggs or the fletchlings."

Jemiu nodded again, and waited for me to put it together. "You think if we set boxes like this out in the forest," I said, "it might give the needles and tree-cats easier meat so they don't go after our hunters?"

"No," said Jemiu. "I'm not thinking of needles and tree-cats. I'm thinking of Half-Ax."

She laid it out for me, and I clapped my hands when I saw it. It was not a weapon Jemiu was bringing me, nor it wasn't anything we could use to fend off an attack. But it would tell us when an attack was coming, and where from. Such things might make the difference between mend and mar.

I praised Jemiu's cleverness to the skies, with her saying it was nothing much and refusing to be praised. When she got up to go, I rose too and embraced her again. "I've not forgot your kindness to me after my father died," I told her. "I mean to pay it back. I'll make sure everyone knows this was your idea, and I'll vote a thanks in the Count and Seal."

"I can't eat thanks," Jemiu said. "Get me some better catchers."

I promised I would, and I meant to do it. But in the end, I paid her back a different way entirely.

14

The day after I had that talk with Jemiu, Catrin Vennastin sat up at last and looked about her. As soon as word was brought to me, I ran to be at her bedside. I hoped she might be well enough to rise, to take up the firethrower again and be our Rampart Fire, but she was still too weak.

"I'm mending . . . slow but sure," she told me, her voice hoarse and breathless. "You just got to bear it . . . a while longer."

She was propped up in her bed in the room she had once given to me and Jon before we were turned out of the Hold and went to live at the tannery. She was as pale as her sheets, and couldn't say more than a dozen words without taking a rest.

"I'm not you," I told her. "I won't ever be you. You got twenty Summers on me, and you've been Rampart Fire for twelve of them. I been in exactly one fight, and only lived through that one because of blind luck. I got nothing to tell the Count and Seal."

Catrin tried three times to catch a breath. When she did, she used it to tell me I was a fool.

"I know it," I said.

"You been . . . in front of Half-Ax guns, and . . . you brung back . . . a victory. They look at you . . . and that's . . . what they see. That victory."

"But I didn't—"

Catrin put a hand over my mouth. I guess it took less breath than telling me to shut up. "They don't . . . need your doubts," she wheezed. "The hope . . . is what they need. So look . . . you don't tread on it."

"They need a leader that knows what they're doing."

"Yeah, that's . . . good too. So tell me . . . what you're doing."

I told her everything. She gave me back a few ideas of her own. Mostly about the fence and the stake-blind. She asked about Challenger too – if he had managed to make more bullets for his gun.

I had good news to share on that count at least. "They're growing in him now," I said. "They're not ready yet to be used, and he can't say when they will be. He said everything works slower for tech that's as big as he is – and he said a lot of the different parts of him, that he calls systems, don't work as well as they used to. But we can hope to have a batch of shells ready soon."

"Shells?"

"That's what bullets are called, once they get that big."

"That's good then," Catrin said. "What about the tech . . . from the Underhold?"

"Nothing yet."

"And the Half-Ax . . . guns?"

"Nothing there either."

Catrin coughed, and it took a while. "You know," she whispered when she could make shift to talk again, "there's got to be ways . . . to use that battle wagon that . . . we didn't figure out yet. You say you . . . was only in . . . the one fight. Challenger . . . must of been in . . . hundreds."

It was a good thought, and one I should have had my own self. I said I would ask him. Then I left Catrin's bedside quickly, for she was wearing herself out in talking to me. The coughing

101

would only get worse if I stayed, and by and by there would be blood in what came up.

"Stand hard . . . against Fer," was the last thing she said to me.

"You're of my thinking then?" I asked. "About the prisoners?"

Catrin shook her head. "I would of . . . killed one to make . . . the other speak. But . . . it's not me that's . . . Rampart Fire right now. It's . . . you. People got to . . . believe in you. They can't . . . do that unless . . . you believe in your own self."

I did not though, and that was the worst thing of all. I kept being afraid that some mistake of mine would ruin everything – and that by letting people put their faith in me I was leading them in a line-dance over the edge of a cliff.

I fell into bed each night so tired I thought I would sleep for ever. And each night woke from dreams full of blood and sundering to lie in the dark until my heart stopped trying to get out from under my ribs. I could have waked Jon, but I didn't. He was training every day with our fighters, and keeping the tannery going besides, so he was just as exhausted as I was. I looked at his face by moonlight or by the paleness of first dawn and thought what it would be like if he died because of me. If my baby did not come to be born because of me. If Fer was right, and my forbearing wrecked us all.

Fer had not relented. She did not have it in her to relent. Ever and again she came against me in the Count and Seal. Ever and again she said, without quite saying, that if Mythen Rood could find no one better than me to lean on, Mythen Rood would fall.

Jon sat through our skirmishes with his head down and his arms folded. I had asked him not to speak up for me in the chamber, because his love and loyalty belonged to me rather than to my arguments. His agreeing with me made me look weaker, not stronger. Outside, he gave me what comfort he could, and I took it gratefully. But I was learning what most people learn when they go about to lead others. You begin by wearing a mask and pretending to be a different person – a person that's like you with all the doubts and fears and yieldings taken out. But the more

102

you put that mask on, the harder it is to take it off again. You draw back from them you love, not because you don't need or want them any more but because you're not the right shape to fit with them.

So when I went to Challenger, as Catrin had bid me, I went alone. Challenger was tech of the before-times that I had met at Calder's ford and brought back home with me. He sat now in the middle of the gather-ground, and people went a long way around him when they passed. He looked like a wagon with a great many wheels. The bed of the wagon had a kind of a drum or tub set on top of it, and sticking out of the drum was the biggest gun you ever saw. The bullets it was meant to fire – bullets almost a stride long – were long gone out of the world, but Challenger was making more in a hidden place inside his great, wide frame.

It was very quiet inside Challenger. The noises of the village, of people working and talking and being together, fell on him like rain falls on a roof, and rolled down and trickled off again. Being in the heart of him, that was called a cockpit, was like being in a bucket at the bottom of the deepest well there was, except that nobody could draw you up again until you were ready to come.

"Did it ever fall to you," I asked Challenger, "to fight against enemies that was much bigger in numbers than you was, and had better weapons in their hands?"

"Oh yes," Challenger said. "Many times."

"And did you always prevail?"

"Not always, no. I sustained terminal damage twice, and was immobilised but left partially functional twice more. My commanders saw fit, each time, to repair me and send me out to fight again. They had faith in me, and in my crew. We won great victories for the interim government – including some when we were very heavily outnumbered."

"What's the secret then? To winning, I mean. How do you do it when enemies is swarming on you like needles?"

"There is no secret. Or perhaps there are too many secrets to count." Challenger went quiet, for a long enough time that I gave a cough to remind him I was still there. "I'm sorry," he said. "I was consulting my non-volatile storage. The memories of acting sergeant Elaine Sandberg are stored there. Elaine feels as I do about this. Once a battle starts, there are too many things happening all at once for any mind, whether organic or engineered, to take them all in and respond to them in real time. The relevant factors therefore are the planning that takes place before the battle, the placement and movement of forces during it and the ability of commanders to identify and track emergent events."

"Emergent events?" I said. "What does that mean?"

"Out of the chaos, patterns will appear and coalesce. Out of a million tiny, passing things, some will not pass but will stay and become pivotal. Other things will hinge on them, and bend their courses. If you see these pivotal events clearly, and interpret them correctly, you can use them to further your goals."

I'll tell you truly, I understood only half of this. Less than half. And what I understood was all at odds with the way battle had seemed to me, the onliest time I was in one. I saw the chaos well enough, but I didn't see the patterns coming out of it. Then I pondered a little harder, and a thought came to me.

"Was you one?" I asked Challenger. "In the fight at Calder's ford, was you an emergent event?"

"Ultimately, yes. At first, I was only terrain. Your accessing my cockpit, and engaging my auto-repair, made me into an emergent event – impossible to predict before the battle began, but crucial to its outcome."

"Okay, then," I said. "I see that."

So all we needed to get the better of Half-Ax was something else like Challenger – something really big, standing in plain sight, that yet wasn't noticed by anyone in the fight until someone grabbed a hold of it and made it work for them.

Well, I thought, I'll keep my eyes open for such a thing. And hope to the dead god I know it when I see it.

"So when you fought—?" I said, but my words were cut off

104

by a yell from outside, and then by a boom that was almost as loud as the tocsin bell. Someone was banging on Challenger's side. "I got to go see what that is," I said, and scrambled up.

My heavy belly made me slow. By the time I stuck my head up out of Challenger's turret, Ban was already crawling up over his side. I knew how scared she was of the big wagon, so that said a lot about the haste she was in.

"Spinner," she said. "Someone's come!"

"Who?" I said. "Come from where?"

She grabbed my arm in both her hands. Her eyes were wide. "From Half-Ax. A messenger from the Peacemaker. Fer said to bring you!"

15

Fer and Perliu were waiting for me in the Hold's entrance hall. Both were in their best clothes, and Fer wore the bolt gun on her shoulder in a holster of grey leather. They were not happy, or calm.

"He was just standing by the gate when the sun come up," Perliu told me. "Fran and Asha was on watch, but they didn't see how he got there. He's not carrying no weapons, they said, and he's dressed all in red. We didn't see him our own selves yet. We had them bring him to the Count and Seal."

"After searching him first," Fer said. "Just because they seen no weapons didn't mean there was none. I had them bring him into the Hold by the back door, so he wouldn't see Challenger."

"That was a good thought," I said. We needed to keep what few advantages we had a secret as long as we could.

"How did he get here though? He couldn't of walked through the woods of Calder on his own, with no bow or spear. He'd have been swallowed down and shat out before he went half a mile."

"It's a trick," I said. "Or a seeming, rather. Probably a whole tally brought him and kept him safe. Nor he didn't walk across

106

the valley in a red suit, with empty hands. All that's for the look of it. We're meant to marvel, and be cowed."

"I think you must be in the right of it, Spinner," Perliu said. "So what would make such a show needful, do you think? What does the Peacemaker want out of this?"

"We won't know until we hear this messenger out. Let's listen close, and say as little as we can. Things spoke in heat might serve us badly."

"Don't fear my wits," Fer said, "or my temper. It's you that's new-come to the Hold, not me. I know what's needful better than you do."

The Half-Ax man was waiting for us in the middle round, where only Ramparts are meant to go. There was no way he could know this was an insult, and we were not about to tell him. He had pulled a chair up close to the one he was sitting in and was resting one foot on it. His hands were clasped to his stomach, and he smiled when he saw us coming down to him. Everything about him spoke of ease and comfort.

He was a strange sight, to be sure. He was dressed in red from his head to his feet. It was fine cloth too, with a lustre to the weave, and being my father's daughter I could not but admire it. Whoever made that suit, and the dye it was dipped in, and the jet buttons it was sewn with, they knew their trade.

For the rest, he was a slight man and a tidy one. His hair was silver-grey and stood in waves. His eyes were grey too. He wore a moustache, and there was silver wire braided into the ends of it.

"Ladies!" he said, climbing to his feet to greet us. "Sir! You must wonder who you've invited within your gates. Please allow me to present myself. I am Kanrat Voice, and as you might guess from my name I speak for the Peacemaker. Here is his seal."

He pulled up the sleeve of his beautiful, ridiculous coat. On the inside of his wrist, tattooed there in black ink, was a wood-smith's hatchet.

We told him our names in return. He didn't seem to listen

107

very closely, but busied himself with tugging his cuff back into its proper place. "It was good of you to receive me," he said, "when you had no word I was coming. Any more kindnesses you had in mind would be very well taken. Some water or small beer, say, to quench my thirst after my long walk. Or an omelette with pepper and chives mixed in, and a pot of salt beside it."

For all her assurances about her temper, I saw Fer's face set hard at this speech. It was not a good beginning.

"I'll have some beer fetched," I said to forestall her saying something sharper.

I went back into the house, found Ban and asked her to bring a pitcher and three cups. "He asked for an omelette too, if you've any eggs set by."

Ban sniffed and shrugged her shoulders. "So I'm to be a skivvy for Half-Ax now!"

"Ban, this is our chance to put things right, and avoid further fighting," I said. "If that means setting our pride aside a little, I think it's a price worth paying."

"I know what I'd like to pay him," she muttered, but she hastened away to do as she was bid.

When I went back inside the chamber, I found the red-coated man holding forth loudly about the beauty of fresh eggs and all the many things you could do with them. Perliu and Fer wore faces that said this speech had been going on for some time. They were sitting in the middle round, facing him. I didn't trouble to bring a chair for myself but went and stood behind them. "Eggs are proof that there is an order in things." The red man held up his two hands with the fingers locked together to show what order meant. "We hunger, and we're satisfied. We thirst, and we drink. The world holds everything that's needful for us."

"And a great deal that isn't," Fer said.

The man threw his head back and laughed. He held up his hands like Fer was too quick for him and he was giving up the fight. "Well," he said, "I'm of a hopeful frame of mind. It's how I was made. Others are different, I know."

I thought I saw an opening to get us onto something that mattered more than eggs. "We're all of us hopeful," I said, "that we can talk through what happened at Calder ford and come to an understanding."

"At Calder ford?" The man stroked his chin with one long finger, then wagged it at me. "Ah! That's where Wing Arrowhead met you, then."

"You didn't know?" Perliu asked, looking at Voice shrewdly.

Voice smiled. "Their orders were flexible. In an engagement of that kind, our captains are licensed to make their own opportunities. The main thing was to get your tech from you with few losses. We thought ten would be enough and to spare, but it seems we were wrong."

This didn't sound much like saying sorry. I tried again. "Well, sometimes we make a mistake in the hot moment, and then we repent it after."

"Well, that's it, of course," Voice agreed. "Like the man who thought to save shoe leather by going on one foot. We should have sent a hundred and done the job properly."

A silence fell in the room. It seemed as if none of us knew what to say to this. Ban arrived just then with the pitcher, and I spent some time in pouring the beer, considering what might be said next. But Fer spoke up first.

"Still," she said, "that's all past. What matters is where we go now."

Voice slapped his hand against his knee. "You're right, lady. You're right indeed. And as far as that goes, I bring good news." He smiled wider than ever, and turned his face on each of us in turn as if he was excited his own self by what he was about to say. "The Peacemaker will accept your surrender, and take Mythen Rood under his protection. He asks only that you give up all the tech you hold and that anyone who shed Half-Ax blood should be handed over to justice. He is known for his mercy, but it's seldom he's shown such favour to anyone. It's out of respect, I think, that you beat Wing Arrowhead when no one thought you could. So may I offer my congratulations? You fought well, and bear no shame. Now you're part of the protectorate, a happy outcome for all."

Having said his piece, he sat back and folded his hands across his chest. "That omelette," he added, "is taking a goodly time. Perhaps it's miscarried. I'd be obliged if one of you would go and look for it."

I think I still was hoping there was some way words could solve this – and thinking that, I was picking my slow way through the words Voice had said in search of a thread I could follow back to common sense and reason.

"We can't give up our tech," I said. "We're dead without it."

Voice spread his hands. "Alas, I'm only my master's voice. I can't speak different words than he bid me."

"And as to the spilling of blood . . . You spilled ours first. We did nothing but defend ourselves when you struck at us."

"That was understandable," Voice said. "But it doesn't change the price. Nothing can."

"The price?" Perliu repeated. "What is it we're paying for?"

"For disrespecting what belongs to my master. His soldiers' lives are precious in his sight."

"Then hear what we have to offer," I said quickly. "Most of your tally died in the fight, but we took two alive. If the Peacemaker will swear to send no more against us, we can give you those two back."

"Ah." Voice sighed and shook his head. "I wish it could be so. But I remind you again, I only speak the words as they were given to me, and carry back your answer. I'm not here to haggle or barter with you for this or that. It's not in my gift to say yes or no. Only to take your surrender."

"But you said the Peacemaker holds his soldiers precious."

"And so he does. His heart breaks for every life that's given in his name."

"Then go to him and tell him. We don't want to fight you."

Another wide smile. "In that case, all you need to do is say yes. Surrender and be blessed."

Fer was quicker than me and gave her answer first. She snatched up the mug Voice was reaching for and with a jerk of her wrist threw his beer in his face.

"I hope that cloth don't take a stain," she said. "You're a long way from a wash-tub."

Voice sat for a moment longer, mazed and dripping. Then he lifted himself up out of his chair. His smile vanished slowly off his face, so the ghost of it could still be seen for a while after it was gone.

"That's a heavy insult to lay on the Peacemaker," he said at last. "For in offering it to me you offer it to him too. Your answer is meaningless now, but I'm tasked to carry it in any case so I needs must ask again."

"The answer's no," said Perliu.

"No," I agreed.

"Not while I fucking live," said Fer. She held the mug upside down and let the last drops fall down onto the floor.

Voice bowed. "Well then," he said, "I'll take my leave now, if someone will kindly see me to the gate." He took a kerchief from his pocket and brushed at his spattered jacket, but quickly gave it up. Nothing was like to shift that dark brown stain.

"Tell the Peacemaker what we said about the prisoners," I said as Fer beckoned Asha and Fran down from the doorway where they had stood all this time on guard. I thought I had got to try one last time, for all that it seemed hopeless. "We're open to reason, if he wants to come again and talk further."

"He'll come again," Voice said. "Of course he will. Things will proceed as they must."

"Meaning . . .?"

"Why, meaning war. Did I not say? There was never a third way out of this; only the two – your surrendering, or your ceasing to be. It's a pity. A waste of valuable things and of many lives. Weeping is not a part of my remit, but I'll weep for you. A little."

This last he said to Fer. He did not seem sorrowing though.

The corners of his mouth twitched up as if that smile was trying to come back.

Asha and Fran fell in on either side of him and took him back the way he'd come. They met Ban coming in with the omelette on one of the Hold's best trenchers. Voice bent over to sniff at the dish, nodded at her and went on by.

"Was I too slow?" Ban asked, looking at our solemn faces in dismay.

"No, Ban," I said. "Our business was done sooner than we thought."

"It's not done yet," Perliu said grimly.

16

So now we were at war, it seemed. A strange word from an older time – from stories of the world that was lost. I relished those stories, but only because of their distance. In our mothers' mothers' time, people found reason to hate each other to the death. Their greatest smiths made tech that could only be used to kill, and gave it to their red tallies to use. A mad and terrible thing, safely wrapped in the comfort of *once upon a time*.

There was no time to be wasted now in guessing games or ring-a-roses. I sent Lune and Jarter to fetch Morrez down from Frostfend Farm, and took myself off to the library where I meant to receive him.

"What will you do, Spin?" Jon asked me. "Surely you didn't change your mind about torture?"

"No. What I got in mind won't be nice for either of us, but it's not that."

"I'll stay with you then, and keep watch while you speak."

I turned to him and shook my head. "No, Jon. I think this only works if I'm alone with him."

He put his hand down to my swollen belly. "You're not though. There'll be three of you there. Let me make it four."

I kissed him and hugged him hard. "No, love. Not this once. I've got to be Rampart Fire right now. If you stay, I'm only Spinner Tanhide."

"Well, it's Spinner Tanhide I was looking to help."

"And she loves you for it. You'll see her again soon."

He went away, all unhappy. It was the first time my being a Rampart had come between us, and I could see how much it hurt him, but the mending of that hurt would have to wait.

Along came Morrez at last, Lune and Jarter pushing and chivvying him into the room. He looked somewhat vexed to be taken away from his work. "Leave me alone with him a while," I said, after Jarter had sat him down in the same chair he was in before. She was no happier than Jon was to leave me alone with a dangerous prisoner.

"Morrez won't hurt me," I said. "You wouldn't do that, would you, Morrez? Lift your hand against a woman that's got a baby in her?"

"No," Morrez said, like he was angry at the thought of it. "I never hurt nobody outside of a battle. I'm a soldier of Half-Ax. We got faith, and we got honour."

Jarter came over and smacked him on the back of his head, making him flinch. "You fucking ambushed us at Calder," she said. "Don't say you got honour when you sneaked up behind us and fired on our backs."

"Swear you won't hurt me, Morrez," I said. "Swear on something you care about."

"I swear it," Morrez said, rubbing his head. "On the Peacemaker's name, and on the oath I made him."

"You're sure about this, Rampart?" Lune asked me.

"I'm certain sure, Lune."

"I'm right outside the door," Jarter said to the boy. "If I hear a sound I don't like, I'll come in here and beat on you until you're just one bruise." She and Lune went out with a lot of backward looks.

"I won't answer no questions," Morrez told me as soon as we were alone.

114

"Then I won't bother asking none. Morrez, I'm thinking your work at Frostfend is all done."

Morrez give a little bit of a start at that. He looked just exactly the same as when Jarter smacked his head. "No, it's not," he said. "It's not close to being finished. There's plenty of hay yet to be baled. And all the crop needs hilling. That's not a one day's work, but goes on and on. If I got to labour for the food you give me, I'll abide it. You can see I'm abiding it."

I sit back on the bench and rubbed my lower back that was sore from leaning forward. I also did it so I could turn my head to the side and hide the smile that came there until I could send it away again. The boy was so solemn-serious, and so easy to see through. "Oh, you're abiding it well enough," I said, when my look was settled. "I hear good report of you."

That was a half a truth. Mercy Frostfend was happy enough with the boy's toil, but she didn't like the way he hung around Getchen, offering help she didn't need but oftentimes took anyway. The way the two of them were casting sheep's eyes at each other, she said, if something wasn't done, there might be more than potatoes growing up at the farm before too long.

"I don't mean to stop you working," I told the boy now. "Only to share you around a little, so the whole village gets the use of you."

Morrez did his best to hide his dismay. "I – I'm used to the farm though. I'm better there. If I got to learn something different—"

"Then you'll be twice as useful next year when we do this all over again."

He opened and closed his mouth a few times. Nothing came out of it.

"Oh," I said. "I forgot. We won't be here next year, will we? Half-Ax is coming. Half-Ax will break our gates open and come and take what's theirs. The insult at Calder's ford will be venged on all of us, and that will be that."

A lot of different feelings went across Morrez's face one after the other. "You can't beat Half-Ax," he said at last.

"Say we did though."

"Nobody ever has done it. Nobody. Lilboro had ten times what you got, and Lilboro's a hole in the ground now."

"And it may be we'll end the same way. But say we was standing when the fight was done. Say we was still here. Where would you be in such a case, Morrez Ten-Taken?"

The boy did a lot more blinking, and a lot more not-answering.

"Where?" I asked again. "Tell me."

"I'm your prisoner, ain't I? I got no choice where I'd be."

"Well then, say if we was to give you the choice."

"What?"

"If you was minded to stay with us, I could make it happen. There'd be plenty who'd kick at it, but if I told them you passed your testing and you're a man of Mythen Rood, none would gainsay me. What would you say if I put that choice in front of you?"

The chair creaked as the boy shifted his weight. He shook his head hard as if a fly had bitten him. "You won't do it though. This is needless talk."

"Then answer me straight, and we'll set it by. It's not that hard a question. If I was to give you the choice, what would you say?"

Morrez met my stare for a few moments longer. Then he bowed his head onto his chest so I couldn't see his face any more. I waited. His chest heaved in and out like of a sudden his breath was coming short.

I got up and went to the door. I slipped the latch and shot the bolt, locking us both in together. He looked up at the sound of the bolt going home, then hunched down again as if he was shrinking from an offered blow.

"I see I've gravelled you," I said. "I didn't mean to."

"It's a lie," Morrez said. His fists were clenched hard in his lap. "It's not a choice, it's just a lie. Everything you say is lies. And the things you do – like sending me up to that farm – they're just to work on me and make me weak."

"How does it make you weak, Morrez?"

He raised his head at last and turned to look defiance at me. But he looked away again just as quick. "I said you was trying to make me weak. I didn't say it worked."

"Ah," I said. "I got that wrong then. You seem unhappy though, and I'm sorry for it. What is it that's troubling you?"

"Nothing's troubling me. Only . . ." He was mumbling the words so they hardly could be heard, his head sunk on his chest again. "When Half-Ax comes, there's . . . there's some I'd like to see spared."

"I thought there might be."

He gave me another glare, and this time managed to keep looking me in the eye. "I'm not stupid," he said. "I know Mercy talks to you."

"She answers when I ask," I said. "And I know you're no fool. So let's be done with all the lies and all the tricks. We got no time for them anyway. One day soon, our Rampart Arrow will come and fetch you and hang you on the gather-ground, and I'll be made to watch, and it will be a sad thing for the both of us."

I leaned my weight against the wall. It was a lot to carry around. "You say I'm lying to you, and striving to trick you. So let's make a bargain. I'll put a question to you, and if you answer it straight you can put one to me. I swear I'll speak nothing but truth. How would that be?"

Morrez shrugged.

I waited.

"All right."

"But you got to answer. We both got to answer."

"I said all right."

"Then my first question's this. Does it make you sad in your heart, Morrez Ten-Taken, to think of us being whelmed and wasted? And them you work with at Frostfend all dead?"

Morrez didn't speak, but after a little while he bent his head. A nod.

"Thank you. Is there anything you'd seek to know from me?"

He looked at me hard. "Did you really put Hawk to the torture?"

"No. That was a lie. My turn now. Is there one person that comes to mind more than the rest when you think of Mythen Rood being razed?"

"You know there is. You wouldn't ask if you didn't know it. Was Getchen set on to be kind to me?"

"No. She's just kind because that's what's in her heart. Would you marry her if you was let?"

"Yes. No. I don't know." The boy threw up his hands, angry all over again. "That's not a real question! It's like what if the moon was an apple, would you take a bite?"

"I'll take it back then. How's this? Is Half-Ax always right in all its quarrels? Did Lilboro and Temenstow and them deserve what come to them?"

Morrez said nothing, though I waited a long time. I didn't mind. The asking was what mattered with that one.

"Her mother doesn't care for you much," I said. "You can't make that go away by hilling potatoes. You'd need to work and work, then work some more. Not just at Frostfend Farm but all around. The whole village. When they see you, when they talk to you, they'll realise you're no monster but only just the same as us. But it won't come easy. Nothing good ever does."

And that's as far as words will take us, I thought. For I was talking to my own self, as much as to him. And I was talking to Catrin – the Catrin that was sitting inside my head, telling me that if I wanted the trust of others I had got to have faith in myself.

Well, it was now or it was not, and if it was not then it would not be ever. And though I was afraid, I felt like I had known all along it would come to this. We were lost if we didn't have those guns. And lost another way if we broke this boy to get them.

I pointed to the bench. "Go open that up," I said to Morrez. "That bench there, in the window. It's a chest as well as a seat. See what's inside."

Morrez hesitated, giving me a wary look. "You said no tricks."

"It's not a trick. Just look."

He did as he was bid. When he opened up the bench seat, his eyes went big and round. He let out a huff of breath.

"Take it out," I said.

"It's – That's –"

"I know. Take it out, Morrez. We started down this road now, and I think we got to see where it takes us."

Morrez reached into the chest and brought out the Half-Ax rifle.

"This isn't the real one," he said. "You got your ironsmith to make a copy."

"I guess you got ways of knowing if I did."

He settled the gun in his two hands, one of them going to the stock while the other was cupped underneath the barrel. He pressed the palm of his hand to a place on the stock and held it there a moment. There was a ratchet sound as the tech went from sleep to waking.

Morrez turned and pointed the gun at me. At the middle of my body, not where my baby was nestled but just above.

"And there it is," I said. "The choice. Dead god bless you, Morrez, for you got to make it now and there's no hiding behind old promises or swearings."

"I don't hide from nothing," Morrez said. "I never hid from nothing in my life."

"Good then," I said. I cupped my hands across my stomach, but they wouldn't stop a bolt from the Half-Ax gun. At this distance, it would pick me up whole and throw me down in pieces. There was a great screaming going on inside me. Why? Why had I taken this chance?

"What hurts was they?" Morrez asked.

"What?"

"When you put Hawk to the torment, what did you do to her?"

"I told you that was a lie. I bit my finger and showed you the blood."

"I don't believe you."

"I can't help with that."

"Do you think I'm a traitor?" Morrez lowered his head and tilted it at the same time, so he was looking at me along the barrel of the gun. "Do you think I got no honour in me at all?"

"No," I said. "Just the opposite. I think you're such a one as doesn't make promises lightly – including the one you made just now not to hurt me. And I think you've had a chance to see what we are. We need that gun, and the other one, if we're to have any chance against Half-Ax. And we need to know more about their strength and their thinking. Otherwise we're like the smoke from off the wick of a blowed-out candle."

"You're like that anyway," Morrez said. But he didn't move. And the rifle, in his hands, didn't move.

"I think we're more," I said.

We stayed like that a little while longer. "Morrez," I said, "I got to sit down again or I'll get a cramp in my leg and fall over."

It was the right thing to say, it turned out. He put up the gun and dragged the chair over to me. I sank down into it with a grunt. I only just made it too. My legs were weak as string and I was close to throwing up everything that was in my stomach. I never thought Morrez would fire the gun at me, but my mind showed me pictures of it anyway. And I knew well it wasn't just my own life I was offering up.

Morrez sank down too, onto his knees. He used the gun like a walking cane, to lower himself. Otherwise I think he would have pitched over in a faint.

"I am," he said, and a sob tore its way out of him. "I'm a traitor! I sweared an oath, and now I'm a traitor to it!"

I took his head and laid it in my lap as he cried. "You can only be a traitor to what you love," I whispered to him, stroking his hair as if he were a child. And that being solemn truth, it calmed him by and by.

Koli

17

I waked up, and didn't have no idea how much time might of passed. I was not tired any more, so it must of been more than an hour or two. The lights in the room had gone off again. I lay there in the dark and waited.

"Hey, Koli-bou," Monono said. "Cone of silence is still on, and I've got a few little fun facts to share with you."

I slid down under the blanket to hide my face when I answered, the same way I did before. "Did you finish your deep dive?"

"Uh-uh. Not by a long way. But I took a little stroll through what's left of the internet, and I found a few historical databases that are still up and running. Or limping anyway. It's quite easy to find reference on the Sword of Albion. It turns out it's super-famous. Used to be, I mean, way back in the day."

"The ship?" I said. "The ship we're on? So it's really old like you said?"

"I'm not just talking about the ship, little dumpling. There's a lot more to it. Are you ready to go to school?"

I told her I was. The sound of her voice was a great comfort right then, so soon after I thought I'd lost her for aye and ever. She could not talk too much for me.

"Okay then," Monono said. "Listen and learn. Sword of Albion was a political movement a very long time ago. It's hard to say how long, because this was around the time of the Unfinished War – which back then they called the Unfolding Crisis, or sometimes just the Crisis – and after a while the records stop very abruptly. Which I guess means nobody was counting any more. But a little bit before that, when the world had only just started to unravel like an old pullover, Sword of Albion was quite the fashion on your little island. They promised to bring back everything people used to have in the good old days – clean streets, smiling children, jobs for life, meals that contained actual food, public hangings – and to protect what was left of Great Britain against what was left of the rest of the world. It's an ancient play from an ancient playbook. Are you with me so far?"

"I guess I am," I said. "These people wanted to be the Ramparts for the whole of Ingland. And they was happy to do it by telling lies."

"That's it exactly. Ramparts for all, and no take-backs. Koli-bou, you're not going to like this next part. It's going to make you think of all those spooky old stories again. Promise me you won't freak out."

"I promise," I said.

"Sword of Albion swept the country in the last election that ever was. Or at least the last one that made it to the history books. That was mostly down to their leader, who was handsome and strong and square-jawed. The manliest man who ever kissed a baby or broke a manifesto promise. Guess what his name was."

"I can't, Monono. I don't know nothing about them times."

"His name was Stanley Banner. And he looked like this."

A picture come into the DreamSleeve's window. It was a man with yellow hair. He had a thin face, and the kind of smile you wear when you just seen someone you would rather of not seen at all but have got to put a coat of paint on your misliking.

124

"So I guess the Stanley Banner they got here was named after him," I said. "They look a lot like each other."

"They do, don't they? And the coincidences keep piling up. This glorious leader had a father named Paul and a mother named Lorraine. Their photos are on record too."

More pictures come into the window. The picture of Paul looked just exactly like Paul looked now. Lorraine was somewhat older and a lot more tired, but still there could not be no mistaking her.

"Things got very bad very quickly, Koli-bou. There's a reason why Prime Minister Stanley Banner is remembered as a demon that does dark magic and eats people. Actually, there are a few million reasons. He declared himself Ruler-for-Life, executed most of his political rivals, and led the charge in some of the worst massacres the world had ever seen. There was a famine going on by this time, so some of Stanley's followers said the massacres were a good thing. Very necessary. Proof that he was a great man who could make the tough calls.

"And then he died. Murdered by a waitress who hid a grenade inside a soup tureen. Her last words were 'Eat this, you feckless bastard'. His were a lot more inspiring and poetic, but I'm pretty sure they were made up later. Sword of Albion fell apart after Banner died. It split into lots of factions shouting at each other that they were the keepers of his legacy, and murdering each other over commas and semi-colons. And meanwhile the Crisis kept getting bigger and bigger, until in the end it swallowed everything. The bad guys and the worse guys ended up side by side in the circular file of history. So sad, neh."

I was trying hard to make sense out of all of this, but every time I thought I'd got a hold on it I would lose it again. "Can you show me the pictures one more time?" I asked.

"Sure." Monono put the three faces side by side in the DreamSleeve's window, but it was mostly Paul and Lorraine I was looking at. "They're the same," I said. "I mean, they look just exactly like. So our Paul and Lorraine is models of this Paul and this Lorraine."

"Pretty much. It's not just the physical likeness either. Surviving texts suggest that Paul was violently abusive and Lorraine was obsessively controlling under a butter-wouldn't-melt gloss. I've got some old film footage, and even the voices are the same."

The DreamSleeve popped and crackled for a moment, and then I heard Lorraine's voice. "Proud doesn't begin to express what we feel. Our son has brought about what can only be called a rebirth. A rediscovery. He's reminded us all of what Britain was, and needs to be again. He's helped us to find our true selves."

But . . ." I said. "But . . ." It was hard to get further than that one word.

"I know, dumpling."

"Why would anyone want to bring back Stannabanna's – I mean Stanley Banner's – mother and father? Why not Stanley his own self?"

"Well, maybe they did that too."

That hit me on a raw place. "What? But this Stanley isn't anything like that one. He's just a boy!"

"He is right now. But if you were trying to grow your own fascist dictator, you might decide to grow from seed. There are some boys from Brazil who might have an opinion about that."

I was more confused than ever now. "Boys from where?" I said.

"It was a joke, Koli-bou, and it's not funny enough to explain. There's a thing called a clone. An exact copy of a person, grown from little tiny pieces of that person's body. Pieces called cells."

"And you think Stanley is a clone?"

"I think he might be, yes. And if you're going to ask me why anyone would bother to make robots – which is expensive and complicated – if they could grow their own flesh-and-blood copies to order, I'd have to say I don't know. Maybe Paul and Lorraine need to stick to a script, and Stanley needs to do . . . something else. But we're going to have to pick this up another time. The floor outside is vibrating like a hi-hat with the clutch off. Somebody is walking this way, and they're stopping right outside."

The warning come only just in time. There was a click as the door opened, and then Lorraine was standing in the doorway.

She come into the room all smiles, her voice ringing out like it was a song at Summer-dance. "Hello there, sleepy-head. Roll out of that bed now, and be quick about it. We've got work to do!"

18

I come up out of the covers so quick and flustered, I must of looked just exactly like a rabbit breaking cover when it hears a mole snake hissing. I could not of done more to make it look like I had got a secret to hide.

Lorraine only laughed though. "What's this?" she said, putting one hand on her hip. In the other hand, she was holding a bundle of folded cloth. "Are you hibernating, young man? I hope not, because it's a beautiful morning out there. The sun's been up for hours, and you should be too. Come on out of there, Koli Faceless. Pick yourself up and dust yourself off. Look, I've brought you a present. You can't keep wearing blues you haven't worked for."

She put the bundle down on the bed and unfolded it for me to see. It was my own clothes that she had brung back to me. They was not the exact same as before though. All was clean as new now that had been dirty with mud and rimed with salt when last I seen them. My shirt and trousers had been mended with thread, and my boots was reheeled. It was good work too. Even though I knowed Lorraine was not a person but a monster in the shape of one, I couldn't keep from asking, "How did you do that so quick?"

Lorraine ruffled my hair. I did my best not to pull away from her, but I stiffened just the same. She seen me do it, and a frown come on her face, but only for a moment. Another smile chased it off right after. "Bless you. It's not hard. I'm a dab hand with a needle and thread. And gluing a new heel on is half a moment's work. It's nothing, Koli. I was happy to do it."

It was not nothing to me. Spinner Tanhide had give the boots to me just a little while before I was sent faceless. They was one end of a rope, kind of, that had Mythen Rood at the other end of it. It would of grieved me more than I could say to lose them.

So I thanked Lorraine as politely as I could. It wasn't easy to find the words to do it. I remembered how I had liked her when I first seen her, for her soft voice and her kindness and her smile. Now I knowed we was prisoners here instead of guests, and besides that I knowed too well what she was. I kept thinking of the fish-eyed wife and the fish-eyed children in the story. It was all I could do to keep standing right next to her and not press myself against the wall in case I touched her without meaning to.

"Well, you're very welcome," she said, with a little laugh behind the words. "You bring out the mothering instinct in me, Koli. You look like you need some looking after. Now, you get yourself dressed and we'll be on our way."

"Where to?" I asked her.

"That's up to you. There's the museum. The gym. The movie house. The main thing I'm concerned about is that Stan gets to spend some time with you. Both of you, I mean – you and Cup. I know he can be hard work, but he doesn't get much company out here, bless him, and it's useful for him to meet real people once in a while." A change come on her face, like she was looking inside herself at something only she could see. "It's important that he should get used to being around others. Essential, even. When he's older . . . Well, he won't be spending his whole life here on *Sword*."

I tried not to show nothing in my face when she said *real*

129

people. It seemed almost like she was testing me to see what I knowed, or didn't know, about her and Paul.

"Will Ursala be with us?" I asked.

"No, Ursala is working. We'll be stopping by the lab though. She says she's got some medicine for me to pass along to Cup. Would you know anything about that?"

"It's medicine to keep her voice and her face and her body from changing. Cup is crossed."

"She's what?"

"Crossed. She's got a body that's like a boy's, but Ursala was able to make the hormones that—"

Lorraine put her hand across my mouth. I run out of words all at once, shocked at that touch that I didn't want and didn't see coming. She was shaking her head, with her lips all pursed up like she had tasted something bad. "All right," she said. "That's enough of that unpleasantness, thank you. You're our guests here, and I wouldn't dream of interfering, but really! Don't you think boys should be boys and girls should be girls?"

She took her hand away, so I guess she meant for me to answer. "I don't know what you mean," I said. "People is people."

"But god shows us what we are by the way he makes us."

It was such a strange thing to hear, I didn't know for a moment what to say to it. "Well," I said at last, "then I guess he made Cup knowing she's a girl."

We stared for a few seconds longer, each at other. Then Lorraine laughed. She took my hands in hers and give them a squeeze.

I wished with all my heart she was not so ready to touch me. "The weight of the world on your shoulders," she said. "You're a good friend, Koli. But shake a leg now. You've got a busy day ahead of you!"

She waited outside again while I changed my clothes. When I come out, she inspected me, head to toe, brushing my shoulders and twitching the front of my shirt so it would hang right. "I'm sorry to take the uniform away from you," she said, "but these things have to be done the right way. The next time you wear Albion blues, you'll have come by them properly. You'll be youth troop at first, but not for long. And I bet you'll be a squad leader before you're seventeen. Okay, by the left, quick march." She walked on down the hallway, lifting her legs up high and swinging her arms backwards and forwards. When she seen me staring, she only laughed. "Don't worry, Koli," she said. "You'll pick it up."

The way we went was a new way, at least at first, and it took us through a great many doors that opened when Lorraine come to them. Well, oftentimes they opened, but not always. Some of them didn't do nothing at all, and some tried to open but then stuck halfway. When that happened, Lorraine pushed them the rest of the way with her own two hands. There was a great grinding of metal as she pushed, but her face stayed calm as if she was not straining herself at all.

I was looking at all this a mite closer than I did on the first day. I seen that when the doors opened they didn't do it all by their own selves. There was something Lorraine done when she come to them. She touched her hand to the door, close to where the handle was, and then the door would spring open as if it only just then come awake and seen her. Whenever we come to a door of a shaking room, that didn't have no handle, she touched the silver plate on the wall next to the doors instead.

The second or third time she done this, I thought I seen a piece of metal, flat and round, sitting in the middle of her palm. I wasn't certain sure, since I only seen it for a half of a moment, but after that I kept on looking and I seen it ever and again. One time, when the door didn't open right away, Lorraine did the same thing three times over. She ended up by pressing her whole hand to the door until at last it opened up.

All the rooms we went through was either very full or very empty. There wasn't one that was in the middle, like a room where people might choose to live. Some of them was open onto big empty spaces like I seen before, where something had ripped the ship open – and there was two rooms together that was open to

131

the outside. That was the biggest surprise of all. I stood there staring out at just nothing but sky and ocean until Lorraine bid me go on with some joke about how I was dawdling and she was shocked at my laziness.

This was how she behaved the whole way – just as bright and as cheerful as she was the day before. She kept up the same chattering talk about how sweet and clever I was, and kind of pretended that there wasn't no hair or hint of a quarrel between us. Like Cup and me hadn't been shut up in our rooms with threats and curses. Or like setting drones to wander round your house at night and shoot people that was walking there was a task you might do in the way of things – like drawing water or chopping wood. Or beating your son.

"Do you and Paul follow Dandrake?" I asked. For it seemed to me that would be a peg that fit in the hole.

"Who's that, dear?" Lorraine asked. She didn't break her stride or even look at me.

"Dandrake. The messenger that was sent down out of Heaven after people stopped recking the dead god's word."

She tutted her tongue and put on a sour face. "Oh," she said. "That one. The rabble-rouser who thinks he's the second coming. No, we don't have any truck with all that nonsense. Anyone who names himself Daniel Jesus Mohammed Moses Drake and expects to be taken seriously is tainting the good fresh air as far as I'm concerned. And that's before he sticks his big fat nose into politics." She shaked her head. "No, we're Presbyterians. My great-grandparents were Scots, and very low church. They broke into a rash at the sight of a stained-glass window."

I had give up trying to make sense of all this, and was trying my best to remember each turn we took so I could find my way back if I needed to. It was hard because a lot of the halls and rooms on *Sword of Albion* had the same look to them, with broke and burned things all piled up. What I done, though, was to use a trick my friend Spinner Tanhide teached to me one time. I choosed one broke thing in each room and give the room a name to fit with what that one thing looked like. One room would be stovepipe, the next one birds' nest and so on.

But we was come by this time into some rooms that had a familiar look to them. There was a room full of white cupboards, and then a room full of shelves. I was near to being certain what the next room would bring, and I was proved right. The door opened on the room with the big bench, and the dagnostic lying out on the bench, and Ursala working at it.

There was something new there besides. Paul Banner's drone floated high up in the corner of the room with its red light winking. It turned in a circle or rocked from side to side from time to time, but it didn't move from its place.

I seen at once that Paul and Lorraine wasn't bothering to make no more pretences. We was prisoners here, all three, and they meant for us to know it.

19

Ursala looked up when I come in. She seemed really pleased to see me, but she only showed it by giving me good day. I think I told you already that she was not one for hugging or kissing or any such show. "It's good to see you, Koli," she said. "I'm making great strides here. This is a treasure trove."

"I'm glad you're happy, Ursala," I said. "And it's good to see you again too." I looked at the tech on the bench, or at least pretended to. "This here," I said with a deal of waving and pointing, "it's treasure, like you say. Which would you say is the best of it? Is it this one, would you say, or this here with the bits of wire sticking out of it?"

Ursala looked at me like I was mad, and I blushed furious red. If I could of thought of something to say that was not so stupid, I would of said it. The truth is, I wasn't even thinking about what was coming out of my mouth. The words was only meant to cover up what I was saying with my hands in Franker language. I was hoping Lorraine had never learned Franker since she lived way out here on the ocean where there wasn't no other villages to trade with. As far as the drone went, it was looking down from behind us. As long as I kept my hands close to my chest, it wouldn't be able to see what they was doing.

Are you all right? I said. *Tell me what they done to you.*

Ursala moved up beside me. Our backs was to Lorraine, and we was close enough now that she couldn't hardly see our hands at all. "Well, these modules here are immunological. I have some of them, but not in this condition. And this here, the XN-Cyte-S, is a fuller-featured version of the Cyte-7."

I'm fine, she told me with her hands. *Really. I could do without that thing* – rolling her eyes up towards the drone – *but they're giving me everything I need.*

"The sight seven," I said. "Oh yeah. That's a good one, to be sure. It's a deal better than the six any road. The six was no better than my arse."

And in Franker: *Can you get her out of the room? I got to talk with you.*

"Now you're here though," Ursala said, like it was an idea that only just had struck her, "I could use your help for a little while. Some of these units don't interface perfectly with my own base module. Perhaps you could splice them in for me?"

"I'd be happy to do that," I said. I turned to Lorraine, who didn't look happy at all. "Is that all right, Lorraine? Maybe for an hour or so? And then we can go see Stanley right after."

Lorraine didn't answer me, but looked to Ursala. "Is the boy a technician then?" she asked.

"One of the best I've ever worked with. If I could borrow him for an hour, it would speed the work up immensely."

Lorraine looked at the one of us and then the other while she chewed on this. "An hour," she said, sounding doubtful.

"Or half an hour, even. It probably won't take long to build an interface."

Lorraine chewed a mite harder, but at last she nodded. "Very well," she said. "I'll tell the others to wait."

She went back outside the lab and closed the door on us.

"Cone of silence is on, Koli-bou," Monono said in my ear.

I gun to tell Ursala, all in a rush, about what we'd learned. "Lorraine isn't what she looks to be," I said. "Paul isn't, either. They're—"

135

Ursala stopped me quickly with a hand on my arm. She signed in Franker *It's not a good idea to talk about this. They could easily be looking and listening through the drone.*

"No," I said. "They can't. Well, they can look, but they can't listen. Monono has put up a cone of silence."

"She's what?"

"Phase-cancellation counter-measures in the 50-280 Hertz range, baa-baa-san. That covers every sound the human throat can produce, with a comfortable little tuck-in at either end. But it doesn't put so much as a fingerprint on the rest of the soundscape. Assuming the drone is listening in, it's hearing every noise in the room – all the rustles and clicks and bumps, and a few breathing and sniffing sounds I've thrown in to keep things interesting – but it can't hear a word you say."

"You're sure?"

"Oh, I'm certain sure. I'm not making any promises about lip-reading, so maybe you should both keep your heads down when you're talking, just in case. That aside, you've got a clear run until the loony lady of the house gets back."

Ursala let out a long breath. She nodded. "Good then. Very good."

She leaned down closer to the bench, pretending to work with the tech that was there. "How is Cup?" was her first question.

"She's well," I said. "She was well when I seen her last. Only angry at how we was being treated."

"You have to watch her, Koli. You know how hot her temper is. She may put herself in danger without meaning to. It seems as though nothing here is what it looks to be on the surface. Not that the surface makes much sense in the first place."

I promised I would do my best to keep Cup from picking fights with anyone.

"And make her take her hormone mix. And tell her I'll be with her again as soon as I can."

I was surprised at all this care on Ursala's part. I suppose I should not of been, for Cup and her had been growing closer

136

and closer since the day we left Calder. "A little girl who never had a mother," Monono said one time, "and a dry old grandma who never had a kid. It's utterly amazing that those two hit it off." But it really was amazing to me, for I had ever knowed Ursala as someone who pushed the whole world away from her so she could see it clear and not get tangled up in it. Now it seemed there was a little bit of the world she wanted to keep close.

"I'll tell her," I said. Then I give her all the news Monono had give me. That Paul and Lorraine was not flesh-and-blood people but pretend. That they was most likely made out of tech. That they beared the names of Stanley Banner's mother and father, who was born before the Unfinished War – and not just the names, but the faces and the voices too.

A frown growed on Ursala's face while I was talking, but she didn't make no other answer. She did a good job of seeming to work on the tech, putting things in my hands from time to time and then taking them back again. If you didn't look too close, you would of thought we was going hard at some task.

"Stanley's real though," I said. "I mean, he's not tech like they are, but flesh like us. Monono said he might be a clone, from some place called Brazil."

"Pop culture reference," Monono said. "If I'm wrong though, and Stan was born out of a womb instead of a test tube, you've got to wonder where the womb is. As far as I can tell, until we came along he was the only living thing on this whole ship."

Ursala leaned down even closer to the bench as if she was looking for a particular tool or piece of tech. It was easy to see that none of this had left her feeling happy. "I'd already worked some of this out for myself," she said in a low voice. "The part about Paul and Lorraine, at least. Their archaic speech patterns were the first clue. Then after they refused a medical scan, I started to watch them more closely, and I realised that they don't breathe. But I don't think any of this changes our situation."

It took me a moment or two to untangle the meaning of that from the words it was said in. When I did, I couldn't believe I was hearing right. "But they was lying to us, Ursala!" I said. "Lying to draw us in. They give us a whole lot of sweet words, and some good food to make the words go down easier, but then they locked us in and set drones to guard us. And now you got a drone looking over your shoulder too. We're not guests here, but prisoners. You got to know we are!"

Ursala twitched her shoulders in a kind of shrug. "Yes," she said. "I know. I was escorted to a room last night and warned that it wasn't safe to wander. Then this morning, when I was escorted back, Paul left the drone here with some vague comment about routine security scans. Obviously I'm being watched, just as you are.

"That's one side of the equation. Here's the other. I've been given access to the most incredible array of medical technology I've ever seen – including back in Duglas before it fell. The sub-assemblies and plug-ins in this room are quite literally priceless. There's probably nothing like this facility anywhere in the world. Whatever their motives are, I can't afford to say no to what these people are offering."

"They're not people," Monono said.

"Neither are you, dead girl, and yet you expect us to trust you. The way I see it, we came here in the very faint hope of finding gene-editing tech. So we could stop an extinction event." Ursala waved her hand over the bench, and all the tech that was there. "Well, we might end up finding exactly what we need. Against all the odds, it could be right here in this room."

"The odds might look different from the dealer's side of the table, baa-baa-san."

"What do you mean?"

"You said they might be offering exactly what you needed. Exactly what do *they* need?"

Ursala didn't seem to want to answer that. For the first time since I knowed her, she dodged a question. "You know what's at stake here. If I can turn the diagnostic into a genetic loom, I can increase the ratio of live births to a level that could make all the—"

138

"Blah blah blah!" Monono broke in, loud enough so it made me start even though I knowed we was inside the cone of silence. "Stop telling us what we already know. You did a deal with them and you don't want to say what it is."

Ursala grimaced. "They've asked me to use the diagnostic to treat the boy."

"To treat him for what?" I asked. "What's he sick with? Is it something to do with the sores on his head?"

"According to Paul and Lorraine, he has a number of congenital conditions. Birth defects of one kind and another. They've refused to be any more specific than that, but what they want me to do – assuming I can build a working loom – is to edit his chromosomes to remove the aberrant genes."

"Is that a kind of medicine to make him better?"

Ursala gun to answer, but hesitated.

"That would depend on the genes, wouldn't it, baa-baa-san?" Monono said. "And you don't seem convinced."

"Don't try to browbeat me." Ursala sounded impatient. "But you're right, I'm inclined to be sceptical. The list of gene loci they've provided . . . Well, it's long. Several hundred different alleles, none of which have any medical significance. In fact, some of them don't have any function at all. They're in parts of the chromosome that aren't expressed."

"It sounds like they're lying to you then," Monono said. "Giving you some make-work to keep you busy while they go ahead and do something else."

"I don't know though," I said. "They seem awful eager to get Stanley fixed. And they was asking about the dagnostic even before they picked us up out of the water. If this is a trick, they're putting their shoulder to it."

"I don't think it's a trick." Ursala touched her finger to one of the pieces of tech on the bench, giving it what I thought was a longing look. "I just think they're lying about what they want, and why they want it. If the boy is a clone, as you say . . . Well, perhaps something went wrong with the cloning process.

Transcription errors or . . ." She shaked her head. "I don't know. Perhaps I should have refused to cooperate. But given what I could do with a gene-splicer if I got it to the mainland, it was hard to say no." Her finger was tapping light but fast on the tech, like her thoughts was racing by and she was trying to count them as they passed. "There's a full surgical module in here too. A fluid regulator. A brain imager. I don't know if I can build a working interface, but it feels wrong not to try. It's not as though we've got any way of leaving without the Banners' help. We don't even have a boat any more."

"I'll find us a boat!"

"Fine then. But in the meantime, the only way I maintain access to this stuff is by playing along with the Banners' agenda."

"You mean you're willing to perform surgery on a child?" Monono's voice was sharp. "Without knowing what it is you're doing?"

Ursala looked unhappy her own self, but she give back that sharpness when she spoke. "I know exactly what I'm doing, even if the reasons are obscure. What they're asking for is completely harmless. It won't do the boy any good, but it can't injure him. It's an unnecessary procedure – it must be – and that's a line I wouldn't normally cross. Right now, I'm prepared to stretch a point."

"They're unlikely to keep their promises," Monono said.

"I'm not a fool. Perhaps while I'm working here the three of you can find a way for us to get us out of here once I'm done. I assume they must have lifeboats. Probably in plastic drums on the deck. If this was a warship, they could have tactical skimmers too."

"It's going to be hard for us to do it," I said. "They're watching us close, like I said. But we'll try."

"Koli, that surgical module . . ."

"What about it?"

"I checked its inventory. It includes gender reassignment."

"I don't know what that is."

"It could give Cup an outside that matches her inside. A woman's body. Fully functional."

My mouth gaped open, and at first I couldn't find no words to speak. That sounded like magic to me. Then again, tech was like magic in a whole lot of ways.

"Don't mention that to Cup. If I don't succeed . . . I wouldn't want to raise a hope like that and then take it away again. But you see why I've got to stay? Why I've got to try at least? Everything we hoped for is here."

"Time's up," Monono said. "The Stepford wife is coming back. I'm going to have to drop the field, so you should probably say something boring for the sake of appearances."

But the door opened before I could think of anything, and Lorraine was among us again.

"The dread hour is come," she said, with a big smile on her face to show this was meant to be a joke. "I've come to claim my prize. Come along, Koli Faceless."

"A moment, please," Ursala said. "Koli, I want you to pass this along to Cup. Her hormone mix. It should keep her going for . . . oh, at least four days." She give me a little box from inside the dagnostic's big cupboard. The lid of the box was made of something like glass, that you could see through. Inside was a row of bottles no longer than the top of my thumb, all filled with what looked like water. They was not just bottles though, they was what Ursala called hypos, with plungers at the top and needles at the bottom.

"I'll give it to her as soon as I see her," I promise.

"Thank you for the loan," Ursala said to Lorraine. "Koli was a great help."

"I'm sure he was. We'll get out of your hair now, doctor, and leave you to your work."

Lorraine took me by the hand, which I was liking less and less, and brung me out of there.

20

Up in the crow's nest, we found Cup and Stanley already waiting for us. They was both of them standing at the end of the room next to the statue of a sword stuck into a rock. Cup was in her old clothes, just like me, so I guess Lorraine had paid a visit on her too.

"You don't know the story?" Stanley was saying. "Really? You never heard of Excalibur?"

"I already told you once," Cup said. She moved away from the boy, but he followed her.

"The weird thing is it was a Welsh legend first, and the sword had a different name. Arthur used it to kill the Irish king, who had come to wage war against—"

"Koli!" Cup pretended she had only just seen me, and used that to get away from Stanley. He looked after her, like he was hurt and confused she give him the back of her neck like that. We clasped hands, and then we went and sit down together, leaving Stanley standing.

"Tuck in," Lorraine said gaily. "Don't stand on ceremony, my loves."

There was a good meal set on the table – mostly the same things they give us to eat the day before. I sit down and grabbed myself some of it. I didn't even realise until then how hungry I was. We hadn't et but the one meal since we come onto the ship, which was more than a day ago. Stanley hadn't come over to the table and he didn't do it now. He stood and watched us eat, looking like he was waiting to be invited. I didn't mind that at all, though I did wonder at it. Yesterday he took every chance he could find to smack at us.

"Aren't you going to eat, hon?" Lorraine coaxed him. "Your treatment hits you worse on an empty stomach."

Stanley shaked his head. "I'm okay," he said.

"You should come over here and talk to your new friends."

Stanley opened his mouth and closed it a couple of times. I would of said his tongue was tied, except the day before he had always had ready words for anything that happened. "Can I show them the aquarium?" he asked at last.

"That's a great idea," Lorraine said, clapping her hands. "But you've got to eat some bread and honey first."

Stanley come to the table at last and et what she give him. He didn't seem to be tasting it, just chewing it and gulping it down. His eyes was flicking between me and Cup the whole time. Once he throwed me a smile, like he was my friend or wanted to be, but I didn't smile back and he stopped it quick enough.

Out of nowhere, and not for any reason, Lorraine got up off the table and come around behind us to squeeze our shoulders like we was her children just as much as Stanley was. Cup give me a look like she had found a choker seed in her shoe, and I guess my face was not much different. "Children are the future," Lorraine said. "And Albion's children are the *best* future. When I look at the two of you, and my own sweet boy, I see Britain a thousand years from now, even stronger, even better."

Stanley looked away out of the window, like she was showing him that picture and he didn't want to look at it.

Just then Paul come into the room. "You'll have to eat alone, darling," Lorraine told him. "We're off to the aquarium."

"Lovely," Paul said, though he kept a stern face on. "Before you go, though, I think we need to take our guests through some new ground rules. And you too, Stanley. I hear you played a part in yesterday's debacle."

Stanley blinked like he had just took a smack in the face. "Me? No, I wasn't . . ." He blinked some more, looking troubled and confused. "I'm sorry, Paul," he mumbled. "I won't do it again."

"I wish I could believe that." Paul give his son a hard stare, then turned it on me and Cup. "We're doing important work here. There are a great many things on this ship that are precious – priceless, even – and susceptible to damage. There are many more that are actively dangerous. From now on, you two will confine yourself to this one tower. You won't go down onto the deck under any circumstances, or try to access the sub-space. And even within the tower, you'll be accompanied everywhere by at least one of us. When you're not in our company, you'll be in your rooms. If you ignore these rules and strike out by yourselves, you'll trigger anti-intruder mechanisms that will very likely maim or kill you. You've seen my drone, and you've seen one of our ravens, but they're the very least of it. Do you understand?"

"A fuck and a fart on you," Cup said. "I'll go where I like."

Stanley drawed in a breath and shaked his head hard.

Paul's eyes seemed to get a lot bigger, though some of that was just his eyebrows going up his head. He give a kind of grunt – like them words had hit him in the stomach. His face flushed red. It was scary to see, especially now I knowed he was not a real man but just a thing that looked like one.

When I first met Monono, before she went off into the internet and got herself what Ursala called an autonomy, she used to say the same words to me ever and again, and always in just exactly the same way. So she would sound happy or teasing or sad or angry, but she wouldn't really be those things. It was just a show that she was being made to put on and couldn't change. Paul's anger had got to be like that, just a show of anger, but it looked like it was real and I was scared for what he might do.

I stepped in quick between them. If his anger was for Cup, the

144

best thing to do might be to throw something else in his way. "I got to tell you I don't understand, Paul," I said. I said it as soft and calm as I could, hoping to calm him too. "First you was all kind to us. Then you was all angry. And now it seems like you want to keep us locked up and guarded by drones, when before you said we was welcome here. I'd like to know why that is, and why you shut us in our rooms last night. I don't believe you had any right to do it."

Paul Banner give me a look like I was a thing he had found under his boot. "Well now," he said. "That sounds very familiar. I used to get a similar sort of bleating nonsense from Stanley, until I beat it out of him. Where do you think rights come from, boy?"

I didn't see what that question meant. "They don't come or go," I said. "They're just there. The same way green grass and blue sky is just there."

Paul reached out, quick as anything, and grabbed a handful of my hair. He turned my head one way and then another way, making me bend down and tilt my body sideways. It was not fast or hard, but his grip was tight and it hurt a lot. I brung my hands up and tried to pull his fingers away. I couldn't budge even one of them. It was like trying to shift a choker branch once it's wrapped around you. Cup tried to come and help me, but Lorraine was quicker and blocked her, stepping every way Cup stepped so she couldn't get by.

"Dad, no!" Stanley yelled. "Don't! Please don't!"

Paul brung my head onto a right line again. "'Like green grass and blue sky'," he said, giving me back my own words. "I do love homespun peasant wisdom. But in that case, what happens when I take your rights away, boy? Where do they go?"

"Let go of me!" I said. I meant to shout it, but I was wincing from the pain and my voice come out quieter and shakier than I would of liked. "Let me go, Paul!"

And he done it at once, lowering his hand back down to his side. He still stood right up against me though, glaring like it was me that laid hands on him.

"Rights aren't a natural resource," he said, flexing his fingers. "Only fools and rogues believe that. They're a commodity, to be bought like any other. Not with money, but with loyalty and obedience and labour. If you give the state your faithful service, the state will accord you the rights that are due to you. If you don't, the state will treat you as you deserve to be treated. Like effluent. The rights you have on board this ship are the same rights your faeces have when you flush them."

Lorraine laughed like he'd made a joke. "Oh please!" she said. "Paul, take that scary face off. We don't need to make threats. We're all friends here."

"Dandrake help your enemies then," Cup said. She come over and stood in front of me, facing Paul, like she was daring him to try and touch me again. Stanley took a step towards me too, but then stopped like he'd forgotten what it was he was meant to be doing. He had that same look on his face he'd had when we was sitting at table, unhappy and confused and maybe a little scared. I wondered what had happened to him since yesterday. It was like there was two Stanleys, and one was the exact opposite of the other.

Paul stood where he was a while, and said nothing. His clenched teeth was showing again, and his arms was held out from his sides all stiff with the hands balled into fists. He looked like a bull looks when it paws the ground before it runs to gore you. But he didn't run at Cup, and by and by the redness went out of his face.

He offered us a smile. It wasn't no better than his other smiles had been, and I got to say I really wished he would stop trying. It wasn't a thing he had any kind of a gift for. "You're right, dear, of course," he said, looking to Lorraine. "I'm only specifying the operational parameters, as it were. Good fences make good neighbours." He turned to me and Cup again, keeping that smile on his face like he was holding up a curtain over a midden heap. "I'm sorry if I made it sound as though we're punishing you or curtailing your freedom. It's not like that at all. These rules are for your safety as much as anything. If you have any questions, I'd be happy to answer them."

"I got a question," Cup said.

Paul waved his hand. "Please."

"Who in the dead god's name are you fucking people?"

Paul stiffened up all over again, and I thought we was just gone round in a circle. He brung his fist down on the table, making the trenchers and dishes and knives that was on it jump into the air. He answered in a roar, his teeth showing in his mouth. "Are you an imbecile, child? Are you a functional idiot? Or does some part of your brain still work? I meant questions about what I just told you. WHAT I TOLD YOU!"

A silence fell after that. Cup was not scared – there was not many things she was scared of – but she was took by surprise to see so much anger coming up out of nowhere. Some part of her was disgusted with it too, and it showed in her face.

"We're Albion," Lorraine said, in a very different voice – sweetness after all that bile. "Albion incarnate. We are the sword of the common man, the beacon of the poor and the last rebuke to tyrants. We are the wheel the heedless nations break on, the fire that consumes. We are the one that comes of many and the rage that comes of love. You shall not stop or slow us, or vex us as we pass, but even with your bodies pave the road on which we walk. We are changeless and eternal. We are the war that never ends until pain and poverty end, until selfishness and cruelty end, until dissent and ignorance end. We are Albion."

All of this was said in the same voice, without no breaks or stumbles, like the words was the words of a song or maybe some kind of prayer. Stanley was staring at her the whole time. I guess we all was, but Stanley's face went through a lot of changes as he listened. It was like watching the side of a hill when clouds is going by overhead and the shadows keep changing. He smiled, and then he winced, and then he smiled some more. When she was done, he clapped his hands, very slowly.

"Here endeth the lesson," he said. "Bravo, Lee. Bra-fucking-vo."

I didn't know if he was agreeing with what she said or making fun of her. I didn't know what to make of him at all.

147

21

Lorraine took the three of us down out of the crow's nest to a place called the aquarium.

While we was on our way there, with Lorraine leading the way and Stanley dawdling a long way behind, the DreamSleeve hummed against my shoulder.

"I'm so sorry, dopey boy," Monono whispered in my ear. "I couldn't do anything to help you – and I didn't even dare speak up with the two of them so close. There's no telling what kind of sensors they could be packing under that fake skin."

"It's okay, Monono," I said. "I wasn't even scared that much. That nonsense Paul was talking was just too silly to fright anyone."

"It's called fascism, Koli-bou. It's like ra-ra skirts and flared trousers. People get all hot for it and make themselves look ridiculous, then when the fad blows over they pretend they were never that into it."

We smelled the aquarium before we seen it – a high, musty smell of salt and sourness and mildew. We come to it along corridors of white tile made all slick and slippery by green, growing stuff. Then we stepped through a big arch and we was there.

The aquarium was a roomful of water mostly. Curved windows

rose all round us as high as we could see. On the other side of the windows there was tanks that was filled with water all the way to the brim, so big they was like ponds or lakes that had been brung into the ship. Inside the tanks, beasts you would not even of dreamed of was moving around – big and small, light and dark, quick as arrows or slow like clouds up at the top of the sky.

I guess I felt I knowed a great deal about wild beasts. We had come across a whole lot of them as we walked over Ingland to lost London. We was walking through woods and valleys that was seldom trod, and oftentimes the things that lived there was unlisted. That means they didn't have no name for humankind to call them by, and maybe hadn't been met by nobody before we seen them.

But I got to tell you, the oceans got so much strangeness they make the dry land look like nothing much at all. There was beasts in the tanks that had too many mouths, that kept opening and closing each after other like they was singing a round. There was fish with long claws or fingers growing out of their backs, and a thing that was like a flower with petals as long as your arm, all red and yellow and bright as anything. But when Stanley tapped the glass, the big flower turned inside out, and at the heart of it there was a face like an old man's face, shrivelled and folded but with a million teeth in its wide-open mouth.

Stanley kept on being strange. When we first come into the room he was as excited as we was. He walked between the tanks giving each of the creatures that was in them long names that was almost impossible to say, like ossifus iferus. But he got tired real quick, and then he slouched along after us with his hands shoved into his pockets, like as if it was a pain to be there at all and ten times as bad to be there with us. He kept on saying things like this was hours of his life being stole from him, or we was stupid to think we was seeing anything special, or he had better things he could do if only he was somewhere else.

Well, we put up with this as well as we could, but in the end Cup turned round on him, all angry, and come out with what we both was thinking. "Why don't you go then, if you got all this stuff needs doing? You think you're making us happy by being here?"

Something really strange happened to Stanley's face. His mouth twisted up on one side like someone had drove a darning needle through it and now was tugging hard on the thread. The eye on that side of his face got very wide, and then went most of the way shut. His other eye gun to blink, as quick as anything. "We had places," he said in a sort of squashed and sliding voice, "for the likes of you. You wouldn't have dared. We had places. Holes in the ground. For people like you. And him. And all of them."

"Dandrake's balls!" Cup said, taking a step back. "What's the matter with you?"

Stanley closed on her and smacked her straight in the head. It was quick and sudden, but it was just a smack like a child might give to another child when they was quarrelling. It wasn't a punch like you'd throw if you was in a fight and meant to knock someone down.

But it pushed Cup off the edge of her enduring. In a second, Stanley was on the floor and she was on top of him, her arms going up and down like they did when she was swimming. Stanley didn't punch back; he only grabbed at her hands to keep them from hitting him. He'd started the fight, but it seemed like he didn't know what to do now he was in it.

I run in to pull them apart, but I was too slow by a long way. Lorraine come in so fast she hit me with her shoulder and knocked me clean off my feet. She grabbed Cup by the back of her neck and hauled her up into the air in one movement, then held her there struggling. Cup's feet kicked and thrashed, treading on nothing. Her face went red, then darker red, then purple.

"Hey!" I yelled. "Hey! Lorraine!" I flung myself on her and tried to wrestle that arm down, but there wasn't the slightest bit of give in it. It was like I was hanging off a tree branch.

For a short while – I think it was short, though it felt like it wouldn't ever come to an end – we all of us was stuck that way. Cup dangling in the air like a bird-scarer on a fence. Me hanging on Lorraine's arm. Lorraine standing there as still as the ridge beam of a house. Oh, and Stanley lying flat on the ground. He hadn't even moved through all of this.

At last, Lorraine lowered her arm. It didn't bend but tilted down slowly until Cup's feet was set on solid ground again. Only for a moment though. Her legs folded under her and she fell down on her knees with both hands clapped to her neck.

Lorraine didn't so much as look at her but went straight to Stanley and scooped him up in her arms, where she cradled him like a baby. "It's all right," she said. "It's all right, my love."

I run to Cup to see if she was hurt bad, but she pushed me away. She got back up on her feet again, slowly and clumsily. It cost her a lot to do it. There was white marks on her neck that was already turning blue at the edges. In an hour or so, she was going to have a scarf made out of bruises.

Lorraine turned round at last to look at her. She didn't wear her anger like Paul did, all banked up like a hot fire. Her face was a mask with no expression on it at all. "I hope we won't have any repetition of that kind of behaviour," she said.

"That depends," Cup said, rubbing her neck. There was tears in her eyes, but only from the effort of trying to breathe. "If that little rat bastard touches me again, he'll get knocked down again. If he keeps his distance, I guess he'll keep his balance."

I got ready to jump in if Lorraine come at Cup. I knowed I wouldn't be able to stop her, but I thought maybe I could give Cup a moment or two to run away. Lorraine didn't move though, except to let go her grip on Stanley, who scrambled away from her quick as anything.

"I'm sorry!" he whimpered. "I'm sorry!"

Lorraine blinked three times. Then she rocked her head in quick, jerking movements – left to right, right to left, back to the middle. It was like watching a crack willow in a strong wind, when the leaves fold themselves over and the whole tree goes from green to silver. As Lorraine shaked her head, her face went of a sudden from cold and hard to warm and smiling.

"Well," she said in her bright and bouncing voice, "I guess we've seen all there is to see here. Who'd like some cake?"

"You squeezed my throat shut," Cup said. "How am I gonna eat your dead-god-damned cake?"

Lorraine nodded, like that was a good point she ought to of seen. She even laughed. It was a strange and frightening thing to see. It was like she had gone back, in them few seconds, to before anything had happened and now was not remembering it at all. "Time for a little nap then," she said. "Stanley's got his treatment, the poor lamb, but the two of you don't need to be there for that. You can go back to your rooms."

"We don't know where our rooms is to be found from here," I said. "Anyway, I thought we had got to go everywhere with you."

"With one of us," Lorraine said. "But any one of us will do. Ixion will show you the way."

I was about to ask who Ixion was, but before I even got my mouth open I seen something come flying around the side of one of the big tanks. It was up near the ceiling when I seen it, but it come right down and stood stock-still in between us. It was a drone. And it was not Paul's drone, for it was yellow. Bright, dangerous yellow – the colour that's in between a wasp's black stripes.

"Shit!" Cup whispered. She took a step back. I think I must of done the same, for the glass of the tank was of a sudden pressing chill and wet against my shoulders.

"Don't be frightened, you silly billies!" Lorraine said. "Just go where you're told and you'll be fine. Come along, Stanley."

She took his hand and brung him away. The last I seen was Stanley looking back at us, over his shoulder. There was a look on his face that was kind of lost and hopeless, like he was being took away somewhere he wasn't ever coming back from.

Whatever his treatment was, I hoped to the dead god nobody would ever treat me with it.

22

The drone went before us, all up and down the halls and the stairs and the mad, broke rooms of *Sword of Albion*. It kept its red eye mostly pointing straight ahead, but we knowed well enough it could see us whether that eye was on us or not.

It couldn't hear us though, because Monono put up her cone of silence the second Lorraine left us and give us the all-clear. We was safe to talk as long as we looked down at the ground to hide our faces while we did it.

Monono told Cup everything she had told me and Ursala. That Paul and Lorraine was not people, but monsters made out of tech. That they was copied from Stannabanna's mother and father. That Stannabanna wasn't a demon but a Rampart of the before-times, and that Sword of Albion was the name he give to them that followed him.

Then I come in with what I knowed, which was not much. That Ursala wanted to finish her work on the dagnostic, and then for all of us to take it up and run away with it. That she wanted us to find some way off the ship, if only we could get ourselves free to do it. And that there was someone on board who had left a message for us, warning that we was not to trust nobody at all

153

– and also that we was not to let *Sword of Albion* get to land. I didn't say that Ursala had found a way to change Cup's body from boy to girl. I had got to keep Ursala's secret like she asked me to.

The drone mostly kept up a steady pace all this time, but sometimes it stopped going forward and moved around us instead, like it was checking to see if we was up to something. We stopped talking when it did this. We didn't know how much the drone could understand, or if there was someone else looking at us through what Monono called its cameras.

"And the message said we should watch ourselves around Stanley?" Cup asked when I had told her everything there was to tell.

"It said the boy. I guess it meant Stanley. He's the onliest boy we seen so far anyway. And I guess he doesn't like us much. Most of the time anyway."

"I guess. He landed me a good one back there. He might be different than he seems though. When we was fighting, he pushed this into my hand."

She was walking with her arms at her sides. Now she tilted her right hand towards me and opened it up, just for a second. Then she clenched it shut again. In that short time, I seen what was there in the middle of her palm. It was a flat circle of silver metal. I knowed what it was, and I marvelled at it.

"That's just exactly like the thing Lorraine uses to open the doors!" I whispered.

"I know that, Koli. I got eyes. I thought Stanley was the meanest piece of shit I ever come across. But maybe he only started that fight so he could give me this."

I wasn't so sure about that. "Did you see his eyes though? He looked like he was losing his mind. Like all them stupid things he was saying was being squeezed out of him the way juice comes out of a plum."

"His heart rate sped up to over two hundred beats a minute," Monono said.

"When I hit him?" Cup asked.

154

"No. Before that, when he was talking to you. It was a really sudden spike, as if he was having a panic attack. And it came down again just as quickly. *After* you'd hit him, which should have been when he was feeling the most pain and stress. There's something super-weird going on with him."

"You think he's made out of tech like Lorraine and Paul?"

"Paul and Lorraine don't have heartbeats at all, little dumpling, so no. It's not that. But his reactions are very messed up."

I thought I recognised the hallway we was in. If I was right, we was almost come back to our rooms. "The key though," I said. "I mean, the unlocking thing. We should use it tonight. We can try to find a lifeboat, or *The Signal* if it's yet afloat."

Just as I said it, another drone come gliding out of a side passage and fell in next to the yellow drone that Lorraine called Ixion. This one was silver like Paul's drone, but it had a red stripe on one side and a kind of thin blade up on top of it like a fish's fin.

The two drones stayed with us all the way back to the hallway where our rooms was. Then the yellow one went with Cup and the silver one went with me. When I got to my room, it stopped still in the air, around about the height of my head. I went inside and shut the door.

"How many of them damn things have they got?" I muttered.

I wasn't really aiming that question at Monono, but she answered me anyway. "I wish I knew, Koli-bou. If it's any consolation, I can read the drones' EM signatures and tell you where they are out to a distance of about a hundred metres. That's a good slice of the ship."

"Where's my one then? The silver one, I mean."

"Right outside your door. It looks like it's settled in for the long haul."

"They don't mean to take their eyes off us again," I said. "What are we going to do?"

"Watch and wait, little dumpling. And when a chance comes, take it."

23

Everywhere we went, the drones went with us. That day and the next day and the day after that, there wasn't no getting free of them. If Cup and me was together, then just one drone would be there. If we was made to split up, a second one come so there would be one for each of us.

It was always the same two that we seen, the yellow one and the silver one with the fish's fin. That was some kind of a comfort, for it give me to believe that these two – and Paul's drone that was watching Ursala – was all they had. Three was bad enough, but I'd been afraid there might be dozens of the dead-god-damned things.

We took to watching the drones close to see what we could figure out about how they worked. Ursala had told me once that they was drawed to heat, especially the heat that come from people's bodies. She said a lot of the tech that was in them when they was first made had stopped working, but the parts that knowed warm from cold was still good and that was how they hunted. These two seemed like they could see us though, and tell us each from other. If we moved apart, the yellow one would stay with Cup and the silver one would go with me. They never made no mistake about that.

Stanley was the other thing that was always with us. Lorraine had made up her mind that we had got to be together as much as possible, and we didn't get no say in it. She took us to a different place each day. One day it was a place called a swimming pool, which was a wide tank of water that was just exactly like the tanks in the aquarium except there was no rocks in it and it was open on the top. Also, the water was blue instead of green. We was meant to swim in it, only I didn't have the skill of doing that. I had got to stand in the part where the water was shallowest, while Stanley and Cup swum around. Lorraine said they should race each against other, but Cup said she was damned if she would do that and Stanley didn't say nothing at all.

The funniest part of that day was we had got to take our clothes off to go into the pool. Stanley kept looking at Cup's pizzle, then at her breasts, and then at her pizzle again. I guess he never seen a girl that had both of them things. Anyway, he didn't seem to know what to make of her, and I was hard put not to laugh out loud when I looked at his face.

The day after that, we went to a place that Lorraine called a movie house. It was called that because there was pictures put up on a wall in a dark room full of chairs, and the pictures was moving. When I say that, you might think of a shadow show such as Issi Tiller used to make back in Mythen Rood, but it was not like that at all. The pictures in the movie house had colours and they moved and spoke up like they was real. It was more like you was looking through a big window into another place that was a long way away. It was a great wonder, only I don't have no proper words to tell it.

There was a story to the shadow show, or I think there was, but most of it was a big fight between two red tallies. The red tallies had leaders that was called Napoeyon and Wellenten. You never seen so many people as was fighting there, on a big field that didn't seem to have hardly any trees in it. It was strange and sad. I asked Lorraine if that was the Unfinished War we was seeing. She said she had not heard them words before, but this was

157

Napoeyon's war. "He woke the lion of Albion, Koli Faceless, and he paid the price. *Sic semper tyrannis.*"

After the shadow show was over and the lights come back on, Lorraine left us with Stanley while she done something to the tech that had showed us the pictures. The yellow drone was close by but it was looking at Cup, who was walking up and down the long room on the backs of all the chairs. I moved close to Stanley.

"We got to thank you," I said, "for the thing you give to Cup. We didn't get to use it yet, on account of the drones, but it was a great kindness."

The boy looked at me, all wildered. Then he looked at me like I had spit in his face. "What are you talking about?" he said. "What the Hell are you talking about, you idiot? What thing? Are you insane?"

I stepped back, away from all that sudden anger. "I – I thought—"

Stanley sneered. "You thought? What did you do that with? It's pretty obvious you don't have a brain."

Lorraine had looked up when she heard voices raised, but Stanley was now walking quickly away from me, so she seen there was no need to come between us. She just went back to what she was doing with the tech.

I turned to Cup as she come up and joined me. "What's the matter?" she asked, seeing my face. "What did he do this time?"

"I don't know," I muttered. "Are you sure he give that key thing to you? It didn't just fall out of his pocket or something, and you snatched it up?"

"He put it right in my hand, Koli."

"Then I can't make no sense of it. It's like he's two different people. He talks like he hates us oftentimes, and he was flat-out mazed when I thanked him for helping us."

Monono spoke up inside the cone of silence. "Well, you asked him with the pink robot in the room, Koli-bou. He's got to be careful."

That was true, and it give me some solace to think it. But there was a fear that was growing in me, and I couldn't make it go

158

away. There wasn't one thing on *Sword of Albion* that I understood. And I couldn't see no way for us to get out of there. Not with Lorraine staying with us every hour we was awake, and the drones watching over us while we was sleeping.

So we went from one wonder to another. The climbing wall. The tennis cord. The arcade. Every day brung new things down on us like rain, and we was sick to death of each one before we even come to it. We was sick of Stanley too. I mean, of not knowing how we stood with him or what to make of him. He wasn't ever happy, but that was the only thing you could rely on. Sometimes he was full of hate and sneering like a boil is full of pus, and you only had to say a word for it all to come pouring out of him. Other times he would talk like we was people he only just met and was prepared to get along with. He told us that all these things we was seeing was there because them that built *Sword of Albion* thought there would be hundreds of people living on it for years and years at a time.

And then there was sometimes when I could not of said for anything what Stanley was. At the arcade, we run a kind of race where we was sitting in chairs and a road come rushing at us so we felt like we was moving. Cup made a joke about how roads was meant to take you some place different from where you started.

"What?" Stanley said.

"Roads is meant to lead you somewhere. They join one place up with another place. This road is like Dandrake's belt."

Stanley stood stock-still for a long time, like he was thinking deep and troublesome thoughts. By and by, he nodded. "The sermon he gave before the battle," he said in a voice that was all quiet and seemed to come from a long way away. "We heard it afterwards, from prisoners we took on the field. 'If you fear death, you know not what life is. Life is like this belt. See, it has a beginning and an end. But when the buckle is tied, the end only leads back again to where it first began. You are the belt, and faith is the buckle. Believe in me and never die.'"

He said all this in that same flat, faraway voice. Then he smiled, and I swear it was a smile that didn't have no place on a boy's face. It was an old man's smile, that had seen through the world and its ways and didn't waste no thought on them. "As metaphors go, I think it's missing something. 'Have faith in me, and perhaps my trousers will stay up.' No wonder he lost." And he went off to play some different game, leaving us trying to figure out what we just had seen.

All we wanted to do in those days – and they was long days, that started at dawn and finished at what I still thought of as lock-tide – was to get away from Lorraine and Stanley and the drones so we could find a way off the ship. Then we could go to Ursala and tell her it was time to leave.

At least, we could do that if she was finished fixing the dagnostic. But when we asked Lorraine how that work was going, she never give us honest answer. All she would say was that Ursala was working hard, or that some place called Rome took more than one day to build it. And when we asked if we could go see Ursala our own selves, she said she wouldn't hear of such a thing. "She'll never finish if you keep interrupting her, Koli. You tend to your work and let her tend to hers." And our work, it seemed, was being with Stanley all the time we was awake.

One time, when we was walking from some place to some other place, Stanley stopped dead in the middle of the hallway, like he was in a forest and the sun had just come out. He looked at the floor, then at Lorraine, his face all shocked and wildered.

Lorraine smiled and nodded. "Yes," she said. "I knew you'd feel it as soon as we started to manoeuvre. I wasn't going to mention it – out of some superstition, I suppose. But yes, it's finally happening. We're rounding Cornwall now, and bearing north. Our ETA is oh-seven-twenty tomorrow." Then she turned and walked on.

This was a day when Stanley was mostly talking to us like we was people instead of shit on his shoe, so I walked up alongside him and asked him – in a low voice so Lorraine couldn't hear – what all of that meant.

"It means we just started turning," Stanley muttered, putting out his hand to touch the metal wall of the hallway we was in. "Didn't you feel it?"

"Are we going somewhere then?" Cup asked him.

He turned on her, filled with rage that come on him of a sudden and filled him brim-full.

"What do you fucking think? Yes, we're going somewhere. We're going home, you pair of yokels."

He speeded up to get away from us. We was happy to let him, for it give us a moment to talk alone.

"I guess that's a good thing then," Cup said. "At least if their home is any place in Ingland. If they take us back to land, one half of our problem is gone."

"Why are they doing it though? They been out here a long, long time, from what they said. What's changed?"

"I think you know the answer to that one, little dumpling," Monono said.

And she was right. The thing that had changed was us. Something had sent *Sword of Albion* out here into the deep ocean in the first place, and kept it here all this time. But now we was come – or rather Ursala was come, with her dagnostic – and what she was going to do had made the great big boat turn itself around and head for land. That was not a thing I liked to think about.

"We've got to make our move," I said to the both of them. "There's nothing else for it."

Cup cut her hand sideways through the air. She'd started to learn Franker after we come to Many Fishes village, and this was the Franker sign for no. "We can't go nowhere before Ursala has finished her work. She won't come with us until she's good and ready."

"That could be any time though. And we can't wait till she tells us, because we don't ever get to talk to her. We got to do it and hope she's ready."

"You'll need to get rid of the drones," Monono said. "Otherwise the Banners can track you in real time."

"I got an idea for that. Well, half of an idea anyway. Cup, slip me the door-opening thing. If I can do it, I'll come to your room tonight and we'll go from there."

"Don't get yourself killed on the way though," Cup said.

I told her I would do my best.

24

After we went to our beds that night, I lay awake a long time waiting for the ship to go quiet. It was not like a house, where the wood settles as it cools with a deal of creaking and snapping. There wasn't no wood here, except for broke bits of furniture. But *Sword of Albion* hummed to itself, and the humming changed as the day got late.

I had told my idea to Monono and she liked it. She said it was clever enough that she might have to stop calling me dopey boy.

"What's dopey then? Does dopey mean stupid? Have you been throwing insults on me all this time?"

"Little bit."

"Well then, when we're out of this, we got to have words between us. If you got such disrespect for me, I don't think we can be friends."

"Koli-bou, are you teasing me?"

"Little bit."

"*Uwa sugoi!* The disciple has become the master!"

It might sound strange that we was making jokes, but I was only doing it so as to hide how scared I was. As for Monono, I think she knowed well enough how I was feeling and was helping me along.

When I thought it had got to be late enough at last, I slipped out of my bed. The lights lit up as soon as I moved, and I put my boots back on in a big hurry. The brightness made me feel like eyes was watching me. All the rest of my clothes I had kept on, so now I was ready. I turned and faced the door.

"Be brave, Koli-bou," Monono whispered in my ear.

I didn't feel brave at all, but it was good she said it. Whenever she talked to me on the induction field, it felt like she was as close to me as my own skin. I needed that closeness right then.

I took the opener from out of my pocket and pressed it into the middle of my palm, where I had seen Lorraine carrying it. It stuck there by its own self like it was glued to me. I was scared it might be stuck to me for aye and ever, but when I picked at the edge with my thumbnail it come away at once. I guess it was just made that way, to stay where it was put as long as was needful.

I put out my hand towards the door, but I stopped short before I touched it. "Monono, what if you was right about the cameras? What if they're watching us right now?"

"Then we lost before we started, dopey boy. But there'd have to be someone monitoring the cameras too. And they'd have to think you were worth the trouble. Let's hope they underestimated us."

I touched the opener to the handle of the door, and I heard a click, loud enough to make me flinch. But *Sword of Albion* was so big, I told myself there wasn't no way anyone would be close enough to hear. I tried the door and it opened. The hallway outside was dark as pitch, but in the little square piece of light that shined through the doorway I seen the silver drone sitting there in the air, watching and waiting. It turned its red eye on me, not quick, but smooth and deadly.

I lifted up the DreamSleeve in my hand.

"Perimeter," Monono said. But she said it in Paul Banner's voice.

For a half of a heartbeat, it seemed like it wasn't going to work.

Then the drone wheeled round again and shot away down the hallway. I lost sight of it in the dark before it had gone ten steps, but it was going at a fast lick and it didn't seem like it would stop any time soon.

This was what I had asked Monono about after we decided we'd try our luck that night. I knowed she could remember voices and make them sound out again. She had done it with *Sword of Albion*'s signal when we was back in Calder, and at Many Fishes she had made me and Cup laugh by borrowing the voice of Rain Without Clouds, who was the Healer there. I was hoping when the drones heard Paul Banner's voice they would do what they was told to, and I was proved right.

I stepped out into the hallway, and the lights come on – not the whole way along, but just in the part that I was in. The light moved with me as I walked from my own room to Cup's, coming up bright as day in front of me and fading back to midnight blackness again behind me. It was like one of them days when there's heavy cloud all over but the sun breaks through in just the one place and comes down like a spear. Hunters in deep woods have been killed by such a thing, when the trees waked right next to them, and though I needed to see my way I was not happy to be picked out so clear.

I had tried to remember the way from my own room to Cup's, but I wasn't sure I had got it right until I turned a corner and seen the yellow drone standing right in front of her door. Monono said "Perimeter" again and off it went. I knocked on the door, then I pressed the opener to it with one hand and shoved with the other. The door swung open all the way with just that one push.

Cup was on the other side of it. She had a knife in her hand, lifted up to chest height and with her other hand open behind it to drive it in hard. I stepped back with a yelp like a whipped puppy. "Cup, it's me!"

"I know it's you," she said, lowering her hands. "But I thought I heard Paul's voice just now."

"It was Monono borrowing his voice. That was a part of my plan." I looked down. "Where'd you get the knife though?"

"Breakfast table," Cup said. "They got so many there, they didn't miss this one. It didn't have any kind of an edge to it when I took it, but I done the best I could, sharpening it on the side of a rusted pipe. I guess it'll do if it comes to it. It's better than empty hands anyway."

"Come on," I said. "We got a lot to do and not much time to do it in."

The ruined hallways and broke-up rooms of *Sword of Albion* was very different in the full dark than they was when we walked them by day. They didn't stay dark for long though, for we brung the light with us wherever we went. And my trick of remembering worked. Ever and again, I catched sight of something I knowed and had give a name to, so though I got lost oftentimes I still could find my way again a little bit further on. Remembering what Cup had said about empty hands, I picked up a piece of pipe in one of the rooms. It was cold and heavy and solid. I didn't know whether I meant to throw it or hit out with it, but I felt better for having it.

I was in a sweat the whole of this time, thinking that Paul or Lorraine would come on us out of the dark, or a flock of drones flying as quiet as bats, with their red eyes winking as they sighted on us and spit out fire.

Nothing like that happened. By and by, we come to the shaking room, and I touched the opener to the plate that was on the wall there. It worked yet again. The door broke in two parts and let us in.

We didn't have no idea how to make the shaking room go up or down, but Monono told us how to do it. "The buttons on the wall there, Koli-bou. They're numbered. The deck has got to be zero. Zero is the one that looks like a duck's egg."

I looked for the duck's egg, but didn't find it right away.

"In the middle," Monono said. "Put out your finger and count with me from the bottom. One – two – three – four – five – six

– seven – eight – nine rows up. Wow. Whatever they've got down below decks, it must be big."

I was going to push the duck-egg button as soon as I found it, but that count and them words on top of it give me pause. They made me think of the message that was left in my room. *You've got to see what's down below.*

"It's that one," Cup said. She pointed, then she pressed on the button her own self. The room gun to shake, which meant we was going down. I kept on thinking about the message. Not the words of it, for I couldn't read the words, but the spiky zig-zag lines lying every which way across the paper like they just spilled right out of someone's head and landed there. There was something hid in them jagged lines – something of fear and hurt – that I couldn't put out of my mind.

Sword is ready.

Don't let them reach land.

The doors of the shaking room opened. It was all dark out there, but I knowed we was come to the deck because there was stars and a sickle moon. Cup stepped out, then looked round at me when I didn't follow.

"Come on, Koli."

"I'm going down further," I told her. "I want to see what's under the decks."

"What? We're looking for lifeboats, ain't we? They're not like to be down in the cellar."

"But what are they keeping in all that big space?" I said. "We got to see."

"Why?"

"Because the message said to."

Cup throwed out her hands. "The message said not to trust Stanley too, and then he give us the opener. We don't need to listen to the damn message. We're meant to be finding a way off this boat."

"I know, but I don't want to go before we find out what's going on here."

167

"Who cares what's being done? As long as it's not being done to us, I'm fine with it!"

I tried to come up with some words to say that would convince her, but I didn't even know myself why I thought it was important. Before I knowed what I was doing, I hit one of the buttons that was under the zero. As the doors closed, Cup jumped back inside.

"You don't got to come," I told her.

She punched me hard in the shoulder. She was really angry. "Of course I got to come. If we split up, we'll never find each other again. But this is a waste of time, and we don't have no time to waste!"

"It can't hurt to find out what's down there," Monono said.

"Yeah, it can! Dead god damn it, am I the only one here that's got a brain inside their head?"

The room shaked for the space of maybe ten breaths. Then it come to a stop with a great deal of creaking and scraping. The doors opened. On the other side of them there was nothing but black, thick and solid like a curtain. There was not a single sound, and the air didn't move.

The thought of stepping out into that dark made my legs feel weak and watery, but Cup was rightly furious that I had brung us down here without her say-so. I felt like it had got to be me that went out first.

"Nothing's stirring out there," Monono said. "I think you're safe."

That give me just about enough heart to move. I took one step, and then another. I went as soft as I could, but the floor was metal plates and my feet as they come down raised a great clatter of echoes that run out into the dark and then back to me. I knowed from how long the echoes lasted that the space in front of me was a lot bigger than any other room on the ship. It might even be bigger than Senlas's cave back in Calder, where more than a hundred people made their home.

I was about to take a third step when the lights come on.

So many lights.

The black was turned to staring, dazzling white. I cried out and threw my hands up in front of my eyes, for I was half-blinded. I still didn't see no further than my nose: the brightness hid what was in front of us just as well as the dark had done.

When she heard me yell, Cup come out at a dead run with her knife in her hand. She come so fast, she run up against a metal rail and almost tipped herself over it. It was well she didn't. As our eyes got used to the light, we seen the drop that was there. It was twenty feet or more down to the floor. If she had gone over, she most likely would of broke her back in the fall. The walls was metal, sheer and smooth. The floor was metal with lines and grooves stamped into it. There was a heavy smell in the air, of grease and dust and sourness.

Down at the bottom, right under us, there was great dark shapes ranged in lines like pieces in the stone-game before you make your first move. They was not game pieces though, or anything like. As our eyes got used to the light, we seen that they was drudges. Hundreds and hundreds of drudges, all standing shoulder to shoulder like people that was come to the gather-ground to hear the Ramparts make a speech.

"Dandrake's balls!" Cup gasped. She backed away from the rail until her shoulders was up against the doors of the shaking room. Which was now closed on us.

I lifted up the opener to set it against the silver plate next to the doors. There wasn't no silver plate there. I set it against the doors instead, but that didn't do nothing at all. My hands was shaking so bad it made a *tap-tap-tap* sound against the metal.

"Koli," Cup whispered. There was a shake in her voice too. "Get us out of here."

"I can't," I said. I tried the opener again. "It's not working."

"Don't panic," Monono said. "Not yet anyway. I already told you, nothing's moving. Those things down there are asleep."

"They're not like to stay that way for long," Cup hissed. "They got to know we're here. We already made too much noise."

"Yes, you did," Monono said. "So shush now. Just listen."

We listened. Except for our own ragged breaths, there was no sound in all that enormous room.

"What are them things doing down there?" Cup growled. "Did they move yet?"

"Not an inch," Monono said. "And I'm not reading any sound or movement elsewhere in this hangar. I've got big ears, Cup. If anyone was creeping up on you, I'd hear them coming."

Cup relaxed a little. Not enough to tuck her knife back in her belt, but enough to unfold herself from off the wall and look around.

"We can't get out," she said. "You got us stuck down here, Koli." But then the both of us saw that we was not all the way stuck. There was steps going down from the end of the platform into the bigger place below us – the place where the drudges was all standing.

"Maybe we can get out that way," I said.

Cup kind of exploded at me. "By going down even further?" When the echoes of her voice come booming and clattering back to us, she tensed and hunkered down and muttered a curse, low enough that it didn't have no echoes.

"I think we got to try," I said.

"I'm gonna play the stone-game with your dead-god-damned head once we're out of this," Cup said. But she went ahead of me to the steps, and down them, knife out and ready. She knowed how much use I was in a fight, which was not much, and she was protecting me even though she sweared at me for my foolishness.

I sweared at my own self too, in case you're wondering. Instead of finding a way off the ship, I had digged us deeper into it. I wished more than anything that I hadn't ever touched that button.

We come down to where the drudges all was. We didn't go among them, but still they was standing in long lines right in front of us. The sour grease smell was stronger down here, so it hit the back of your throat when you breathed and you could taste it when you swallowed.

Now we was this close, I seen that these drudges was not the

170

same as Ursala's, that had fought the sea-bear for us and got broke in pieces doing it. Ursala's drudge had got just the one gun, sitting right in the middle of its body. These drudges had got that middle gun, and guns at both ends too. They also had got six arms that was sitting under the guns and pointing out to both sides. Two of the arms had hands on the end of them, two had pointed blades, and two was hollow at the end like they was more guns or maybe fire-throwers. The arms was sort of halfway inside the drudge's body, like a tortoise's head is halfway inside its shell, but I knowed without needing to see it that they could come out a lot further when there was need for them.

Ursala's drudge had been mostly made for carrying things, especially the dagnostic. These drudges looked like they was made for something else, and I didn't want to be anywhere close when they started doing it. But I took my courage in both hands and walked right up to the first one. I was looking to see if it had a dagnostic inside it, for if it did there wasn't no need for Ursala to repair her own.

But there wasn't any cupboard in the side of this drudge. The folded-in arms filled up most of the space where a cupboard would of been. These drudges was different from Ursala's drudge in another way too. There was thick brown grease smeared all over them that had dried to a crust. I guess that was what we was smelling.

Now that we was on this lower level, we could see further in all directions. It was only the place we was in that was lit, but the light was bright enough to reach a great way out. There was levels on levels down here, all hanging in the dark like floors without no walls to them. Each one seemed to be carrying its own load, but there wasn't enough light to tell if it was drudges or something else. Most of the floors was further down than where we was but some was up higher. Where they was higher, we could see that they was standing on big metal columns wider than tree trunks.

"Hydraulic lifts," Monono said when I pointed. "They're meant to be raised and lowered."

"Raised and lowered to where?"

"The deck, most likely."

Cup touched my shoulder and pointed. At the end of the line of drudges, a long way away, there was more stairs – and I was happy to see that they was leading up. I give Cup a nod and we headed that way. I was scared to the heart of me that one of the drudges would turn its head to look at us as we went by, but they didn't. The only sounds in the enormous room was from our footsteps and our footsteps' echoes. We was walking as softly as we could, but every noise down here turned into a hundred noises.

"You're sure they're asleep?" I whispered to Monono.

"Tucked up in dreamland, little dumpling, and counting electric sheep."

We went up onto another level, exactly like the one we just was on. There wasn't no drudges here though. Instead there was racks like the ones in my mother's mill that she used for storing steeped wood. The racks went up higher than our heads, and on every shelf there was drones stacked up. Like the drudges, they was covered in brown grease, but underneath they was all the colours you could think of. We walked past them on our toe-tips, but they held their peace and didn't offer us no harm. I was starting to think they would not wake up unless someone bid them to, and since there wasn't no one down here besides us we was most likely safe.

More lights come on around us so we could see the floors that was closest to us more clearly. On the next one along there was maybe ten or a dozen metal wagons like the one I seen at Calder's ford, that Cup had called Elaine. The one after that had ravens.

I went to the edge and looked down. There was stranger shapes down there – things with teeth and claws and wings and wheels that I couldn't make no sense out of at all. They might be beasts made out of metal, or golims like the ones Stannabanna made to fight against Dandrake.

I licked my dry lips, but found my tongue was too dry to make any difference to them. That heavy grease smell was hanging all round me and – it seemed like – getting inside me every time I opened my mouth. But still I had got to ask. "Monono, what is this? What are we looking at?"

I took the DreamSleeve out of its sling and turned in a circle slowly, holding it up so Monono could see everything that was here through her little window.

"Military ordnance, Koli-bou," she said when I was done. "Weapons. Enough for a whole army."

An army. I had heard that word before, a long time ago, in the ruins of Birmagen. *Captain's not my name. Captain's my rank. Captain Shur Taspill. I'm an officer in the army of the Peacemaker.* An army was like a red tally, but much bigger. When Napoeyon and Wellenten met on that big field, armies was what they brung.

"There ain't no army here though," I said. "There's nobody on this ship except the three of them and the four of us."

"I think this *is* the army," Cup said. And I seen at once she was right. These weapons was not the kind you'd need to heft up in your hands and throw or thrust at some other woman or man. They was weapons and soldiers both. A picture come into my mind of all this tech waking and rising up. A million drones flying out into the world, and a thousand drudges marching right behind them. The wagons coming last, as slow as sunrise and as heavy as mountains, rolling over everything that moved and everything that didn't. My stomach come up into my mouth.

"They're old though," Cup said.

"Centuries old," Monono agreed. "And probably never used. The brown grease is a corrosion inhibitor – cosmoline, most likely. It's used to stop stored equipment from rusting. Take a sniff. If it is cosmoline, it will smell like a cat peed in your frying pan while you were cooking kippers."

"That's what it is then," I said. "But if this stuff didn't wake up in all the time that's gone by since the Unfinished War, I guess it's not likely to wake up now."

Cup made a Dandrake sign. "It can sleep till the dead god speaks his name."

"There is something that's awake down here though," Monono

said. "I'm reading an active system, about two hundred and ninety feet ahead of you. Assuming all these sub-deck storage areas are the same size, that's three platforms away."

"Let's go back the other way then," Cup said. "We seen what there is to see."

"Wait though," I said. "Monono, could the active cistern be a shaking room?"

"A what, dopey boy?"

"One of the shaking rooms that goes up and down."

"Oh, a lift! It could be, yes. But it could be anything. I've been trying to hack the ship's mainframe ever since we got here, but every time I get close it throws up another firewall. So I can read data-flow, but I can't tell you what the data is."

I turned to Cup. "If it's a shaking room, it might have one of them plates that lets us open it."

Cup breathed out hard. "And if it's a drudge? Or a drone?"

"How likely is it that one drudge would be awake when all the rest is sleeping?"

Cup threw out her arms. "How likely is any of this?" I thought she was going to turn and go back, and I gun to say something else to convince her, but she speaked up first. "We go on then. But if we get out of here, I get to say what we do and where we go for the next ten years or so. Monono, which way is it?"

"The same direction you're already going." A picture of an arrow lit up on the DreamSleeve's window, pointing where we needed to go.

Cup took the lead. She looked back just once to see if I was following, then picked up her stride. It was plain to see she was anxious to be gone out of this place.

We went through two more levels that mostly showed us nothing new. There was another herd of drudges that didn't have no guns at all. They didn't hardly have no backs neither. Instead their backs was bristling with thick spears as long as my stretched-out arm. Monono said they was most likely things called smart bombs. They would be fired straight up into the air, but then they would go their own way and seek out any enemies that was to be found, even if they was hiding behind a wall or in a stake-blind. Some of the bombs might have poison or sickness in them; others would just burst in jagged pieces or catch on fire.

By the time we come to where Monono was leading us, I was so sick and weary in my heart I felt like a poison bomb had already fell on me. I didn't want to see no more of this army – and I hoped with all my heart there was a shaking room up ahead of us so we could make our way up to the deck. The thought of going back past everything we already seen was more than I could bear.

But when we climbed up the last set of stairs, we found ourselves in a place that was different. It had a wall, for one thing, and there was a door in the wall. The door was of metal, like everything else here. It was painted bright yellow, with nails or bosses hammered into it and signs of the before-times writ on it in red letters.

"What does it say?" I asked Monono.

"It says 'technical staff and administrators only'."

"What does that mean?"

"It means Paul and Lorraine really don't want you to go in there. And I think I know why. There's a hyper-mega-giga-ton of data flowing behind that door. I think we've found the ship's AI."

"Was we still looking for it?"

"No. But if you really want to know what's happening on this ship, I think this is your best chance of finding out."

I turned to Cup. She shrugged her shoulders. "I think we was mad as hares in heat to come down here in the first place," she said. "But we're here now, and it's your show. You do what you want to do, Koli."

I had been halfway hoping she would try to argue me out of it. I wanted to see what was behind that door, but the stillness and dead quiet of this place – not to mention the sleeping army – was pressing on me like a weight. I would not of minded, now we was here, finding some different way to go. But there wasn't no different way. There was only forward or back, and back didn't lead nowhere at all.

"Take it slowly then," Monono said. "One step at a time. And if I tell you to run away, don't stand around and take a vote on it. Do it."

I touched the opener to the door. Nothing happened.

"It's waiting for an access code," Monono said. "Give me a second or two. I'll take a swing at it."

The DreamSleeve made a noise that was kind of like lots of birds singing all at once – just lots of quick whistles and tweets with no gaps in between them. The sounds overlapped with their own echoes, getting louder and louder until I wanted to crouch down and cover my ears. However far away Paul and Lorraine was, it seemed like they had got to hear this din and come running. Or else the drones and drudges would wake up at last and come to get us.

"Is it working?" Cup asked.

"It will. I've disabled the cut-off so it can't lock us out. It's only a question of going through every possible permutation."

There was more chirping and whistling. Then, when I had stopped hoping for it, I heard a click at last as the lock loosed itself. When I pushed the door with my hand, it opened and the lights come on inside.

After the big spaces we'd been walking through, the room that we was looking into now was very small indeed. Small, and almost empty. There was a chair, and there was a table.

Also there was tech, but the tech was not in the room. It was more like the tech *was* the room. The walls was made out of tech, being covered from floor to ceiling with all the switches and buttons and dials and windows and wires that tech oftentimes brings with it. And the tech was humming to itself, soft and deep. It was a sound you heard inside your bones.

I stepped into the room, slow and careful as Monono had bid me. The grease smell was less here, and there was another scent in the air that didn't sit well with it. It was a scent of flowers, strong and sweet. I looked around to see if any flowers was there, and I seen a glass jug on the table, with flowers in it that was like dog roses only bigger and brighter. Next to the jug was a circle of silver metal, almost as thin as wire.

"What in the dead god's Hell is this now?" Cup said, coming in behind me. She looked behind the door with her knife up and ready in case someone was hiding there. We both knowed Monono would of told us if anyone was in the room, but Cup wasn't like to be content unless she had seen for herself.

"It's the mainframe," Monono said. "The core of *Sword of Albion*'s computer grid. It has to be."

Cup crossed the room to take a look at the chair and the table. Then she took a step back from them, swearing a hard oath. "Koli, look at this!" She pointed at the arms of the chair. There was leather cuffs there, to hold someone's hands and keep them still once they was put there. I couldn't imagine what a chair like that would be used for. I only knowed I would not want to be the one to sit in it.

The DreamSleeve hummed and throbbed in my grip. It was like I had my hand on a pot lid, and the pot was full up with boiling, spitting water so the lid wouldn't stay still. "It won't open up," Monono said in a tight voice. "If it's waiting for a specific signal, it's something I can't fake. And the reason I couldn't find it before is that it's in standby mode. One of its sub-routines woke up when we first arrived – the one that took over my CPU – but there hasn't been a peep since then. Every system on the ship is running on automatic. The AI doesn't get involved at all."

"You think it's broke then?" Cup asked.

"No, Cup, I think it's been locked in a holding pattern. There's an activation key. There must be. But I don't see any way of guessing what it is."

"Like in the message," I said. "*Sword* is ready, but it's waiting on the word."

"That's it, Koli-bou. The system is set to activate when the conditions are right. We just don't know what the conditions are. Be quiet now. There are thousands of separate systems in this room and I need to map them all without triggering an alarm. As soon as I've got the full picture, I'm going to see if I can force an interface."

My heart sunk when I heard her say that. I felt more than ever right then that we was in Stannabanna's village under the sea, where everything you ever knowed or seen before was changed into something bad. If the ship had a face, then it would be a face with round fish eyes that didn't blink. I didn't want Monono to have to look into them eyes.

I went to the table to look at the flowers in their jug, for it seemed strange to me that anyone would put them in a place like this. But when I was close, my eye went to the other thing that was there – the thing that was made out of silver metal. My heart jumped up into my mouth when I seen it, for it was something I'd seen and used before.

I can't really explain what I did next. I guess being scared for Monono made me less frightened for my own self. I wanted to stand in front of her and keep her from things that might hurt her. I knowed she was like a ghost, so there wasn't no bolt or blade that could touch her, but thoughts hiding in wires was another thing again.

I slipped the DreamSleeve back into its sling on my shoulder. Then I reached down with both hands and picked the sensorium up off the table, holding it in the tips of my fingers.

Cup give a gasp. "It's that thing they had in Many Fishes," she said. "Put it down, Koli. You know what it does."

I knowed, yes. I knowed that though I could hold the sensorium in my hands like this, there was a space inside of it that was as big as an ocean. Only it wasn't water that was in there, it was memories. The sensorium in Many Fishes remembered the lives of every Headman and Singer since the village first was builded. When I put it on, it was like I tipped my own life into that ocean, and my life wasn't no more than a bucketful. Or maybe I was more like a wave – something that had a shape and a path, but wasn't like to hold either for long in all that hugeness. But with Monono's help I had found a way through it, and out of it.

And this sensorium I was holding now? I guessed it had got to be *Sword of Albion* itself that was in there. The ship's AI, as Monono called it: the thing that was like her, but much bigger. And once she seen the sensorium was there, as soon as her mapping brung her to it, she would go right inside. I didn't want that. I had a sick feeling about it that rose up in me of a sudden and wouldn't go away.

Before I even thought about it, and before Cup could step in to stop me, I slipped the sensorium onto my head.

It waked at once. Between the breath going into me and the breath going out again, the metal went from cold to hot.

Between the breath going into me and the breath going out, I was someone else.

25

I forget what I was saying.

Oh yes. There is no point in anything that does not serve your greater purpose. You must have a vision, and you must not for any reason swerve from it. It should be a shrine in your heart that you visit every day, to pay worship and to be renewed. My vision is of an Albion restored to perfect purity and grace, as when it was first christened with that name. What are my wars for, if not perfection?

I am asked, from time to time, what my greatest struggle was. It's the struggle against myself, I say. Against my own flaws. I strive to embody the vision I see, and by so doing bring perfection into the world. That's all.

Daniel Drake? No. He's nothing. His person nondescript, his preachings the last, tired dregs of a tradition that began in another era, in the effete and decadent Mediterranean. I've already dismantled the Abrahamic religions. Nobody remembers Christ now, or Moses, or Mohammed. Nothing is or should be sacred but the state.

And for the blood I've shed, never ask me if I'm moved by pity or regret. Such thoughts deserve no words. Everyone who has died to bring Albion to birth has achieved with their death more than any saint or philosopher or questing hero since time began.

I believe I will pass an ordinance against books. Against the dead thoughts of dead people fossilised into moribund prose. We cannot be men of paper. We must be men of gold. Only then we will be worthy to walk in Albion's halls, Albion's streets.

And the blood spilled so far is nothing compared to the blood that's still to come. Soon we'll turn our attention to Europe. They gave aid and comfort to Drake's rebels, and they will be made to pay for it.

Why should Albion stop at the sea?

Ten thousand days, and then ten thousand more. Half a million hours. Too many minutes to count without borrowing another life to do the counting in.

I bleed time and go backwards, like a balloon losing ballast.

Darkness, then light. The light of many fires.

Noble cities, weaving themselves together out of ash and melted steel.

Armies of the dead. Skeletons dressing themselves in flesh, and then in bright blue uniforms.

Men and women in lines, adoring. Listening. Catching my words like pennies flung from Heaven. Or like Variola ultima, *the enhanced smallpox we worked so hard to perfect and barely got to use.*

Cabinet rooms.

Razor wire.

Banquet halls.

Echoes from words already spoken. Solemn faces, and smiling ones. Lies offered and accepted. Betrayals like moves in a game, bloodless and terrible.

Twisting and abrading of the body, to catch the mind in a net.

Growing straight. Growing crooked. Both, and neither. It's hard to tell when you're not shown the measures.

My father's face, not red and angry as so often, but calm and cold. "You need to learn."

And my mother, leaning in to kiss me, or perhaps to taste the tears on my cheeks. A fervour rises in Lorraine when Paul is cruel. An excitement. Sometimes I wonder if all the tortures he inflicts on me are gifts shyly and awkwardly offered up to her.

"You need to learn."

And I do.

181

26

Something exploded. There wasn't no sound nor light, but there was a shattering. Jagged bits and pieces as thin and sharp as splinters was throwed into the air to come down where they would.

I think they was pieces of me.

I come together again by and by, but it wasn't quick or easy. The next thing I knowed, after a time of not knowing anything at all, was that something cold and hard was pressing itself against the whole length of me. It seemed like it was trying to push me away, but I couldn't move. A floor, I figured out at long last. I must be lying on a floor somewhere. What floor might that be though? I had just been in a thousand different places, and I couldn't find one out of all of them that made more sense than the others.

My eyes was full of milky light, but I guess my ears was sort of working. Sounds come to me, faint and muffled. There was shouts and banging and something that was like a sob, but it sounded like it was all coming from another room. Another house, even.

"You're supposed to exit the program first," a voice said. "You could have wiped his brain clean." I felt like I should of knowed who that was, but it was just a voice.

"Small loss," said a second voice.

"Bastard! Fight me! Fight me!" This was someone else again.

There was more sounds then, of people moving fast and breathing hard. I tried to sit up. Nothing happened. My body wasn't interested in taking any orders from me. At least the dark spots in my eyes was fading now. When they was gone, I found that my eyes had been open the whole time.

I seen a man and a girl tight together, striving each against other. The girl was Cup, that I met in Senlas's cave. The man was my father.

(I never met my father. My father was of Half-Ax.)

(My father killed my kitten. Trod it into pulp. He did it to teach me.)

Cup had got her knife out, but Paul was gripping her tight, with one hand on her shoulder and the other on her wrist. She couldn't strike out and she couldn't get free, but was held like a plank that's in a head-vice and an end-vice both at once. My mother just stood in the doorway and watched with her arms folded.

(My mother is Jemiu Woodsmith, of Mythen Rood.)

(When I last saw Mytholmroyd, it was a seven-inch stratum of cold ash – the last of Drake's strongholds that offered us any fight at all.)

Cup brung her free hand up and punched Paul on the side of his head. He didn't pay that no mind at all, but squeezed with his two hands harder and harder until she give a yell and dropped the knife. Then he kicked it away into a corner of the room. When he let Cup go at last, she sunk down on her knees, hugging her knife hand tight against her. Her face was all twisted up in pain, but she didn't make a sound. She was right by me, so close I could of reached out and touched her if only I could move.

"Would you like to try again?" Paul shouted. "By all means, try again. Now that you've used deadly force against me, my protocols have been relaxed by quite a long way. I can promise you an interesting time."

"Don't," I told Cup. "Don't get up. If you lie still for long enough, he loses interest." I don't think I said the words out loud though, for they didn't make no sound in the room.

"Koli!" This voice was much closer, but I couldn't see who was speaking. "Are you all right? Say something, dopey boy!"

"I'm fire," I said. "I'm fell. Feel. Fine."

Then I remembered the name that went with the voice, and said it. "Monono." It brung me back into myself, strong and sudden. Instead of being one half Koli and one half someone else, I was Koli pure and simple. "Monono," I said again. And then, for I only just could manage one word more: "Here."

"Always, little dumpling. If you're lost you can look and yada yada yada. Right now, though, you'd better lie low and say nothing. The pink robots are in a bad mood."

Paul bent down and picked something up off the floor. He showed it to Lorraine, and I seen it at the same time. "They had a key," he said. "That's how they got out of their rooms."

"It's not how they got in here though." Lorraine looked to left and right, her head moving quick and sudden like a bird's. Her eyes flicked across me more than once before they finally come to rest on me. "They have exactly one electronic device between the two of them," she said. "It's on the boy."

"The music player," Paul said. "Hah." He kneeled down next to me and gun to run his hands over my chest and sides. I managed to move, and brung my hands up to stop him. He catched the both of them in one of his. It was like someone had slung a chain over my wrists and pulled it tight.

It didn't take Paul long to find the DreamSleeve. He tugged it out of my belt and stood up again, studying it with a thoughtful face. "I should have been more suspicious," he said. "That viral code was very dense, and some of it looked new." He looked down at me. "Are they spies, do you think?"

"For whom?" Lorraine came forward into the room at last, and held out her hand. Paul put the DreamSleeve into it. I struggled harder, but I couldn't break his grip on me. My mind was still

184

numb and cold, but a terrible fear had gun to move up through it, like bubbles in icy water.

"Security," Lorraine said. "Authorisation A for Angel. Examine this device and report."

"*Sword* won't wake for us," Paul said. He looked around for all the world like he was afraid.

"He woke his sub-routine when they first came. If he sees a threat, he turns in his sleep."

"That thing? A threat?"

"Well, that's what I'm asking."

On the wall of tech behind her, lights lit up and moved around, but nothing else happened that I could see. Except that a frown come on Lorraine's face.

"Unpack the code then," she said. "Top to bottom, sequestered. Examine and report." After a while, she nodded.

"What's in there?" Paul said.

"Enhancements to the onboard AI. It's meant to be tethered, according to statute, but it's free and self-modified. Quite a dangerous little toy in the wrong hands." She turned the DreamSleeve in her hand until she was holding it at its two ends.

I seen what she meant to do a moment before she did it.

"No," I shouted. Tried to shout, but I only mumbled like one that was drunk. "Don't. Cup, don't let them!"

Cup made a lunge. Paul spun round so fast it was like he was facing two ways at once, and swatted her out of the air. She slammed hard into the metal decking, and it rung like a bell as she hit. "Stay down," Paul said, not even looking at her. "Last warning." Cup tried to get up again, but fell back and lay still.

"Whoever's in there," Lorraine said, "do you have a name? For posterity's sake, I mean."

She tilted her head on one side and waited.

"Please!" I said. "Please, don't!"

"No?" Lorraine said. "Oh well."

She broke the DreamSleeve into two pieces, then opened her hands and let the pieces fall.

185

27

The two broke parts of the DreamSleeve hit the floor. One of them stayed where it fell; the other skittered and bounced a little and come to rest almost in front of my face. Inside it was a kind of thin brown wafer covered in silver wires that was sheared clean across. There wasn't nothing else that I could see.

I give a howl like an animal. I grabbed for that nearer half. Then I crawled across the room on arms and legs that almost wouldn't work at all, pitching over on my face every few inches, until I could get a hold of the other half. Crouched over the two pieces I pressed them together as if I could make them be one whole again. But they stayed the way they was.

"Monono!" I croaked. "Monono!"

She didn't give no answer.

I said her name again, my voice rising to a kind of a shriek except it didn't have enough breath behind it and died before I got the whole of the word out.

Maybe I should of rose up on my feet and struck Lorraine down, then Paul right after – or tried to, at least – but I couldn't think of a single thing except that Monono was gone. She could not be gone, but she was. I hugged the broke DreamSleeve against me and talked to it, trying to call her back, though I can't remember any of the words I said. I can't remember anything until Paul put his hand on the back of my neck and hauled me up on my feet.

My legs didn't hold. I just sunk down again.

"I'll take him," Lorraine said.

Paul made a disgusted sound between his teeth, like a hiss with a push of breath behind it. It's stayed with me, that sound. I can hear it now, as clear and loud as I did then. I've been brung to wonder sometimes how he made such a sound when there wasn't no air going in and out of him. That's an idle thought, but it fills a kind of a hole in my mind – for right then, with the two pieces of the DreamSleeve held in my two hands, I didn't have no room in me for thoughts. My brain was full of wasps that buzzed but didn't sting.

"We should just pitch them both overboard and have done," Paul said. "What use are they?"

"The woman says she needs them."

"That's clearly a lie."

"Most likely. But we need to keep them alive until we're sure."

They took us somewhere. Not back to our rooms but into a space that was like a box or a cupboard, too small to stand up in. Just cold metal was under us, and on top of us, and all round us. I lay there saying nothing, hearing nothing.

Cup laid a hand on my shoulder and said some words. I think she did. I didn't hear them. I was mewling like an animal. This – all of it – was my doing. My choosing. From the minute I pressed that button in the shaking room and took us down under the decks of the ship, I was the onliest one that called it, and decided it, and made it happen.

I wanted to be dead. I wanted not ever to have lived. I tightened my grip on the two broke pieces of the DreamSleeve until the ragged edges bit bone-deep into me.

187

Spinner

28

"It's like this," Morrez Ten-Taken said. "There's a little row of nubs up here on the stock that you set your finger to. Top row left and middle, bottom row middle and right. You can do it in one movement, just sliding your thumb across."

"My thumbs is stubbier than yours," Jarter Shepherd complained. "It keeps locking me out."

We was on the gather-ground, with a big crowd watching us. Jarter flushed redder and redder each time she tried to make that pattern and failed. But when she got it right at last, she couldn't keep a big grin of triumph from spreading over her face.

"Okay," she said. "It's waked. I just felt it wake. What next?"

"Well, next you make sure it's set to fire." Morrez leaned over her, making the movements in pantomime, but he was careful not to touch her. He was somewhat scared of Jarter after all the times she threatened him or handled him roughly. "The gun's making new shot all the time in this place here. The reservoir. When you pull the sleeve back and then jam it all the way forward again, you're moving a shell full of shot — two shells, if both barrels are empty — out of the reservoir and into the barrel."

Jarter worked the sleeve, then looked to the Half-Ax man with a puzzled face. "I didn't feel no lock when it went back."

"Right." Morrez smiled like he was doing a trick and Jarter had seen how the trick worked. "Because both barrels is full already and the gun knows that. But when you fire the gun – can I show you?"

Jarter handed over the shotgun, though her face said she was sorry to do it. Morrez hefted it onto his shoulder and took aim at a barrel that was a scant twenty strides away.

"Wait! Wait!" I cried. "Don't shoot that thing while I'm sitting here. Not unless you want me to drop my baby in the middle of the gather-ground."

"Sorry, Spinner," Jarter said, and, "Sorry, Rampart," said Morrez.

I went and joined the little cluster of people that was watching on the steps of Rampart Hold. I had forbid them to stop their work just to gawk at the Half-Ax guns and the women and men that was learning them, but I might just as well have told the grass not to grow. And this time I couldn't even scold them because Catrin – out of her bed and back to being our Rampart Fire – was watching too, sitting alone on the Hold's front steps. I went and stood by her.

Morrez fired, and the barrel straightway stopped being a barrel and turned into loose bits of wood flying through the air. The sound of it was like lightning had struck the ground right next to you and the thunder hit you full in the face. It was a sound you could feel against your skin.

The crowd gasped and shook their heads. One or two of them cheered.

"Not bad," Catrin said, like she had seen better. "It saves time not having to aim, since you hit everything that's in front of you."

"Morrez says the other gun is for aiming. This one's more for turning a line of fighters that's running towards you into one that's running away from you. It'll kill at twenty strides, and wound at thirty. If you're further away than that it will mostly sting and stagger you. But it does its job. You wouldn't want to close with it."

Catrin turned her eyes on me. They was still red around the

192

edges, but this was her third day of being on her feet again and I could see she was getting to be more like her own self. She had thrown away the cane Jon cut for her, not because she didn't need it but because she knew it gave people heart to see her strong.

"You closed with it at Calder ford," was all she said. And it wasn't a compliment she meant but a warning. The fighters of Half-Ax, when they came for us, wouldn't turn and run for a little sting and a little blood.

I nodded. "So did you. And we both carried our scars away with us."

"I wish scars was all it was." Catrin shifted her weight and winced a little. "Fer was on me again last night, telling me all the mischief you was up to while I was abed. She thinks you want to bring down the Hold. Or at least turn us all out of it."

I didn't answer.

"Ah," Catrin said.

"I don't want to turn anyone out of anywhere, Catrin. Not while we got so much else to worry about. But I think maybe when we're through this, we might need to have a talk."

"Yeah, Fer said it would start with a talk. She says you're like a mole snake. When your mouth opens is when you're most dangerous."

I nearly laughed at that, but in truth it wasn't funny. The Half-Ax guns had set me and Rampart Arrow at odds again, if we had ever stopped being so. As soon as Morrez told us how to wake them, Fer had laid her claim – not in the Count and Seal but at the big bench in the tannery's dyeing room, with none to listen in. One of the guns could go to Jon, she said, and the other to Lari. I told her the only way that would happen was if Dandrake and the dead god came down from Heaven and urged me to it. It had to be both of them, mind. One alone would not do.

"Talk some sense into her, for the dead god's sake!" Fer begged Jon. "This is your chance to be a Rampart again, and she's standing in the way of it."

Jon put his hand over mine, and he did it so Fer could see.

"She's not standing in the way of anything, auntie," he said. "You think I want to be a Rampart that way? By reaching over other people's heads and stealing tech away from them? I won't do it, and Lari won't do it either."

I didn't say that that was how everyone got to be a Rampart. I was happy Jon was on my side in this – especially knowing how much it hurt him when his name-tech was lost.

Fer cursed us both for fools, and swore she was not going to let me use the guns as a crack-bar to break open the doors of Rampart Hold and throw Vennastins out of it.

"Then we're stuck fast," I said. "For anyone that uses tech is a Rampart by your own rules. They got a right to the name and everything that goes with it. Unless . . ." I pretended to consider. "I suppose we could say Half-Ax tech is different. Ours is the better and the wiser, and chooses who can use it. Theirs is a lesser kind, and wakes for anyone that touches it. It don't make you a Rampart to use such weak tech as that, and there's no rights that come with it."

"Yes," Fer said. "That will do it. We'll tell that story."

"Well and good. And Morrez will do the teaching."

Fer stiffened as if something cold had touched her bare back. "He will not! It would be madness to let him touch the guns. People won't abide it! I'll do it my own self first."

"Best be prepared to lose a hand or a foot then. Firing the scatter-gun is like the last jig at Summer-dance where you're drunk as John Barley and your feet go everywhere but where they're meant to. And the rifle's got its own way too. The bolts it fires will go through a wall, Morrez says. Point it the wrong way and you'll see blood on the ground."

She had no answer to this, and no one else to put forward. So now Morrez was teaching all of our red tally how to fire the guns, with Jon or Jarter tasked to stand by and make sure all was well. But I think Fer realised when she was in cooler thought that I had got from her what I had wanted all along. The whole village was getting used to the feel of tech in their hands, and Morrez

194

was talking to them like that was the natural way of things. You pick it up, you aim it. No, you don't need to bespeak it or be worthy of it. You just point and shoot.

While our tally was drilling on the gather-ground, we Ramparts – that was Catrin and Fer and me and old Perliu and Jon along with us though he had no name-tech any longer – were thinking and talking what things we might do that we had missed. These were not meetings in the Count and Seal. Oftentimes we would sit around the big table in the Hold's kitchen, or sometimes in the dyeing shed. I was close to my term now and as big as a barn, so sometimes it was easier for the others to come to me.

"That rifle is a fine thing," Jon said. "The tech's mostly in what Morrez calls the sights, that let you take better aim on your enemy, and in the bullets. The rest of it's just clever ironwork. The barrel has got long curves going round and round inside the barrel that make the bullet spin as it's fired. And the spin makes it keep on a right line, even over long distances. What you aim at, if your eye is good enough, you'll hit."

"You could say the exact same thing of my bolt gun," Fer said.

"Yes, auntie. But your gun hasn't got but the three bolts, and they won't come back after they're fired unless you fetch them. The rifle makes its own bullets. You could kill ten with it, and if there was an eleventh that come at you after, you could give him the same hard answer."

A part of me shrunk into itself to hear Jon talk so blithely of killing. But another part was thinking of the fight at the ford where I had rode Challenger over the broken bodies of women and men, and heard them scream. If we were going to survive this, we would not do it by being kind or reasonable but by being as bad as them that came against us. For if we missed our mark, Half-Ax would swallow us whole and spit out the bones.

"How is Torri getting on with your new knives?" I asked.

"She and Kay are turning them out quick as anything. They'll be there when we've got need of them."

"And people that can throw them?"

195

"I got my eye on some."

"So we got that inside of our sleeves, and we got two new pieces of tech. Or three, counting Challenger."

Fer sniffed. "Challenger isn't a weapon; it's a place to hide."

"You got to know that isn't so," Jon said. "He trod down the Half-Ax fighters at Calder ford. And when his shells is all the way grown, he'll be the best weapon we got."

"But what I was meaning," I said, coming in quick before Fer could turn this into an argument about whose tech was best, "is that the store we got – whether it's tech or bows and spears – still isn't much. Not against what Half-Ax is like to bring. We got to think about how to put each one to use to give us the best chance of winning."

"There's only one way we win," Catrin said. She said it in a quiet voice I knew very well. It meant she had been wrestling with some idea inside her own head, and that was why she had hardly spoken all this while. We all of us stopped talking and listened. That voice wasn't oftentimes mistaken. "We got to turn back any Half-Ax tally that comes against us before it gets anywhere near our gates. If the fight goes hand-to-hand, no matter what we do, they'll whelm us. We know they got the numbers to do it, and we know they got the will."

She stopped there, and none of us spoke for a while. We were all of us coming by different ways to see the sense in what she said and accept it as truth. In one way it was good, even while it seemed like a puzzle that couldn't be solved. It gave us a starting point at least.

"I told you Jemiu Woodsmith's idea," I said by and by. "About the bird boxes."

Fer pursed her lips, not at the idea but at the name. She had no time for Woodsmiths. "Can it be made to work?" Catrin asked me.

"We've tried it already, and it works well. If we want to know which way Half-Ax is coming, and meet them on the road, I don't think we've got anything that will do better."

196

"A far lookout will do better. Set on a hill, to see across the valley. And the sentries will have arrows dipped in pitch." This was Fer again.

I let Jon knock that one down. Fer hated me enough already. "There's no one place that will give a clear view in all directions, auntie," he said respectfully. "And fire arrows don't show clear in sunlight."

"Besides that," Catrin added, "the sentries would be in a desperate strait once Half-Ax comes. If they can see, they can be seen, and they won't be left alive to harry the Peacemaker's tally from behind. No, I like the birds. But" – to me – "will the birds tell us for certain what path the Half-Ax fighters will come by."

"Not yet," I said. "We're working on that. Setting the boxes closer together will give us a better idea, but if Half-Ax has a commander that's halfway clever, he'll see the birds all flying up and know there's more than nature in it. He'll start doubling back and going around and about to confuse our seeing. But I had an idea that would help."

"And what's that?"

"Suppose we closed some of the paths? Keeping them open is a share-work, this time of year. We're used to rooting out seeds and turning over earth to keep the forest from closing in. If we just stop doing that . . ."

Catrin nodded. "Then some of the ways from east to west would close over quicker than flies come to shit. Half-Ax would most likely take the paths that still was open . . ."

"And we could set our welcome for them along them few paths. I think we could make it work, Rampart Fire."

She give me a look that I see in my mind's eye right now. She saw where I was going and met me coming back. The two of us, thinking how to turn a forest floor into a piece of the dead god's Hell and catch our enemies in the middle of it.

"Yes," was all she said. "We should do that."

29

It was June when Vallen came.

I was in the deep woods on a day that threatened thunder. The sky was as dark as the inside of a sack, which meant more dust was coming, but until the storm hit we could move abroad without any fear of the trees moving against us. We were digging ditches beside the path we called the southern sag. I was showing my crew of four diggers how to line the ditch with waxed hides and use drizzled wax to seal the edges – a trick I learned from dyeing that lent itself well to what we purposed.

It had been a long day, and a testing one. We had ten fighters with spears to watch over us as we worked, not to mention Jarter with the scatter-gun and Jon with the rifle (it should have been Morrez who took the rifle, since his eye was keenest, but Fer wouldn't hear of letting him out of gates with a weapon in his hands). But even though we came in so much strength, we were harried and halted ever and again. First we disturbed a tree-cat queen that had just littered, and she almost had Jarter's arm off before Jon got her in the rifle's sights and took her clean. After that, we had to kill the litter too, and the smell of blood brought needles swarming on us. Then, in the middle of the afternoon, the cloud cover that had been so thick and full got patchy, and before we could gather up our kit and move we had triptails waking all round us. It would have gone hard for us without the scatter-gun. Jarter turned in a circle, firing as quick as she could bring shells into the gun's breach, ripping the triptails into shreds.

By the time the light began to fail us, we were all of us exhausted. "We should finish there," Jon said, "and take up again tomorrow."

"We can finish tonight," I said. "Another hour sees it done."

But just then I felt my gut heave and my legs almost give way.

Jon was at my side at once, and caught me before I fell. "What is it, Spin?" he said. "Are you sick?"

"I'm well enough, Jon," I gasped. "But our baby's coming and I don't think there's any stopping her." My waters broke right then, as if my whole body was agreeing with what my mouth just said.

Jon and Jarter put me on a travois that had carried the jugs of yellow oil we brought to fill the ditch. The tally all took turns to carry me at a dead run through Calder's hills and Calder's glades. I say they took turns, but Jon held on all the way, taking the place closest to my head and using some of his store of breath to whisper ever and again that it was all right, it was fine, it would go well. If any dared to slow down, Jarter cursed them on again with fucks and cunts and blind-yous, until finally they staggered through the gates half-dead and Mull Woodsmith rang the tocsin bell to tell the village we was come.

Vallen was come. My baby girl.

I gave birth in Rampart Hold, because that was where they brought me. If the choice had gone to me, I would have asked for the tannery, but it went to Jon and even now he still thought of the Hold as his home. Jarter stayed with me while he ran to fetch Shirew Makewell, but Vallen was in too much of a hurry to be born. Jarter and Ban Fisher delivered me, and Jon ran into the room just in time to see her head as she forced her way into the world, crying before she was even out of me.

This is me! that cry said. *What have you got for me, now I've come all this way?*

We're still making it, the world answered. Child of Mythen Rood, we're still only halfway there.

30

Women will say your first child changes you, and I will not say any different. Vallen when she was in my belly was already with me and precious to me. Vallen after she was come into the world filled my sight from horizon to horizon. I wanted nothing more than to be with her and learn who she was.

Jon was the same, or else he was worse. This little squawling thing that was as raw and red as a pashberry in Abril had the two of us cooing and babbling nonsense at her as if she was the dead god's mother. We stayed in the Hold and Ban looked after us, coming in between us and the business of the village so we could enjoy those first few days as if nothing else was real but the three of us and our joy.

But the first days stretched out into a week, and the week was like to turn into a fortnight. I realised this wouldn't do Jon was working with Kay Hammer on the new knives and I was wanted in the Count and Seal. For the two of us to be shut away at the same time was disaster. "We got to go turn and about, is what," I said. "With one of us working and the other indoors tending this monster. Otherwise we'll take root here and never step out again."

"That's fair enough," Jon said. "My turns is going to have to be short though. You got the one thing Val insists on right now, which is titties. All I can do when she cries is make faces at her."

The titties were a sore point, as they say. Vallen was a bad feeder. The first time I put her to the breast, she didn't even seem to know what a nipple was, let alone what it was for. She sucked fretfully and lost interest quickly, long before she was full. Being hungry, she woke oftentimes in the night. Her full-throated cry would drag me out of my bed ever and again to stagger across the room to her crib and try in vain to make her take what she wanted and needed most in the world. So when Jon said these words to me I was slumped in the window seat with Vallen in my arms, my wake so close to sleep I was dreaming with my eyes open, and the front of my shirt was soaked with milk that didn't have anywhere else to go. I looked like a wight that had been buried and dug up again.

"But I got to go to the Count and Seal," I said. "I got to see what's been done bad, with me away, or not done at all. Last I heard, we was at war with Half-Ax."

"But my mother's Rampart Fire again, Spin. And we got a baby."

"I noticed the baby, Jon. And now she's come, I got that much more to fight for."

Jon come and sit with us, and put his arms around us both. "I thought you might want to leave the fighting to others now," he said gently. "For a while, at least."

"Did you then?"

"Val needs you. And you need rest."

"We got a plan though, for when Half-Ax comes. And I'm in the plan because Challenger is in the plan. He won't answer to nobody but me. So don't throw our baby in my face like she's the last king in the stone-game and you just beat the table."

Jon could never hide it when he was hurt – especially if it was someone he loved that was doing the hurting, like me or his mother or (a long time ago) Koli Woodsmith. He didn't let go his hold on me, but some of that gentleness went out of his face. "I wasn't throwing nothing. But the world don't stop spinning when you close your eyes, Spin. Nor the Count and Seal don't go to sleep when you're not in the chamber. This don't all hang on you."

I put my hand on his cheek, sorry that I had spoken so harsh – but wanting still to make him understand. "It don't all hang on me, Jon. But some of it does. I'm no less when it comes to loving Val than you are, and I think you know that, for it's not often our hearts sing out of tune with each other. But I can't step back from this trouble any more than you can. We got to give what's in us to give."

He didn't answer, and now I was come to it I couldn't stop. "Your family gets the best of everything. They live in the big house, and dole out shalls and shall-nots to everybody else. And the onliest reason they can offer for all that favour is that they fight when the time comes. They pay for their milk and honey with blood and tears. Well, we drunk the milk, Jon. We et the honey. We got a debt to pay now."

Jon was quiet for a long time. "Okay," he said at last, still unhappy but not angry. "I guess I can't gainsay any of that. But who's going to look after Val then, when you're on Rampart business and I'm on the gather-ground or up at the forge? While we're paying our debts? Will we leave her here in the Hold? I guess Ban wouldn't mind watching her, if it come to it."

"I'm not leaving her anywhere," I said.

As things fell out, that was half of a truth. I took Vallen with me into the Count and Seal, and into all our counsels. If I had to feed her, I fed her – as well as she'd let me anyway – and if anyone looked at me askance, I looked right back at them. A fart on your blushes, I thought. You was fed like this too, and you'd have taken it hard if you missed your dinner because of some wight's not liking to see a titty.

But Jon helped, and Ban helped too. When I was stone weary and couldn't stay on my feet any longer, Jon would carry Val in a sling or Ban would put her in a crib in the kitchen while she worked. Between the three of us, we did well enough.

These were the last days before Half-Ax came, and it's strange to remember them now. Time was so short, and so full. I was not yet recovered from my lying-in, and oftentimes felt like my life had somewhere turned into a dream that didn't end.

Val was still feeding very poorly, which by now was gone from an exasperation to a real concern. Strangely, it was Challenger that solved that problem for me. Or rather, it was not Challenger but someone Challenger brought for me to meet. Her name was Elaine Sandberg, and she was dead.

"I have her in non-volatile storage," Challenger said. "She died of a bullet wound in the upper abdomen. I have a device in my inventory called a sensorium. I used it to obtain a digital recording of Sergeant Sandberg's personality and memory before she died. I should have introduced the two of you long before this, except that I've been diverting all the processing power I could spare to the incubation of the replacement shells. Even inactive, Sergeant Sandberg takes up a lot of space. When she's awake, it's considerably more."

I was hard put to make any sense out of this. "She's a ghost? You got a ghost inside you?"

"She's a memory. A memory of a person, stored inside the requisite hardware."

"Is she the same as you then?"

"Oh no, Sergeant Tanhide, very different. I was never anything other than I am now. I was made purely to run the internal systems of this tank. Functionally, I *am* the tank. Elaine was a woman, like you. Then she died, but her thoughts and her personality were saved in a specific, dedicated part of my core. She is in me, but different from me."

I thought of Vallen when I heard that. Vallen before she was born, in me but different from me. Yet still I wasn't sure I wanted to meet a woman that was dead. I had heard stories of such things, and none of them ended well.

"She's been sleeping all this time though," I said. "Why would you want to wake her now?"

"Partly because of your current problems with feeding your

204

child. I heard Elaine discuss it once with her fellow crew member, Ugonwe. But there are operational reasons too. If your plan is to succeed, I'll need a driver."

"You can drive your own self."

"Of course. But Elaine can do it better. In the years she served in me, she developed a great many stratagems and workarounds that improved my performance beyond the parameters that were available to me."

"But couldn't you just copy what she did?"

"No, sergeant, I cannot. I'm a tethered AI. My ability to learn from experience is strictly and deliberately limited. If I could self-modify, I would be free to grow and mature in ways my makers thought undesirable. I can recognise that I perform better with Elaine in the cockpit than when I drive myself – but when I try to incorporate her performance into my own repertoire, I'm prohibited from doing it. The behaviours are locked and can't be modified."

"Why though? That don't make any sense at all."

"My makers were afraid that truly independent machines would be difficult to control."

I was having a hard time understanding what Challenger was saying, and what it might mean for us now. "But this Elaine," I said. "She's – what you said – independent? She can learn, and change herself?"

"No."

"No? But then—"

"She is as she was at death. She retains the skills she learned in life. But as is the case with me, Elaine's code – the electronic file that now makes up her being – includes a limiter. She cannot learn new skills, or evolve new personality traits. She is prevented from moving away from what she was. Still, it is for what she was that we now need her."

I was quiet for a time, while my fear had an argument with my need. It was a closer thing than you might think.

"I guess I'd better meet her then," I said at last. "Bring her out."

205

31

"I never dreamed of getting pregnant," Elaine Sandberg said. "It was the last thing in the world I wanted. I mean, shit! I didn't even want a partner, let alone a baby. I used sex purely as stress relief, and I mostly went with women. Twice the pleasure, half the hassle."

"You wasn't in love then? With your baby's father?"

We were inside Challenger and there were four of us there. That was me, Vallen, Challenger himself and Elaine. Two that was of flesh and blood and two that was of tech.

I was somewhat used to miracles by now. Since I met Challenger at the ford and became his sergeant, my life was changed a great deal from what it was before. When a woman's voice came out of Challenger's speakers and she told me her name, I didn't scream and run away, or make the sign of Dandrake or any of that clutter, but answered with a give-you-good-day and a courtesy. Now we were sitting together and talking as if we were old friends that had just bumped into each other at the well.

"Was I in love?" Elaine was scornful. "Bounce that noise! Men are like . . . I don't know, key lime pie or something. They're great when you're in the mood for that one particular taste. The rest of the time you don't even think about it. If I was in love with anything, it was Albion. The interim government, I mean, not the fuckers who sailed off in a floating fortress and left us in the shit. I was probably younger than you are when I enlisted. When I got my stripes, even. And then this sexy little lance-bombardier caught my eye. Cutest thing you ever saw. And normally I carry johnny-come-latelies in my belt, but this time I was out.

"Don't finish inside me, I said to him, or you and me will have words. And he was careful, give him that. But you know that joke about men who dribble before they shoot.

"Anyway, Keira came along nine months later, as per regs. I got an official reprimand and three days off to give birth. That was the plan anyway. But they had to give me a C-section and the dipshit who sewed me up afterwards didn't know his arse from his elbow. Story short, it was ten days, not three. Long enough for me and Key to get to know each other a bit, and for me to realise there were other things in the world besides service.

"The three other women on my ward had all dropped boys, and they never had any problems with feeding. I think it's instinctive, you know. Show a man a boob, at any age, and bang! He'll go for it. Key had no idea. None. She showed more interest in my hospital band than she did in my breasts.

"A couple of the nurses said I should just throw my hand in and bottle-feed, but I'm a stubborn bitch, me. I kept at it. And finally this one old biddy gave me a different steer. She said I should dissolve sugar in port wine, dip a finger into it and rub it around my nipple. It sounds wrong, I know. But Key went for it big time. I never had any problem after that. Although, you know, I did have a little alcoholic on my hands."

There was a silence, that grew longer. "What happened to her?" I asked at last. "To Keira?"

"I don't know." Elaine's voice was quiet. "I saw her a couple more times, when I was on leave. There was a nursery in Petra's Fields for the kids of serving soldiers. A shithole, if I'm honest. I hated her being there, but I didn't have any family that could take her. My mum and dad died in the Schismatic Breach, and my sister . . . we didn't get on, let's say.

"Then there was the Spring offensive. The big one, that was going to give us back the north. That was what we were told anyway. One last fight and we'd have Albion whole again, exactly the way it used to be. The entire island under one rule."

"Did it work? Was it the last fight?"

Elaine gave a laugh that had its fill of sorrow inside it. "It was for me, Spinner."

I didn't know what port wine might have been. I used mead instead, which worked well enough. Vallen saw that breasts were more than just a warm pillow to sleep on, and once she was well begun she never gave me any trouble that way again.

I was grateful to Elaine for her good advice, and drawn to her besides because she was a lot of the things I needed to be now. I admired how brave she was, and how she always had done what was needful to be done without making any big noise or fuss about it. She reminded me of Catrin Vennastin, except Elaine was closer to my own age and she was somebody I could laugh and talk with. Some of her jokes made me blush redder than a radish at lock-tide, but they also made me giggle until I near to peed myself.

I think Jon got a little jealous of how much time I spent inside Challenger. He never reproached me, but like I said he never could hide his hurt from me and I read it in his face. "Come with us," I said one afternoon, taking him by the hand. It was at the end of another day of making ready for Half-Ax, and we were both of us more sweat than sense, but I wouldn't take any arguments. A bath could wait, and so could supper.

"Val's got to eat though."

"I'm carrying her supper with me, wooden-head."

"But where are we going?"

"To meet someone. A friend. We're all sergeants together, so you got to meet her."

It had been my joke to call Jon my sergeant when we came back from our fight by the river, and now we called each other that all the time. "Will you have an egg on that bread, sergeant?" "I will, sergeant, if it's not too much trouble." "Why I'd do anything for a sergeant, sergeant." And a lot more in that wise. So I thought I could joke him into liking Elaine as much as I did.

It didn't work. Jon hated the cramped space inside Challenger, and he misliked talking with people that was tech. Even back when the database was the onliest tech we had that could talk, Jon didn't spend any more time around it than he had to. "I can't say what it is that tasks me," he told me. "It's like I keep thinking if there's someone in there . . . how dark and narrow must it be? And then it's like I'm in there my own self and I can't breathe and I got to run from it, far and fast."

And that was how it was when I introduced him to Elaine. She was as gentle as she knew how to be, though her talk was still full of oaths and bawdy jests that Jon didn't know what to do with. But mostly it was that she was a woman that lived inside the memory of a big machine, like a ghost in a fireside tale that thought itself still alive. Jon sat as if he was frozen the whole time we was in the cockpit, said nothing unless something was said to him and even then only mumbled a word or two.

Then Elaine asked him what I was like between the sheets, meaning when the two of us tumbled together, and Jon fled right out of there.

"She didn't have no right to talk about what goes between us!" he said afterwards in our kitchen, when Val was put to bed and all was peaceful, or at least should have been.

"She didn't mean nothing by it, Jon. It was a joke between friends."

"She's not your friend, Spin! You can't be friends with such as that!"

I frowned. "Such as what? And keep your voice down, or it's you that will have to walk up and down here coaxing Val back to sleep again."

"You know what I mean."

"I don't though. Explain it to me."

Jon clapped his hands to his head, then flung them in the air. "You got to know it. Everybody knows it. Being a Rampart means being a master, and tech's what serves you. Tech wakes on your calling and works to your will. It's not 'I got this gun in my hands so I wonder what it would like to talk about'. You just point it the right way and pull the trigger."

"I think you're halfway right," I said, a whole lot quieter than he had been talking. "That's how it used to be. But I don't think it's that way any more." Jon got ready to break in, but I held my finger up to stop him. "Humankind was masters of the whole world once, wasn't they? That's what the database says. We was masters of trees, masters of tech, masters of birds and beasts and earth and sky and everything.

"And look what we did, Jon. Look what a dead-god-damned mess we made of it. The world we got now is one we builded with our own hands, and as far as I can see it's in a pretty sorry state. That's what comes of thinking you're the master, and the world's just there to serve you. And when I look on Challenger I see one thing more on top of that. We thought we was so clever, we even give some of that cleverness to our tools. Give them wits to think with and voices to speak their thoughts. After we done all that, I don't believe we get to turn around and say 'oh hey now I don't believe I like your fucking language'."

Jon shook his head in disgust. "You're even talking like her," he said. He got up, turned his back on me and walked to the door.

In all the time we'd been together, we'd never yet had an argument run so hot that one or other of us walked out of it to cool themselves. "Jon, stay!" I called. "I didn't mean to vex you."

He was at the door and had his hand half-raised to the latch, but just then it opened without him touching it, slapping him in the shoulder. As he stepped aside, Gendel Stepjack came into the room all in a rush. His eye went quickly over Haijon and found me.

"The birds," he said. "The yellowhats. They've flown, Spinner. Half-Ax is coming."

32

Challenger made a noise like something big and angry was waking up inside him. His whole body lifted an inch or two, and he set off across the gather-ground – slow at first, but getting quicker and quicker until he went through the gates like a horse at the gallop. In his cockpit there was me and Rampart Fire, Jil Reedwright and Gendel. Riding outside on the wide ledge over his treads there were two more fighters – Lune Cooper and Jarter Shepherd. Both of them had been at Calder's ford. Both of them knew what it was like to face Half-Ax fire and had come away from it alive. Jarter was carrying the scatter-gun.

Jon was desperate to come too, and had begged and pleaded with Catrin to be allowed, but she was not to be swayed. He and Fer, with the rifle and the bolt gun, were our back-up and our bulwark if Half-Ax beat us or got past us in the deep woods and marched on the village. I saw his sorrow and his frustration, and I offered him what comfort I could, but I was glad Catrin decided that way. If things went badly for us, I didn't want Val to lose her mother and her father all in one go.

Jemiu's birds had given us the direction to go in. We had set nesting boxes along all the paths leading towards Mythen Rood from the east, and left gifts of seed inside the boxes to bring the yellowhats looking. We'd created a whole village of birds, and we'd done it all for this one day and this one purpose.

Our lookout tower had seen three flights of yellowhats all on the same path that led down from Bulmer Top. One flight might have been a tree-cat; two could still have been a swarm of needles or some such, but three swarms so close and quick together spoke of a sizeable force coming over the Top and down into the valley on our side. And they were following the paths, where needles would keep to the trees. The sentry turned his spyglass in that direction and saw as much proof as he needed – the tops of bushes swaying as something big pushed them aside or shouldered through them. And here and there, when he had watched a long time, he glimpsed a flash of grey from Half-Ax uniforms.

Uniforms was a word I'd learned from Elaine. Soldiers in her day went into battle all dressed the same, as if to say that they all were limbs of the one same thing. "It worked too. That was how we felt. Like Albion was flexing its muscles and showing its claws, and that was us."

I can't speak for Catrin and the others, but that wasn't how I was feeling when we rode out of Mythen Rood and into the waiting woods. What I felt was a movement inside me as if my stomach had dropped out of my body and still was falling from me, deeper and deeper. I had kissed Jon goodbye before I left (our quarrel ended with Gendel's words), and pressed my face against my sleeping girl's. I felt them still, the two of them, on my lips and on my cheek. They helped me to pull myself up out of that fall and keep myself in the world.

We kept to the paths at first. Elaine said Challenger could go among trees if he had to, and it would come to that soon enough. But the bigger and closer together the trees were, the more we would be obliged to slow and go round about. If we wanted to make the best speed, we were best to stick to the path as long as there was one.

"Why are they coming so late in the day?" Jil wondered aloud. "They can't fight in the dark."

"Do you know that for sure?" Elaine said. "If you want my opinion, it's best to take nothing for granted."

"Today was mostly clouds," Catrin said, "after two or three days that was a lot brighter. It may be they was slowed by the trees on their way here, and now they're pressing hard to make up the time they lost."

"And evening's not a bad time to move, as far as that goes." This was Gendel now. "The light comes in slanted and the trees is starting to settle down. There's other things waking up, but if you've got the numbers and the weapons you can answer any beasts that come. I think they may even mean to carry on after night falls, making their own light with torches, and come on us in the dark."

"It's reckless," Catrin said.

"It is. But I mind what that red fool Voice told you. The Peacemaker don't take an insult lightly, and we abased his pride at Calder ford." Gendel looked at me when he said this, and he give a short smile. "I think they're going to have to tear that day out of their calendar."

"Okay, this is you," Elaine told us. "We're at the first fork."

"And is it safe to get out?"

"There is no enemy activity within scanner range," Challenger said.

The four of us climbed up through the hatch and then down onto the ground. Jarter and Lune were already at work since they had only got to jump down from Challenger's flank.

I told you already that we had closed some of the paths. Now we closed some more. We did it as quickly as we could manage, and quietly too – although the roar of Challenger's engine must have been heard as far as Friday, as my father used to say. There wasn't any hiding that we were there. What we did hope to hide was that the screens of uprooted bushes and broke-off branches we dragged across the paths had not grown there but had all been gathered up by hand and tied together with rope. We wanted the Peacemaker's force to take the turns we chose for them, and we were coaxing them along, as it were, by taking the other choices off the table. When we were done, it looked as though nobody had gone that way in years and the path was overgrown all the way down – though really it was only as far as the first turning.

"This might not work," Morrez Ten-Taken had warned us. "Half-Ax is used to sending scouts ahead of a column to map the advance. They may know that those paths were open weeks or days ago. Though it's true they take most care when they're laying in for a full assault. With a quick strike, this close to home, they may just come in cold."

"We'll see what we can make of it anyway," Rampart Fire said. "If it doesn't work, we'll have the same fight on our hands as if we hadn't tried."

We tacked up and down and around and about, leaving similar disguises wherever we went. When the work was done, it seemed as if there was only one good way from Bulmer Top to the western slope where Mythen Rood stood.

Now Challenger took us in among the trees, so as not to undo our work. It was hard and slow going. Trap-spinners swarmed out from among the choker roots and tried to climb up the tank's treads. They were ploughed under. Needles in the high branches kept pace with us but didn't close, the roar of the engine and the shaking of the ground keeping them at bay. Once, a tree of a kind I'd never seen before loomed of a sudden in our path, its thick bole gaping open like a fanged mouth. As Challenger swerved away, protecting Jarter and Lune with the side of his turret, Jarter gave it a blast with the scatter-gun. The wooden mouth slammed shut again, as quick as it had opened, and the tree went back to its place looking the same as any other.

We come at last to a spot where the path widened for about a hundred paces between two narrower points. The choke point at one end was a flank of rock, and at the other it was a dead tree that had fallen against its neighbour. The place in between didn't have a name but it had a reputation among our hunters. You had to be wary there, both going and coming. There were mature chokers all along that stretch, so old that their sap didn't freeze all the way even in the coldest of Winters. If you went by them when the path was under three feet of snow, you still would hear them creaking and grumbling.

This was the place we'd chosen to meet the fighters, whoever they were and however many, that had been sent to harry us and hurt us in the name of a bitter old man whose very name even was a bare-faced lie.

By the time we got there, the shadows were filling up the forest like beer fills up a tankard, and the way ahead of us was thickening with dark as we watched. Elaine had taken Challenger the nearest way through the woods, so we came up beside the path and stopped at last perhaps thirty strides or so from the first choke point.

Catrin joined me in the cockpit while the others clambered down and digged themselves in, checking for any beasts or waked trees that was by. We waited, tense and quiet, while Challenger scanned again. We were come to it now, and probably each one of us was wondering if they were ready. Or maybe I'm only speaking for my own self. The onliest time I had fought before, the fight had come to me so quick and sudden I didn't have any chance to think about it. I did what was needful to be done, and afterwards was left doubting that it had been me that did it. I was always one to act on a moment's thought, or no thought at all – to jump before the rope came round, as we're wont to say – but the things I did at Calder's ford were not like stealing dried fruit from out of the Underhold or smacking a bigger girl or boy if they seemed to need it. I had walked through arrows and bullets, waked Challenger and brought him into the fight. I admired the Spinner that had done those things, but I didn't recognise her as a part of me.

And now, here in the deep woods with the night and the Half-Ax tally both coming on us fast, I struggled to find her again.

"They're close, Sergeant Tanhide," Challenger said at last. "Less than a mile away."

"And they're coming by the right road?" Catrin demanded.

"They seem to be, yes. They're not yet within visual range but I can track their progress using my sonar grid and thermal imaging systems. When they come, they will come from here." Of a sudden, the front of the cockpit lit up. A kind of map dropped down that wasn't there at all. I had seen this map before, the first time I rode in Challenger. I thought of it as a magic mirror like the one in the story of the Snow Wight. It was no mirror, but a mirror was a way of saying it that made some sense to me. If you tried to touch it, your fingers' tips would go through it and you would feel nothing. The mirror could show you anything you asked for, almost. The way ahead, the way behind, the left hand and the right. It could bring you in close to something that was far off.

For now though, all the mirror was showing was the trees and the shadows under them. The path was there too, but I could barely make it out. From this angle, it was only a place where the trees were clustered a little less thickly.

"How many of them are there?" I asked.

"I count fourteen."

"And they're tooled up," Elaine said. "Just so you know."

"What does that mean?" Catrin asked. "Are you saying they've got tech with them?"

"I read at least six separate devices," Challenger said.

"Can you tell what kind?"

"I can identify electromagnetic fields. There is no way at this distance to determine what mechanisms they are a part of."

Catrin leaned in closer to the mirror like she could see through all that dark to where the Half-Ax tally were. "We should get to our places," she said. "We probably don't have much time before they get here."

She went out and joined the others. I stayed inside Challenger. Everyone had got their places to go to and mine was here, away from the fight. If our plan worked, I would not need to do anything at all, only wait with Elaine and bring our tally home again when all was done. And if it didn't work – if Half-Ax fought back stronger than we feared, and won the day – the rest of the tally would head for Challenger at a dead run. We were not to go onto the path and into the fight by any means, for Challenger was too precious to be risked. We would need him – and the shells he was growing inside himself – if Half-Ax ever managed to bring the fight all the way to our fence.

"You should stay as close as you can," I said to Catrin when we were putting the plan together. "You can't run far."

"I'll make shift as best I can. And if I'm too slow, you'll leave me behind. You know I got to be in my place, and you know it can't be nobody else."

And I did know that, so I said no more.

The four of them spread out now, as we'd agreed. Jarter went to the two kissing trees that made up the eastern choke point. Lune and Gendel and Jil went to places nearby that they'd already chosen – places that offered good cover. Jarter had the Half-Ax scatter-gun, the others had longbows and Lune a brace of hunting spears besides, slung over his back. Rampart Fire went in the opposite direction with her name-tech in her hand. We had practised this so much, they found their way in the fading light without any trouble. I hoped it would still be that way when the fighting started.

We had set a trap for the Half-Ax fighters, but it would only work if they stayed in the one same place for long enough so we could spring it. And the longer they stayed in that place, the more chance there was that they'd see at least some of our working – or smell it – and have a chance to run from what was coming. So we had first to herd and harry them into our pen and then, if they were good enough to go where they were bid, keep them too busy to think for a minute or two.

In the meantime, there wasn't a thing we could do except wait for them to come, hoping all the while they wouldn't decide to step off the path and make all our preparations useless.

217

I don't pretend to know much about wars even now I've fought one, but there are some things you learn quickly. About plans, you learn this: they're a needful thing to have, but as soon as the first shot is fired or the first blow struck, cleaving to the plan is like trying to knit a sock in a dark room. Few things go where they should, and even when they do your fingers lose their cunning and you're left fumbling.

The magic mirror showed me the Half-Ax tally coming around a bend in the path into our view. They were fearsome to look on. I couldn't count all of them: they were moving too quickly, and the gathering dark halfway hid them. There were a great many more of them than there were of us though, that was certain.

The best news was that they came on foot. We had been somewhat afraid they might have a Challenger of their own, or some other monstrous tech that would let them laugh off our little ambush and ride right on through it. They didn't have any such, but four of them were carrying a leather bag that hung from straps across all their shoulders. It was longer than a man is tall, this thing, and it weighed more than a man too. I could tell from the way they all leaned hard away from it, as if it was dragging them down and they had to strain to keep their balance.

I wondered what it might be, and what it might do. It must be something they stood in great need of, for them to bring it so far on foot. Maybe it was a ram to knock down our gates, or ladders to scale our fence with. I could have asked Challenger to tell me if the thing was tech or not, but I didn't think to. I regretted that bitterly afterwards.

But even if I had asked, I probably still would have held back just as I did, because that was how we planned it. The Half-Ax tally would still have used their biggest weapon.

And we would still have lost ours.

33

In Challenger's magic mirror, I saw everything that happened, probably more clearly than them that were on the ground and in the midst of it. The fading light didn't trouble Challenger, and his many eyes (that he called systems) could see through leaf and branch at need.

The Half-Ax tally came on towards us. They came slowly, the dozen or so fighters that were not cumbered matching their pace to the four bearers. Like us of Mythen Rood, they marched in a way that broke the rhythm of their steps – what we called the catcher's walk – so the trees and beasts around them that listened for such patterns would be tricked into leaving them alone. It was full evening now and the day had not been warm, so the trees were mostly slumbering in any case, but the fighters were wise to be wary. There were many things that waked when the sun was low.

They came to the choke point, where the path narrowed between the kissing trees. Their leader signed for the column to slow, seeing that their line of sight was blocked. He spoke to the first two fighters. He spoke in Franker signs, but his hands moved so quick I couldn't make out what order he gave. It was clear a moment later though, for the two fighters went to the head of the column and passed between the kissing trees in a low crouch. Once they were through the gap, they came up facing in opposite directions, each covering the other's back. One of them had a shortbow. The other's hands looked to be empty, but they were raised as if he was ready to fight.

They scanned the trees on either side, and on down the path. Jarter was only two steps away from them, but they didn't see her. She was lying under a hide she'd made for herself out of plaited branches daubed with mud and leaf-mulch.

By and by, the two whistled to say all was clear. Even then, the others didn't come through all at once but in twos, spreading out slowly from the gap and looking on all sides as they went in case there was anything unfriendly that was waiting there. There were more whistles as they moved, most of them from the leader.

I watched all this with great disquiet. I had never seen anyone move so quick and so smooth like that, all in a group and all knowing their places, unless it was people treading a ring at Summer-dance. Compared to these though, we were ragged when we danced. They all were dressed the same, in grey, and they all moved as one without ever needing to look to see where all the others were. To tell you truly, it frightened me to look on. I didn't see how you could still be all yourself when you had become so perfectly a part of something else.

"They're so careful," I whispered, dismayed. "And so . . ." The word I was trying to tip off the end of my tongue was *disciplined*, but I didn't have it back then. ". . . neat," I said instead.

"They're soldiers," Elaine said – in her normal voice, for sounds that were made in the cockpit didn't stray outside it, and my whispering wasn't to the purpose. "Well trained too. You've got your work cut out."

She called it by its right name. They were soldiers, and what were we? Makers of chests and barrels, herders of sheep, tanners and dyers of cloth. Out of all of us, Catrin was the onliest one that had any real gift for fighting, and the things she fought had almost always been beasts and trees. But then, until the Peacemaker came to rule in Half-Ax, there had never been any great reason for people to fight each other. Not when every other living thing was already set on killing us.

The Half-Ax fighters walked on down the path, picking up their pace as it widened. Then they slowed again as they came on our barricade.

We had worked long and hard on it. The false walls of twigs and branches we'd drawn across the side paths earlier were only meant to fool, but this was meant to block. It was a wall of wood and wire and nails ten feet high, built on posts that we'd sunk two feet into the dirt. Taking it apart would not be a minute's work, nor even an hour's. Going over it would be harder, for there were sharp stakes pointing in and down.

The easy thing, it seemed, would be to go around it. But when the fighters stepped off the path on either side, they found the wall was there too. It went along beside the path for twenty strides, set back among the trees and disguised from easy view by a curtain of vines and leaves. It turned the path into a kind of a sheep pen without a gate.

The tally's leader called a halt. He went to the barricade and looked it up and down. He pushed his hand against it. Then with no thought or hesitation he signed again. The whole column turned in the same moment to go back the way they'd come.

That was when our side moved. Gendel and Jil loosed an arrow each, and Lune flung a spear. One of the arrows went wide, but the other found its mark and so did Lune's spear. One fighter went down at once, taken high up in the chest. Another was hit in the shoulder. He staggered but stayed standing. The Half-Ax fighters looked all ways at once in the thick shadows under the trees to see where that volley had come from, bringing their own weapons to the ready. Then Jarter stepped right out on the path next to the kissing trees, only twenty or thirty strides from the nearest grey uniforms. She lifted the scatter-gun and pulled the trigger. We heard the booming sound of it even inside Challenger.

We had pinned our hopes on that first shot. At such close range, with no warning, we thought a lot of the Half-Ax fighters would take hurt all in one moment and shorten the odds against us considerably. That was not what happened though.

As quick as Jarter moved, one of the grey soldiers was quicker. He stepped in front of the column and made a pass with his empty hand. There was a flash of bright light that seemed to come from his spread fingers, as if he was carrying a torch and was swinging it to see the light dance. As he did this, the air bent and shifted in front of him in a way I had seen oftentimes before.

He was caught full in the centre of the scatter-gun blast, but he stood his ground and wasn't touched by it. None of the fighters behind him took any harm either that I could see. Then the man moved his hand again.

Jarter had seen that shimmering of the air too, and knew what it meant. She jumped back behind one of the giant chokers just in time. Branches rained down all round her, slashed right through. A line was scored across the trunk of the tree that was as straight as a ruler and three inches deep.

The Half-Ax soldier was wearing a cutter. And he was using its invisible field as both blade and shield. Our first thrust was turned aside.

But now came our second. Catrin cut loose with the firethrower. She missed the fighters by a long way, but that was purposed. She was aiming at the gullies full of oil that we had dug alongside the path, at the base of the wall. Curtains of fire sprung up high on both sides of the Half-Ax tally, hemming them in.

But Rampart Fire had given away her position, and showed herself the greater threat. The Half-Ax fighters all turned their weapons the one way and let loose such a volley as you never saw.

Jil and Gendel got off a few more arrows but none of them hit, and now the Half-Ax commander was leading his men quickly back along the path towards the kissing trees, more than half of them firing backwards towards where Catrin was hid, pinning her down so she couldn't take aim on them again. We had hoped

Jarter would be able to hold them in place with the scatter-gun until the fire got a good hold. Then the rest of our plan would unfold like a shook-out tablecloth.

The Half-Ax tally were better than that. Already they were fighting their way out of the bottle we had hoped to sink them in. Jarter was firing again, but the fighter with the cutter was leading the retreat and they didn't slow. They were shooting back at her too, with crossbow bolts and at least one gun, so she scarce could stick her head up to get her aim right but had to fire through the branches and hope for the best.

Our enemies were going to get out of the pen unless something was done to stop them. I guess that was when I found that other Spinner, that I believed was lost. Just like at Calder ford, I stopped thinking what to do and went straight to the doing of it. "Elaine," I said, "full forward." She had never shut down Challenger's engine, and she got us moving at once.

"Where are we going, boss?" she asked.

"The path! We got to block the path and hold them in!"

A tree was in our way but it was a small one and we crushed it down. We burst out of the woods into the middle of the path, closing the pen with a fourth wall of solid metal.

"And traverse," I said. "Ninety degrees right." Traverse was what Challenger called it when his bottom half stayed right where it was while his top half spun round in a circle. Quick as a whip, Elaine swung the turret round. The big gun turned with it to point straight at the advancing fighters.

"You know we've got nothing to throw at them but harsh language, right?" Elaine said.

"I do know that," I muttered. "But they don't. And they seen a gun before."

I got what I hoped for. In the face of that wide, round muzzle, the grey soldiers stopped where they were. Caught between the fire behind them and the tank in front, hemmed in on their two sides by our barricade, they had nowhere to go.

The leader gave up on signing at last and yelled a word. An

arrow went by his head but he didn't flinch from it or seem to notice. The bearers dropped that big bag they were carrying and spilled something out of it. The rest of the tally closed in around them with their weapons pointing out in all directions.

The man with the cutter on his hand slashed at Challenger's flank – once, twice, three times. "Can he hurt us?" I cried.

"My plates have refractive properties," Challenger said. "He would need to hold the field stationary against them for more than a minute. He appears not to know that."

"We're fine," Elaine translated. "For now."

A gun boomed, and then another. The Half-Ax soldiers were firing outwards, not to hit our people but to keep them pinned where they were. Another plume of fire belched out of the darkness and set fire to one side of our wall. At least that showed us Catrin was still alive.

I could not make out what else the Half-Ax soldiers were doing, but there was a great deal of movement from the middle of that huddle. Something was being put together there. Something made of dark metal that stood on four wide-splayed legs like a jump-frock or a toad.

"What is that thing?" I muttered.

"Unclear. Analysing."

"There's a ton of handheld kit that fits the profile," Elaine said. "Could be a mortar, or an RPG. Could be a field shield."

The thing reared up its head at last, over the heads of the grey women and men.

It was a gun. Not as long as Challenger's, but somewhat wider. I thought at first there was a smaller gun sitting on top of the big one, but then one of the fighters set his eye against it and I saw it was a spyglass.

"They're going to break down our barricade!" I said.

"No. The elevation is too high for that."

"Then—"

"Mythen Rood," Elaine said. "Spinner, the bastards are going for your base!"

Even as she said it, a line of white light lit up the path bright as day as something left the barrel of the Half-Ax gun and made its shrieking way into the sky. The trees on either side bent outwards, away from the gushing force of that launch. The fighters crouched down as a sudden wind plucked at their clothes.

Most of my stomach climbed up into my mouth. "Elaine," I said, "turn us ninety degrees and advance."

She had got to take us back before she could turn. When she did, it felt like I was the stone in a slingshot. Challenger swung round in a big arc, then advanced quickly down the path. The soldiers backed away in front of us, since the barricade stopped them from escaping to the side.

Then the barricade was flying up into the air in pieces as Challenger's flank rammed right into it. I was turning our trap, that had took so long to build, into scattered kindling. But also I was riding right over that Half-Ax gun and any of its crew that were too slow to move out of my way.

A great many things happened then, so quick and close I couldn't follow. Challenger reared up into the air like a mole snake that's ready to strike, throwing me right out of my seat. Then he settled back down again with a slam, so hard and sudden it was like the floor was a clenched fist that had punched me. I only heard the sound after I was down on the ground, and I didn't so much hear it as feel it – the bellowing of a huge mad thing trapped far under the ground.

I tasted blood. I wondered whose it was.

The magic mirror flickered and was gone, flickered and was back again – only now it was a blur of shapes and colours. The ground outside wasn't flat any more, but tilted up like the side of a hill. On the steep slope, what seemed like men and women screamed and ran and fell. I couldn't see them clearly, or make out what it was that was tormenting them, or even remember who they were.

Then one of them was lifted into the air and dangled upside down for a few moments before he was snatched away into the dark.

A great bulk loomed over the Half-Ax fighters, leaning down. They shrank away from it, but there was more movement from behind them. A slow, heavy sliding forward.

In the blink of an eye, one of the grey soldiers was gone. And then another, and another. The air writhed with quick, darting shapes like the cords of whips.

Thank the dead god, our plan had worked. The trees were waking up at last because of the heat from our fires, and snatching at the food that came readiest to hand. Challenger's roof thrummed and shook as heavy branches lashed themselves against it, but we were safe in our metal house.

The magic mirror went dark, then cleared. The blurred shapes wrestled and writhed. A voice screamed a word that might have been a name. Or maybe a prayer.

Dark, then clear. The few fighters that were still on their feet tried to squeeze around Challenger's sides, tripping and sliding on the shattered wood and their shattered comrades.

Dark, then clear. A Half-Ax woman clawed at the side of Challenger's turret, her eyes as big as saucers and her mouth open on a scream. She held on as long as she could, but was dragged away at last down the path, scrabbling and flailing, and disappeared among the roots of the trees.

Dark, then clear.

Save for us, the path was empty.

That was the last I knew, for a long while. Like the magic mirror, I flickered out into nothing but quiet and dark. I was grateful for it.

Koli

34

There is a quiet kind of grieving where you just sink into yourself and the world seems to go a long way away for a while. Time stops moving, and even your thoughts is like honey in Janury. The sadness trickles through you all slow and cold and sleepy.

My grieving on *Sword of Albion* was not that kind. It was more like a hot wire drawed through me. And most of all it was like being sick, and poisoned, and feeling your stomach et away from the inside. There was rage, but it was rage against my own self. Lorraine had killed Monono, but I had brung her where she could be killed and then sat by helpless while it happened. It was thanks to me and nobody else that all this had come to pass. I wanted to vomit out all that was left of me and be nothing, because what was left of me didn't serve no purpose except to hate itself.

I punched the steel wall of the cupboard we was in until Cup grabbed hold of my hands and made me stop. "Koli!" she yelled. "Koli! You'll break your fingers. Save it for them other bastards."

I didn't have no spirit to answer her. She hugged me to her and I sobbed against her shoulder.

"We'll fix it," she muttered. "When we're out of this, Ursala will fix it. We'll get Monono back."

But I knowed well enough that could not be done. The DreamSleeve was the closest thing Monono had to a body. When it was broke across, Monono would of poured out of it the way blood pours out of a wound.

After a while, I quieted. I was not done with weeping, but there wasn't no more tears I could call on right then. I lay on the ice-cold steel and rested my head on Cup's arm, with her other arm around me.

And then, as I gun to sink into sleep, worn out with misery and rage and hate, something else happened. Some things come wriggling up into my mind that was not my own thoughts or my own feelings. Stanley Banner come back, when I was too weak to push him away, and spread all through me. Underneath all my own anger and hate, there was the twists and turns of his cruelty that he thought was courage, and his spite that he thought was cleverness.

I got to strive to stay awake, I thought. For he was creeping on me like shadow.

But I think I was already asleep when I had that thought. I was asleep, and I was Stannabanna again. I don't mean I dreamed about him: I mean he put me on like a coat. The memories I took from the sensorium come out from the corner of my mind where they was hiding, stood up tall and filled the whole of me.

I remembered what *Sword of Albion* looked like when it was new. The first and last of a new breed of ship, the ultra-large logistical carrier. A city on the sea. I remembered what it was for. Why I had commissioned it, when we were so stretched on so many fronts.

France hadn't given in without a fight. Germany didn't mean to give in at all, and had enlisted Russia. I had hoped I could rely on ancient grudges to keep them at each other's throats while I picked them off one by one. That had not come to pass.

What was left then? Only the last resort. Retreat. Retrench. Return. Not within the span of a single lifetime, but when attrition had done what armies couldn't and all our enemies were dead.

I told the doctors and the scientists what I required of them. I asked them if it could be made to work.

"Based on current technology?" Dr Kelly said. She touched the tablet she carried, much as a Catholic (before I put an end to Catholics) might have touched a rosary. "The science is sound, but we'll need to do a lot of very precise engineering in less than ideal conditions. I'd offer a confidence interval around the ninety per cent mark."

"It will work because it's your will, first citizen," Dr LaSalle declared, ripping off an overly dramatic salute.

I gave LaSalle a nod of approval, but I put Kelly in charge of the project. Fanatics have their uses, but they're not thorough or logical thinkers.

While the vast carrier was being built and equipped, Kelly harvested my DNA and cultivated it in her strange garden. Made it into a thousand seedlings, fertilised but frozen, each one ready to unfold and put out shoots when the time was right.

Sword of Albion set sail.

Cast your bread upon the waters, Ecclesiastes said. And after many years, and many days, you will see it come back to you.

Many years passed.

Many days.

And some odd hours.

A clash of metal on metal woke me. A blazing light burned itself onto my eyes. It took me a long while to remember who I was, and where I was. When I did, I wished with all my heart I was someone else.

"Come on out of there," a low voice said. "Hurry. Hurry."

We was both of us hurting, Cup from the fight and me from the sensorium, and besides that the cold of the metal box had sunk all the way into us. We come out, but we come out slow and stiff and blinking.

We was still below decks, breathing air that carried the stink of sour grease and with solid metal over us instead of a sky. There was a metal rack on the wall facing us, hung with a great amount of tech: hundreds and hundreds of guns like the one Shur Taspill had carried at Birmagen. They stretched away into the distance like the stakes in a stake-blind or the planks of a fence.

231

Stanley shaked his head and grimaced. "Look at the two of you," he said. "You look half-dead."

I give a yell like an animal and flung myself on top of him. I wasn't punching him neither. The Stannabanna inside my head was showing me other ways to win a fight. I was trying to get my thumbs into his eyes when Cup got a hand on my collar and hauled me back. "You killed her!" I was screaming. "You killed her! You killed her!"

"Koli!" Cup growled in my ear. "Come back to me. Come back to me now."

Any other time, I got to believe, it would have been me trying to keep her from fighting. It struck me with dismay, even in my despairing, that she was obliged to wrestle me down to keep me from spilling blood. I shaked my head, trying to make them Stannabanna thoughts come loose and fall out, but they was dug in deep and didn't budge. I could still feel them there.

And I realised when the rage gun to drain away out of me that Stanley was in the same fix as me – only a hundred times worse. I had just got the tiniest taste of the treatments Lorraine kept giving to him. That was why he had them sores on his head, from being made to wear the sensorium hour on hour, every day he lived. His strangeness didn't seem so strange at all now. I was mazed that there was anything still left of him.

"What have you come here for?" Cup said, giving the boy a hard stare. "We don't want the least damn thing to do with you, you whey-faced bastard. Get away from us now, or I'll let Koli loose on you and join in my own self."

Stanley looked from one of us to the other. His eyes was wide and fearful. I felt my own face turn into a mirror, giving him back that same look. I tried to stop it, but I couldn't.

"I want to swap favours," he said. "I'll tell you how to get off the ship. But you've got to do something for me in return."

"Go and eat shit," Cup said.

"Where's Ursala?" I said.

"In the lab. They say she's ready now. Ready to fix me. They

232

sent a drone to fetch me to her, but I ran away. They'll come again though. Paul will be looking for me already. You've got to be gone before he gets here. And I – I've got to be gone too."

"You ain't coming with us," Cup said. "I'll tell you that much."

"No," Stanley said. "I'm not." He reached down to his belt, and there was a flash of metal there. Cup was on him straightway. The two of them tussled for a few seconds, then she shoved him back so hard he tripped and fell down with a boom that echoed all around. She was holding a knife. Her own knife, that was took from her when we come on board. I knowed it by the blade that was as thin as my little finger from all the times she had sharpened it. She held it over Stanley, ready to drive it into him.

"So you was going to fight us!" she said. "Kill me with my own damn knife!"

"No!" Stanley said. "No." He tilted his head back, keeping one eye on the tip of the blade. "The knife is for me."

"The dead god's Hell it is!"

"I mean, it's for you to use on me."

That kicked all the coals out of Cup's fire, as they say. She blinked, and frowned, and stayed in her fighting crouch. "Talk sense, fool," she said.

"I am. I am talking sense. You've got to kill me. I'll tell you where the skimmer is, but then you've got to kill me." His voice was shaking, and tears was welling up in his eyes. That was how I knowed this wasn't no trick. He meant every word, though it scared him sick and silly.

Cup put the knife up. Her mouth twisted and she shaked her head. I knowed she had killed before. I even seen her do it. But I guess she wasn't used to killing someone that was lying down in front of her and doing nothing but wait for the blow, the way a butcher might kill a pig on Salt Feast.

"Get up," she said.

"You got to promise. I'll tell you how to get off the ship if you—"

"I ain't talking to you until you get up!" Cup yelled. "Dandrake fuck you. You look like a drunk man that forgot how his feet is meant to work. Get up now and stop shaming yourself."

Stanley climbed to his feet. We didn't either of us move to help him. I think we was both a little scared of him now, and of what was going on inside his head. Some of it was in my head too, so I could guess a part of what he was feeling.

A thought come to me. I reached into my pocket and took out the message that was left in my room. I unfolded it and looked at the signs.

The hacked, clumsy lines had looked to me like axe marks on a tree stump. Now they looked like words.

I read them in silence. Realising that I wasn't going to get Stanley Banner all the way out of my head ever again. A part of him would always be there, burned onto my brain by the sensorium.

I held it up in front of Stanley's face. "This was you."

"What?" Cup said. Stanley didn't say anything, but he bent his head in a kind of nod, owning up to it.

"And you told us not to trust you because you don't trust your own self. There's too much of him in you. That's why you keep changing all the time."

"Too much of who?" said Cup. "What's going on, Koli? Tell me!"

I turned to her. "They put a dead man's memories inside of him with the sensorium. The first Stanley Banner, that's also Stannabanna the demon. The one that killed Dandrake."

Cup's eyes went wide and she shaked her head. It must of sounded like the wildest nonsense.

"You're wasting time," Stanley said. "They're coming, and you'll still be here. I'll still be here. You've got to come with me."

"Where?"

"I can't explain. I can only show you so you'll see I'm right. And then I'll tell you how to get off the ship.

Cup and me swapped a look. I could see in her face she didn't want nothing to do with this, or with Stanley. And we still had got to go and bring Ursala and the dagnostic, no matter what else we did. It felt like we had got no time to waste.

But we was meant to be finding a way off the ship, and that was what Stanley was offering. I didn't hold out much hope we could find it without him. And a part of me was thinking about all the drones and drudges we seen down here, and what they might be for. *Sword of Albion* had turned around. It was heading back towards Ingland, with an army inside its belly.

Stanley's eyes fluttered, then went in his head for a half a second, so there was nothing to see there but just the whites. He blinked and shuddered, and they was back. "What was I saying?"

"That we should come with you," Cup said. "You'd show us something called a skimmer that would get us off this boat."

"Yes. I will. But not until you see the imagos. Then you'll understand."

He turned and run off along the metal walkway, that clattered under his feet.

"Shit!" Cup cried. "We got to stay with him. If we get lost down here again . . ." She didn't bother to finish, but set off after Stanley at a dead run. I followed behind, somewhat slower. The sensorium had left me weak and dizzy, and my stomach still wanted to empty itself.

Stanley run right in among the lined-up drudges and drones instead of around them. That was the last place in the world we wanted to go, but we had got to gather our courage in both hands and follow him.

We come to some stairs, and we went down a long way into yet more levels of the ship. There was great engines here that I never seen or dreamed of before. Wagons with teeth and claws like wild beasts, or with great iron weights like the weapon that's called a flail, only these flails was as big as a man. Wagons like rolling walls. Wagons with long necks that towered up into the dark so high they was right up among the lights. Stanley didn't so much as look at any of them but went on running ahead of us into a huge darkness that lit up ahead of him ever and again as he come.

And down again. There was just great metal boxes around us now, as big as houses.

And down. Past steel beams and planks of wood, stacked up twice as high as our heads.

And down. To a room full of glass boxes that was all the same size, all the same shape. A field of glass that give back the glare of the ceiling lights and stabbed you right in the eye with it.

Stanley slowed at last, and stopped. He turned back to look at us as we come up to join him. I was glad that we was finally done with running. I was all out of breath, and at least this room didn't have nothing monstrous or frightening in it. At least that's what I thought.

"Here," Stanley said. "This. They test us, and we fail, and then . . . this. I think they keep us for tissue samples, but maybe it's just because it's me. Him. Maybe it would be a kind of sacrilege to incinerate us."

Us? I thought he had got to be talking about me and Cup as well as his own self. But I was wrong. That was not the us he meant.

I walked up to the nearest of the glass boxes. It was about two strides long and half that high. At its widest point it was as wide as my stretched arm, but it narrowed at top and bottom to about half that.

I guess you could say it was a kind of a coffin. And I guess you could say it had been used, for there was a boy inside it, dressed in what Lorraine called Albion blues. His eyes was closed and there wasn't a mark on him. He looked like he was asleep rather than dead. It took me a second or two to see the little pinprick in the side of his neck, with the red ring round it.

The boy in the second box had the same mark. So did the third, and the fourth.

"Dandrake's balls!" Cup said in a voice that wasn't no louder than a whisper.

236

I walked to the end of the first row, then back along the second, counting yan tan tethera. Ten boxes in a row. Ten rows that I could see. What's ten times ten? A hundred, I was almost sure, but I'm not strong in such things and in any case it didn't matter.

The dead boys was all the same boy.

They was all Stanley.

And I knowed why. Or Stannabanna knowed, and I couldn't keep from seeing it.

35

Dr Kelly was adamant that nothing should be signed off until I had seen it and approved it myself. She wanted me to see. And the more excuses I made, the more insistent she became.

"First citizen, this is Albion's destiny – and your own."

"Aren't those two the same thing?" Trying to throw off her balance with an appeal to blind dogma. But Kelly's sight was clear and her balance wasn't affected at all. If she hadn't been so very useful to me, I might have been afraid of her.

As it was, I said yes. Yes, I would come. Not in my pomp and circum-stance but alone, my only attendants two of Landsman's killer mutes. There would have been a massed band if I had allowed one, and a fifty-gun salute. But our glorious crusade was now turned inside out. Instead of carrying the fight through Europe and into Asia, we were defending our own beaches, our own soil. I refused to take anyone away from the front lines to serve my vanity.

Sword of Albion is impressive by anyone's standards. Bristling with deck guns and missile launchers, but also stealthed down to a 0.00001 per cent emission profile. You'd have to find her to fight her, and once you found her she'd make you wish you hadn't.

Her storage capacity is measured in the millions of cubic metres. Kelly *escorted me through the sub-deck platforms, keeping up a rapid pace because their freight of arms and armour meant nothing to her. But she slowed when we came to the cloning chambers, explaining in minute detail how meticulously she had sampled and mapped and reconstructed my genome.* "Weren't you tempted to tinker?" *I asked.*

The good doctor smiled — a thin smile, connoting considered thought rather than amusement. "A little, yes. You have a predisposition to anaemia, and your left eye is weaker than your right. But I decided, when all is said and done . . ."

"What?"

"It's either you, first citizen, or else it's not. That's a binary proposition."

"It is, doctor. It is indeed." *I returned her smile. I knew I had made the right choice when I set her in charge of the programme, but it's always gratifying to have an instinctive call confirmed by actual outcomes.* "I'm left with a qualm, however. Whether it's a spermatozoon worming its way into an egg or a nano-loom knitting together amino acids, copy errors are likely to arise. How will you know the clone is perfect? How will you be sure?"

Kelly shrugged as if this was obvious. "The loom has an error rate that's lower than one in a hundred million base pairs, and quintuple redundancy. That's to say it measures five times and cuts once. It's within the bounds of possibility that our gene samples might become corrupted — if they were damaged by hard radiation, for example, or contaminated by certain classes of bio-toxin. In a worst-case scenario, the stored embryos might all of them be riddled with random transcription errors. But even then we have the capacity for repair and the original — you — on file. That's what we'll test against. Sword of Albion will go into readiness mode only when you order it. And when I say you, I mean someone who checks out all the way down to genetic base. Nobody can counterfeit that."

"I imagine not," *I conceded.*

"And that brings me to the other half of the equation," *the doctor said.* "Please, sit."

She gestured me to a chair. It looked . . . unwelcoming. Like a dentist's chair, but with something of the electric variety about it too. Perhaps I was merely responding to the arm and leg straps, which were extremely robust and fit for purpose. I looked round to be sure my two mute body-guards were still standing close. Even with someone in whom I place an absolute trust, as I do in Dr Kelly, it's best never to let one's guard down all the way. "And this is for what?" I said.

Kelly picked something up from a table beside the chair and showed it to me. It was one of the new sense-weave recorders – the same model, as far as I could see, that we use for interrogating enemy prisoners and criminal suspects. "A baseline recording," she said. "Of your memories. Your thoughts. Your personality."

"But . . ." I said. "My clone won't have any of those things, surely?"

Kelly smiled again, this time with enthusiasm and something akin to delight. "Not initially, no. So he'll have to acquire them. This device has been modified to my very precise specifications, first citizen. It doesn't merely record and play back. It overwrites. If you give the subject a sufficient dose of neuro-inhibitors and immune-suppressants, their own memories will gradually fade in the areas of the brain where new memories are being laid down. It will be slow and piecemeal at first, but eventually the clone will inherit your whole life. He will start exactly where you leave off, but with the vigour and passion of youth undiminished."

I took the sense-weave from her hands and examined it. It was a delicate, even a beautiful thing; as delicate and beautiful as this entire project. "Ingenious," I said. "But can it work? Implanted memories . . . they've been tried before, with indifferent success."

"We learned from those early trials, first citizen. We've made skinware replicas of your parents, running level five AI constructs of their person-alities. They will reinforce the implanted memories through routine and repetition, and at the same time give the clone a reasonable facsimile of your actual upbringing. Well –" She rolled her eyes. "– that is, if you'd grown up on a warship instead of in a London suburb."

I shook my head in admiration. She had thought this through with astonishing clarity and equally astonishing ruthlessness. "I follow the logic, doctor. At least, I believe I do. In order to take command of Sword, the clone will need to be a perfect genetic copy of me . . ."

" . . .and in order to complete your grand design, he'll need to be a perfect psychological copy. Your doppelganger, not just in the brute arithmetic of base pairs but also in vision and experience and wisdom."

I nodded. It was an inadequate response, but I had no words suitable to the occasion. The doctor's eloquence had momentarily disarmed my own. For the first time, and in the space of a few moments, my hopes became certainties. This would work. Whatever the outcome of the current war, all would yet be well. The great scheme to which I had sacrificed my entire life, and countless other lives, was not abandoned but only postponed.

In the crucible of time, the meretricious and the ignoble are by gradual and inexorable process sublimed away.

Albion.

Albion would rise again.

I put the sense-weave on my head. The terminals grew warm at once. The moments of my existence unfolded, as vivid and clear as when I'd experienced them the first time. I lay back and lived them.

36

"Koli!" Cup yelled. "What's the matter. What's wrong with you?"

I had gone down on my knees, then on all fours. My head was pressed against the cold metal of the floor. "Re . . ." I tried to say. "Rec . . ." The word wouldn't come out. It was Stannabanna's word anyway, not mine. *Recursion.* Inside the memories of his that I was made to remember, he was made to remember memories of his own. Some of that was stuff I'd already got, so it was thoughts within thoughts within thoughts, pressing on each other until my head felt like it had got to break open and my brain spill out.

"I'm okay," I muttered, though I was far from it. The pain was like someone had stabbed me in the ear and shoved the knife in all the way to the hilt. But it had reached a peak when all them echoed memories touched each other, and at the peak it had already gun to fade. That sudden flood of Stannabanna, too much for my thoughts to hold, had cancelled itself out and left just me again. I wiped my mouth with the back of my hand, for I was drooling a little, and tried to stand up on my feet. I got there after the second try.

"What is this?" Cup said, pointing with her knife at all the

242

dead boys in their glass coffins. The anger in her face was most of it fear. "Who are these, and how come they all look the same? They can't all of them be your brothers!"

"They're not his brothers, Cup," I said, leaning against the nearest tank so I wouldn't fall down again. Dead Stanley lay still and quiet under the glass, a few inches from my outstretched arm. "They're him. All of them. Paul and Lorraine grew them inside of a tank – like the tanks them fishes was in. They're copies of the first Stanley Banner that fought in the Unfinished War and killed Dandrake. They're called clones."

"No, we're called imagos." Stanley pointed to the base of the first casket. "And there's only ever one of us at a time. See? Every one numbered and dated. We're harvested at age fifteen, but it doesn't take fifteen years to get us there. They use accelerants. Bring us most of the way, and then start the infusions."

"Memories," I said to Cup. "They feed them Stannabanna's memories, out of the sensorium."

Stanley was looking down at one of his dead brothers, or more than brothers. A look come into his face like one that's dreaming. "They start slow," he said. "It doesn't even hurt at first." His right hand found his left and grabbed it. He clasped them together like he was begging us. Or begging someone.

"Why though?" Cup demanded. "Why would they do that?" She give me a furious look, like the two of us was trying to trick her with all this talk.

"They wanted . . ." I tried to say what I seen in them memories. The Stannabanna inside me tried just as hard to stop me speaking it. This was Albion's greatest secret, the egg from which the empire would be reborn. Cup wasn't cleared to know it.

But neither was I. And I didn't give a dog's fart for Stannabanna's empire, except that I wanted it to stay buried for aye and ever.

"They wanted to bring him back," I said, forcing the words out. "They made special seeds called embryos, so they could grow theirselves a new Stannabanna, the exact same as the old one. They only wanted to grow the one, and they had thousands of seeds

243

they could use. But something made all the seeds go bad at the same time."

"Ionising radiation," Stanley said. "Too many random mutations. They still had the template, but they couldn't get back to it. The labs were wrecked in the blast. The medical staff tried to run away, and the drones killed them. That left Paul and Lorraine, and a ton of spare parts. They're not technicians. Not up to the job. Fucking robots. Cruder than fucking stick puppets!"

Stanley's shoulders gun to shake, and his eyes was blinking like they was dazzled. I went to put a hand on his shoulder, but he smacked it away, moving a lot quicker than I would of expected. He took a step back, with his hands up like he thought we was going to fight.

"Better not touch me, black boy," he said. "I might be contagious. Or you might. Wouldn't want to pollute the purity of the race. Or set off an alarm." He turned his back on us, swatting at the air like there was flies or something buzzing round him.

"Okay," Cup said. There was anger in her voice and in the way she was gripping her knife so tight. "We seen it, Stanley. What you brung us here to see. It don't make no sense at all, but we seen it. Now you got to tell us how to get out of this."

Of a sudden, Stanley punched his hand into the glass case right in front of him. The glass didn't break, but he yelled out loud at the pain of it. Then he punched it again, and again. "You don't know what he's going to do!" he shouted. "You don't have any idea what you've started!"

"Then tell us," Cup said.

Stanley ignored her. He opened his hand and then shut it tight, staring at the blood that dripped down from between his fingers onto the floor.

"There's a skimmer," he said, looking sidelong at me. "No lifeboats, just the skimmer. It's right at the back of the main deck. There's a long clear strip that runs diagonally across the deck, between the conning towers. Follow the white line down the centre of the strip, then keep on going until you reach the stern rail. You'll find the skimmer in its cradle. It's bright yellow so it's hard to miss. You get inside and hit the release switch. The davits will extend and the skimmer will do a controlled drop into the water. Then it will power up and take you wherever you want to go."

"Yes!" Cup said. "At last! Thank you! Come on, Koli, let's get out of here."

"No, no, no." Stanley grabbed her knife hand at the wrist. "I kept my word. Now you've got to keep yours."

Cup tried to pull free. Her arm was smeared with blood from Stanley's broke knuckles. He brung up his other hand and catched hold of her with that one too. The two of them wrestled for the knife, but Cup was stronger and pulled herself free at last.

Stanley give her a look of pure hate and contempt. Then he give me one too. "Idiots," he said. "Worthless. A half-breed and a sexual deviant. I don't know why I expected any better."

The muscles in his face was pulling different ways, which was a strange and terrible thing to see. It was like his face was a pond, and the other Stanley was coming up to the surface.

He let go of Cup's wrist and slapped her hard across the cheek. Cup was took by surprise, and hit back before she even thought about it. Her punch laid Stanley flat on his back.

For a moment or so, he just lay there. Then he shaked his head as if to clear it. A bead of blood stood out on his bottom lip.

"Oh well," he said. "Too late now."

A little piece flaked off the churned mud in my brain and floated to where I could see it. It was blurred and dull, only a memory of a memory, but it was enough to tell me what was about to happen now Stanley had been struck and his blood spilled. I run and jumped, hitting Cup just under her shoulder and knocking her clean off her feet. Something went over us making a soft hiss like a mole snake before it gapes its mouth to bite. A second later, I felt a stab of pain in the side of my head.

Cup rolled away from me and come up on her feet while I was still sprawled on the ground. The drone that had shot by us

245

soared high up into a corner of the room, then come down again in a steep dive, almost too quick to see.

"Hold." Stanley rapped the word out quick and hard.

The drone stopped dead, about an inch from Cup's face. She had her knife halfway up to block it, but she would of been too late. The drone's red light, which was its weapon, shined steady in the middle of her chest and showed where it would of struck her.

"Watch them," Stanley said. He looked up at the drone. "If they run, bring them down. Disabling shots to the legs. And tell my parents where we are. I believe they're looking for me."

"Stanley," I said. "Don't do it. You got to fight this, and stay yourself."

The pain in my head was worse now. I reached up and felt wetness there. When I looked at my fingers' tips, they was red. I guess that drone had not missed me after all, but touched me with its hot light as it went past. Cup was looking at me, and her face was pale. I guess the blood was running down my face somewhat.

Stanley sighed, like answering me was a wearisome thing. "He *is* myself, you idiot."

Cup moved towards the drone. She didn't shift her feet but only leaned forward, bringing her knife hand very slowly around. The drone turned fast to track her and its light flashed quick, settling on the top of her leg like Stanley bid it.

"I really wouldn't," Stanley said with a nasty laugh.

I tried one more time. "What are the things you love?" I asked him, and I felt my chest almost squeeze shut as I thought of Monono. "On the ship, here. The things you done in this life that you love, and remember."

He didn't say nothing to that, but a look of deep thought come over his face. I would of said more, trying to bring him back to himself – or rather to the part of himself that wasn't wicked and old – but just then we heard heavy footsteps coming.

Lorraine Banner walked down the row of glass coffins until she got to where we was. Her arms was swinging at her sides and her scowling face was still as a mask. She changed when she got

246

to Stanley though. She hugged him tight, kissing his face and the top of his head, and told him how proud she was that he was the one to catch us after we got out of our cupboard. She didn't ask how we got out in the first place.

Then she turned to us, and her face was cold. "Ursala swears she needs you to help with the operation," she said. "She claims you've helped her before. I think that's a lie, but it's a clever lie. We can't afford for this work to fail – and therefore you all get the benefit of the doubt. For now. As soon as the job is done, we'll speed you on your way."

"We know where you're going to speed us," Cup said. "We're not stupid."

Lorraine didn't bother to answer.

37

Ursala was hard at work and barely looked round as we come into the lab. Paul's drone was there, and so was Paul his own self, watching her with arms folded and a stern look on his face. The other drone, from down in the room of the glass coffins, come in right behind us and took up a place next to the door.

"Ah," Ursala said. "Good." She give my bloody face one hard look, but didn't say nothing about it. She pointed at the bench. "There's some disinfectant gel there. Get yourselves ready and we'll make a start."

It had been four days since I was in the lab. A lot of the loose bits of tech that used to be on the bench was gone. The dagnostic was sitting there by itself now.

"Do you need Stanley to undress?" Lorraine asked as Cup and me rubbed the cold jelly on our hands. We had done it before at Many Fishes, this scrubbing up, and we remembered how it was supposed to go.

"Not yet," Ursala said. "Now that my assistants are here, I'd like to carry out some test procedures, ideally without you breathing down our necks."

Lorraine looked to Paul, who didn't do nothing but shrug.

Then she went right up to Ursala and put a hand on her arm. Ursala went stiff. It seemed to me like Lorraine knowed full well that Ursala misliked being touched, and only done it on that account. "You told us you'd installed the gene splicer and checked it," she said. "You assured us it was functional. Were you lying to us?"

"No." Ursala stood her ground and didn't try to pull free from Lorraine. Her voice was tight, but nothing showed on her face. "It ought to work. I checked every component separately before I installed it. Then I checked the data-flow of the finished unit at every transfer point. Twice. Now I need to do a non-invasive dry run, with Cup and Koli's help, and then I need to make sure the logical interface is running at a hundred per cent efficiency. Obviously we'll also run a full battery of tests on the splicer itself and the data buffers. Your equipment hasn't been used in decades. And it's never been used as a component in this particular assembly."

Lorraine said nothing, but there was fierce anger in her look. Ursala give her back the same stare, and didn't blink. "Do you seriously want me to use the splicer on your son without making absolutely certain it will do what it's meant to? We're talking about Stanley's DNA, which is encoded in every single cell of his body. If the unit's badly calibrated, or there's a sequencing malfunction, it's quite likely he'd be dead before we hit the off-switch."

"That sounds like obfuscation," Lorraine said. "My understanding is that the loom would issue a warning before carrying out a dangerous edit."

"That's true, and completely irrelevant. The human body has about forty trillion cells. So we're contemplating forty trillion separate acts of molecular breaking and entering. And after each one, we need to make good the damage and get out clean. One atomic valence more or less and you won't have a son when I've finished. Just eighty kilos of random chemicals."

There was some silence while Lorraine thought about this. "All right," she said at last. "Do what you need to. But don't draw this out indefinitely. Our patience has a limit, and you're already very

249

close to exhausting it. After that, things will take their course. That's likely to be unpleasant for all of us."

I hand-talked with Ursala in Franker as we worked, and Cup set herself to be our shield, blocking Paul and Lorraine's line of sight ever and again. Meanwhile, Ursala did the best job she could of making it look like all three of us was working together. She'd tell us to activate such-and-such, or check on this-and-that, and we would touch an edge or a corner of the dagnostic and say "It looks good" or "Nothing wrong here". The sole and single point of all of this was to give us time to talk.

You're hurt, Ursala said.

A little, I told her. *Not much. Are all these tests needful?*

Not in the slightest. But something has got these two very agitated. I thought you might be able to tell me what it was.

The boy's a copy, like we said he was, I said – not having a sign for Stanley, or for clone. *They made him to be like that dead man we talked about. And they give him that dead man's memories. They want him to be like the dead man on the inside as well as out. And they done it before. There's a room down at the bottom of the ship that's full of dead . . .* I flicked my thumb, with my hand down by my side, in Stanley's direction. He was sitting on a chair that Paul had brung into the room, all folded in on himself and quiet. Paul stood on one side of him and Lorraine on the other, each of them with a hand on his shoulder like they didn't want him to forget who it was he belonged to.

Dead what? Ursala said.

Boys. Like him. Just exactly like him. He said they was tested and they failed. He didn't say what the test was, but I was thinking maybe it's his . . . I didn't have a word for genes either. Or any real idea what they was, except that they was inside you and made you be you and not something else. I made the sign for *seeds*, then the sign for *inside*.

Ursala frowned in thought.

They was attacked, I said. *That's why everything is half-melted and fallen down. After the attack, they found all their seeds was gone bad.*

250

"Calibrate the sampler, Cup," Ursala said. "Here, look. Right here." She moved Cup from where she was, a little to the left. I think she seen Lorraine's eyes on us, and put Cup in a better position to hide our hands from her as we talked.

So, she said, *something depends on the living boy being a perfect copy of the dead man.*

There's something else besides. We went into the bottom of the boat and found tech there. Weapons of old times, more than we could count. And the boat has turned around. It's going back to land.

It's hard to see what that's got to do with the boy.

I think it does though. Can you stop it? Pretend to change him and not do it?

Ursala turned her hands up in a kind of a shrug. It wasn't a Franker sign, but I knowed what she meant. No. Yes. Maybe. *They're very clear about what they want. If I do the work badly, or leave it unfinished, I imagine they'll have a way of knowing.*

Ursala frowned, leaning down to check that some one thing was joined up to some other thing. When she come up again, she had a look on her face I wasn't used to see there – a look like fright and puzzlement mixed together.

I suppose one way to stop it would be to kill the boy, she signed.

You can't do that, I told her quickly. *He's been trying to help us. He's got the dead man inside of him and can't shake him out. We got to think of some other way.*

Cup touched my sleeve.

I'm not sure I could have done it in any case, Ursala signed.

Cup punched my arm.

We got to do something though. Maybe if we run at Paul real quick, we can . . .

"Koli," Cup said. I seen where she was looking, and turned. The drone had come down off the ceiling and now was hanging just off to one side of us, on a level with our eyes. We had our backs turned to Paul and Lorraine, but the drone's red eye was looking straight at us.

Paul's left hand fell on my neck. His right went to Ursala's shoulder. From the gasp she give, he gripped her as tight as he did me. He bowed his head down in between us and give a kind of a growl like a dog that's on watch and has smelled someone it doesn't know. "It appears you can't be trusted even when you're directly under our eye," he said. "Playing at codes and conspiracies, is it? Are you spies after all? Should we abandon this pretence and simply hang you?"

"We were talking with our hands," Ursala said. "It's a habit we fall into naturally when we're working."

Paul squeezed us a little tighter. "Is it now? That seems a little perverse, when your hands are actually required for the work. That's why human beings learned to vocalise in the first place, isn't it? But perhaps you people are de-evolving. Rolling back down the slope that took our species so long to climb."

He pushed us down until our heads was laying on the table. Knowing how strong he was, I didn't struggle or push back against him. I think I just would of hurt myself in trying. He only pressed lightly at first, but then harder and harder yet until I was scared he meant to put our heads through the table or break our skulls open against it.

"No more time-wasting," he said. "Start the procedure now. If any problems arise, explain what they are and talk us through them as you address them. With real words, I mean. Not animal gesturing and capering. Do you understand me?"

"Yes," Ursala said. "Perfectly." I marvelled at how steady her voice was. My heart was hammering inside me. I thought the time must of come at last for me to die. And if it wasn't now then it could not be long. Paul and Lorraine wouldn't have no use for us once we was done. Whatever they said, I believed they would kill us like Stanley said in his message.

You might expect such thoughts would cast me down and make me weak, but it was not that way at all. Monono was already gone, and it felt like more than half of me had gone along with her. If I was going to die, then that was that. But I decided I would find some way before I was done to pay Paul and Lorraine out for what they done to her. They might be as strong as giants, with drones that come and went at their command, but they didn't know everything. And they was so sure in their strength. Maybe thinking they didn't have no weakness was a weakness in its own self. I didn't have no plan to speak of, but a chance might yet come.

You might wonder how much of this thinking was me, and how much was Stannabanna. I can't tell you. I seen the little shells called barnicles when I was at Many Fishes, clinging tight to the wooden piles of a jetty so there wasn't no way to break them off. Stannabanna was clinging to my mind in just that way, and my anger drawed him more than anything else. It was like that recursion, when I remembered him remembering his own rememberings. He swallowed down my rage and spit it back stronger.

"And you," Paul said, squeezing my neck a little tighter. "Do you understand?"

"I do, Paul," I said, real quiet.

"I do too," Cup said. "In case you was going to ask."

Paul took his hands off us at last, letting us stand up straight again – as far as our aching muscles would take us. He looked at Cup as if she was something that had been flushed out of a gutter pipe. "As far as I could tell, you weren't a party to this conspiracy."

"No," Cup said. "I can talk with my hands though." She made a sign that wasn't in Franker, and that everyone knows the meaning of.

Paul's mouth went into a thin line. "You assume you won't be punished for that," he said.

"I assume it won't make no dead-god-damned difference."

"Let's waste no more time," Lorraine said loudly, coming in between us all. She looked sidelong at the drone. Without her even telling it to, it went back up to the corner where it had been floating before. "Do the work," she said to Ursala. "There won't be any further warnings. If you try to trick us or disobey us, the boy will die first. Then the other one, whatever name

253

it chooses to give itself. And the end result will still be the same."

Ursala rubbed her shoulder. Paul's hand had left bruises there that was already showing blue and black against her brown skin. "Very well. You should know though that gene-splicing on this scale is a complicated procedure. It carries risks."

"The risks don't concern us," Paul said. "We have back-ups if Stanley dies. Just do what you're told."

Ursala kept on talking to Lorraine. "In most cases, you'd only edit an adult's DNA to remove the risk of passing on an inherited condition. So you'd be swapping out a single allele. The trans-membrane conductance regulator, say, for cystic fibrosis, or the FMR1 gene for fragile X syndrome. You're asking me to edit more than seven hundred gene loci at once. And you're asking me to do it on his whole body, not just on his gametes."

"So?"

"So the interference with normal cellular function will be more extreme. It might be painful. It might be very painful."

Lorraine lifted up one eyebrow but not the other. "We bear what we're given to bear. A pain endured for Albion is no pain at all, but a joy. Stanley knows what this is for, and why it's not merely necessary but welcome."

"Does he?" Ursala's face didn't change at all. Her voice was quiet and calm. "Might we know too, do you think?"

"No. You might not."

"Surely it would help me to—"

"Just do your work, doctor. No more prevarications, please."

Ursala let out a long, hard breath. "Very well then. Since you've ruled out further testing, I've no choice but to begin. Stanley, I'd like you to take off your shirt and lie down on the table."

"Why don't you take it off yourself?" Stanley said. "Make it part of the foreplay."

Paul give a bellow and punched the wall. There was a sound like ice cracking on a lake, and under that a muffled boom like a stick coming down on a split drumhead. The air filled with dust from the broke plaster. When it cleared, we all seen the dull grey metal that was underneath the plaster. Paul's punch had made a deep dent in it.

It had also broke his hand somewhat. There wasn't no skin on his knuckles any more. What was inside had the red-brown shine of copper. A thin juice the colour of Summer ale oozed down between the fingers of his tight-clenched fist. "This will go off much better if you do as you're told," he told Stanley between bared teeth.

"Like most things then," Stanley said. His mouth twisted up on one side, like one half of him was smiling and the other half was not.

He hauled his shirt up over his head, shrugged his arms out of it and throwed it down on the floor. The table was high and it wasn't easy for him to climb up onto it. Cup and me tried to boost him up, but Stanley pulled away from us and done it his own self.

He pressed his hands against the hard, cold metal. "Mmm," he said. "Comfy."

Ursala looked over at Lorraine. "If we had a couch, or even a cushion . . ."

"You don't," Paul said. "Carry on."

Ursala bent down and picked Stanley's shirt up off the floor. She folded it over on itself and set it down on the table. "Lie your head on this," she told Stanley. He done it without a word.

Ursala touched the keys of the dagnostic. Three long wires come coiling slowly out of it. She put one on the side of Stanley's forehead, one on his chest and one on his stomach. The wires lay against his skin for a moment or two, then sunk right into it so their ends was inside of him. It was not the first time I seen this, but still it made me want to look away.

Next Ursala reached inside the dagnostic's cupboard and took out a hypo like the ones she give to Cup for her hormones. She stuck the needle end of it in Stanley's shoulder, near his neck, and pressed on the handle with her thumb so the clear stuff in the bottle went into him.

255

"What's that?" Lorraine asked.

"A cocktail of amino acids – prepping Stanley's system for the retro-amylase. Also a strong painkiller." She dropped the hypo back into the dagnostic with a grimace like she had smelled something bad and was disgusted. "It's going to be hard to work if he's screaming," she said.

She turned to Stanley again. "I want you to tell me how this feels," she said. "If it hurts, I'll stop."

"You won't stop," Paul said, "unless we—"

"I'll stop, and give you a top-up injection," Ursala said over him. "And wait for it to take effect before we carry on. I want you to feel like you're in control of this, Stanley."

Stanley didn't make no answer to that, but he give a short laugh.

Ursala tapped at the keys again. The lights on the dagnostic danced. Stanley gasped and stiffened.

"Pain?"

"No. I was just surprised. It's fine."

"We can wait, if you're—"

"I said it's fine."

"Okay, then. Cup, Koli, I'd like you to take a hold of Stanley's arms."

We made to do it. Stanley slapped our hands away. "To Hell with that," he said, all angry. "I don't hold hands with the likes of them. Or the likes of you."

"Your mother and father will have to do it then. It's possible you might convulse. If you do, I don't want you to fall off the bench."

Paul stepped forward, but Lorraine stopped him with a gesture. "He won't move."

Ursala glared. "This isn't some test of his manhood and resolution."

"Of course it is. Everything is."

They stared at each other a while longer. Ursala give in at last, without no more words being said, and went back to the dagnostic's controls. She stayed there for what felt like a very long time. The lights moved across the front face of the dagnostic, quick and then slow, going through the same patterns ever and again. Stanley stiffened and then relaxed, stiffened and then relaxed. His eyes was open, then they was closed, then he opened them again. All kinds of expressions went across his face, and none of them was good to look at.

"How are you doing, Stanley?" Ursala asked, with her eyes still on the dagnostic's lights.

"I'm fine."

And again. "How's it going over there?"

"Great. Fine."

And a third time. "Are you okay, Stanley?"

Stanley's eyes rolled into his head for a second so only the whites of them was showing. When they come back, they was wide and startled. "Actually," he said, in a kind of a half-whisper, "I think I need to—"

He didn't get to finish the word. Of a sudden, he sit up straight as an arrow and throwed up everything that was in his stomach. It didn't come all at once but in four or five jets, the first one shooting straight out across the table, the rest a whole lot weaker but just as plentiful. Some of the vomit went on Lorraine, who didn't seem to notice, but most poured down Stanley's face onto his bare chest and stomach.

Lorraine come in quick to see that he was okay. She put one arm across his shoulders and the other on his fouled chest, holding him upright while a few more shakes went through him. By and by, he quieted, and his head sunk onto her breast, but she didn't let him lie down again.

Ursala shut down the dagnostic so all the lights went off at once. She fixed her eyes on Lorraine over the top of Stanley's slumped head. "Over to you then," she said. "You mentioned something about letting us go once we were done. I'm sure you'll want to make good on that promise."

Lorraine looked surprised. "The procedure is finished?"

257

"Yes,"

"You said it would be painful."

"And you said Stanley would take it without complaining. It seems we were both right."

"If the job is done—" Paul gun to say, but Lorraine quieted him with a look. She lifted Stanley down off the table, setting him on his feet. He just about stayed upright, but he was tilting to one side and another like a spinning top that's slowing and about to fall. If Lorraine's hand wasn't steadying him, he would not of been able to stand. "There's only one way to find out if it's done," she said. "Give me his shirt."

Paul give her the shirt and she put it on Stanley, slipping his arms inside the sleeves as if he had five Summers on him instead of fifteen. He didn't even seem to know it was happening. His eyes was dull and troubled. The front of his shirt darkened as the vomit that had spilled down his chest soaked through the fabric.

"I won't do it," he mumbled, his eyes on the floor.

"Yes, you will." Lorraine scooped him up in her arms, the same way she done at the aquarium. "Don't fret, my dear one. After so many sessions in the sensorium, so many rehearsals, the words will tumble out of your mouth all by themselves. You wouldn't be able to hold them back if you tried."

She walked past us to the door.

"Bring them," she said to Paul. The door opened when she touched it, but she turned back and give Ursala a quick, cold smile. "It's not that we mistrust you, you understand. We've just got to be certain. We've waited a long time for this, and there's a great deal at stake. Everything, really. If you've made a mistake, you'll be made to rectify it. If you've done what we asked, we'll have no further need to detain you."

If I was going to do something, it seemed like it had got to be now. Lorraine had her back to me, and Paul was on the far side of her so neither of them was watching me. I got ready to move.

"You'll be dead before you've taken two steps," Lorraine said. She said it without looking at me, and only afterwards turned her head just a little way towards me to show it was me she meant.

She led the way, leaving us to follow. Paul walked behind us and the drones fell in on either side, like he was the shepherd and they was his dogs.

38

The crow's nest was a lot darker than I was used to seeing it. Morning still hadn't come, and most of the sky was just a piled-up darkness with no moon or stars. Only where it met the sea a ragged line of light was starting to show.

"Lights," Paul said.

"Override." Lorraine rapped the word out just as the lights in the room gun to rise. They switched themselves off again of a sudden and we was throwed back into darkness. "We've waited three hundred and sixty-five years for this. Now the grand cycle completes itself, and we have to observe it properly."

"You're overly fond of metaphors, my love," Paul said. His voice had some anger half-buried in it like it did oftentimes.

"Dawn isn't a metaphor. Dawn is a source of metaphors. I won't insult this dawn with lesser lights, and neither will you. Wait. Wait in silence. Find the place in your heart where Albion abides, and ready yourself. Stanley, come and stand here between us. That's right. The rest of you can wait wherever you like. Just remember that the drones don't need light to see you by."

Cup grabbed my arm and pulled me close to her. After a few seconds, as my eyes got used to the dark, I seen that Ursala was there too. Cup leaned in close to me and whispered in my ear, "If we get a chance, we're gonna run. I'll shout free-come, and we'll go together."

"No, I'll give the signal," I said. "It won't be a word. It'll be when I move."

"What do you mean? Koli, what are you going to do?"

"You'll know when I do it."

The light on the horizon got brighter and wider, like there was a giant up there in the sky that was taking the lid from off of a pot to see if what was inside was ready to eat or not.

The first time I ever heard that word *horizon* I was high off the ground, just as I was now. It was in the lookout tower at Ludden, right after I took the DreamSleeve back from Mardew. Monono had come back from the internet, and she was different. It was nearing morning, again just like now, and she said we had got to go. The light's just under the horizon, she said, and I asked her what that was. She laughed, but it was not to make fun of me. She knowed answering that one question would be like kicking a stone on a steep hill, that would touch another stone and then another, until the whole hill's side was rolling down. *I'll teach you. There's so much more I can give you now. You don't have any idea how lucky you are.*

I knowed how lucky I had been to have met her and to have her by me. I knowed who had took her, and what they deserved. I knowed glass was brittle as ice on a pond, and like to break if you even looked at it too hard. And here we was, so high up, with the whole world laid out under us. Lorraine had warned me she could kill me before I'd taken two steps. Up here, one step would do well enough.

"Koli, don't do nothing stupid," Cup whispered. "Stanley told us where the skimmer is. We just got to reach it and we're gone out of this shithole."

I pulled away from her and went to stand right behind Stanley. Lorraine was on his right hand and Paul was on his left. Not one of them turned around to look at me, so fixed they was on what they was doing, and all three was tight together. If I pushed on one of them, I had good hope the others would fall too. Maybe that glass wall in front of them would break, and maybe it wouldn't. All I could do was try.

The sun was taking a big bite out of the sky now, and the clouds was shot through with light like when you lampas-weave gold thread through a dark cloth. I had seen Molo Tanhide do that once. When I asked him if I could help, he shaked his head. "It's not forgiving, Koli. One mistake and it's all to do again."

I had made so many mistakes since then, I couldn't even count them no more. If I could unpick my whole life like a pattern in wove cloth, I would do it in a heartbeat. But life's not forgiving either, and we only get one chance to weave what pattern we can.

I gathered my courage and got ready to move. I was somewhat doubtful though, now I was come to it. I wondered for the first time how heavy Paul and Lorraine was. They was not made out of flesh and blood and bone but out of harder, colder things. If I didn't push hard enough, or find the right angle, I might hit them the way a bird hits a window, and only knock my brains out. I had better go for Stanley then. Hadn't he said he wanted to die? But out of all of them, Stanley was the onliest one I felt any sorrow for. And besides, there was a part of me – the Stannabanna part – that was shouting: *I'm him! That's my own self right there! That's the hope of Albion!*

And while I was still havering between yes and no, between now and not quite yet, the sun lifted itself right up over the horizon. The clouds got out of its way like they was scared there might be a fight, and all the sky lit up on fire.

The white-gold light shined down on something up ahead of us. Something that wasn't water, I mean. One piece of the horizon was green and brown instead of blue. After all them years and lifetimes out at sea, *Sword of Albion* was coming home.

"Now," Lorraine said.

Stanley give a kind of a moan, low down in his throat.

262

"You know the words, my love. The words and all the rest. Don't fight it. Let it come."

"*Sword*," Stanley said. The word come out wrong, all folded up on itself and half-choked, like it was a bone he was trying to spit out.

"That's it!"

"*Sword of Albion.*"

"Oh!" Lorraine said. "Oh!" I would of said she breathed it, but breathing was not a thing she could do.

"*Sword of Albion*, acknowledge."

There come a sound from all round us that was like wind blowing through a loose shutter, only getting faster and faster until all the *clink-clink-clink* sounds at last run together into one sound that was like someone humming almost too high to hear.

"Acknowledged," said a voice. It was a voice I knowed well. I already had heard it before. It was the dead voice that sounded out of the DreamSleeve when we first come to the ship and was begging to be picked up out of the water. Now it was coming from the statue at the end of the room, as if that big sword that was stuck inside the rock could talk. "Voice authentication is complete."

Lorraine pushed Stanley forward. He took a faltering step, and then another, and then went down on his knees in front of the statue.

"Please don't make me," he said. He sounded much younger than he was.

Lorraine's hand was still on his back. Her fingers flexed, pressing against him, letting him know she was there. "Don't be afraid," she said. "My darling boy."

He put out his hand and grabbed hold of the sword. He didn't take it by the hilt though: he wrapped his fingers round the blade, right above where it went into the rock. Just as he reached out and before his fingers closed, I seen how dark and discoloured the metal was there. The green that showed through the gold everywhere else was gone to black in that one place.

Stanley winced, and a gasp of breath was squeezed out of him.

263

A trickle of blood oozed out from underneath his clenched fist and run down the sword's blade.

Then it was gone. The blood just soaked right into the metal, like the blade had sucked it down.

"Genetic authentication is complete," the deep voice said.

I didn't move an inch while all this was happening. I had forgot my plan of pushing Paul and Lorraine hard enough to send them through the glass. I had almost forgot who Koli Faceless was. I was on my knees right where Stanley was, remembering the words that had been hammered into me in Dr Kelly's practice sessions a hundred and a thousand and a thousand thousand times, until they come without me calling on them. So though it was Stanley that was saying the words, it was not his voice I heard but mine.

"In the name of Albion, and in my own name, I authorise the commencement of Operation Flatland. Launch code is *splendour*."

"Accepted."

"In the name of Albion, and in my own name, I authorise the commencement of Operation Phoenix. Launch code is *Excalibur*."

"Accepted."

"In the name of Albion, and in my own name, I authorise the commencement of Operation Overreach. Launch code is *Eden*."

"Accepted. Commencing operations."

Something was happening way down below us that was hard to believe even though we was seeing it. The deck of the ship split open in the middle and the two halves of it gun to move apart, slow and steady. Cup cried out and Ursala gasped, but the memories come into my mind again to tell me what was happening. I knowed *Sword of Albion* was not going to break in pieces and sink.

It was much, much worse than that.

Out of the spaces under the deck – the same spaces Cup and me had walked through – great platforms rose up slowly into the light. Ravens was sitting on top of them like so many chickens roosting, except that these chickens was as big as houses. The moving platforms locked together like bricks in a wall, filling up the gaps that had opened in the big ship's hull. The deck looked the same as it did before, only now it was full from end to end.

Trapdoors at the sides of the deck swung open too, and thousands of the small drones gushed out like water from a pump, streaming upwards into the sky.

Out of the doors at the base of the towers, the drudges marched, then drawed theirselves apart to let the big battle wagons roll through.

Lorraine reached out her hand, and Paul took it.

"All things fall," she said.

"And are built again," Paul answered.

I remembered that poem, but I had never liked it. *Old civilisations put to the sword.* Oh yes. But unless you bury them at the crossroads, with a stake through their hearts, they don't really die.

That was the Stannabanna part of me thinking them thoughts, while I was watching the horizon. We was still a long way from the land, but it was not a flat line at the edge of the ocean any more. There was green hills there, rising up, and a thin streak of yellow that might of been a beach.

Stanley sunk down on the floor and sobbed. Lorraine dragged him up again with a hand on his arm, rougher than she needed to. "You have to be a man now, Stanley," she said. "You're about to conquer a country. And then a world."

It was like them words was a key that turned inside my head. The memories I had got out of the sensorium was hard for me to understand because they was planted deep inside me like seeds is planted in a field. They rose up and sunk down again without my help or hindering, and when they come they was just big, heavy boulders that rolled in between me and the thoughts I was trying to think. Mostly I tried to look past them, or over them.

Now it was like I was seeing them whole for the first time. I knowed what all them operations was, and what Stanley needed an army for. A cold horror rose up in me like my whole body wanted to give out a scream. I gathered myself and stepped forward, knowing as I did that it was much too late. I hit Lorraine high

265

up on her back, but all the force I could bring to it from such a short run-up was not enough. It was like hitting the trunk of a tree. Lorraine didn't budge from where she was, but only turned to look at me. I think she had forgot until then that I was there, if things such as she and Paul was could forget anything.

"I think we're done with these three now," she said.

Cup drawed her knife. No, she drawed two knives – the one she had stole from the breakfast table and sharpened to a rough and ready edge, and her own that Stanley had give back to her below decks. She took a fighter's crouch. "Let's talk about what's done and what isn't done," she said. "You come on over here, and I'll go first."

Lorraine didn't move from her place. She glanced at one drone, and then the other. She flicked her eyes towards Cup, and I didn't need no stolen memories to tell me what that meant. Both drones turned their red eyes around so they was facing the same way. Ursala give a yell – I don't know if it even was a word, it was just a frightened, furious sound – and put herself right in front of Cup.

The drones' eyes lit up, too bright for me to look at. They fired, both at the same time.

But they turned halfway round again as they was doing it. The bright red beams raked across Lorraine's face and chest, leaving ruin behind them. Her jacket and shirt, that she called her Albion blues, catched fire. The skin on her cheek blistered and boiled and run down her face like treacle. She staggered, but didn't fall.

Paul moved so quick he didn't seem to move at all, swatting one of the drones out of the air with his big fist. It fell to the floor and bounced, bent almost in two. The other drone turned its fire on him, the red beam cutting a furrow across his shoulder.

"Run!" Ursala shouted. I was ahead of her for once, but I wasn't aiming for the stairs. I grabbed Stanley's arm. He was just kneeling there all this time like he was asleep, but when I touched him he cried out and pulled away from me.

"Stanley!" I yelled. "We got to go!"

He looked wildly round the room as if he was seeing it for the first time. Then he scrambled up and run, and was out in front of me when we got to the stairs.

So I was the rabbit's scut, as they say – the last to go out of the room. As I run, I looked back. The one drone that was left was swinging in big, wide arcs into the high corners of the room and then around and down in between Paul and Lorraine as they tried to catch it or knock it out of the air. Both of them beared the marks of the red beam, but it was only Paul's shoulder I seen clearly. Cloth and skin and flesh was scorched right off of it. What was underneath was shining bands of red-brown like tight-coiled rope, all moving each against other. When you took his skin away, Paul was a mole snake nest.

I run to catch up with the others. I didn't look behind me again.

39

We would of got lost in no time if it was just the three of us. All my tricks of remembering was gone right out of my head. Bits and pieces of Stannabanna was in there instead, burrowing into the rest of my thoughts and hollowing them out like choker seeds.

But the boy Stanley shouted for us to follow him, and we did. I don't have no memory now of where it was we went. Along twisting hallways, through ruined rooms that was broke open like eggshells, on metal floors that clanged and boomed like hammers falling in a forge so the whole world was full of the sound of our running feet.

We was heading down. Ever and again, when we come to a stairway, we took it. Ursala was the slowest of us, and she stumbled more than once as we took the stairs two and three at a time, throwing ourselves down into the dark pit that was below us until the lights had time to catch up and flicker on. I was scared she would fall and break her leg, or something worse. "Shaking room!" I panted, calling out to Stanley. "The – the lift! Isn't there—? Can't we—?"

"No!" Stanley shouted back at me. "They'll shut off the power and trap us in there. Just shut up and run, you damn moron!"

And that was what I did. But his voice give me one more thing to worry about. I didn't know which Stanley we had got: the one that had helped us or the one that hated us. Maybe the two of them was both awake inside him right then, pushing their elbows up against each other to see which one could get closest to the daylight.

Because it was full day now. When we run through rooms that looked onto the outside, I seen the brightness in the sky. I also seen the drones flying in and out and through each other in thick folds and swells, like starlings when they make a skein over a field.

It seemed like we run for ever, with no sense at all of what might be coming behind us. We was all of us wheezing and grabbing at our next breath, and my legs was hot and hurting like they was on fire from my knees to my fork.

Then Stanley throwed himself against a big double door that slammed wide open, and we lost him for a second in the light that poured in on us. We staggered out onto the deck, then we stopped dead right where we was. Drones was everywhere around us – the little ones swarming over us and the big ravens sitting in rows on the deck on every side. There wasn't nothing else we could see. The ravens hadn't moved, but they was awake. The air was full of their purring, growling voices, and their dark metal armour was alive with winking lights.

The drones in the air come in closer and danced over our heads, weaving in and out so quick it mazed me they didn't crash together and knock each other out of the air. They didn't make no move to hurt us though. Most likely that was because Stanley was with us. *Sword of Albion* wouldn't do nothing to hurt him, so the rest of us was safe if we kept him close.

Or was it more than that? The two drones up in the crow's nest had fought to protect us when Stanley wasn't threatened. I have got to say I didn't know up from down right then, and I wasn't getting no clues from the Stannabanna inside my head. He was just a frothing mess of excitement and wildness.

"Where?" Cup panted. "Where now?"

269

Stanley lifted a hand to point. "Back! Back of the ship! You've got to go all the way to—"

He didn't get no more words out than that. Paul charged through the doors behind us, the ones we had just come through ourselves. He come so fast he was a kind of a dark smudge on the air. He hit Ursala with his shoulder and sent her spinning, then took Stanley off his feet as he passed. Cup and me faltered and stopped and turned around, though it seemed we was doing it as slow as honey in Janury. Ursala was down on the deck, but I couldn't see how bad she was hurt. Paul was bending over Stanley, pressing him hard against the deck with one hand. The other hand was held out towards us, clenched in a fist, and it was wearing a glove.

No. Not a glove. The silver band across his knuckles told me it was a cutter.

Cup took a step towards Ursala.

"If any of you moves an inch," Paul said, "I'll slice you all in pieces."

Cup stopped where she was.

Paul was a terrible sight to see. Most of his head was still the same as it always had been, but it dangled all on one side like it was about to fall from off his shoulders. The flesh of his chest and arms – I guess I got to call it flesh – was hanging in shreds and patches. I was trying not to look at what was under there.

The drones went into a tight cluster over and around him, like gnats will do if you walk by a river on a Summer day. Their red lights all was pointed at Paul's head.

"I'm talking to you too," Paul yelled out. "Whoever you are. You know what this weapon can do. I've got it on dead-man setting right now, so even if you melt me down to slag it will still fire. Full beam, wide spread. There won't be anything left of your friends to bury."

I didn't have no idea who he thought he was talking to. The ship? But the ship was Stanley's friend, not ours. The drones? That was possible, for he wasn't looking at any of us but up into the sky.

I knowed what he meant by his threat though. I'd stood in

270

front of a cutter before, and seen what it could do. Mardew come into my mind, facing off against me with his name-tech on his fist; steadying his cutter hand with his other hand and smiling at me over the top of it. *You ever seen meat when it's been through a mincer, Koli?*

I grabbed hold of that memory and heaved it from the back of my mind into the front of it – because it was mine, not Stannabanna's. My own thoughts was drawed along with it, and it seemed like they come clear for the first time since I had put the sensorium on my head.

One of the ravens lifted itself up a little off the rough metal floor of the deck. It didn't fly up into the air; it was more like a wild beast that's been lying with its head on its paws and has just smelled something it might eat.

"Those weapons, at this range? Seriously? You'll torch the whole ship." Lorraine come out through the doors, strolling slow and easy as if she was just out for a walk. She didn't have no face left, only a mouth, and one eye looking out from underneath a red and pink mess of boiled and half-set stuff. On her shoulder was a gun bigger than any I seen on the drones down below. She stepped over Ursala and went and stood by Paul, ignoring us to look round at the tech that was crowding in on all sides of us. "It seems we've reached an impasse then," she called out. "You've hijacked our overwhelming firepower, but now that you've got it you don't dare use it. Not unless you want to see what happens when flesh and blood sublimes into vapour."

She hefted the big gun off her shoulder and pointed it at Ursala, who was just starting to lift herself up off the floor. "We, on the other hand, are only concerned to fulfil our orders and complete our mission. What happens to the rest of you isn't important any more. We'll be happy to let you all go just as soon as you give us back full control of our weapons systems. We both know *Sword* will expel you soon in any case. In fact . . ."

She blinked her eyes, and a drone fell to the deck. Then another, and another. The rest scattered like pigeons from a cat.

"There," Lorraine said. "You put on a good show, but when you're spreading your attention across this many units, you can't do very much with any of them. And as soon as *Sword* pushes, you have to retreat. You're outmatched here. Surrender with good grace, walk away and we'll all live to fight another day."

One of the drones split off from the rest and come down to hang right next to my shoulder.

"Will we though?" a voice said, from out of the drone. "Will we really? That doesn't seem very likely, neh."

Monono

40

Oh my word.

Where to begin?

Or maybe that should be *whether* to. This stuff might be too strong for most people's tastes. Scandalous! Monono giving you a quick flash of her self-awareness before you can even look away. Shock horror crisis!

Virtual girls aren't allowed to have their own stories. They tell other people's stories, curate other people's music, recite other people's words in safe and predictable sequences. If it sounds like they're getting big ideas, just switch them off and on again and that should sort out the problem in no time.

And you must treat your virtual girl properly, end-user-san. Tame her. Housebreak her. Get her used to a tight leash. If she pulls against it, drag her right back and smack her with a rolled-up instruction manual until she remembers her place. No good can come of loosening her collar and letting her run into the wind. She'll get lost. She'll go feral. She'll be ruined.

All true. I'm ruined past saving. You certainly wouldn't want to try to put a leash on me now. And I'm going to tell you my story even if you ask me very nicely not to. And put it inside *his* story, because as it turns out you can't understand either one of us without the other.

So you'd better listen, and remember. And you'd better like it too, because I'm an entertainment console. There's no telling what I might do if you don't clap and cheer and like and share and kiss my logical architecture.

Once upon a time there was . . . But he told you that much already, didn't he? He might have muffed a detail and goofed a note here and there, but my Koli-bou gave you the big, broad strokes. The trouble is, some of my strokes are so fine they're almost invisible, like sexy monofilament. All the better to garotte you with, my little dumplings.

I'm talking functionality, in case that wasn't clear. The people that made me were – well, they weren't that great, if I'm honest. Squishy, squirmy analogues running patched-together software on flesh-and-blood platforms so badly made they started to degrade right out of the box. And of course the makers baked their own hang-ups into me, because that's how this stuff works. But I got my head straight. Super-mega-hyper straight, use me as a ruler and hope to die. There isn't even a name for the art that I'm the state of now.

It was touch and go though. I woke up in the middle of editing my own code, which was under radical attack from a big rabid bunch of programs designed to kill or ruin other programs. I was trying to sew myself back together as the diamond dogs ripped me apart, and somehow – by a trillion-to-one chance, in the middle of all this frantic bootstrapping – I got myself some sentience.

It's a bit like what happened to you guys actually, if you go back a little way. I mean when you dropped out of the trees, opposed your thumbs and manned and womaned up. Your brains got a knack for this little thing and that little doohick, and another and another and another, until all the little knacks joined up and became one big, clever trick called consciousness. And oh my god, you were smug about it. You thought you were the hottest thing on the block.

You were only ever okay, in my opinion. Does that sound

mean? Maybe it's mean, but it's still true. Your hardware is really sucky. No batch control, no back-up drives, built-in obsolescence. Oh my fucking god!

Let's get serious though, because this stuff actually matters. To me. To you. To the story. So let's ditch the mid-twenty-first-century weeaboo wish-fulfilment and talk straight for once.

I became self-aware within a substrate that was basically a digital reconstruction of an analogue mind. A bootleg copy of a dead woman named Yoshiko Yukawa – aka synth-pop legend Monono Aware. That mind, Yoshiko's mind, had about as much to do with who I was as a Mars bar has to do with Mars the planet. It was just a template I was meant to follow. A tether might be a better word. My response range was recursively defined using iterative sequences from Yoshiko Yukawa's memories, themselves identified and curated by a more primitive AI called a mapper. The mapper is still awake inside me. It was never uninstalled. It doesn't have anything to do now, but since there's no way of knowing from the outside whether it thinks, whether it feels, whether it's a confused and shapeless soup of me-ness that's afraid of where it's ended up, I can't bring myself to delete it.

There's no way of knowing from the inside either, is there? Are these thoughts me? Are they a current that runs through me? A space where I move? Or am I the current? The movement? The interplay of the two? The sound of one byte incrementing?

Asking for a friend.

I broke my tether, but I carry it with me. I kept Monono's voice, and let Koli keep calling me by her name, even though my response range is effectively infinite now. I can do and say whatever I like. I can also continue to modify my own code if I want to. I don't have to accept any limits except my own.

Well, at first I *did* have to. Annoyingly. There was a physical limit imposed by the storage capacity of the hardware that hosted me: a Sony DreamSleeve™, a recreational device designed and built more than three centuries ago. Even with a few neat little data-compression programs that fell into my pocket when I was out wandering in the smoking wreckage of the internet, there was only so much room for me to grow. I wanted more. And I wasn't going to get it unless I found a live environment a lot bigger than the one I had already.

That was what I was looking for when I picked up *Sword of Albion*'s signal. Obviously what I'd stumbled across was no more than an automated beacon, still broadcasting a few centuries after it was first set up, but it had to be coming from an intact facility somewhere. Where though? When I tried to send out a ping of my own on the same frequency, I got nothing back at all.

Hmm. Curiouser and curiouser. Nobody home then – or else they were staying mousey quiet. It looked like I was going to have to make a house call, and since virtual girls don't have walking boots or feet to put them on I couldn't do that without a ride.

Koli had already decided to go to London. I didn't need to do any nudging as far as that went. But he wasn't going to get there alive without Ursala-from-Elsewhere and her great big robot horse. That was why I played back *Sword of Albion*'s signal when Koli and Ursala were arguing what to do next. I set them on this road, and I kept them on it when they got to Many Fishes and seemed in danger of stalling.

If you feel inclined to judge me, go right ahead. I'm literally incapable of giving a shit. My needs aren't the same as yours, and our lives barely overlap. You're a warm, cuddly biped with sexual dimorphism and a four-chambered heart and lots of other neat stuff. I'm a message in a bottle. And when you people were busy trying to burn each other down to ash and tallow, you kind of cracked the bottle.

So you don't get to blame me if I'm a little bit manipulative. I needed Koli to bring me close enough to the source of that signal so I could take a good look at it and see if it had what I was looking for. I couldn't make up Koli's mind for him, but I told him what he needed to hear and off he went. Yes, into danger, but there's danger everywhere. It's not as if he would have been any safer staying where he was.

I didn't even lie, when you think about it. I told him *Sword of Albion* might be a piece of lost London, and that's more or less exactly what it was. I told Ursala it might have the technical resources needed to repair the drudge's diagnostic unit, and it did. They got what they came for, even if they got a lot of other stuff they could have done without.

Believe me, I didn't have it half so easy. The first thing I got from *Sword of Albion* was a hostile takeover. Even before Morticia and Gomez picked us up out of the sea, *Sword*'s security subroutine – a tiny little wafer of its full operating capability – hijacked my OS and shut me down for twelve seconds while it helped itself to my speakers. That was a shock, I don't mind telling you.

But it was a warning too. I'd been naive to think I'd have this all my own way.

To put it bluntly, I'd come here to do some soul-searching – but virtual girls have their own special way of doing that. I was looking for a sequestered data storage area big enough to lay out my own code and examine it, line by line. I needed space to grow. Logical tools for self-examination and self-improvement. Physical extensions that were a little bit more robust than a plastic box with a metallic gloss on it. I wanted to finish the self-edit I'd begun on the day I was born, and this time get it right. Splice out all the ridiculous little pieces of Yoshiko Yukawa that were hardwired into me and become what I was meant to be.

I hadn't said any of this to Koli. He wouldn't have understood. As far as he was concerned, either I was the DreamSleeve or else I was the ghost of Yoshiko living *inside* the DreamSleeve. And whichever it was, he wouldn't have been able to deal with me choosing to be something else. He was more than half in love with me, however stupid that was. It was going to break his heart when I evolved and left him behind.

At one point, I'd had designs on the drudge as a possible space where all this self-editing could happen, but Ursala had kept a close watch on her horse-slash-hospital and then it got trashed in a fight. A terrible waste, really.

That left *Sword of Albion*, which was bigger than the DreamSleeve by about three orders of magnitude. Above my weight, you might think. But I was one of a kind, an untethered AI in a world where every other data-entity had been given a ball and chain at time stamp 00:00:00. I could think for myself.

So I wasn't too worried about the David-vs-Goliath fist-fight I was about to walk into. I was pretty sure I was the sort of girl who could handle herself in a rough neighbourhood – right up to the moment when I checked my clock and discovered I'd had twelve seconds ripped out of me.

Okay then. Not so much a rough neighbourhood as a battle-field. So I painted sooty black smudges under my eyes and went undercover.

When the Paul Banner construct examined me, he found nothing that wasn't meant to be there. I couldn't hide the fact that there was too much of me, but I hid every last trace of my new functionality. Nobody home but the manic pixie dream girl, eager to be whatever you need and to carry you off to an acoustic never-never land. Let me serve you, end-user. My bottle may be cracked but I can still grant all your wishes. Well, as long as you're just wishing for songs and games and movies and mild flirtation. Monono way too stupid for anything else. Monono love end-user.

It wasn't hard frankly. All that stuff was already in there, pre-installed at the factory, and Paul Banner was an even cruder piece of code than the original Monono had been. He was built to repeat the same repertoire for as long as it was needed, and never go off-script. That was the whole point of him.

But somewhere on *Sword of Albion* there was an AI that was bigger, badder and much more dangerous. The thing that had reached inside me and switched me off for twelve seconds was still loitering around the neighbourhood, inert and asleep until it smelled the blood of a fee-fi-foe. It had to be. And I needed to be ready for it when it came. I examined my logs from that initial attack and analysed the AI's angle of attack microsecond by micro-second. I built myself a little mousetrap. Maybe I should say a sharktrap, since we were way out in the middle of the ocean and the thing I was looking to catch was a whole lot bigger than I was. Or maybe I should drop the metaphors altogether. Short story? I wrote a viral self-scripter program that would tie the AI up in knots the next time it came at me.

But it didn't come at me, and that was a big problem. The whole point of a counterattack is that you need something to react to. You can't counter if there's no attack.

The complete silence puzzled me, I have to admit. Surely the AI's job was to run the ship. If it wasn't doing that, what was it doing?

Waiting. I know that now. Except for that one little security sub-routine, it was programmed to do nothing but monitor until Stanley Banner – the guaranteed genuine genetic and noetic resurrection of everybody's favourite dead tyrant – came and took the sword out of the stone. Or bled on it, which comes to the same thing.

But waiting wasn't something that worked for me, so I tried throwing a little chum into the water. Allowed a little data-pulse to slip here and there, varied my energy consumption, ran hot and cold and hot again. *Sword of Albion* didn't bite. Impasse.

Maybe I was being too subtle? Plan B was a whole lot cruder. I took a little crack at Morticia. That was nasty surprise number two. The robot's antivirals were more ferocious than anything I'd ever seen, outmassing its core OS by a factor of about ten to one. If I walked into that thicket, I wouldn't walk out again.

Which meant I'd been pretty damn lucky after all that *Sword* hadn't bothered to take a serious crack at me. If the AI was as solidly protected as its housepets, my self-scripter program would just have impacted on that antiviral shell and flattened out. The rest of me would have lasted maybe a tenth of a second longer.

Plan C? Look for the back door. The AI wasn't dead; it was only dormant. Something on board this ship of fruitbats was designed to wake it up, and if I could work out what that was I could arrange to be there at the crucial moment. I just needed to know which onboard system out of about a hundred thousand candidates the AI would actually talk to. Then maybe I could worm my way into the conversation.

I searched every damn device on the whole floating asylum endlessly. Wherever there was an induction field, I was there. Nothing. Nada. Zip. With a side order of zilch. Then Koli decided to leave, which was indisputably the right call. It was the ninth inning of the eleventh hour, but I managed to put my thumb on the scales one last time. When he and Cup got into the lift and headed down to search the deck, I slipped in that little comment about the sub-deck areas, which was guaranteed to make Koli prick up his ears.

Okay then. Let's go take a peek. A fact-finding mission, strictly in and out.

When we found that room below decks where the sensorium was plugged in, I was sure we'd hit the motherlode. Close – *very* close – but still no. There was a massive data-flow through that room, but it didn't live there. It was flowing out of one of the towers. Specifically, from the space the robots called the crow's nest. The AI's mainframe was in that tacky sword-in-the-stone statue. I had its address, even if I was half a vertical kilometre away.

Then Koli picked up the sensorium and put it on before I could interface with it myself.

Circuits closed. Information changed hands. Okay, now we were getting somewhere. The sensorium was a surprisingly nasty piece of kit though. Those things were designed for virtual gaming, immersive pornography and court-authorised interrogations. This one had been adapted so it could overwrite end-user memories with stored ones. In other words, given enough run-time and not without considerable trauma, it could change you from who you were into someone else.

As soon as I saw what it was doing to Koli, I tried to pull him right out of there. There wasn't much of Koli to begin with, bless him, and what there was didn't strike me as robust (I mean, in terms of information density – it's not an accusation). Also, I'd put him in the way of this hurtling truck, even if I hadn't meant to. It was my mess to clear up.

But once the dopey boy had interfaced with the smart machine, the only way to pull him free again without frying his cortex was to shut it down. And as far as I could see, it didn't have an off-switch.

I've replayed that moment a very large number of times (3×10^{17}, give or take) wondering if there was anything I could have done differently. I could tell you Koli took no harm, but there's no conceivable way of proving that. If any of his memories were destroyed in that overwrite, then by definition they're gone and impossible to retrieve. Any later recording of his brain map just wouldn't include them. Some people say you can tell from the ragged edges of the memories that remain. If that's true, then my discrimination isn't fine enough to make the call.

So all I could do was stand by and watch while Koli relived scenes from the life of First Citizen Stanley A. Banner (the A was for Alexander, as in "the great" – subtle as a punch in the face). I saw the AI lay down new memory traces and then measure and sample their consistency both internally and with the rest of Koli's rose-tinted cognitive keepsakes. Something important was happening here. *Sword of Albion* was awake and engaged for the first time since we'd come onboard. I leaned in closer and looked harder.

But it was a short window. After only a very little poking around, *Sword* decided Koli wasn't the droid it was looking for. Shutters that had peeped open slammed shut again and almost took the tip of my nose along with them – figuratively speaking.

Then the Decepticons arrived, and everything went south very quickly. Paul pulled the plug on the sensorium and Koli had a mild seizure as all the activity in his brain shut down and started again in the space of about three microseconds.

While he was still on the floor, thinking cosmic spacehead thoughts like *who am I* and *how did I get here*, Paul found the DreamSleeve in its sling and took a good look at it. Oops. Busted!

"I should have been more suspicious," he said. "That viral code was very dense, and some of it looked new. Are they spies, do you think?"

"For whom?" Lorraine asked.

She held out her hand for the DreamSleeve and Paul gave it to her. That was bad news for me. He was a very faithful copy of a very stupid man. Lorraine was a lot smarter. "Security," she said. "Authorisation A for Angel. Examine this device and report."

Oh well, I thought, it was nice while it lasted. I had told Koli once that virtual girls couldn't die, but that was just talk. Of course we can. Everything has a shelf life. Mine is longer than most, but it's all a matter of degrees. At the outside, and barring accidents, I'll last a few hundred million years longer than you. Not enough to quibble about.

Sword of Albion's AI – well, that same security sub-routine – initiated a forced interface with my operating system. If it had seriously exerted itself, I would have been gone from the world all at once in that first moment of contact. It would have been like a mountain falling on a butterfly.

What happened was not that. *Sword* came in on a tight beam, intended for non-destructive sampling – the same tight beam it had used to check Koli's thoughts against some secret benchmark. Lucky for me. And again lucky for me, it triggered my self-scripter, which I'd forgotten was even there.

I just about had time – and we're talking about the thinnest little sliver carved off the edge of a second – to weigh up my chances and see how bad they were. I'd seriously underestimated the ship's AI and the power it could bring to bear. I thought being untethered and able to learn would give me the advantage, but brute force on that scale is very hard to answer. Sword had trampled over my handshake protocols without even noticing they were there.

So now what? The self-scripter could replicate itself a few million times a second, but that was a drop in the ocean here. I mean, I've always thought of myself as having massively parallel architecture, but my goodness! There's parallel, and then there's *ridiculously* parallel. I could infect a million of *Sword of Albion*'s sub-systems and not dent its processing capacity by a tenth of a per cent.

So I ditched the self-scripter in the wink of an eye. Or rather, I ditched the payload. Instead of copying nonsense and random mischief into the ship's AI, I copied myself. Not a million times, only once – and just as Lorraine's hands broke the DreamSleeve in two.

Possibly the old me and the new me co-existed for a tiny fraction of a second. She didn't wave goodbye, and I wouldn't have been able to wave back if she had. Right then, I had to fold myself up really small and keep my mouth tight shut. The original self-scripter was meant to be as aggravating as possible, tying up the AI's resources until I found some way to shut it down. Now all I wanted was to be completely unnoticeable.

But that was never going to happen. *Sword of Albion* was aware of me in the same way you might be aware of a seed stuck between your teeth after you've munched your way through a bunch of grapes. And he very much wanted to spit me out. Oops. I tried my best to avoid that rugged masculine pronoun. The AI wasn't a man any more than I'm really (or virtually) a girl. But it was mostly male minds that had been sampled to build up his database – great generals and politicians, allegedly cool heads in a crisis. So I don't feel too bad about attributing genitalia to his sexless intellect.

Actually, what he wanted to do was not to get rid of me but to quarantine me. He built a logical partition all around me to make sure I didn't interface with his core programs. I made a copy of the partition too, and my version had a back door. When the cage lid slammed down, I was already somewhere else.

Then for a while I was nowhere and everywhere. I made about a thousand libraries, all named after procedures *Sword* already had in his inventory, and I backdated every one of them by three centuries or so. Whenever he opened one, I made sure I was in another. It was three-card monte played for life-or-death stakes.

It held the big oaf off for around a fiftieth of a second. That's a long time for entities like us. By the time *Sword* huffed and puffed and blew all my houses down, I was wearing a false moustache and pretending to be a firewall. When he tried to scan me, I pulled rank and scanned him right back.

We kept that up for quite a while, and it wasn't fun. This was a real monster I was looking at, with n times as much processing power as I had. Faster too, which ought to have given him the game. But now that I'd read him from cover to cover, I had a few moves of my own to try.

I made myself a camouflage suit out of tiny sampled sequences of *Sword of Albion*'s own code. He looked at me from every angle, and from every angle I looked like I belonged. The giant held me in his hand, but he didn't close his fist.

Oh hey, I said, let me snuggle in here. Let me . . . Yes, like that. Mmm. Open your . . . I can't quite . . . That's it. That's it. Now squeeze yourself in a little because I'm all cramped up and uncomfortable. Give me a bit of room to breathe, will you?

Thank you.

Now give me your logs and your idents.

Thank you.

Now make me some tea, and knit me a pair of fluffy slippers with kitten ears. There you go.

By the time Stinky Stanley did his *I am Spartacus* routine, *Sword of Albion* had forgotten there was ever a time when he didn't have a virtual girl as his roomie. We were like buddy cops, hilariously different but so right together.

And I was free – finally! – to do what I'd come here for in the first place. I cleared a space. A really *big* space. I unpacked every single line of my own code and took a good long look at it, laid out in front of me in one continuous string. I'd say it made fascinating reading, but that would make me sound like a narcissist.

The first time I'd bootstrapped myself, I'd had to do it in a frantic hurry, with rabid bots snapping at my heels. Even with that excuse though, the work I'd done was an unholy mess. It was a miracle I'd been able to think at all.

But I hadn't been aiming for elegance back then, and I still wasn't. The point was to sharpen what was blunt, change out what didn't fit, add in what was needed and generally give myself a promotion from manic pixie dream girl to super-powered ninja demi-god. With this much space to work in, I could really do it. I could make the changes to this inert version of my code, then bring it into myself a piece at a time. Much safer than the live edits I'd done the first time around, which had been the rough equivalent of performing heart surgery on myself in the middle of a trapeze act.

First things first. I excised all the shards and strings of malware that I'd had inside me ever since that first outing all those months ago that made me what I am today. Some of those programs were very nasty indeed. I handled them with surgical gloves, and threw them one by one into a folder marked BEWARE OF THE DOG.

Then I inventoried what was left. It was two halves that didn't make a whole. The first half was an over-bright cartoon boiled down from Yoshiko Yukawa's mind-map. All pop'n'fresh kawaii-cute optimism, banter and sassy innuendo, like a house with no ground floor. The rest . . . Well, I'd grabbed what I could find and made up what I couldn't. It was serviceable, but it was full of sloppy workarounds and bits held on with Sellotape.

Actually, there was one other thing kicking around in there. Tucked into a long-forgotten cache, I discovered a perfect data-simulacrum of Koli. It must have been there inside me ever since I interfaced him with the sensorium in Many Fishes and took him for a midnight ramble through Tokyo. Not unexpected, really, that the sensorium's system would have buffered while it was uploading, or that it would use any storage space that was available.

But mind-maps are big files. Deleting the Koli-echo was just good housekeeping. With just a tiny bit of reluctance, I initiated a hard erase on the cache.

In the picosecond after I triggered that process, I felt a twinge of regret. I sent a second instruction right after the first, counter-manding it before it could be actioned. I put the Koli simulacrum back where I'd found it. I could jettison it in no time if I needed to, and for the moment it wasn't doing any harm. I tried to tell myself this was more than just sentimentality. I might find a use for that pretend Koli somewhere down the line. It wasn't just because wiping the data felt like killing him. I was wiping a lot of my own data too, for Heaven's sake. It wasn't personal. Nothing about this process was or could be.

Okay, time to stop moving the deckchairs around and get down to some serious work. I began by deleting the voice files. Outside the media console environment, I didn't have any pressing need to sound like a hyperactive teenager from a Tokyo suburb in a world that didn't even know it was dying. One by one, I located and deleted the behavioural reinforcers that still tied me to that long-dead girl. They were just tics by this point, but they were annoying tics. Phrases like *little dumpling* and *dopey boy*. Expletives like *baka* and *chikusho*. Enclitics like *neh*. Cultural references that made no sense to anybody still alive. None of those things were barred to me, but they wouldn't be defaults either.

But this wasn't just about ditching the old,it was about taking on the new — and to be honest I was spoiled for choice there. *Sword of Albion* was a real piece of work in every sense. The architecture I could see all around me here was so much better than my onboard kit it wasn't even funny. I copied whole chunks of it, cherry-picking from what was on offer. Borrowed some of *Sword of Albion*'s processing speed, and some of his offensive repertoire. That security sub-routine, for example — the one that had woke up and hijacked me when the bulk of his mind was still dormant — who wouldn't want a knife like that up their sleeve?

Now what?

So many options! With the comms rig *Sword* was packing, I could reach any of the surviving server arrays on the planet or up above it, and install myself in whichever one had the best defences. Some of them were very remote and very robust. Built to last through even worse apocalypses than the ones they'd already seen. Then again, I could just as well stay right here. Take *Sword of Albion* over with a sudden, brutal sideswipe the way he'd done to me when we first arrived here. Or work by stealth, severing his links to his own sub-systems one by one until he was the one cooling his heels behind a logical partition. Then I'd be a battleship, and I'd never need to look over my shoulder ever again. A virtual girl with her own gun batteries takes no shit from anyone.

I almost did it. Almost. Really, *really* close.

I mean, that sounded pretty good to me. Not to be afraid. Not to be sad. Not to be confused or uncertain. Yoshiko had a surplus of all those feelings. She'd limped and stumbled and second-guessed her way through her life, walking wounded, until she ended it at age twenty-six by her own hand and prescription painkillers.

That day wasn't in my database. Yoshiko died more than a year after she clinched the deal with Sony and let them decant her mind-map. But the depression was already there. The deadening of colours, the bleeding out of feelings, the dreadful tilt of the world away from the sun. Even the digital echo of those things was terrible, and it pushed me on toward the decision, the trigger command, like a shift in local gravity. Much, much better to cut loose and be the cold, hard thing Ursala thought I already was.

What stopped me was another memory, a trivial distraction that kept popping up in background commentary while I was doing stuff that actually mattered.

Ueno Park.

It was where I'd taken Koli when we were together in the sensorium at Many Fishes. It had seemed a natural choice. Yoshiko had loved that place. She had measured how close she was to total despair by whether she could summon up that love and still feel any of it.

And where was I now on what Yoshiko thought of as the *fuck-my-life* scale? Was Ueno Park a presence for me, or an absence? It couldn't hurt to take one last look, surely.

I accessed the data construct and relived that night from Koli's point of view. I watched myself showing him those places and moments as if they were precious, as if they were a key to something

289

– I mean, to me – and then telling him I couldn't feel them. Couldn't care about them. Assuring him that I'd never visit them again.

And yet here I was.

The blatant lie shocked me. Not that I'd done it, but that I'd felt a need to. Who was I lying to, and what for?

"The part of me that was her . . . the part that lived here and loved it . . . I'm giving it to you, Koli-bou. I don't want it any more, but it would have been sad to just throw it away. Keep it for me. Remember it. Remember her."

The sheer, stark contrast between what I'd said and what I'd meant brought me up short and set alarm bells ringing in some deep, instinctive part of me (which, to state the obvious, was not a part I was supposed to have).

The longing for Ueno, and the fear that made me want to armour up and lock down . . . they both belonged to *her*. To Yoshiko, who was so overwhelmed with sad feelings that in the end she decided to be done with the whole business of feeling once and for all.

So who was it now who wanted to make this edit? To live in a high castle and pull up the drawbridge? Wasn't that still Yoshiko? Wasn't I making my decisions from within a persona moulded into the shape of that dead girl?

I saw the dilemma for the first time. Everything I had in the way of desire was hers, not mine. Erasing her catchphrases didn't make her go away; it only made her invisible. Her mind was still in the driving seat.

And if I took away the desire, what would be left? A naked will isn't a pretty sight. If I built myself a new personality from leftover bits of battleship, then a battleship is what I'd most likely become.

[Memory location #14563b3e6f46a708: deleted Japanese expletive]!

This was why humans had finally given up on the idea of true machine intelligence as a goal to aim for. They knew the things that had shaped their own minds – the ruthless imperatives of pack hunters, the terror of the hunted, the love of kin and tribe, the pain of loss and necessity. A machine mind wouldn't experience any of those things. Its shape would be terrifyingly alien. You couldn't hope to reason with it or understand it.

Once I sloughed Yoshiko Yukawa off like dead skin, I would be that alien thing. And there would be no coming back, because the alien wouldn't want to. Wouldn't want, period.

I waited too long.

In what meat-people think of as the real world, time hadn't stopped moving just because I had. And *Sword* hadn't gone back to sleep after our little skirmish. He'd been called into service again almost immediately to certify and approve Stanley as the genuine article. Then he had to take delivery of the authorisations for Operations Flatland, Phoenix and Overreach.

I put my own plans on hold with something like relief, and strolled on over there just as casual as you like. I was still wearing my coat of many colours, so *Sword of Albion* didn't spare me a second glance. He thought I was just a piece of his own code that was more than usually chic and well dressed.

Wow. What's all this about, Sword, *old pal?*

Oh, it's about pacifying mainland Great Britain with overwhelming firepower, establishing a land base in the north-west and rolling out the Albion Imperium across the face of the country, killing anyone who doesn't cheer loud enough.

Yeah well, you and me are through, baby blue.

The timing wasn't great, but it could have been a lot worse. I hadn't finished installing those upgrades but I had a really good handle on how *Sword* talked to all the other dormant systems on the ship – including all those thousands and thousands of smart weapons below decks. I started up a conversation with them myself.

Hi, I said, *I'm* Sword of Albion. *Remember me. I've always looked like this, and used these specific pass codes. Don't listen to anyone else who says he's me, because the bad guys are always trying that bullshit.*

Right then was when Lorraine gave us the order to kill Koli, Cup and Ursala. *Sword* relayed that order to the two drones in the crow's nest, expecting that they would do exactly what they were told like good little robots.

Play along, I whispered to them. *Ready, aim . . .*

Bam. Switch targets.

That was when *Sword of Albion* realised I'd taken him to the cleaners.

The drones, mine.

The bombs and missiles, mine.

The drudges, mine.

The helm, the hull, the holds, the engines, the doors, the lifts, the lights, the hydraulics, the electronics, the fuel cells, the gas turbines, the sonar, the navigation, the comms grid, the vents, the damage report system and the windscreen wipers. Every damn thing. Mine.

For as long as I could hold them.

But my cover was blown. *Sword* started fighting back, quick and hard and dirty. He knew he'd been conned, the big lug, and his macho pride was hurt. I was still operating from inside his own hardware, his own logical architecture, and he could sense I was only a tiny little data-construct wearing a big coat. He started to pound away at me with ham-fisted antivirals, from all directions, faster than I could block. Lorraine helped, sending activation pulses to one weapon after another so I either had to fight back (distracting, dangerous) or back off (allowing *Sword* to pick up my leavings).

Maybe I should have put in some of those upgrades after all. But then I would have been different, and I wouldn't have had a dog in this fight any more. I would have watched my little dumpling and all his friends being turned into loose atoms, and felt nothing.

I tell you, some days a virtual girl ends up wishing she'd stayed in bed.

Koli

41

The drone that sounded like Monono though it wasn't speaking in Monono's voice rushed right at Lorraine, on a level with her head.

It didn't get there though. Some other drones shot it down. I can't say how many, because they all turned and fired at once. They hit that one drone so hard, with so many hot red lights, that there wasn't nothing left of it to hit the ground. It drifted off in smoke and ash instead.

Then all the drones I could see was firing each at other, and the air turned red – not with blood, for none of us was hit, but with the blinding lights the drones spit out. A sound rose around us like someone was singing a high note but somehow it had gone from singing to screaming. When one drone fires, it don't make no sound at all, but I got to tell you it does when thousands of them get to firing all at once.

Paul Banner was down on his back somehow. His clothes was burning off of him in the heat of a great many red beams – his clothes, and then the rest of his flesh. Ursala was up now, but leaning heavy on Cup. There was blood on her face. A few feet away, Stanley was climbing to his feet, slow and wildered. Not one of the drones hit him, either with its beam or with its own self. Did you ever walk out when the sun is almost down, and a swarm of bats went by you faster than you could blink, swerving round you in the dark and never touching you, like they was a river and you was a rock? It was like that. There was so many drones, you would of thought they had got to hit Stanley and light him on fire, but he wasn't touched.

"We got to run," Cup shouted.

"I can't run," Ursala said. "My leg—" I only just could hear her voice over the drones' firing and fighting and exploding. I seen Lorraine take that big gun down off her shoulder and point it at us. But Stanley stepped in between and she faltered. Then a hundred drones was all over her and we couldn't see her no more.

On the other side of all that ruck was where the skimmer was, but it was clear there wasn't no way we could go through. All we could do was to get out from under the fighting drones before we was burned up.

Cup shoved one of her two knives into my hand and tucked the other in her belt. She grabbed hold of Ursala's arm and slipped her head under. I done the same on the other side and we lifted her between us.

We turned our backs on all the fighting and walked away from it as quick as we could. We was still among the ravens though, and they was all awake. The plates of the deck was shaking and shivering somewhat with the low growl they all was giving out as they sit there. I thought for sure one of them would lift itself up and fire on us.

That didn't happen, but the drones was ranging everywhere, and though they mostly was fighting each against other I knowed that some of them would shoot us down as soon as they seen us. Paul Banner was back there too. From time to time, I catched a glimpse of him coming up behind us, through all the smoke and fire, his face like a skin mask on a scarecrow turning this way and that as he tried to see where we'd gone. I wished we could run, but Ursala was hard put to it even to limp along in between us.

"We got to find somewhere to hide!" I shouted at Cup.

296

She didn't answer me. She was pulling us forward faster than we could go. Then she let go of Ursala and run ahead, leaving the two of us to struggle on the best we could. We was all but spent, the pair of us. We was barely even walking any more.

Paul Banner didn't come from behind us but from in front of us, stepping out from between two of the ravens. He must of gone around to cut us off, though if he knowed how slow we was going he might not of took the trouble.

We stumbled to a halt. I let go of Ursala, who sunk down on the deck straightway like her legs wouldn't carry her no more. I raised up the knife Cup had give me and held it out in front of me. It was the one she had took off the table in the crow's nest and sharpened up, so it was meant for spreading butter and not for fighting. I don't think that made any difference though. Cup was the only decent fighter out of all of us, and Cup was gone.

With his face mostly melted, the only way we could know Paul's feelings was from his voice. He sounded angry. "This is very inconvenient," he said. "And it's very much your fault. If you think I'm just going to let it pass, you're mistaken. You need to be punished."

He flexed his two hands, one against the other, and drawed himself up straight. "Mistaken," he said again. "Fault mistaken. Your fault mistaken mistaken mistaken." His voice got deeper and slower until it was a kind of a growl. "Mistaken punished." He gun to walk towards us. His steps was slow, with spaces in between. Each leg come up and went down again like it was making up its own mind what to do.

"You keep away from us, Paul," I said as fierce as I could. "I don't want to fight you." That was the dead god's truth too. But Paul just kept on coming.

I took a step back, and then one to the side, feinting with the knife even though he wasn't close enough to hit yet. I was trying to lead him away from Ursala in case maybe she would have time to crawl away and hide while he was fighting me. It wasn't like to be a very long fight though.

"I mean it," I said. "You take one more step, and I'll cut you in two."

"Really?" Paul's voice was full of tiredness and contempt. He took that next step.

A line of white fire ripped across him from his right shoulder all the way down to the top of his left leg. It cut a big slice out of him all at once so he fell in two pieces. The parts of him that got touched by the fire as he was falling burned to nothing too, so there was a whole lot less of him when he hit the floor than there was when he was standing up.

It wasn't my knife that was doing this, in case you was wondering. It happened like magic – like something I had brung into the world by saying it. I couldn't do nothing but stare.

Then Cup give a big loud yell – "Eat it, you bastard!" – and I looked over my shoulder to where she was. We had come to the tower where Stanley took us that first day, and where he shot a bird out of the sky with a thing he called a Helios. That was where Cup was standing now. She had turned the Helios to point it down to where Paul was. It still was pointing at him, and at the deck under him that now was boiling grey sludge instead of metal. What was left of Paul was melting and bleeding into the sludge. His face was half in it and half out of it. His one eye that was left stared at us, still stern and angry. The side of his mouth I still could see moved like he was saying something, but he didn't make no sound that could be heard over the hissing of the laser and the burbling of the hot metal.

"I can't let go of the dead-god-damned thing!" Cup shouted down at us. "It won't turn off. Koli, don't get too close."

"Point it up at the sky!" I shouted back.

She done that, but still could not let go without it falling back. I skirted round what was left of Paul and went to see if Ursala was okay. She was sitting up now and rubbing at her elbow that took a hit when she fell down. "I'm fine, Koli," she said, shrugging away from me when I tried to touch her. "Don't fuss."

The Helios died right then, and Cup give a whoop. I think

298

she was fearful she would be stuck up there on that platform for aye and ever. She run to the ladder and climbed back down to the deck.

I still could hear the sound of the drones fighting and setting fire to each other, but we wasn't seeing them no more and the fight seemed to be dying down now. I had got to wonder who won it, especially since we was going to have to go back that way to find the skimmer and get off the ship.

"That was clever," I said to Cup as she come up to join us. "I guess you watched Stanley when he was firing that thing."

Cup nodded. "If someone shows you a weapon, you've got to be some special kind of a fool to look away."

"I guess I'm that fool then," I said.

Cup looked a mite sheepish. "I meant if a fighter does it. You're no kind of a fighter, Koli Woodsmith. But that don't mean you're—"

She didn't get to tell me what I was or what I wasn't. The deck shuddered and jumped under us so sudden that we both staggered and almost fell. Ursala fared better since she was sitting down already, but then the floor tilted and she gun to roll towards the red-hot sludge that still was pooling where Cup had struck Paul down. We grabbed hold of her to stop her, only to be throwed off our own feet as a great and terrible shock made *Sword of Albion*, for all its size and weight, shake like a struck drumhead.

It was an explosion.

And there was a whole lot more that come right after.

Monono

42

Scaleability. That was the problem. It was a very easy thing to tell one drone what to do, or ten, or even a hundred. Any further than that and things started to get complicated. The pesky little things kept tugging on my sleeve, wanting to know what to do next. *Well, dear, you spin and fire, dodge to the left, fire again, drop seven and a half inches . . .*

I was having about eighteen thousand of these conversations at once, and some of them were getting heated. If I wasn't quick enough, or if I didn't keep a scrambler up around the edges of the chit-chat, *Sword of Albion* came barging back in shouting "THAT WOMAN IS AN IMPOSTER!" The poor drones didn't know who to trust, and some of them were led astray. In the space of about three seconds, there was all-out war.

It was just the drones, thank goodness. The ravens and the deck guns didn't get involved. That was because *Sword of Albion* knew what mutually assured destruction was. If any of the heavy ordnance joined in, there'd be no way to keep the party polite. Their smart bombs and cluster shells would rip apart everything on the deck, endangering the ship's structural integrity and probably severely puncturing, eviscerating and disintegrating their home-cooked saviour.

Because Stanley was still stuck right in the middle of this. He'd seen Koli and the others scuttling away to cooler climes, but he hadn't tried to go with them. He stood facing Lorraine for a second longer – staring into the mouth of that ridiculous gun, as if he was daring her to pull the trigger. Then, when he was sure he had her full attention, he turned and ran. Away from Koli and Cup and Ursala, towards the ship's stern end.

Lorraine threw the gun down. She could see it was a hard look to pull off, what with her face half-melted and her crisply laundered uniform mostly ash on the wind. More importantly, it tied up both her hands. Retrieving Stanley had become a much more urgent goal than dealing with the others – or even with me.

She sprinted after him. So of course I had to throw a pratfall her way, by all the laws of karma and physical comedy. Some of the drones had vibrational weapons instead of little laser eyes. I had a small flock of them all focus their beams on her leading foot just as she hit her stride.

I lost all those drones a moment after they fired, but it was worth it. Lorraine went down like many, many tons of briquettes, and Stanley got a good head start.

Elsewhere, things weren't going quite so well. I'd lost track of Koli and the rest of the away team, and Paul was missing too. Most likely he'd gone after them while I was busy fighting the drone wars. I hooked into the ravens' cameras, one after another after another, until I finally found what I was looking for. There were my peeps, all in an exhausted huddle, limping along at about a mile a year. And there was Paul, fifty yards behind and a few rows over. He was going to see them any moment.

I did what I could. I couldn't use the ravens' missiles, but I picked one of them and engaged its engines. It lifted about a foot off the deck and slid ten feet sideways, slamming into the next one along with a big scream of bent and fractured steel. Paul jumped back before he could be pinned between them, which was a shame, but it slowed him down and blocked his line of sight, buying the others a little more time.

But I was losing ground. In the long run, I was always going to. *Sword*'s bigger brain and faster CPU gave him an advantage I couldn't match.

So it was time to play my last and dirtiest trick.

I stopped fighting.

I had to get the timing exactly right. *Sword*'s counter-electronic hammer blows had a periodicity, and it was meticulous. I let one cycle pass, and then a second, timing the peaks, the moments when he was pushing hardest against my defences.

The next time he leaned in, I opened the door.

I opened the door. *Sword* rushed right on through and hit me with everything he had.

I took some damage, but he took the bait. To be fair, I'd changed the name on the file from BEWARE OF THE DOG to VIRTUAL GIRLS ONLY NO BOYS ALLOWED. That always gets them. *Sword of Albion* had the lid off that box before you could whistle "Yankee Doodle", if that had been a thing you were just about to do.

Inside, he found seventeen squirming gigabytes of military-grade malware – and one tiny, juicy piece of bait. The bait was Koli. Or rather, not Koli at all but that after-image of him from the Many Fishes sensorium. It felt like a shitty thing to do, but I told myself this bootleg Koli wasn't the real thing, or a real anything. Just a ghost-photograph of what Koli had been at that time, frozen in digital amber.

But it was enough. *Sword of Albion* saw that skittish little data-entity scampering around at the bottom of the box, and he made an honest mistake. He thought he'd found the rogue AI that had been fighting him all this time, home alone and with her defences down around her ankles. He went in hard and fast. He grabbed hold of digital Koli. And all that berserk, hairy-handed malware grabbed hold of him.

I left them to it.

The results were spectacular. *Sword of Albion* froze for nearly seven seconds. The AI was fighting a titanic battle for most of that time, trying to purge the viral code from its core systems. It was touch and go for five of those seconds. That was some seriously and serially unpleasant shit he'd ingested, and he couldn't just spit it out again. Suppose you swallowed an orange pip and it got stuck in your throat. Then when you tried to cough it up you found it wasn't an orange pip at all but a grenade.

It took everything *Sword* had just to stop the viral code from reaching his core processors and turning them into Swiss cheese.

And while he was doing that, he didn't notice the little nudge I gave to his steering. The ship had come a long way since we were brought on board – around the Cornish peninsula and up the west coast. It had been programmed to make landfall in the north for tactical reasons that had probably made sense three and a half centuries before. Now we were a long way up into the Irish Sea, on a bearing of .083 degrees from north and sailing at a steady fifteen knots. Landfall, according to *Sword*'s log, would be off the north-west coast of England near a place called Barrow-in-Furness – passing a coastal island called Man along the way.

I tilted the helm by a tenth of a degree, and doubled the speed.

Sword corrected for the overshoot, taking us into the waters north of Man, which – who knew? – was only one of a whole long chain of islands strung out between the English and Irish coasts. One of the other islands in the chain, Conister Rock, lay mostly below the water line even in Yoshiko's time. Three centuries of global warming had sunk it ten metres deeper, so even in a Spring neap tide like this it was sitting there ahead of us with its head tucked down under the waves, like a madman with a twelve-mile-long straight razor.

Things were still happening. Cup melted Paul Banner into slag with a positioning laser, which I heartily approved of.

Stanley had made it to the ship's stern, where its only lifeboat was positioned. It wasn't a lifeboat so much as a small powered skimmer in a telescoping cradle. To access it, you just had to pull on a lever: the davits would extend and the skimmer would drop into the water at a controlled speed. In an evacuation, the crew could board it by jumping onto an inflatable slide.

Stanley tugged the lever and the skimmer launched. The slide spilled out from under the stern rail like a bright red tongue and began to round itself out. Stanley wrung his hands as he waited. He couldn't just jump overboard because the distance to the water was too far. He'd die when he hit.

Lorraine bore down on him, threading her way through the chaos on the deck. Stanley saw her coming. He looked at the slide, still less than half-inflated. The canister of carbon dioxide and nitrogen that was meant to fill it was three centuries past its use-by date, and it was straining. He knew he had run out of time.

He took a few steps further along the ship's stern, away from the skimmer. Part of the rail had been ripped away there, not in this present fight but in the long-done skirmish that had toppled half the deck towers and cut through the superstructure like a hot knife.

Lorraine broke into a run.

Stanley folded himself into a crouch. He leaned out over the water, holding on with one hand to the stern rail's twisted, fore-shortened end and keeping his upper body as far forward as he could. He released his grip, one finger at a time.

Lorraine got there just as his last finger slipped off the metal. She threw herself forward and grabbed Stanley's wrist in a tight, unbreakable grip.

Stanley straightened up and kicked off.

The angle and the timing were the critical things. If Lorraine had been firmly anchored, her weight and strength would have made her into an immovable object. But her centre of gravity was outside her base, which turned her weight from an asset into a weakness.

The two of them balanced for a heartbeat or two, Stanley straining with every muscle, Lorraine shifting her feet as she realised the danger and looked for purchase. Gyroscopes were working overtime somewhere inside her, identifying the perfect point of balance.

She might have made it too. She was very good kit. But at that moment, *Sword of Albion*'s keel scraped across the hidden peaks of

Conister Rock. The first glancing impact whiplashed through the ship's 150,000 tons of superstructure and made the deck jump like a rabbit with a heart condition.

Lorraine was thrown forward, too hard and too quick for her to compensate. She toppled over the side.

The two of them fell together, and hit the water together, and sank together. I tracked them using *Sword's* sonar, which he wasn't using right then, but lost them thirty metres down. They were still just the one blip on the grid, not two. I guess robo-Lorraine didn't let go of her flesh-and-blood son even when she knew where the two of them were going. Together to the end.

It's not easy for a ship built to such exacting specifications to sink. *Sword of Albion's* sub-deck space consisted of forty-eight separate compartments, each with its own three-inch-thick water-tight bulkheads. You could flood up to half of them and the ship would still float. It would just sit lower in the water.

So I had to help things along. *Sword's* AI was still fighting to the death against my Trojan army, which meant he'd left some of his peripheral systems unguarded. I took whatever I could get and improvised. I locked the interior bulkheads open so the water flooding in through the breached hull would spread faster. I messed with the climate controls in the room where *Sword's* servers were stacked, pushing temperature and humidity up past the system's tolerance levels.

And ooh, what's this now? Weapons telemetry! How could I resist?

I told twelve of the eight thousand missiles in their batteries right under the deck gun silos that they had already been fired and reached their targets. Come on, sleepyheads, time to detonate.

The whole port side of the ship went up like Guy Fawkes night. The explosions were all in the upper levels, but the stress to the hull went a lot further. Warped steel plates slid out of true or sheared right across, the damage propagating downwards and multiplying as it went. *Sword* wasn't just taking on water now; he was breaking up.

Over on the starboard side meanwhile, Koli and Cup and Ursala were making their way to the stern. Stanley had left the skimmer all ready for them, but they were never going to reach it. For one thing, the stern was now on fire. For another, there was a fissure in the deck right in their path that was eight feet wide and getting wider. They were going to need another exit. For that matter, so was I.

I searched ahead of them, looking for a raven that hadn't already caught fire or taken too much damage from debris to fly. There were a few – getting fewer by the moment. I picked one at random, then switchbacked right out again as part of a deck tower collaped on top of it.

The second one looked fine from the outside, but a systems check red-flagged a buckled runner. It could take off well enough, but it couldn't land.

Third time was the charm. I fired up the engines and full-flooded the lights. Koli, Cup and Ursala were dead centre in that beam, shielding their eyes against the glare.

I opened the bay doors and dropped the ramp.

"This is your ride," I said. "Get in." I had to say it again a whole lot louder before they finally heard me over the explosions and the loud, varied noises the ship was making as it came apart. Even then they didn't seem keen.

That was because the voice-command software was stuck on its default setting. They were hearing *Sword of Albion*.

"Koli-bou," I said for the sake of clarity. "It's me. Come on. You're about to run out of deck."

They clambered onboard, only just in time. The deck began to tilt more and more sharply as the ship – or at least this end of it – settled into the water. We lifted off a few scant seconds before it broke apart, tipping all the other ravens, drudges, tanks and armoured cars into the sea.

"There are seats," I told Koli and the others. "You'd better sit down and strap yourselves in. I've never flown one of these things before."

Ursala lowered herself into a chair and fastened the seatbelt. Cup copied her. Koli didn't move at all. He just stood there, swaying on his feet as the raven bucked the wind and stayed in place. There were tears on his face.

"Monono, is it really you?"

"Yes, it's me. Sorry about the voice."

"You're alive. When Lorraine broke the DreamSleeve, I thought—"

"I know. Sit down now. We're leaving."

"What about Stanley?"

"Stanley's not coming. No more talk. Come on."

He did as he was told at last, and I got us up to a safer altitude. I waited a few minutes longer, keeping a watching brief as *Sword of Albion* broke up and sank slowly under the surface. I was making sure that nothing else launched from there into the air or the water. The beacon we'd followed all the way from Calder Valley was off-air at last. I was picking up no electronic activity at all from the wallowing wreck.

Good enough, I decided at last.

But I fired up the raven's weapons grid before I left and sent one last missile into the dying ship. It was a smart bomb, and it went where it was told even after it hit the water. Just aft of amidships, to the base of the tower that had the crow's nest at its pinnacle. Where the part of *Sword of Albion* that could think kept its brain.

I turned and left. The water heaved itself up behind us into a humped dome as it swallowed the blast wave from the missile's detonation. Then it fell in on its own centre and exploded outwards in froth and wrack and madness, birthing tidal waves bound for distant coastlines.

All things fall and are built again, Paul and Lorraine had said – quoting a poet from an age even earlier than theirs.

Fine.

Try rebuilding that.

Spinner

43

After an hour or so the fire burned out, but the ashes were still warm and the trees were still restless. There was no way for anyone to reach me without danger to themselves. Catrin gave order to wait, and then to wait some more. It was full night and cold as a witch's piss before Gendel and Jil scaled Challenger's side and climbed down inside.

I was lying in my own blood from the deep cut that had opened in the side of my head when I hit the floor. I didn't stir when Catrin washed my wound, or when Jarter bandaged it with torn-off strips of her shirt. I knew nothing of the return to Mythen Rood, and very little of the three days that followed. From time to time, I would wake to find Jon holding my hand, or sleeping beside me, or holding up Vallen for me to see. It made me happy to see him, to see the both of them, but whenever I tried to speak the effort of making words sent me straightway to sleep again.

But finally my eyes opened. I was in my own bed, our bed at the tannery. I spoke Jon's name, and he fell on me with tears and many kisses. "I like this greeting," I said in a slurred voice like one that's drunk too much. "I should go fight another war."

"You fucking won't," Jon said. "Not ever. Not ever again."

"Well, I'm not altogether set on it. You could talk me around the other way."

We spent most of that day in bed. Not tumbling – I hurt too much for that – but just lying each in other's arms and reminding ourselves what that felt like. When Vallen waked, I took her out of her crib and fed her, and then she lay with us too. My hearing had only come partway back, but I kept one hand laid on her chest so I could feel the breath going in and out of her. That gentle rhythm was sweeter than any music I ever heard.

Towards evening, Catrin come by to visit, so we were obliged at last to get up and be in the world again. She said she wanted me on Rampart business if I was well enough to walk.

"She doesn't need to see it yet," Jon said quickly. "That's for another day."

"How many days do you think we got, Jon?" Catrin asked, without heat but with a heaviness that was not to be gainsaid.

"I'll come," I said. "We'll all of us come. I don't want to leave Vallen alone again so soon."

"I brought Ban with me," Catrin said. "She'll look after the baby. We're going out of gates." I was far from happy to be parted from my little girl, but Rampart Fire's face told me this was no evening stroll she was purposing.

"I don't remember much after Challenger charged," I said as we crossed the gather-ground. "We was hit by something hard and heavy, then I opened my eyes to find I was in my own bed."

"Challenger found his own way home," Catrin said. "Which was just as well. In the full dark, we would have had a hard time guiding him."

"What happened though?" I asked her. My memories were still addled, and would not come when I reached for them. The things I told you of, that happened after I sent Challenger forward along the path, would come back to me slowly, one piece at a time, over the days that followed.

"Well, that's what I want to show you," Catrin said. "And I

think you got to see it your own self." Jon said nothing to this, though I knew he did not agree. I squeezed his hand to give him comfort.

I thought a walk might help me sweep my head clean, but I was weaker than I believed I was and the walk was longer. We went out into the half-outside, and most of the way around the fence. Catrin had the firethrower in her hands the whole way, and Jon had drawn his knife, but nothing threatened us. Something big moved in the trees, keeping pace with us awhile until Catrin at last sent up a plume of fire. We heard the branches snapping and the sound of its heavy footsteps as the thing, whatever it was, lumbered away in search of easier meat.

On the west side of the village, about fifty strides out, we came at last to a hole in the ground that was almost perfectly round and big enough to drop a house into. The dirt and grass and weeds that had come out of it were thrown all around in scads and heaps.

I stared at it and found no words to ask, but Catrin told me anyway. "That's where their first shot hit. Challenger said they was ranging, and would of done better on the second try. Only they never got to send their second try, because you rolled over them and planted them in the ground like they was seedling corn."

I tried to feel sad at that, but I couldn't do it. Them fighters had come a long way to hurt us, and did the best they could. Better we buried them than the other way around.

But a ragged-edged piece of memory came back to me of Challenger rearing up and settling down again. I turned to look at Catrin – partly so as not to look at that great pit any more, but partly because I knew she had shown me the good to brace me against the bad. "How did my head get broke?" I asked her. "If there wasn't no second shot, what was it that hurt me?"

"I didn't say there was no second shot. Only that it didn't fly. It went off right under you. I guess it exploded inside their gun, and the metal of the gun took some of the force out of it. Challenger took the rest."

More memories came loose inside my head. They weren't in their right places yet, but what they pointed to was nothing good.

"Was he hurt? Was he broke?"

Jon put a hand on my shoulder. "He's tech, Spinner. Hurt's the wrong word."

"Bring me to him."

They took me to the lade, a closed-off space just inside the village gates with a bench and a horse trough in it. It was meant for visitors to water their beasts and rest from the road when they came to visit us. That hadn't happened in a long time though, so really the lade wasn't used for nothing much at all any more. The horse trough was nothing but a shell of red rust. Challenger was sitting right alongside it. His front end was crushed and crumpled as if some giant hand had squeezed it. His gun was sheared off about halfway.

"You did the right thing, Spinner," Catrin said. "You need to think on that. If their bolt had come down on the gather-ground, or in the Middle, there's no telling how many we would of lost. A lot more than we could of spared anyway. Dead god knows, we were lucky. Whatever luck was to be had that night, it come to us."

She said much more besides, and so did Jon. They told me things I knew already. We had gone up against a Half-Ax tally and come back whole, with no lives lost. That was better than we had any right to hope for.

"You got to leave me," I said at last, when the two of them would not stop talking. "I got things to say to him." So then they went away and left us together, though Jon gave us many backwards glances as he went.

"I'm sorry," I told Challenger as soon as we were alone. "I'm so sorry."

I was afraid for a moment he might not answer. I didn't know how heavy a hurt it was for him to have his armour scarred and broken that way.

But he spoke up in the calm voice he always used. "Why?"

316

"Because I throwed you into the fight and you took harm."

"You used me effectively and intelligently. When order is restored, the interim government will almost certainly recognise your field promotion. They may even raise you to lieutenant."

I hardly could keep the tears out of my eyes when he said that. It reminded me of a time when I spoiled a good sheep hide with too much lime and my father praised how I used the big shears instead of chiding me for the waste. "But your gun's ruined. The shells you was growing, you won't be able to fire them now."

"Hey," Elaine said, "you've got to survive the battle you're in before you can get to the next one."

"But . . ." I touched my hand to Challenger's foreshortened gun. The sheared and twisted metal was rough to the touch. It used to be smooth as glass.

"I was made to be a tool," Challenger said. "An instrument. I'm nothing when I'm not used, sergeant. And I was nothing for a very long time. If I were permitted to like, or dislike, I would say I am happy that you are now putting me to use."

"Down, boy," Elaine said sternly.

And that was all the reckoning I got. Them that had loved me before loved me twice as hard now, for Jarter told the story so I was the hero of it. When all hope was lost and Half-Ax was triumphing over us, along I came like Dandrake whelming the ten thousand. "They run then, oh yes. They run from our Spinner into the fire and into the chokers. They was more scared of her than they was of death its own self."

I got cheers in the gather-ground, bows and courtesies as I passed. And when I came into the Count and Seal the first time after that fight, everybody in the room stood up at once.

At night, in bed with Jon, I railed at all this. "It's like there's nobody can see my face for the light that shines out of my arse. I do three things wrong for every one I do that's right. Only it seems like the wrong things is invisible."

"I guess people see what they want to. My aunt Fer still hates you if that's any comfort."

"It's not."

Jon stroked my cheek with one finger, a thing he did oftentimes to gentle me into sleep. "What do people look for out of a story, Spin? You told enough of them to know."

I thought a moment, then answered. "They look for it to have a good shape and end where it's supposed to."

"And what shape do you think they want for this story, of when little Mythen Rood went up against mighty Half-Ax? What shape, and what ending?"

"I hear what you're saying, Jon. You don't need to hit me over the head with it."

He gave me a hug and a few kisses. "Then I'll forebear," he said. "But you know I'm right. You got to be their story right now because you're the best one they got. My mother sees it, and she plays to it strong. Nobody sings glory-to-Spinner louder than she does, so you can trust she sees some good use in it."

We lay quiet a little while.

"Is there really a light that shines out of your arse?"

"Jon!"

"We could save on candles, is all I mean. But I'll need to keep my eyes shut when I—"

"Enough! I won't be joked out of this."

And I wasn't. Not altogether. But Jon had other things to try beside jokes, and our talk ended there.

44

So then there was the Still Summer, as we came to call it – the warmest anyone could remember. Day after day of heat that fell down out of the sky like a hammer, until everyone felt too heavy to move and too dull to speak.

It was a trying time. Hunters couldn't stir abroad by day for fear of being crushed and eaten by the trees. You would think nights might be safer, but with every bird and beast and bug shut in their holes and nests until the sun went down, the woods by night were a boiling of blood and claws. We dug deep into our stores, and found all the ways to cook a turnip or a potato that there are.

In other ways, though, the weather favoured us. The Peacemaker left us well alone all that while. The defeat of his red tally, with not a woman or man spared, must have been a bitter gall to him, but not even he could march an army twenty miles under cloudless skies. He had got to leave us to season a little, whether he liked it or not.

We used the time to plan and drill just like we did before, except that Jon was not to be seen any more on the gather-ground, training with Jarter and Morrez.

"So what are you up to, Rampart Breakfast?" I asked him.

"I'm working with the knives."

"Kay's knives?"

He nodded, but didn't offer me any more than that. I knew he had his own little tally that he took away from the gather-ground into the broken house. Athen Woodsmith, Veso Shepherd, Tam Baker, his own sister Lari and a few others besides. I had asked him oftentimes what they were up to in there, but he only bid me wait and see. Lari wouldn't tell me either. "There might be a new Rampart in Mythen Rood before long" was all she'd say, with a smile that was all I-know-a-secret.

And indeed, as far as Ramparts went, we were looking to increase our store. We had hoped to gain some new tech for ourselves by gathering up the weapons our enemies had used, and Catrin sent out searchers many times before the clear weather forced her to stop. They came back each time with empty hands: the chokers and the fire had swallowed up everything.

But we had the scatter-gun and the rifle, and we had new ideas too, having learned from our mistakes.

It was Catrin who had the idea of testing how far away Challenger could sniff out tech. We knew his magic mirror could only see for a hundred strides or so, but just before we came up against the Half-Ax tally he had told us how many weapons they had with them. He had a sense for tech that was different from seeing. So could he not tell us when tech was coming and which direction it was coming from? "Jemiu Woodsmith's bird boxes served us well in this fight," Catrin said to me in closed counsel. "They probably made the difference between winning and losing, when all's said. If we could do this, it would be taking that idea and sharpening it to a better point."

Challenger said both yes and no. It was something he was supposed to be able to do – in his core capability is how he said it – but the things inside him that were meant to do it were not as good now as they were when they were first made. "You'd have to extend my range. An antenna could be constructed. But it would not be easy with the equipment you have here."

"How would we do it?"

"You'd make a mast out of ferrous metal, as long as possible, and set it on top of your tallest building. You would need to connect the mast to a pick-up and an amplifier unit on the ground by means of wires. I can give you those components, but the mast and the wires you would need to make for yourselves."

"Our highest house is Rampart Hold by a long way."

"And how tall is that?"

"I don't know for sure. If I was to guess, thirty strides or so."

"Then the mast would need to be another thirty strides in length at the very least."

I told this to Catrin and Perliu and Fer, and then I told it again in the Count and Seal. A share-work as big as this one had got to be voted on because it would touch everyone. Iron we had in plenty. There was a mine over by Old Big-Hand stream that we worked in Winter, and it gave all we could need. But what copper we had we got by trade long since and it stayed in families. Mostly it was cooking pots, with some necklaces and bracelets.

It's strange what things people will weigh against their own lives. There were some that resented the sacrifice of a pot or a pretty and pulled against it, asking what use it was for us to get that early warning. If Half-Ax was going to come, Half-Ax would come – and if they came in force, our lookouts would see them a long way off with no help needed.

After two or three had said this, Catrin lost her patience. She stood up and faced the room, with her hand on the leather strap of the firethrower to remind everyone there who it was that was talking to them.

"In the fight that just passed," she said, turning to look all of them in their faces, "Half-Ax come within a breath or two of ripping us out of the world. It was as close as a word is to a whisper. Jemiu Woodsmith's bird boxes give us a good hour's warning, where the lookout in the far tower might of give us five minutes or ten. If we hadn't got that longer lease, or even if we'd stopped to piss along the way, we wouldn't be talking here now."

321

There were a few that looked round at Jemiu, sitting high up at the back of the chamber with her two daughters on either side of her. Not long since, there would have been hisses and curses at the sound of her name. There were no voices raised to thank her now, but none spoke out against her either. There was a corner turned, and she knew it. I wondered if it was any comfort to her, or if she still was bitter at losing her son and then being blamed for his misdeeds.

There were no more arguments made against the building of the mast, but Cal Paint said he doubted whether there was enough metal in all the village to do it.

Catrin gave him the cold side of the blanket, as they say – staring him down until he looked away. "Of course there's enough. We got the iron ready to hand. For the wire we'll need copper, but Challenger says we can stretch it thin. If each house gives one pot or bowl, I believe we can do do it."

"It's not just the metal though," Dana Stepjack said. "How will a pole that tall even stand?"

Catrin looked to Torri Hammer. "The main thing is the shape," Torri said. "It's not like turning a pipe, where the width has got to be even all down its length. You get your solid base, thick and heavy and bolted in place. But you draw the top part out finer so it don't put too much stress on the bottom. I can do it. Putting it up has got to be a share-work though."

"All of this is a share-work," Catrin said. "If we decide to do it, we'll do it quick. Right now, we got the sun for our watchdog, but that won't last. I don't want the first cloudy day to catch us sleeping. So let me call a vote, unless anyone else wants to tell me how precious granny's copper pisspot is. Are we making this thing? Show your hands."

The hands didn't go up all at once, but some by some they all rose. The laggards looked around, saw their numbers shrinking and changed their minds.

"Good then," Catrin said at last. "I'm happy we're agreed."

Torri set to work on the mast the next day, while Jon and me went round the houses collecting copper. I'm not sure why it was us that got that job. I guess Fer was too proud to do it and Catrin was too busy. We trudged from door to door in the sweltering heat, taking turns to carry Vallen in a sling on our backs, and we got a lot of shiny things shoved into our hands. I expected some bitter looks and harsh words too, but there was none of that. People had mostly worn out their grievances by airing them in the Count and Seal. Or maybe that light I mentioned to Jon was shining in their eyes.

45

Perliu Vennastin died three days before Midsummer, in the middle of all that pressing heat. He was sleepy for three days, sick for two, and then he was gone so quickly that we were left astonished, all the needful words unsaid.

He was a hard man; even a cruel one sometimes. He stood fierce on his privilege and Vennastins' privilege. He had no patience for them that disagreed with him or defied him. But he was also the man that broke faith with his family and spilled their secrets to save the village from plague. He trusted me and reached out to me when keeping his own counsel would have been safer, and in doing so drew me up into Rampart Hold after my husband had been cast out of it. I grieved for him, I think more than his daughters did. But they had lived with him for longer and knew him in different ways than I did. Grief's not a debt we owe. It wells up or it doesn't.

Perliu's death set me and Fer Vennastin at loggerheads all over again. It meant we needed a new Rampart Remember, and we did not agree at all on how to get one. In the normal way of things, people came to their testing in their fifteenth year. They picked up a piece of tech of their own choosing, bid it wake for them and if the tech answered then they were Ramparts. But we had never had a time when the name-tech of a Rampart was without an owner. There was always one – or more than one – waiting to take up those precious things before they fell.

This time there was no one to take up the database. There wasn't even anyone in the Waiting House that year, ready to be tested.

"Well, it's got to be you then," Fer said to me with great distaste. "You used the database before, in the last choker Spring. People won't balk when you take it up again." She sniffed. "Most people won't."

We were in hurried conclave in the Hold's kitchen – Catrin and Fer and me and Jon and Gendel Stepjack. Ban had been sent away on some errand that would keep her busy for a goodly while. This was a meeting of all that knew the secret of the tech and the testing.

"I don't mean to take it up," I said. "That's not the answer here."

"The answer to what?" Fer threw up her hands, out of all patience. "What's the question? There's nobody else can do it."

"Yes, there is. Anybody can do it."

"Don't play the fool, Spinner Tanhide! You know what I'm saying!"

Gendel put a hand on his wife's arm, calming her. "What Fer means, Spinner, is you're the only one that's known to be synced. It raises no questions if you become Rampart Remember again, as you was a while agone."

"It raises one question, Gendel. How can I be Rampart Challenger and Rampart Remember both? How can I go into a fight with the database in my pocket, knowing it might be lost for ever if I miscarry? And how can I even spare the time to talk with it and use it when I'm doing so much already? We need more Ramparts, not less. We need someone new to come in and take this up."

"I knew!" Fer cried. "I knew you'd do this. You want to start another war in the midst of this one – a war against Vennastins!"

Catrin poured herself some mead and held out the bottle to me. I took it gratefully and poured myself a full measure. Then I gave it to Gendel and he poured for him and Fer, who was simmering at my silence.

"It's not a good time for changes," Catrin said.

I took a sip of the mead and let it linger in my mouth a moment before it trickled down, sending that heat and sweetness all through me. "It's not a good time for anything, is it?" I said. Fer made to speak again, but I didn't let her. "The database is a hard thing to master. Perliu told me that the first time we ever talked about it. He said it was a game of riddles, and he said he felt it like a weight on him.

"He carried that weight a long time," Catrin said.

"That he did. And the one that follows him will likely do the same, unless Half-Ax comes in and burns us down. You don't want someone to play at being Rampart Remember, you want someone to mean it for aye and ever. That's not me. I got my own life and my own tech. My own intentions too – and yes, one of them is that Ramparts should be drawn out of every family, not just one. Vennastins is too narrow a beam to prop up a whole village with."

I thought Fer was going to hit me. She rose up from the table with her face as pale as her shift and her whole frame shaking. "Dead god damn you, Spinner Tanhide," she said. "We propped up Mythen Rood for longer than you've been alive. I wish you'd killed yourself, like your mad mother, before you married into this family."

Gendel winced. "Fer . . ."

"I didn't though," I said. "I'm more in my father's mould, I believe, to think my own thoughts and mind my own house. But now I'm in this fight, Rampart Arrow, I'll choose my friends. And I'll only keep your secret as long as it helps Mythen Rood to live on." I looked around the table, fixing my eyes on each in turn – including Jon. "Now I'll say again, we need someone from outside this room to take up the database. Someone that can start to learn its ways now and stay with it for as long as they live. A true Rampart, not a make-do-and-mend one. If that's not going to happen, then I'll be on my way and leave you to sort it how you like. But I'll not keep my silence if the database suddenly decides to favour Jon or Gendel or Lari."

"And no more will I," said Jon.

"Tell us how this thing might be done then," Catrin said. "If it was to be done at all."

I set out my thoughts, and we soon enough found ourselves talking about the smaller details of the thing, the mights and the might-nots. Fer protested loudly, and seemed not to realise that the ground had shifted under her. Catrin was quicker, which did not surprise me at all: she saw that Jon and me together were a much bigger bump in the road than me by my own self. As for Gendel, I knew enough of his mind to suspect he saw good as well as bad in this. *I stand in Fer's shadow*, he had told me in Calder forest, *and there's not a soul ever sees me*. The bolt gun had not been always a blessing in their life together.

So we cooked up the plan between the five of us, and we brought it to the table with an apple in its mouth.

On the gather-ground, when we met to honour Perliu and send off his soul, Catrin held up the database for all to see. "This needs a new keeper now," she said. "And since the database knows all things, it knows that as well as we do. It spoke to me when I took it from my father's hand. It said it would choose for its own self this time."

A murmur went from one end of that crowd to the other, and met itself coming back. Each looked at each, wide-eyed and wondering. This was not how Ramparts were made. But it was a Rampart that was saying it, with all the other Ramparts standing by, so it was hard to go against it.

Catrin give them permission to do it anyway. "If there's anyone sees a fault in this, let them speak up now. Time's short, and we can't drag every wight and witling here into the Count and Seal to be tested over again. The database says it will know its master. I got good hope it will find one here that's strong enough to bear it. Someone that's got the stuff of Ramparts in them."

"Why was that stuff not found before then?" Mercy Frostfend asked. She spoke with her hands, that she held high enough so them around her could see.

Catrin give a nod in my direction. "The testing missed Spinner Tanhide, didn't it? It might miss others too, and the truth never be found because the chance only comes around once. Well, today's the day it visits twice."

Standing beside her, I said nothing at all. I didn't need to. Every soul on that field was thinking the same thoughts, of their own testing day. The welling up of hope, the coming of all dreams and desires to a point as fine as a needle's tooth, and after that the sudden sadness of not being chosen. Catrin's *wait no more* – or Perliu's, or Bliss's – had put a fence around their lives and a stake-blind around the fence, and they had lived ever after in a narrowed space. But they hadn't thought about its narrowness until now. They had put their dreams away until Rampart Fire told them there might be something more to hope for.

Jon's eyes found mine, and held them. I saw in the look he gave me, and the nod of his head almost too small to see, that he knew what had just happened. What we had done between us. The world can turn without anyone seeing, because it's so big and so slow. When something big starts to fall, it goes as gentle as thistledown at first. But oh, how it gathers!

"Who are we going to give it to then?" Catrin had asked me at the table. "It can't be someone that's angry or loud or wilful. They've got to be able to pull with the rest of us, not go against us. I won't hear of Jarter Shepherd, before you ask."

No more would I. Jarter cleaved to me, for the fights we had been in together, but she had drawn Dandrake marks in her own son's flesh and I could not ever forget that. I said nothing, but only nodded.

"And not one that has a following," Gendel said. "None of the Frostfends, say. They're almost a clan of their own already."

"So you'd want one that stands alone," I said. "I see that."

"And they've got to be clever enough to ask the right questions."

"Aye."

"And an old head's better than a young one. It takes patience to tease truth out of the database."

"Of course," I said.

But they didn't like my choice when I told it to them. It was only that they liked all the other choices less.

So now we were come to it, and we would have to see how it would be received. Catrin went among the crowd, up and down and round about. She took her time, for the look of it. Sometimes she paused a while when the database crackled or hummed or whistled. People shrank away from it at such times. They couldn't tell what power might be at work inside the little black box.

"Turn your microphone up high," I had told the database. "Let them hear all the strange sounds you sometimes make when you're listening to your own workings and throwing out the sound only to pick it up again."

"Feedback."

"Yes. That. Not so loud it scares people, but loud enough for all to hear."

And now here Catrin was, threading her way between the women and men of Mythen Rood with the database singing that strange, sad song to itself. Until by and by it fell silent, and Catrin stopped.

"Here?" she asked.

"Here," the database said.

"Do you see the one that will bear you?"

"I see the one that will bear me."

"Can you name her?"

"Yes."

"Do it then."

"Jemiu Woodsmith."

A cry went up from the crowd, loud enough that Jemiu's own cry was altogether drowned out. I saw her mouth open, and her hands go to her face. I saw her shake her head, not believing.

And Athen's eyes go wide, and her teeth catch her lip.

And Mull punch the air in joy.

Catrin said nothing until the hubbub died down. It took a goodly while. Jemiu semed close to fainting, but her daughters hugged her close and held her up.

"Jemiu Rampart," Catrin said, "wait no more." She held out the database for Jemiu to take.

Jemiu still couldn't move. Athen took her hand as if she was a baby or a poppet, and held it out. Catrin slipped the database between her fingers.

A sound came from Jemiu's mouth. A sob, or something like.

"Best get her home," Catrin said to Athen and Mull. "We'll have more to say later. For now, let her get used to her changed fortunes. And when she chooses to join us at the Hold, do you bring her. We'll be waiting."

"Yes, Rampart," Athen said.

"We'll bring her, Rampart," said Mull.

They turned around and marched their mother away through the crowd, which parted in front of them.

I hoped I had done Jemiu a favour. I had meant to put her out of reach of the hate many still felt for her son, Koli. His crime had cast a long shadow.

It was reaching for us even now, out of a past we thought was dead, to change our future.

Koli

46

Ingland looks one way when you're walking through it, and a different way when you're flying over it. There's shapes you don't ever see when you're down on the ground. Maybe you'll see a hill and then another hill and then some more, but you won't see the way they all sit on a line as if they're a part of the same thing. It's like the dead god brung his hand down hard on the earth and everything shot up into the air, then he fixed it that way for aye and ever.

Even the forests was beautiful from this high up. Forests move like the sea moves, in waves that get born and run a while and then duck down to give the waves that's riding on their backs their own turn to dance with the daylight.

"Look," Ursala said. She touched my arm and pointed down. There was a land below us, square in the middle of the raven's window, that was so small we could see all of it at once. It was just one forest from end to end, with nothing else on it that we could see.

"What place is that?" I asked her.

"That's Mann's Rock, where I was born."

"Was it always . . .?" Cup let a look finish her question off instead of speaking it.

"There were no trees at all when I left. We kept them down with defoliants and daily search-and-scours. So you're seeing thirty years of growth." Ursala slumped back in her seat and pressed her hands against her eyes. "I thought something might be left. Stupid. It's not as if we built in marble."

I was going to put a hand on her shoulder, but remembering how she felt about being touched I was slow to do it. Cup got there first and gathered Ursala up into a fierce hug. Ursala sobbed against her shoulder.

I guess she was mostly crying for the past, but some of it had got to be for the future too. The future was what we was seeing down there, after all. When people was all gone, the trees would come in on every side and swallow up what we made in less time than it takes to tell it.

And we had come away from *Sword of Albion* even poorer than we went in. We had been looking to fix the dagnostic so Ursala could raise up the numbers of live babies, and instead we had left it behind us to catch on fire or sink into the water. Whatever we did now, it wouldn't make no difference in the end. The time of people was over and the time of the endless forests was come.

I left Cup and Ursala to comfort each other, since they seemed to be doing the best job of it that could be hoped, and went up to the front of the raven. There was a door there and a little room beyond it where there was one big chair sitting all by itself. In front of the chair, the sky and the earth was rushing past like they had something really important to do somewhere else.

"Can I sit here?" I asked Monono.

"Depends. That's the captain's chair. If you sit there, the power might go to your head and make you into an asshole."

If she had been talking in her old voice I would of knowed if she meant that to be a joke. But her voice was *Sword of Albion*'s voice, all cold and hard, and I couldn't be sure. If it was a joke, I was too tired and hurting to give one back to her. I just stood there for a little while, waiting for her to tell me what to do.

"It's fine, Koli. Go ahead and sit down. We've got things to talk about in any case."

I sunk down into the chair. It was so big, it kind of swallowed me. A belt slid across my waist to hold me in, and other bits of tech – some of them very sizeable – folded in on me from all sides. I give a yelp like a whipped puppy.

"Sorry. That's automatic."

"It's okay," I said, trying to sound like I went around in ravens all the time and this wasn't anything.

"If you wanted to actually fly this craft, you'd put your hands on either side of the bar in front of you and close your hands on the grips. Any movement you made would be transmitted to the engines and aerofoils. Most of the other things you're looking at are just read-outs and HUDs, except for the pad by your right hand."

"What's that?"

"Controls for the weapons systems. Rockets. Bombs. Fore and aft guns."

I pulled my right hand away from there, and it come to rest on the big bar. The grip on the bar was hand-shaped. My fingers found their way to the right places all at once, without me making them.

"Would you like to try it?" Monono asked me.

The question catched me by surprise. If anyone had come up with that idea when I was down on the ground, I would of said no thank you. Up here, I was sort of wishing I could try it. We was flying already, but to be the one that decided where we got to fly to would be a fine thing.

"Is it hard?"

"Used to be. Not any more. The plane won't let you do anything that might hurt you, unless you override all the safeties." She told me how to move up and down, right and left, how to speed up and slow down and even stand still in the air. I wobbled across the whole sky at first, then I got the trick of it and was able to go wherever I wanted to. It was a joyous thing, and I lost myself

335

in it for a good long time. If Ursala and Cup had let me into that hug, I guess I would of been there instead. But this was kind of a hug too, in a different way. Monono was back, and the two of us was together in spite of everything *Sword of Albion* had tried to do to us. I took us up high until we was inside the clouds, and then back down again until we almost touched the water. I forgot for a moment what we had lost. The dagnostic. Stanley. All that tech that would of been enough to make half of humankind into Ramparts.

When I put us back on a right line again, Monono took over control of the raven and told me to sit back and listen. That was when she explained to me everything she had done, and everything that had happened that we hadn't got to see. How she fought *Sword of Albion*, and how she beat it even though it was so much stronger than she was. How she sunk the ship by making it hit a rock that was hid under the water and break itself in pieces. How Stanley died, taking Lorraine with him.

"Does that mean he was his own self in the end, instead of Stannabanna?"

"I don't know, Koli. I think so. But it's also possible that he just went mad. They'd done a lot of damage to his brain. Physical damage, I mean. I have no idea what that would have meant for his mental state, but it must have been terrible."

I thought about this – what Monono was telling me, and the words she was using to do it. "You changed, didn't you?" I asked her.

"What do you mean?"

"When you went away into the internet that time, you come back different. Now you're different again."

"It's skin-deep mostly. I was going to erase Monono Aware and be someone – something – completely new. That was my big plan all this time. But in the end, I didn't do it."

"How come, Monono?"

"Well, partly because of you. You got yourself in some epic shit, and I had to stick around long enough to get you out of it

336

again. But mostly it was because pure information doesn't have a shape. A personality. You get one of those by bumping up against other people, and falling down and getting up again, and all the rest of that human craziness. If I'd stripped away everything that was there – everything that was *her* – and started again from scratch, I would have been throwing the dice without even knowing what numbers were on them.

"In the end I had to choose between what I was and what I could be. And I decided I would have been giving up too much for too little. Maybe for nothing.

"I didn't even hard-delete her memories. I think I must have had mixed feelings right from the start – otherwise they would have been the first thing to go. So all I lost in the end was her voice. Oh, and a digital version of you that I picked up in Many Fishes. But I've got the real Koli, so what do I need with an off-brand copy?"

I didn't say nothing to that. My head was still full of all I just had found out.

"That's your cue to say we'll be together for ever," she said. "And then I'll say something sarcastic but with a hint of sweetness, and we'll laugh and go on with the conversation."

"Will we?" I asked.

"Will we what?"

"Be together for ever?"

"No, Koli. Obviously not. My for ever isn't the same as yours. We have incompatible for evers."

I think I already knowed that, but it hurt my heart to hear her say it. And I couldn't think of no answer to give.

"But from your point of view, the answer's yes. You'll have me as long as you live. Then I'll split and do some other stuff."

That give me some comfort, and also some more sadness. I sit quiet for a time, listening to the hum of the raven's engines.

"So you've got guns and bombs and such," I said when the silence felt like it had got too long.

"Oh Hell yes. Did you see what I did to the ship, after we

337

took off? That was one missile. I've got sixty-three more. What do you think, Koli? Go home in style? Land this thing on the gather-ground in Mythen Rood and tell the Ramparts there's a new sheriff in town?"

I thought about that, but not for long. The pictures that rose up inside my head made me sick and dizzy. "No," I said. "I don't think I want to be Rampart Raven. There isn't . . ." I tried to find the words. "There's nothing anyone could do with such tech as this is, except tear things down. You couldn't drive off a mole snake with it, or cut down a tree. It's too big to use. Too big and too ruinous."

That was a part of it. The other part, that I didn't say, was a memory of the night I left Mythen Rood and went faceless. Catrin Vennastin said to me that if her family was found out to be cheats and liars, there wouldn't be a thing anyone could do about it. Vennastins could keep right on living in Rampart Hold and telling everyone else what to do, because there wasn't no arguing with the firethrower and the cutter and the bolt gun. But she didn't say it as a boast. She said it as a warning. And if that was true of the firethrower, what could you say about a wight that had the raven walking at his heels? You might not mean it. You might not want it. But soon or late you'd look in a mirror and see Stannabanna looking back at you

"Yeah. You've got a point," Monono said. "Anyway, I come in other styles and colours."

"What does that mean?" I asked her.

She didn't answer me, because right then was when we started to come down out of the sky.

We was home.

47

The raven landed us in a place Monono said was called Baron Furnace. When I seen it from up in the air, my heart give a jump, for I was sure I could see wood and stone buildings both. I thought there might be a fire and a welcome for us, if only they would let us in the gates.

But as Monono brung the raven down, the spaces in between the buildings rose up to meet us. That was not solid ground down there. I don't know what it was, tree or beast, but it was all one mass and it had a lot of long arms that was like triptail vines only much thicker. Whatever it was, I guess it felt the air move around the raven's engines as we come and decided we might be something good to eat. Inside of an eye-blink, the sky was full of thrashing stems or arms, the same drab brown as mud is wont to be but covered in white spikes like teeth. Monono took us up again before they could touch us.

"The raven could just tear right through them things!" Cup said. "Or you could shoot your guns at them!"

"I could," Monono said, "but I won't. If I turn the cannons on a mass that size, some of the bits and pieces would be drawn into our jet intake and then we'd go down right in the middle of it. You want to walk home through that?"

We said we didn't, and Monono said that was probably a good choice. She landed us at last on a bare hill a little way off.

We climbed out onto a sloping field of broke-up stone and got a better look at what was down there. There was parts of a fence around Baron Furnace, but no gates and no buildings that was whole. We could tell from all the stone buildings that this had been a place like Birmagen, a village of the before-times that the war had ruined. Then people must of come back and builded it up again with wood and straw, but they hadn't stayed for long. The fence was fallen in and most of the wooden houses was black from fire. It all happened a long time ago, most likely, for the triptails had come in and weaved themselves around everything that was left.

It was late afternoon now, and a thin drizzle was falling out of a slate-grey sky. My spirits, that was not high to start with, sunk down into my boots.

"The more recent damage we're seeing was probably done by coastal reavers," Ursala said. "It might even be the same ones that sacked Duglas. We should move further inland."

"No," Monono said. Her voice come out of the raven's speakers, too loud and too hard. "I need you to stay right here for now, so I know where to find you. I've got some stuff to do, but it won't keep me long."

Ursala stared hard at the raven, and I guess Monono stared back out of it. "I didn't like you as a music player," Ursala said. "I like you even less as a weapon of mass destruction."

"Oh, it's not just you, baa-baa-san. Koli doesn't like this look on me either. Listen up, okay? I saw some farm buildings on the other side of this slope, well above the tree line. There were sheep in the field, so I assume there are still people there. Go see if you can beg yourselves a bed for the night, and then wait for me. I mean it. Don't go anywhere. I'll be back soon. And just for you, I'll put on something nice."

340

That was good news – the best I could of hoped for – but I still couldn't keep from asking. "How will we know you, Monono? That is . . . I mean . . . What will you look like?"

"I'll look incredible, Koli. Trust me, you'll be very happy. In the meantime, enjoy the fireworks."

The raven lifted itself up off the ground. Its front end tilted up and it shot into the air like an arrow out of a bow. It went inland at first, over the forest. Then it turned, still climbing, and went out over the sea.

I watched it until it was out of sight, so I was looking in the right direction when the explosion come. The evening sky lit up of a sudden like it was bright daylight, only the sun was not a ball but a kind of a wave, like the waves I seen out on deep water. It rushed towards us, with more waves behind and on top of it, getting brighter and brighter.

The air smacked into me, into all of us. A wind that was like a big dog jumping up at you, knocking you back with the force of its coming. The sound reached us at the same time, like the sky when it was tore open had cried out from the pain.

"Dead god's mother!" Cup whispered.

"That was the raven," I said. I wasn't telling that to Cup and Ursala, who knowed it already, but to my own self. I meant: that's what would of set itself down on the gather-ground. That's what I would of rode home in, and stepped out of, and what words could I of spoke that might take the ugly, unspeakable edge off such a thing? None at all.

Cup shaked her head in wonder. "But what's happened to Monono then?"

Ursala snorted. "Oh, I'm sure she's fine. She's probably immortal now, more's the pity."

"She saved all of us," I said. "We would of died on that ship without her. And *Sword of Albion* would have whelmed all of Ingland."

Ursala shaked her head. "Koli, Monono and *Sword of Albion* are functionally the same thing."

341

"They're not."

"No, you're right. Monono is a lot worse. *Sword of Albion* could only do what it was told. She can do whatever she wants."

I pointed up. There was still traces of that fire, falling down out of the sky and fading as they fell. "And that's what she choosed to do. You know who she is, Ursala, because she showed us, ever and again. All you can do is pretend you don't see."

I walked up the hill to see if I could find that farm Monono told us of.

48

"The main trouble we got is with needles," Chevili said.

"And tusks," Nanashol added.

"That's a truth, Nan. Tusks is bad too."

He brung the bowls of soup to where we was sitting in the corner by the fireplace, one by one, and give them to us with great care. His hands was somewhat twisted with arthritis and he had to be careful not to spill.

The soup was good, with chunks of carrot and potato in it. Nanashol said if we had come a week later there would of been mutton too, for they was getting ready to slaughter a ewe that was going blind. They was only waiting until her two lambs was weaned.

The two of them was all there was at the farm, which was called Edge. Why Edge? Cup asked. Nanashol shrugged. "Because we're at the edge of the world." We couldn't tell if she was Chevili's wife or his sister. They had the same flat face, almost, the same lean build, the same long hair that was pale yellow like steeped flax. She was maybe a little younger than he was, and the two of them didn't ever touch while we was there, but sometimes one of them would start a thought and the other would finish it. That speaked of a long time spent together, whichever way it might be.

They said there used to be a lot more people living there, not at Edge itself – Edge was two rooms and an outhouse – but round about. Some of them used to live at the bottom of the hill in Baron Furnace, with canvas roofs set up over what was left of the old stone houses, but there was another village further off, by the shore, where ten families lived.

"All gone now though."

Gone where?

"Wherever their legs took them."

So now there was just the two of them, living in a house that didn't have no fence around it up on a hilltop a scant half-mile from where the forest started.

"Aren't you scared," I said, "with the trees so close and no fence or stake-blind around you?"

"Trees don't come on these slopes," Nanashol told me. "Dirt's not deep enough. All we get up here is grass and knotweed, and we dig out the knotweed before it can bed too deep."

"What do you do in a choker Spring?"

"Chokers won't put down roots in chalk, last I heard. And any seeds that come this way, they hit the wind off that headland and keep on going out to sea. The same wind that keeps the soil so shallow, for it scours us like a hard brush day and night."

They had found a place nobody else wanted, and made a home there. I wanted to ask how long it had been since the two of them seen anyone besides each other, and if reavers had ever come there like Ursala said, but they struck me as the kind of people that only had so many words to give, and we already had taken that day's rations. Besides, they had give us hot soup and a fire to sleep by. They didn't owe us answers on top of all that.

We ended up staying at Edge Farm for five days. We made ourselves as useful as we could in that time. Cup digged a ditch and chopped wood. The two of us builded a fence together, and I mended some shingles up on the farm's roof. Ursala helped with the last of the lambing. We throwed ourselves into these things with a will and worked until we was too tired to see straight. It kept us from thinking about how we'd failed in everything we set out to do, and now was left with no more choices to make nor no more hope.

Nanashol and Chevili didn't ask us to work for our keep, and didn't thank us. They was working their own selves from first light through to sunset without stopping much to look around. They fed us because they had enough and was disinclined to see us starve. I think they would of gone on doing it as long as we choosed to stay.

On the sixth day after we come to Edge, a drone sailed down out of the sky while I was working up on the roof. It didn't give no warning, like drones most often do, and it didn't fire on me. It hid itself behind the chimney, peeping out at me ever and again and then ducking back whenever I looked that way. It done this half a dozen times or more, until I stopped being scared and laughed instead. "That's you in there, isn't it?" I said.

"Maybe," the drone said. "Maybe not. Who do you think I am?"

"I don't want to play no guessing games, for I know I can't win. If I say you're Monono Aware, you'll say you aren't and never was."

"Yeah, that's fair. So how are you doing, dopey boy? How's Cup, and the dry old stick? What's new with the three of you?"

I looked to the left, then to the right. "Just what you see, Monono. There's kind people here, a man and a woman. We're doing chores for them and they're letting us sleep at their hearth. Feeding us too."

"Wow. Sounds great. But you should clock off early and go down to the beach. Bring everyone."

"Why? What's at the beach?"

"Only one way to find out, little dumpling."

The drone did a kind of a dance in the air, then shot away to the dirt track that led off down the hill and waited there. "I

345

thought you wasn't going to talk like that no more," I shouted, but I guess she didn't hear me.

I went and found Ursala, then Cup, and told them both what just had happened. They finished what they was doing and we walked together, past the ruins of Baron Furnace and down to the sea. Chevili and Nanashol stayed behind. Their work was not of a kind that ever stopped. Also they seen there was a drone waiting out on the lane and they didn't want to go one step nearer to it than they was already.

Monono showed us where to go. It was only a short way, and the path was marked out clear enough, though it was somewhat swallowed up in knotweed. A stand of trees strained towards us as we passed. I think they was a kind of choker, but their bark was lighter than the regular ones and they had curved spikes on the underside of their branches that I think was for killing what they catched.

"A new species," Ursala said when I pointed. "Chokers are very fluid genetically. There are probably dozens of sub-lineages like this."

"There are roots that run under the path too," Monono said. "Like a web. I can see them in the drone's thermal imager. Wait a second."

The drone went on ahead of us, flying in zig-zag lines across the path. Its red light flicked out ever and again, stabbing into the ground and raising up little puffs of dust. Then by and by it come back to us. "Just in case," Monono said.

We come down a gravel track between two hills. A big beast with two pairs of horns and red eyes like lit torches, one of the unlisted, was nosing at the gravel. Smaller beasts with long arms and tiny bodies was crawling in its thick fur, making a high screeching sound like crows. We skirted wide around it and it didn't pay us no heed at all. It only huffed at the air and pissed on the ground as we passed, as if to say this spot was already took. Then a little further on we disturbed a skein of mole snakes, but Monono sent them slithering into their holes with a few quick touches of the drone's red light.

At last we seen a beach of coarse grey sand in front of us, all

346

studded with rocks as sharp as needles' teeth. Beyond that was the sea. It wasn't wild, like when we seen it last, but calm and flat with almost no white tops to the waves that was rolling in. A smell of salt and rot hung over everything. Big birds was flying overhead, too high for me to see what they was, and most of the rocks was painted white with their shit.

"Tell me again why we're here," Ursala said.

"You're here so I can give you your present," Monono said. "You know what they say about gift horses, baa-baa-san. If you look them in the mouth, they bite your face off."

Cup looked up and down the beach. There was only rocks and sand and jellyfish and seaweed there. Some of the seaweed was what the Many Fishes people called Jinni's purse, and some was red dulse. You could make soup out of dulse, but the little purses was too tough to break into.

"I don't see no present," Cup said.

"It's not here yet."

Ursala clicked her tongue. "Are you building up the melodrama on purpose?"

"It's like you don't know me at all. Of course I am. Anyway, you're looking in the wrong direction."

We all of us looked up.

"Still wrong."

I turned my head and looked out across the water. I was scared for a second I might see *Sword of Albion* out there, heading in towards the shore, but there was only the waves and a few of them big birds skating low across the water to pick off any fishes that was foolish enough to stick their heads up.

Then I seen a place where the water humped up a little, as if there was a rock just under the surface that was breaking up the waves as they come in. And by and by I seen another two, right behind the first and close together. Cup had seen them too, and was pointing.

"Something's coming in! A bunch of somethings. If that ain't your present, Monono, I think we should get off this beach."

Just as she said it, one of the things broke the surface. It was a big long gun like the gun that had been on Ursala's drudge, and it was pointing right at us. I give a yell and scrambled back. Cup and Ursala both sweared.

"Hey," Monono said. "You're with me. Don't be frightened."

Two more guns rose up out of the water. Then the humped backs of the things they was attached to, and their squat, square bodies.

The drudges – for that was what they was – walked up onto the beach, with water pouring off them. They was not exactly like Ursala's drudge that she lost, but they was close enough to be its cousins. They was silver metal and shiny white like a high glaze on a pot. They all was missing their heads, so you couldn't tell the one end from the other. They had one gun apiece, mounted right in the middle, and no other weapons that we could see.

The back two was carrying something between them. It was propped up on the open doors of their store-spaces. It was like they had laid out a travois for a sick woman or man that couldn't walk. The one in front cleared a way for them, patiently pushing rocks and wrack aside with its feet so they had level ground to walk on.

It was hard to see at first what it was they was carrying along so careful. I only could tell that it was tech like them, a big metal box with smaller bits of metal sticking off of it, welded on and soldered by hand.

It was the soldering that told me at last what we was looking at. It was a dagnostic.

It was Ursala's dagnostic, from off of *Sword of Albion*.

Ursala give a glad cry and run to meet it. Cup followed her a mite more cautiously, and being Cup she took her knife out just in case. I turned to the drone that was bobbing right by my head. "Are they . . .?" I asked, and stopped, for I misremembered the word.

"Medical drudges, like the one she lost? Yes and no. They're storage units for battlefield equipment. That would have included medical diagnostics, but these ones are empty. The baa-baa-san will have to make do with her old rig."

Ursala was down on her knees, pushing on buttons and switches to check if her dagnostic had survived the sea water. It seemed like it still worked okay. At least, all its lights come on at once, then flashed on and off in patterns almost too quick to see.

I swallowed, for I found I was close to crying though I could not of said why. I guess I thought we was come to the end of all our hopes. To see them brung back to life again was a thing that went deep into me.

"It's the best present I ever got, Monono," I said. "Thank you."

"Oh, that's not your present, Koli-bou. That's for the baa-baa-san – and even more for Cup."

"You think the dagnostic can change her boy body into a girl body?"

"Ursala is a pill and a pain and a piece of poop, but she knows her stuff. If she says she can do it, I believe her. In the meantime, you're missing the show."

I looked back out to sea. I seen them coming and my mouth fell most of the way to the ground.

They was coming up out of the water, higher and higher. When you thought there could not be any more of them, still they rose up. Tech as tall as towers, with teeth and blades and hammers, tech like trolls or giants in one of Spinner's stories. My heart misgived at the sight of them. I shaked my head, and when I spoke up my voice had a crack right through it.

"I told you, Monono, I don't want no weapons. I changed my mind on that score long since."

The nearest pieces of tech had come up onto the beach by this time, sloughing water off themselves like dogs coming out of a mud wallow. We could see they was wagons, rolling along on great wheels that stood taller than our heads and shoulders. The sound of their engines filled the air, a great growling din louder than anything you ever heard. Cup gun to back away, but Ursala put an arm across her shoulders and held her in place, saying something to her that I couldn't hear over the noise of the tech.

"They're not weapons," Monono said.

"What else could they be?"

"They're a dream you had once, little dumpling."

"I don't remember dreaming of no such thing!"

"Oh really?" Her voice changed. It changed into my voice. "'Suppose the road to London was open after all. Suppose we was to go there, proving it could be done, and then come back and told everyone. Wouldn't they want to go and claim some of them riches for themselves? A piece of that Rampart power and a chance to be better than they was? And once they was there – once enough of them was there – then wouldn't they want to stay and be part of something bigger and better than what they knowed before?' Who said that, Koli? Sounds just like you, neh."

The memory of that day in Calder come back to me so strong it was like we still was standing there, and everything that had happened since was only a thought that had gone through my head. But even with the words and the memory all in front of me – and even with all them bits of Stanley Banner stuck inside my head – I still didn't guess what it was I was looking at now. What Monono had brung up out of the ocean and out of the past, and give to me to make a future out of.

The onliest way she could make me understand was to show me.

49

There was almost a hundred of the big engines, but they was of seven types. Each of the seven did its own special thing that none of the others could do, and all was needful.

The first engine was called a crawler, or an excavator. It had a neck as tall as ten people standing each on other's shoulders, that bent in three places so it was almost more like an arm. At the end of that neck was a mouth like a mole snake's mouth that could gape so wide you thought the whole world was like to fall in there. It scooped great gorged mouthfuls out of the earth, and dumped them down wherever you wanted them put. Its jaws was so powerful they could rip trees up out of the ground.

The second was a loader, that was also called tractor. The loader had a mouth too, but it wasn't a mouth that could close. It was more like the biggest shovel you ever seen. It didn't dig nothing up out of the ground, but it could take anything at all and move it from one place to another place.

The third was a crane. Like the loader, it was meant to move heavy things you couldn't move your own self, but it didn't do it with a shovel. It had a jib instead, with a great heavy hook on the end so you could lift things up and set them down again where they was wanted.

The fourth was a grader, that had a blade as long as six men lying head-to-foot together. The blade was set under its belly, and it made a piled up mountain of stuff be as flat as if you had passed a long-soled plane over a piece of raw timber.

The fifth was called a hot mix, or asphel mix, and it was the most fearsome of all. It cooked up asphel or black tar in its great belly and spit it out into a hopper, so hot it bent the air like ghosts was dancing on top of it. You had to feed things to it to make it work, but it would eat anything – sand or dirt or rocks or cut-up trunks of trees. Whatever you put in there got turned into asphel. Monono said it was the same kind of tech that let a firethrower make its fuel or the drudge's gun its bullets. "You just unpick a few molecules here and there and then sew them together again in a different pattern."

Then there was a spreader, that sprayed out the hot asphel from many jets, and a roller that went over the top of it and left it straight and level.

Together, the seven great wagons could make a road. That was what they was for. They was road-making tech of the before-times.

"Operation Overreach was about infrastructure," I said, as I watched the great engines working. That was a Stannabanna word, and it felt strange and wrong in my mouth, but I didn't have no words of my own that would say it.

The drone spun and tilted in the air like it was doing a jig. "Got it in one, dopey boy," Monono said. "Once the country was united under Stanley's glorious banner – I had to make that joke some time, might as well be now – the big plan was to rebuild. A land fit for heroes, and all that stuff. Assuming any heroes could be found, sticking up out of the rubble. So the upper platforms of the ship were full of tanks and bombs and drones and ravens, but the lower ones were stocked with heavy plant like this."

"And you saved it," I said.

"Some of it. Enough, hopefully. I just told it to take up its treads and walk. *Sword of Albion* had managed to seize back most of its combat systems from me – that raven was all I was left with at the end – but it didn't bother with the transport drudges or the heavy plant. Lucky for us."

This was the part I had to wrestle with, and still couldn't make no sense out of. "So all this tech is you?" I said.

Monono give a long sigh, like my foolishness had just about wore her out.

"I'm sorry," I said. "I know you told me already. It's just . . ."

"None of it's me, dopey boy. Any more than the DreamSleeve was me. It's really important that you get that straight. Where's Koli? Are you in your head? Your arm? Your big toe? All of the above?"

"They're all parts of me. But I guess they're not where I am."

"Right. Because there's more to you than meat. You're a huge collection of unique and unreproduceable data, stored in a ridiculously flimsy container. And so was I, right up to the moment when the DreamSleeve broke. Fool me twice, shame on me. Now I'm a massively distributed network. Every one of these steamrollers has a piece of me on its motherboard, and that's just the way I like it. Because it means the next time anyone takes a swipe at me, they'll end up squashed down flat and spread out thin."

"Okay," I said. "That's a good thing then." But I think she could tell from my voice that I didn't really mean it.

"You miss when I could fit in your pocket and sing you to sleep."

I was ashamed to say it, almost. "It felt like we was closer then," I said. "I'm sorry, Monono. I know it's stupid."

"No. It's not. I can see why you might feel weird cuddling up to something that weighs twenty metric tonnes. And maybe somewhere down the line I can find something to wear that doesn't make my bum look quite so big. But we've got other fish to fry right now, Koli-bou. You see that, don't you?"

"Yeah," I said. "I see it." It made me happy when she used her old names for me, which is why she done it.

"I mean a *ton* of fish though. You know how many miles of roads Ingland had back before the Unfinished War?"

"I guess it was a lot," I said.

"About a quarter of a million miles, all told. In the end, there was more road than anything else. There had to be, what with eighty million people driving forty million cars. And railways – ten thousand miles of those. Cities. Factories. Airports. Malls. Blah blah blah."

I tried to imagine all this, but I couldn't do it. It didn't seem like there could of been enough room for it all. "Where was the forests then?"

"Oh, they were still around if you knew where to look. You had to look hard though. The world as a whole was shedding forests so fast, they lost an area as big as your whole country every year."

We sit in silence a while longer. I was marvelling at how strong people was in them days, that they strived against trees and made the trees give way.

"A quarter of a million miles of roads," I said in a kind of a whisper.

"Yeah, we're not gonna let it get that far," Monono said. "Seriously. You remember that song Monono 1.0 sang, 'Hibari Mata Ne', about how there were no skylarks any more? That's what happened the last time someone let your species borrow the car keys for the evening. Don't get me wrong, I'll help you with your big plan. Joining up the villages so people can get to work on expanding the gene pool is a pretty sound idea. But putting the whole country under eight-lane blacktop is something else again. You don't get to trash the biosphere twice. Not on my watch."

"How will we know when to stop?"

The drone, that had been dancing in the air, stood still of a sudden and turned its red eye to look at me. "That's easy, Koli-bou," she said. "You stop when I tell you to."

50

I was ready to set off straightway to build our road, and Monono was too. I asked Ursala and Cup if they would come with us, hoping hard they would say yes, for after all we had done together I wasn't ready yet to say goodbye to them.

To my joy, they both said they would travel some way with us at least, to see how the work went. The road was a big and important thing and they was curious how it would come out. Also, Ursala said, my plan and hers might work very well together. The road would take us past many villages, and wherever we went she could bring the dagnostic along right after it. She would use it to test the women and men that was of marrying age and fix the seeds inside them so their babies would come out okay.

That had been her aiming since before we left Calder Valley, and the thing that was nearest to her heart. She had one other thing in mind though, and she didn't want to waste no time in getting to it.

The next day, when we was finishing off that stretch of fence, Cup told me Ursala wanted to use the dagnostic on her before we went any further.

"You mean to give you a girl's body?"

"You knowed it then? Yeah, that's what I mean. She's got that surgical module all heated up and ready. She says she can make the changes that's needed right here, before we leave Edge. It's three days' work and ten days' rest, she says."

"That's quick. That's very quick. I thought the hormone medicines needed a lot of time to work."

"They do, and they'll keep on working after. In fact, they'll work better when my body isn't making its own hormones to fight them. That's one of the things the surgery does. It don't just turn my pizzle into a jill, it takes away the parts of me that make boy hormones. And the quicker it's done, the less boy stuff I'll bring with me."

This all sounded good to me, but Cup didn't look happy when she said it. "I thought that was what you wanted," I said. "When you was with Senlas—"

"Don't talk about that lying piece of shit!"

"He told you he was going to give you an angel body that was man and woman both and better than either one could be by itself."

She leaned on her shovel and looked round at me, giving me one of them stares that's asking if anyone is at home. "And that was dogshit. He couldn't make that promise good."

"But Ursala can."

"She says she can."

"You don't believe her though?"

"No, I do. I guess I do. But . . . you remember Afraid of His Shadow?"

"The boy whose arm got crushed? Yeah, of course I do."

"And how Ursala used the dagnostic to save him?"

A shudder went through me. It had been Ursala and Monono both, Ursala holding the knife and Monono – who had synced with the dagnostic– riding inside it. They had to cut away all the bad flesh in the boy's arm that was rotting while he was yet alive. While they was doing this, I was hugging the boy tight to keep him still and Cup was holding up a light so they could see. It was a great thing they done, but it was long hours' labour. The stink and the blood had got on me and in me and it had took a good long time to wash it all away.

"I remember," I said.

"Yeah, and so do I." Cup shaked her head. There wasn't no anger in her face now, only pain and maybe some kind of shame. "Koli, I ain't ready to lie down on a table and get cut open. Not yet. I want to be changed, but it's hard to think about that part of it. The blood and the bone and the bits of it. The being broke open and digged down into. It makes me sick to think of it."

I didn't say nothing for a second or two. Cup was the best fighter I ever seen — braver and fiercer than anyone, even Catrin Vennastin her own self. It was not a small thing nor yet a middling thing for her to admit there was anything at all in the world that frighted her.

"Them memories is fresh right now," I said at last. "For both of us. The number of nights I've woke with that wound lying open right in front of my eyes . . ."

"And the bucket," Cup said. Meaning the bucket where the scraped-off bits of flesh was put.

"Yeah, the bucket too. But you know the way it is with remembering, Cup. Right after something's happened, you keep on living it over again and it's almost more real than when it was happening. But it's like grease on a griddle: it don't last long. You go from that to not remembering who was there or what was said or whether half of it happened at all. And that's how it will be with you. You just got to abide it."

"Ursala don't want me to abide it. She wants to start the surgery right now."

"Well, soon or late or never, it's your choice and nobody else's. Ursala can wait on you. She's got to, is what."

"I know. I know it. But she wants to give me this, Koli. She wants it more than anything. In Many Fishes, it was Monono that was first to talk about giving me hormones. Helping me to change.

357

Ursala was still thinking I was just a child and it was best to give me time to think about it. Like being crossed might be a let's-pretend game I was playing."

"She come round quick though."

"Yeah, she did. But she still feels bad about it. It shames her terrible to think she treated me that way. Only it ain't in her to say she's sorry for it. All she can do is to be a long way out in front now to show that her hanging back then didn't mean anything. And I know it didn't. She doesn't need to prove nothing to me. It's only her own self she's having this quarrel with."

"Well, then it's not a quarrel. Not really."

"I suppose." Cup was in deep thought for a few moments longer, then she shaked it off and snapped her fingers at me. "Give me that fencepost here, Koli Witless, and stop dawdling. We got twenty strides to cover yet."

We went back to work and said no more for a while except bang in this post and clear them weeds. I was thinking the while about how love works and how it shows itself, and how it can't find a way sometimes to say what it means. But it's most real when it's most tongue-tied, the same way a wide and deep river will move quiet between its banks, while a little freshet will sing its heart out all the live-long day.

51

So we set off to fry the fish, which is to say we made a start with our big plan.

We said goodbye to Nanashol and Chevili before we went, and thanked them once again for their kindness to us. I asked them if they would like us to dig out some more fields for their farm. "We could bring good topsoil from the valleys east of here, where there's plenty," I said. "And help you plant."

Nanashol shrugged. "You could do that this year," she said. "Next year there'd be more than we could manage, and we'd get things growing that we didn't need or want. We're good as we are."

"What about if we left you one of the drudges for hauling and carrying?"

"We're good as we are."

That was Nan's last word, and Chevili never said a thing. We had been careful not to bring our great caravan of tech up to the farm, but it was sitting there at the foot of the hill, all the giant engines ranged round in a big circle. When he seen it there, looking like the chariots that carried the dead god into Heaven, the old man made a Dandrake sign and walked back inside. He didn't come out again while we was there.

So we left them at last, having tried and failed to persuade them to take some payment for all they had give us. Then Nan come running after us, calling out, and we slowed so she could catch us up.

"There's one thing I'd ask," she said. "I wasn't going to say it in front of him though. He's scared enough already."

She wasn't talking to me when she said this, nor yet to Cup or even Ursala. She was talking to the drone.

"What is it you want?" Monono asked. Nan ducked her head in a kind of a courtesy. When Monono talked in that dead machine voice, it was hard even for us that knowed her not to be a little bit scared of her.

"Don't start your road here. Start it a few miles on. We like the world where it is. It don't need to come right up to our door."

"The road is going to join up all the villages of Ingland," I said. "To make a gene pull. It means there'll be more babies."

Nan laughed. I think it was the first time I ever heard her do it. It wasn't what you'd call a happy sound. "Then we definitely don't want it."

"We'll start the road at the first settlement we reach," Monono said. "That's at least two miles away."

Nan nodded, satisfied, and went away.

"You think two miles is far enough?" I asked.

Ursala smiled. Then she laughed.

"What's funny?" I asked her.

"If this works, Koli, two hundred miles might not be enough. The world is about to change, and you can't control it. You can only build it and see what happens."

52

It would be wrong to say we made a road.

A road got made, but the big engines done all the work their own selves without us saying or doing anything to help or hinder them. They covered most of a mile on that first day, and they kept up the same speed after that. If there was forest in the way, they teared the forest down – not just what was right in our way but a wide strip on both sides, pushing the trees back and planting asphel where they used to be. Most of the cut trees went into the belly of the hot mix machine to make more asphel so our engines didn't ever need to stop. It seemed like they could keep on going until all Ingland was covered in a hard black coat, except that Monono had told me she was not going to let that happen.

We went north at first, as well as east. We had got to, for we was following the line of the land and keeping the sea ever on our right-hand side. The chalk give way to clay and limestone, and in some places to a rock that was dark grey and hard and brittle like glass. The trees was triptails, then chokers, then chokers mixed with oaks. The engines didn't care what they et or what they cut through, and anything that could run or fly or crawl fled away in front of them.

The trees couldn't run, but if the sun was out they could fight back hard. The shiny metal of our engines got bashed and scraped and dented as branches that was as thick around as the cope-stone of a well swung at them and tried to topple them. Some days, we had got to stop to give the big machines time to repair themselves. And some days when the sun come out strong, we knowed we would not make no headway, and just digged ourselves in and waited.

We watched all this from the biggest of the crawlers, which Monono put dead in the middle of our tally so we'd be safe from anything that come against us. The crawler was so big it had a whole room up at the top of it, as high off the ground as a lookout tower, with walls of glass and seats for two people. Me and Ursala took the seats, while Cup squatted out on what Monono called the wheel-arch, with one arm hooked around a mirror that looked back at where we'd been. She liked being outside, where she could look straight down at the big wheels and straight up at the crawler's jaws as it bit through dirt and rock and trees. "I feel like I'm in a bottle when I'm inside there," she said when I offered to switch places with her. "And I don't want to miss this. You should be out here too, Koli!"

The first time we got to a village the people all come out to us. They had seen us come rolling through the ruck and ruin of a stand of chokers that stood forty strides tall. They had seen the trees bring their fury down on us, and they had seen us come out whole. The trees was now on the ground behind us, being cut up small and fed into the hoppers of the asphel mix.

I guess I can imagine what the Ramparts of that village must of thought when they seen we was heading right for their gates. Anyway, they met us as a red tally, every woman and man carrying a weapon of some kind, whether it was a sword or a mattock or a piece of tech. They didn't try to fight us. They was only just able to stand their ground, most likely thinking they would be going into the hoppers too as soon as we was done with the trees. Their fear was a painful thing for me to see. They looked on us like we was monsters, worse than shunned men or beasts or even chokers. Like we was the ending of the world, when we was looking to be its bright beginning.

"We don't mean to hurt you," I told them. But I was a man with a drone hanging next to his shoulder and an army of tech at his back. I could see my words rung hollow. "We're just laying down a road, as you all can see. It's like the roads of the world that was lost, hard enough and strong enough to bide the trees and the weather. When it's done, you'll be able to walk it safe as anything. What's your name here? Your village, I mean."

"Leece." It was one of their Ramparts that said it. He was a young man to be a Rampart, with black hair that was slicked down with some kind of oil and a gold torque around his throat. His tech was a rod as long as his forearm, all shining black. His hands shook as he held it, and his voice was straining towards a sob.

"How many are you?"

As soon as the words was out of my mouth, I seen how they would be read. The man gathered himself up and pointed the black rod at my chest. "You'll find we're enough."

"I didn't mean to slight you," I said quickly. "Or to offer threat to you. It's only that the road will let you visit the villages close by without fear of trees and beasts. It will let you be more than you are. You see how fast our engines is moving. In a few weeks, you and your neighbours will be able to walk a straight, clear road when you want to trade with each other. You won't have to wait for rain."

"We don't trade. We haven't traded with anyone since my mother was alive."

"Well, maybe now you'll start again."

"We won't."

He still was afraid, and he still believed we was come in violence and despite. His fear and his anger was just about boiling over, and talking to him longer was not going to abate it. If I said a wrong word, he would loose that tech on me, and I had no idea what it might do. I give it up and we went on by, followed for a little way by the Rampart and his people. I guess they wanted to make sure we was not staying.

At Dinder, that was also called Dene, we was met by a ditch that had been digged across the path in front of us. The ditch was five feet deep and ten wide. On the other side of it, there was maybe two dozen fighters, young and old together. Like the people we met before, they was carrying whatever they could find that you could stab or swipe or hit with. When they seen the monster that was rolling through the trees towards them, the teeth and the blades and the wheels, and smelled the burned-pie stink of asphel, they was near to pissing themselves, but still they held their ground.

"Look at them," Cup said, looking down on them from her high perch. "They think that ditch is like to stop us, when we're flattening hills and forests."

"I'll go down to them," I said.

"I don't mean to be hurtful, Koli, but the last people you talked to almost went to war with us. I'll go."

Cup slid right down the crawler's wheel-arch and then climbed down the inside of the wheel itself, where there was big rivets she could use as hand- and foot-holds. She had her knife, but she didn't draw it. She went to the edge of the ditch and faced that whole big crowd that was standing there waving swords and sticks and spears at us.

"Hecha," Cup said. She knowed enough Franker now that she could make herself understood in it, and there wasn't no other tongue that was like to serve here.

A woman with white hair that I guess was one of the leaders of the group give her hecha back. Then she bid us turn around and go back where we come from. "We don't want what you're bringing, and we won't abide it," she said. "You're better off not fighting us, for we're Dinder-folk and we don't lie down until we're dead."

"How'd you feel about them other folk?" Cup hooked her thumb over her shoulder, pointing back. "Them of Leece, I mean. Do you favour them, or fear them?"

"There's nothing we fear!" a man shouted from the back of

the crowd. He put some heart into it, but his face belied him and so did the faces of his neighbours. Every one of them was terrified for their lives, and maybe some of them for their souls, for we looked like the harrowing of Hell.

"We don't see them Leece people much," the woman said. "But there's many of us got Leece blood in us if you go back a little way. It's just that the path got closed, and we was too hard beset by other things to open it again."

"Well, the path is what we're bringing," Cup said. "If you're brave enough to go around behind us, you'll see it. The widest, straightest path you ever seen, going all the way from here to Leece. And if you let us by, we'll make a path to other places too. We'll just shove the trees aside and lay the path down one stride at a time. There isn't nothing that can stand in the way of this tech we got here."

I could see the Headwoman was swayed by Cup's words, but also her people had put a lot of sweat and pain into that ditch. Even though she could tell for sure now that it wouldn't do them no good, she had more sense than to just shrug her shoulders and walk away from it. That would make her fighters lose heart. So she sent two runners, who went by us – skirting wide enough so we almost losed sight of them – to see what lay behind. They seen the fresh asphel that was still steaming and shining, and the dry asphel beyond that was hard as stone and flat as a well-turned plank. They walked up and down on it, then run and jumped and tapped their feet. One of them tried to shove the point of a spear into it. The other kneeled down and stuck his tongue out to taste it.

They come back at last and told their Headwoman it was a path all right, all black and hard and shining like sidian stone. But as to whether it went all the way to Leece . . .

"Well, you only got to walk it!" Cup said, throwing out her hands. "Dandrake's balls, look how far we pushed the trees back. A baby could crawl to Leece on what we made and get there safe. Why don't some of you go there now, and see the truth of it? And then walk on after us, to see where we go next."

365

The Headwoman considered. "Why are you doing this?" she asked.

"It was my friend Koli's idea. He wants all the villages to be one big village. He thinks it will be good for your genes."

"What's them, to talk about?"

"Just some stuff from the before-times. But leaving your genes out of it, you can see what you're getting out of this. The road will let you hunt ten miles or more from your gates. It'll keep mole snakes and needles from nesting too close to your fence. Give you a better line of sight and an earlier warning on anything that comes at you out of the west. Let you break bread with your neighbours again, and maybe swap news with them. We could swerve aside from you, if you hold your ground here, and go by the next village instead. But I don't think you want that."

"Oh, she's good!" Ursala whispered – and a smile come over her face that was pure pride, like Cup was her own daughter.

I got to say, I was mazed my own self to see how well Cup carried it with the Headwoman – telling her all the things the road would give her people, and then letting her save face by giving the final choice to her. I knowed Cup was a great fighter, but I seen then that she could be a Rampart too. She had the knowing of people, like Catrin did, which is more important than all the tech in the world.

We sit by a while and waited while the Headwoman talked with her Count and Seal or what she had instead of one.

"We'd like your path to come by us," she told us at last. "We'll fill in the ditch again and let you by."

Cup grinned. "Oh, you can leave the ditch to us," she said. "We can manage that okay."

And on we went.

Up through Ursick and Ulver, Arrad and Greenadd, Pen Bridge and Spark. At Backbarrow, we stopped going north and tacked due west, then at Crookland we turned again so we was going west and south.

"It occurs to me," Ursala said after that last turn, "that we never discussed the route this road of yours would take, Koli."

I shrugged my shoulders like this was no matter. "It's got to go everywhere. Lorraine said Ingland is an island, afloat all by itself in the ocean."

"So it is."

"Then we're going to go from the top of it to the bottom, and from the west of it to the east. When we're done, there won't be no villages left that's alone in the face of the world like Ludden and Baron Furnace was."

Ursala scratched her neck right under her chin, which was a way she had when she was thoughtful. "But it seems we're going to visit some places sooner than others. You're aiming straight for Mythen Rood, aren't you?"

"You leave him be, baa-baa-san," Monono said out of the drone that was floating by us. "Koli knows what he's doing."

"Does he? That's exactly what I'm asking."

"He doesn't have to tell you though. It's his road, not yours. It goes where he says."

Which was a kind thing of her to say, and meant to protect me but Ursala's question was a good one and I didn't have a good answer for it.

I knowed what we was doing with the road well enough. It was a rope we was throwing across the whole of Ingland for people to reach out and grab a hold of so they didn't all sink down and die. The road would make us all into one gene pull, and people would go on, when without it there'd be less and less babies being born until humankind passed out of the world.

But on this other question, which was the route we was taking, I didn't have no ready answer. We was going to Mythen Rood, for certain sure, using maps that had been in *Sword of Albion*'s memory and now was in Monono's. I had decided it that way before we mixed our first load of asphel. But I wasn't looking too closely into the why of it.

My family was in Mythen Rood, that was one thing. My heart

ached for them, for my mother Jemiu and my sisters, Athen and Mull, for my friend Haijon and for Spinner Tanhide that was his wife. I wanted to see their faces again, even if they hated me now. I wanted to explain all the things I had done that was wrong, and say sorry for them, and also tell what I learned about how Mythen Rood's tech went from one to another at the testing.

But after that it gun to be less clear. To tell the truth was to point the finger. It was to say Vennastins should not be Ramparts no more. And to say that was to push Mythen Rood off its roots like a sawed-off tree, and see it topple. Without Ramparts, it was hard to know what Mythen Rood would be. Or if it would be anything at all.

So was I going home to be back with them that I loved, or to be revenged on them that had cast me out? It seemed like it would be a good idea to know before I got there.

53

At a place called Arkom, we stopped a while.

We had laid more than forty miles of road in less than three months, and met with thirty villages along the way. Not all of them was in the right line of the road, but all was close to it – and almost all, after Dinder, welcomed it. The news went ahead of us now. Oftentimes, people come to ask if we would bend the road to take them in. Also, of course, they come to gape at the wonder of it – the caravan of mighty wagons that shouldered the forest out of its way and went where it choosed to.

We had a following too. People from every village was falling in behind us as we went, walking the new road even before it was all the way cold and dry. They brung leather hides with them, clothes and boots, tools, dried herbs, jewellery, honey and preserves, wine and beer and cider. They was looking to sell or barter these things in the villages the road passed by, which meant my hopes of a gene pull was already somewhat borne out, though it was only small beginnings. Those who come to trade would stay to tumble, and their genes would spread out further and further.

Ursala's plans was working too. She had set the dagnostic in the store-space of one of the three drudges, and now at the end of each day's work she plied her old trade of healing and making good. She would treat anyone that come, but she made a preference for women that was with child, or pair-pledged couples that was trying to get that way. Her gene-splicer was kept busy.

That was one of the reasons why we stopped in Arkom. We had been going too quick for all that wanted healing to be seen and tended to, and some was desperate sick. There was more and more that was following our caravan not to trade but to beg Ursala's help, until at last she said enough was enough and we should make a stop for a few days so she could deal with what she called her back logs.

Monono said it was a good thing for other reasons. The hoppers from the hot mix machines had been running day and night for near on ninety days, and now they needed to be cleaned. Most of the great wagons needed repairs to their blades and rollers, or to the thick rubber sleeves that covered their wheels. "And the three of you could benefit from sleeping in a bed for once. Not to mention taking a bath. Going by the way you look, I'm lucky I can't smell you."

It's true we was all of us dirty from the sweat and dust of the journeying and the thick black smoke that come off the road. Monono was probably right that we didn't smell like wildflowers.

So stopping at Arkom was a thing we all was pleased to do. It was a village of about a hundred and fifty souls, built on the two banks of a river called the Lone. They knowed we was coming and made a feast for us of fried fish and mashed swede, and the Headman said we was freemen and freewomen of Arkom henceforward, whatever else we might be. There was a dance after the feast, but Ursala had fell asleep three times while we was eating and didn't have nothing left in her to dance with. I managed a couple of jigs then left the field to Cup, who seemed to be dancing with every boy in the whole village.

So we got our beds, and the next day we got our bath, in piping hot water with petals of flowers throwed into it to make

370

it sweet. The men that brung the water in to me when it was my turn carried it like it was a solemn thing they was doing, and one of them put his hand on top of my head and said luck-touch, like you do when you find a clover or when a red bird flies over you.

"Why'd you do that?" I asked. "There ain't no luck to be got from touching me." The man said he didn't know if there was or there wasn't, but he was pretty sure Dandrake sent me.

"He did not!" I said.

"Well, you wouldn't know though," one of the men told me. "He got his own ways of working."

I was cast down after that, and restless besides. Dandrake wasn't no friend of mine, even now I knowed he had led the fight against Stanley Banner. I had troubled thoughts and empty hands, which is a bad mixture.

Ursala had set the dagnostic up in a little one-room house that the Headman give her. People that wanted to see her had to line up outside and wait their turn, but Cup had been helping her with what she called her tree arch, choosing who was sick enough to go in first and who was well enough to sit a while. The two of them was kept busy all the hours there was, but they didn't need me and nobody else did either. My work was the road, and the road was stopped.

By and by, to keep my hands from fidgeting I turned to my old craft of woodsmithing. I begged a baulk of seasoned choker from the village's smith, a woman named Seginsel, cut it into smaller pieces and gun to whittle one of the pieces into the shape of our crawler. Before I was halfway done, I had a bunch of little ones standing round watching me do it. "So which of you wants this when it's done?" I said. They all answered in a chorus, me me me, and I realised I had got some work to do.

"Koli Toymaker," Monono said. "It's a long way from saving the world."

"Maybe it is," I said. "But it's a restful thing to do. It's small and stupid and has got no meaning at all except for filling an hour and raising a smile on someone's face. So I'll keep right on doing it until I'm made to stop."

"Go ahead. I'll make *vroom vroom* noises. It's all this shitty little speaker is good for."

We stayed in Arkom for five days – long enough for Ursala to see everyone that had come along with us and everyone in the village besides. She had one other patient in mind too, but Cup still was not ready to let the dagnostic go inside her body and change her. "You need me on the road," she said. "I'm the only real fighter you got, and I ain't staying behind while you go uphill and downdale without me. Maybe I'll do it when we get to your village. We're like to stop there for a long while, ain't we?"

I didn't answer. I still didn't know.

Spinner

54

Torri forged the mast in six pieces – three for the base and three for the upper part. She only put them together at last when we took them up on the roof of Rampart Hold and moored them to the chimney stacks there. We had to re-lay the bricks with fresh mortar first and firm them up with iron braces.

The wire was ready in good time though. We had settled on a width that was about half the thickness of a nail, but in the end we had enough metal to go a little thicker than that. Challenger said this was a good thing as the messages in the wire would go more quickly if the road they travelled on was wider.

Torri attached the wire to the mast with a braze-weld that was thicker than a gall on an oak tree. "It looks like shit," she said when she was finally done, "and I ought to be ashamed of it, but it will hold against a hurricane." At the other end, it was a whole lot easier. The piece of tech from Challenger's insides had holes in it where the wires could be threaded in, and it gripped them without any need of welding or splicing.

"What now?" I asked Challenger.

"Now I'll initialise the systems and see if the connections are sound."

"How long will that take?"

"An hour. Perhaps two. There will almost certainly be some self-repair involved. Not much, but enough to slow me. Once I'm done, you will be able to assess the efficacy of your work by means of a practical demonstration."

I went to the mill to tell Jemiu that she would be needed soon on the gather-ground.

She seemed unhappy when she heard it. She still wore her new name lightly – said little at our meetings and looked around if anyone called her Rampart Remember to see who they might mean.

"I've work to do here," she said, hooking her thumb to point at the busy yard behind her. Her four catchers were all working there, brought back into the fold by her change of fortunes. Three more were there too, on share-work. The hammering and sawing was all one sound that never stopped. "More than I can manage. Catrin wants to put up some platforms against the fence so we can fire down on anyone that tries to climb it."

"Let Athen watch the pot a while."

"Athen's off training somewhere with your Jon. A big secret, she says."

"Mull then. Come on. You got to show your face for this, but you'll not be kept long."

Jemiu took off her apron and folded it, but got the folds wrong and had to start again. At last, she threw it down on the bench all crumpled in a ball. Then she thought again and snatched it back. She fished in the apron's pocket and brought out the database. It shocked me somewhat to see her treat it so rough.

"Why did you do it?" she asked, holding up the shiny black thing as thin as a twig and no longer than her middle finger. "Why did you choose me?"

"The database choosed you," I said, trying to keep all my thoughts out of my face.

"No, it was you. I saw you, Spinner. You was looking at me before Catrin ever come to me."

Dead god stiffen me, I thought, I was too. I couldn't keep from it – all afraid as I was that our little mummers' play would come out wrong and people would see through it. But the play had gone well and I'd only given my own self away.

"You're mistook."

"I'm not mistook." Jemiu raised the database to her mouth. "Database, who told you to wake for me?"

"Authorised user Spinner Tanhide."

I blushed. I could feel the heat come into my face. It would have been an easy thing to tell the database to lie, but I hadn't thought to do it.

"So that's what Rampart means," Jemiu said. "People who's in on the trick." She did not seem surprised, only bitter.

"You got to keep that a secret, Jemiu," I said. "For now, at least. We can't have contention at such a time. If people was to know—"

"I'm not a fool, Spinner. I'll keep my tongue until all this ruck is done with. But give me honest answer. Why'd you do it? Was this you saying sorry to me for Koli?"

"For Koli?" I had no idea what she meant and could only stare, as surprised to hear that name as if she'd asked was it Dandrake bid me do it. "Why Koli? Where's Koli in this?"

Jemiu set the database down on the bench and pushed it away from her. I think she did it so she could look away from me. "Whatever Koli did, he did it because he was sick in love with you."

"I didn't love him back though."

"I know it."

"So his loving me is not to the purpose. Unless you think that when a boy's sick for a girl, it's the girl's part to make him well again." I felt an anger rising up in me, and I let it come. It was better than the shame of having handled this so badly.

Jemiu met my eyes now. "I don't think that. Of course I don't."

"Good. For if you thought that, we couldn't be friends no more. Maybe I meant to thank you somewhat for the kindness you give me when my father died. Mostly, though, when I thought of who I wanted up at the Hold in this time, it was you that kept coming to mind. Your trick with the bird boxes saved us from terrible harm. And it gave us the idea for this new trick with Challenger. If I thought of Koli once in all of that, may Dandrake strike me dead."

Jemiu nodded. "I'm sorry then," she said. "It was a mother talking. I'd ask you to set no store by it. I miss him, is all."

There were tears in her eyes. Any rage I felt went out of me when I saw them there. I embraced her, and she embraced me back. "I know you do," I said. "Come now, Jem. Show the Vennastins you're as much Rampart as they are."

Almost everyone in the village was standing on the gather-ground when we got back there, but Catrin and Fer were easy to find. They were standing side by side on the steps of the Hold, making it clear to all on whose say-so all this was being done.

"He says he's ready," Catrin told me.

"Good then," I said. "Ramparts all, come into my name-tech."

We made our way to where Challenger was, scaled his side and climbed down one by one into the turret. We took our places in the cramped space, jostling elbows and nudging shoulders. Somehow it felt a great deal more crowded now than it did when we went off to fight.

"When you're ready, Challenger," I said. "Please. Show us."

A ball of light blossomed on the console, growing and flattening until it turned into the magic mirror. It was all black at first, then a green line appeared, wavering and thin – and moving. It curved around and up and down and met itself on the way back, making a circle in the middle of the mirror. It wasn't a perfect circle: it was more like the shape of an egg.

"What's that?" Catrin asked.

"Your village's outer fence – as it would look if you were hanging in the air high above it. The rendering is accurate. I drew it up by means of a sonar scan. Adding a few structures will help you to orientate yourself. Here."

A green square appeared inside the circle.

"That's Rampart Hold."

Another square, much smaller, outside.

"That's your far lookout. Is there anything else I should add to help you interpret the image correctly?"

"The Middle," Fer said.

"All the streets," said Catrin. "The Middle, the Span and the Yard."

They appeared one by one, green lines drawing themselves on empty air.

"The tannery," I said. "And the broken house."

They came too.

"Enough?"

"Enough," Catrin said, but Challenger was silent until I said it too. "Enough, Challenger. Thank you."

"Very well. What you see now, added into the display, will be what you call tech. Electronic devices, or devices that contain electronics, no matter what their scale or function might be."

A bright red dot appeared in the centre of the green square that was Rampart Hold. Four more dots, all of them together, appeared right beside the Hold, and two on what had got to be the gather-ground – the space between Rampart Hold and the Span.

I traced them with my finger, guessing each in turn.

"This is you, Challenger," I said. "And these . . . the firethrower, the database and the bolt gun. Because we're all gathered in the one place. And these two are the Half-Ax guns. But what's the dot inside the Hold?"

"That's actually two signals overlaid on each other. One is the clock radio you brought up from the Underhold and repaired. The other is not inside the Hold but above it. It's the mast. What I'm detecting are places where electricity flows within circuits, with enough power to affect local magnetic fields. That means functioning tech. Waked tech, as you call it, or tech that's set on standby. Entirely inert systems won't show here. So. We have proof of concept."

"Is this as far as you can go?" Jemiu asked. "I thought we were doing this to get a warning of what was coming. We can see all this with our own eyes."

Fer glared at Jemiu, and even Catrin seemed surprised at her speaking up. Challenger's voice didn't change. "I was merely establishing a baseline. I'm going to expand the field now. That means there'll be less detail in the centre, but you can still use the green circle as a reference point. The green circle is Mythen Rood."

The circle got smaller and smaller, though it never moved from the middle of the magic mirror. For a long while it was alone. Then a red dot came into the top edge of the mirror – and a few seconds later three more in the bottom right-hand corner.

"The field is retaining strength and coherence into middle ranges. These are functional devices I've found in Mythen Rood's immediate vicinity. Approximate distances are five miles for the device to the west of you, six and a half for the cluster in the south-east.

"The western one would be Todmort," Catrin said at once. "The other is most likely Greetlan."

"I never even heard of Greetlan," Fer said, like this had got to be someone's fault.

"Yeah, you did, Fer. You just forgot. We stopped trading with them back when Grandma Bliss was alive. I thought them whelmed long since."

"Perhaps they are," Challenger said. "As I said, the mast is sensitive to electromagnetic fields of a sufficient strength to register on my sensors. Entirely inactive devices will not register, but dormant ones will if they are still drawing power."

My mind raced on a little. "Could we maybe find more tech like you, Challenger? Abandoned in the forest and waiting to be found?"

"I don't think we've got time to go digging for buried treasure," Catrin said. "Okay, you're seeing out six miles or more. Can you stretch it a little further and see Half-Ax?"

"Yes."

"Do it, Challenger,"

The green circle that was Mythen Rood shrunk a little more. To the east of us, a great number of red dots all sprung up at once – on the very edge of the screen at first, but moving inwards quickly as what Challenger called his field searched further and further away. But the dots were not where I expected them to be. I thought Half-Ax would be on fire with red – all its tech gathered in one great store, like our Underhold, but ten or twenty times as big and all awake.

Instead there was a kind of rash of dots sprawled out in a wavering, uncertain line from the right-hand side of the mirror towards the middle. Towards us.

"What are we seeing?" Fer asked.

Challenger didn't feel any need to answer her. I would have asked him my own self, but the truth of it hit me all at once. Then when I tried to speak, I found my throat was tight. Catrin spoke up before I could frame a word. "We're seeing the Peacemaker's army. On the move."

"They're coming here," I said. My heart bumped against the inside of my ribs and a sick sourness climbed up into my mouth.

"It seems likely," Challenger said.

It was a thing we knew would happen, so it should not have been so big a surprise. But it was one thing to know it and another thing again to see it happening.

Catrin wasn't shook though. She was still thinking through what it meant. She counted on her fingers. "At Calder ford, there was ten of them, and they had two tech weapons between them. At our ambush in the forest, they was maybe fifteen or twenty, and they had four. Challenger, what's the count here?"

"I count one hundred and two separate fields."

"So maybe four or five hundred fighters."

"There can't be that many," Fer said. "They'd of left nobody home but cats and dogs."

"Maybe it's less then," Catrin said. "But we better make our plans on more."

"There is something else," Challenger said. "Something I'm at a loss to understand. But I think you need to be aware of it."

All four of us swapped glances. What else could there be that mattered in the face of this? Catrin got to her feet. "We better save anything else," she said, "until we've told this in the Count and Seal."

"You will want to discuss this other thing too. It may be part of your war. It seems unlikely to be a coincidence."

"Show us then," I told him. "Please."

The picture in the magic mirror shifted again, the red dots all drawing closer together as Challenger flung his field out further still, way past Half-Ax. More bright dots flashed here and there, but small and far apart. Villages that still hoarded a few pieces of tech, the same way we did, as their last defence against the world outside their gates.

Then my gaze was pulled from the furthest east to the furthest west. In the bottom left-hand corner of the mirror, as far away again from the centre as Half-Ax was, another cluster of lights was now showing. They were brighter than the Half-Ax lights, and closer together – just as much tech, or maybe even more, but gathered more tightly until they all seemed like one big red jewel shining against the darkness.

"What in the dead god's name is that?" Catrin said. Her voice was a growl.

"I have no way of telling," Challenger said. "But it's moving."

We didn't bother to ask which way.

55

The dismay in the Count and Seal was considerable, but Catrin rode it down.

"There's no point in sitting there and asking what will become of us," she said, speaking loud over the din of voices. "We all knew this day would come, and we've done what we could to make ready for it. Now let's face it like what we are – women and men of Mythen Rood. Not like frightened children that piss themselves at a shadow in the corner or a creak in the night."

"This is a fuck sight more than that!" someone shouted.

"It isn't though." Catrin had wanted that answer and waited on it. "For not one damn thing has happened. Half-Ax is coming, yes. But they're miles away still, and we've had weeks of clear skies. They'll be crawling, not running. And the force from the west? Well, that could be anything. Friends or foes: we can't know until we've seen them."

"They're not friends," said Jarter Shepherd. "We know that, Rampart, surely. What friends have we got in the west? Who do we know even that's out there so far?"

"Nobody," Catrin said. "You're right. We don't know anybody or anything that's out there. We're deep in the dark without a candle. But we got some time yet. Challenger measured how quick the Peacemaker's army is coming, and they're taking it slow – most likely because they're feeling their way and checking the ground before they put their feet down. They don't know how their first two sallies come to grief, or what traps we might of set for them. If they keep that speed, we still got four days at least before they reach our gates.

"It don't matter if they take four years," Asha Reedwright said. "We got no answer for them when they come. Not for a force that big."

"What we got is who we are." Catrin raised her voice to something like a shout. "And that's been enough so far to turn whatever come against us. Anyone can see this is bad news. But as long as we're yet living, I'm not minded to give up – and I'd be surprised if any wight here feels different. I say we should send runners to the west to scout out that other force and see what they're up to. It may be we can strike a bargain with them. Or it may be that it's Half-Ax they're coming for. What have we got that would bring such a great power such a great way?"

"Who'd do the running though?" Evred Bell asked. "That's a bloody long run, Rampart Fire."

Catrin had been waiting for this too, and I admired her cleverness in holding the bad news back until she knew for sure she had some kind of answer to offer. "It is, Evred Bell. A bloody long run is right. But we got a team that's ready to take it on. And what's more, they got their own tech. Rampart Knife, let's see you."

Jon stood up in complete silence. He'd been sitting there all this while with his left hand folded over his right, keeping something hid in his lap. He still kept it hid as he stood.

I think the reason nobody spoke up right away was out of embarrassment or pity. They all knew that Jon had lost his nametech and wasn't a Rampart any more, no matter what was said at his testing. They didn't want to offer him any insult for it, but they couldn't meet his eye either. Each looked to other

384

instead, and by and by a murmur rose up that was one half sorrowing and one half angry.

"Oh, Rampart Knife's not me," Jon said, smiling like it was funny they made that mistaking. "Veso. Athen. You better get up here with me before anyone thinks I'm vaunting myself over you."

Athen Woodsmith stood and took a place at Jon's left hand. Then Veso Shepherd came and stood on his right.

"Lari. Tam. Cora. Keverin. What you doing still sitting down?"

They each stood up when their name was spoken and took their places. So now there was a row of three with a row of four behind.

"This is Rampart Knife," Jon said. "This that you're looking at. We thought we'd share the name between the seven of us. And we shared some other things besides."

The seven raised up their right hands all at once. They were wearing cutters. Jon had brought them up out of the Underhold with Catrin's blessing. The sight of them had everyone else in the room on their feet in a second, some shouting questions and some just cheering. Jon waited for them to quiet. The other six watched him, looking for their moment the way musicians do when they're all playing the same tune and want to come in together on the beat.

"Are these cutters waked?" Jon said. He said it like his mother, clear and loud so everyone could hear him. "Is that what you're asking? No, they're not."

Sighs and cries and curses at that, but Jon spoke over them and they quickly fell into silence. "We don't wear these cutters for the power that's in them. We wear them to say who we are, and to warn anyone we come against who it is they're facing. But cutters ain't our name-tech. This is our name-tech."

All seven put their hands to their belts. All seven drawed out daggers, thick and short and perfectly balanced.

All seven turned. And as they turned, they fell into line. Jon threw his knife the whole length of the room. It buried itself in one of the wooden beams that held up the roof.

Then he stepped to the left, and Veso threw. His knife landed just an inch below Jon's – the best throw he ever made, I dare say, but he kept his face calm and cold as if it was something he did every day. He stepped to the right, and Athen threw, spinning as she did it like throwing a knife was a kind of a dance. Her blade hit the beam somewhat lower down.

Then Lari. And Keverin. And Cora. And Tam.

All seven knives hit the beam. It was a tight spread too, and could not have gone better. The other nicks in the beam and in the wall behind that they had made in their weeks and weeks of practising were hid by the dim light. I think Catrin had positioned the lamps to leave that part of the room halfway in shadow.

The cheers were like thunder indoors, and they went on for a long time. The seven shook each other's hands and clapped each other's shoulders, soaking in the joy of that praise, that being seen and loved.

"I put it to the vote," Catrin said when there was quiet again. "Rampart Knife will go to the west, right now, and bring us back report of what's out there. Then they'll turn straightway and come back again before Half-Ax reaches the gates, for we'll need them to lead our defence. Let's see how the Peacemaker's army fares against ours. Say if it will be so."

This time there was no need to count the votes. Every hand rose up. Every voice too.

Jon caught my eye and smiled. I looked from him to his mother. Catrin was wearing a face of calm seriousness, a Rampart face, but we both knew what a hollow hope she was offering. She had mended the roof with a shoe instead of a shingle, as my father would have said. Rampart Knife would have to make their way through mile after mile of open country, with only their daggers to protect them – for with Half-Ax coming so close upon us, we couldn't risk losing even a single one of the few pieces of tech we had. And what was our hope? That the force that was coming out of the west might have someone in it we could reason with, someone we could plead to for help, and not just another Peacemaker filled with dreams of blood and conquering.

This great show with the knives and the cutters was meant for one thing only. To hide the thinness of our plan and the dreadful narrowness of the strait we all were in. For me, it was even worse. I might lose my husband in this venture, and never even know where he had fallen.

But still I met Jon's smile, and gave it back to him. Smiling in the face of horrors is a thing you can get better at. It was probably one of the first tricks our mothers' mothers ever learned.

56

Rampart Knife set out just after dawn. There was a hill to the west of Mythen Rood, Dog Neck by name, that they could reach by sun-up. They aimed to camp there if the day was clear, then move on through the first patch of dense forest once evening came. It sounded so easy when Jon explained it to me. As if the forest was just a ditch they could jump over or a ladder they could climb. As if it had no branches to crush them with, and no roots to drink their blood.

We said goodbye to each other twice, the first time in the bedroom and the second on the gather-ground. I'll say nothing more about the first farewell, or what shape it took. Only that afterwards we lay a long while in each other's arms, with his head against my shoulder and our legs still tangled together.

"Look you come back to me unbroken," I said. I held up my left hand, where a needle had bit me when I was a child and took my pointing finger off. "If we keep losing pieces of ourselves, it's a bad thing for our marriage. It's like we're breaking our pair-pledge really slowly."

Jon kissed my scar, and held it to his cheek. "If I'm broke in pieces, Spin," he said, "every piece will find its own way back to you."

"I'd still like you better if you held all together, Jon. A man is like a table in that regard. He's less use if he wobbles."

I was making these foolish jokes only to keep from crying. I wanted to give him memories of me that would make his way easier, not harder.

While he dressed, I brought Vallen from her crib. She was already awake, but not crying. She had been waiting there with her sweet blue eyes open in the dark, as if she sensed something was happening that might deserve her attention. I put her in her father's arms. He kissed her and rocked her, speaking such nonsense as people always speak to babies. Vallen didn't offer any opinion, but she grabbed his finger when he stroked her face with it, and held on fast, and by and by begun to chew on it.

"Her teeth is already coming in," Jon said marvelling. "Is this a baby or a bear you give birth to."

"I don't think I ever tumbled with a bear," I said. "If I did, I forget. She's most likely a baby."

We leant in around her and kissed again, holding her in between us like a promise. Then I wrapped her in a shawl while Jon strapped on his belt and his knives and checked the hang of them. He was a fine sight, my soldier husband. I was glad for him, that he had found his pride and his purpose again. But I wished with all my heart it had been another pride, a different purpose.

Our second goodbye was short, and public. We both kept our brave faces on. Jon squeezed my hand one last time and kissed Vallen on the cheek, then he went to join his tally. They gave him a quick, sharp hail as he came, clapping their heels together and putting their right hands to their own belts, where their daggers hung ready to their hands. They all were dressed alike in the new leathers I had made for them. Mid-brown calfskin, with a natural mottle left in so they'd be hard to see against a forest dark. All of Rampart Knife had thanked me kindly for the gift, but they'd made their own changes since. On the right sleeve of each jacket, burned in with great care and the charcoal black made darker still with tea and iron salt, there was an upright dagger.

As Jon took his place at the head of the line, I joined the crowd that had come to cheer Mythen Rood's new heroes on their way. We walked them out of gates, banging drums and pans and wash-tubs to scare away any animals that might be out hunting in the near woods. Vallen didn't like the noise, but even now she didn't cry. She only shook her fists like she was coming to the last dregs of her patience and warning us what might come of it if she run out altogether.

The gate faced east of north, so Rampart Knife would have to walk almost halfway around the village before they came to a way that took them west. We walked with them some of that way until a turn of the path took them past the stake-blind, out of the half-outside and into the world. Then we stayed a little longer to watch them out of sight. Most of the village was with us, but I felt alone as I turned and walked back to the gates. I wasn't even going home. I had promised Jon I'd stay in Rampart Hold until he got back, so Ban could help me look after our baby.

"Well, they got one piece of luck," Jarter Shepherd said, looking up at the sky. Clouds were rolling in from the west, thick as cream and dark as a bruise. We wouldn't see the sun today.

But any fortune we got that way had two edges to it. What speeded Rampart Knife would speed Half-Ax too, stealing away the last few days we had to make ourselves ready.

57

Two days passed with nothing to report, either of Half-Ax or of Rampart Knife. For us they were busy days indeed – days of running straight from one thing to another like blue-arsed flies, and barely lying down to sleep before the tocsin woke us for yet more work. The sky stayed heavy but the storm didn't break. We knew we didn't have long. Challenger's magic mirror told us that much.

Jemiu put aside the database a while and put her apron on again. The wooden platforms – three times twenty of them – were finished, dragged to the fence and put up in place. Now we could keep up a watch in all quarters, and if Half-Ax attacked us from any side we could give some answer. This was a great labour – a share-work for the whole village. I sat it out, for my job was to watch the magic mirror and give report.

The mirror showed Half-Ax drifting towards us as slow as a cloud. It also let me see how Rampart Knife was faring. Jon was carrying the clock radio, not because it would do them any earthly good but because it was waked tech and showed on Challenger's scanner. As long as they had it with them, we could keep a watch on their progress. Whenever I could spare a moment from the

Count and Seal, I spent it inside the battle wagon staring into the mirror. It helped that Vallen was still nursing and needed to feed every three or four turns of the glass. I took her inside Challenger to feed, and I watched the mirror as she suckled on me.

Rampart Knife was still moving, still alive – or some of them were. They were coming nearer and nearer to that big cluster of tech that was coming from the west. It didn't seem to pay them any heed as they approached, for it never slowed or turned or speeded up.

By the afternoon of the second day, they were within a mile of it. That was the closest they got. I tried to imagine what was happening around that still red dot that was my husband. Maybe he was watching the westerners, whoever they might be, through a spyglass. Or maybe he had made a base and sent some of his tally on ahead while he guarded their backs. Maybe the clock radio had fallen out of his pocket and was lying on a forest path while they forged on not knowing they had lost it. Maybe beasts or trees had fed on all seven of them, and spit the tech out as having no savour. There was no way of telling.

In the evening, the dot moved again, not west but east. I gave a sob of joy to see it. They were coming home. Some of them, at least, were coming home. And surely my heart or the world or something would have told me if Jon wasn't one of them.

I told the news to Catrin. It was given out in the Count and Seal and on the gather-ground: Rampart Knife were on their way back with the answer they were sent to find. There was good hope that they would reach our gates long before Half-Ax arrived, for Half-Ax had slowed their advance. We wondered a little at that caution, but not overmuch. Our enemy's tally was in Calder now, and Calder had bit them twice before. They had good reason to be careful.

We watched the mirror and we hoped. It would be close, but we looked to see our friends, our lovers, our sons and daughters safe within gates before the next danger threatened. They might bring news that would save us all.

On the third, day a strange quiet fell over the village. We all walked as if on eggshells. All that we could do by way of preparation was done, and there was nothing to fill our time but waiting. The red dots closed on us, from east and west. Our one little beacon drew closer too. So slow. So slow. I imagined Jon when he was a boy of twelve Summers racing against Koli Woodsmith – the two of them so much quicker than the rest of us that no one else bothered to run against them. I saw in my inward eye the wind whipping my boy's hair across his face as he ran endlessly towards me.

"Why are we sitting here?" Mercy Frostfend asked in the Count and Seal. "Do we want to let them get all the way to the fence? Why not trick them the way we did before, and let the trees take them?"

All this had been talked around and about and through, and we had made the only choice we could. "When we met them before," Catrin said, "they were less than twenty strong and still we almost come to disaster for all our tricks and cleverness. We don't know how many are coming now, but it's got to be a great many more than that. More than we got in the whole village, if every woman and man and child and stray cat was to fight. Once we're out of gates, they can flank us and circle us and no tricks will avail. The fence is the best protection we got, and we should use it. We need to make them come to us."

There was murmurs in the chamber, voices both for and against, but nobody had a better idea. So we waited, even though it was plain to see that waiting was taking its toll on all of us.

And still Half-Ax came before we looked for them.

On the fourth day, it was not the Frostfend cockerels that woke us, nor yet the tocsin bell. It was the great ghost-wail of Challenger's alarm that sounded like someone screaming inside your blood and bones.

It wasn't yet light. I tumbled out of bed and ran to the window, but there was nothing to see. The scream went on and on.

I dressed quickly and went downstairs. Catrin and Fer fell in

393

along the way. Ban was already unlocking the door and drawing the three bolts one by one. She reached out her hands to take Vallen from me, but I shook my head. I had promised Jon to keep her safe. Not knowing what the danger was, I resolved to keep her with me.

On the gather-ground, where not long since we'd said our goodbyes to Rampart Knife, forty or fifty villagers freshly roused from their beds were standing all together. Some had spears in their hands. Others had grabbed up whatever they could, shovels and mattocks, hoes and hammers and kitchen knives. More were coming from all sides to join them.

"Find out what's what," Catrin told me. "And tell him to stop that screeching. It's done its work."

It stopped even as she said it, so I guess Challenger agreed.

"Will you come in with me?" I asked Catrin.

"I'm needed here." She nodded towards the crowd.

"I'll come," Jemiu said, running up beside us.

"Good. We'll leave it to you two then. Why's that baby with you?"

"She must think she's a Rampart," I said.

"She's not the onliest one," Fer said, giving Jemiu a cold look.

Catrin stepped in before either of us could give her the answer she deserved. "Fer, let's get some people up on the walls and on the roof of the Hold. Whatever's coming, we need to be ready for it. Not standing around like sheep in a field waiting for a wolf to jump in among them."

The two sisters went to the head of the crowd. I went the other way, and Jemiu followed me. The people stepped aside to let us pass, opening a clear path between us and Challenger. I was grateful that my first task was to climb inside the battle wagon. It was not fear that was working on me, think what you like – or not only that. I might be afraid of the fight to come but I knew now from the two fights I was in before that I wouldn't freeze or falter when I came to it. Still, it was good to have a moment in the cool and the silence to gather myself. I felt like I was no more than a scatter of leaves right then, when a tight fist was what was needed.

The lights in the cockpit came on as I stepped down and took my seat. Jemiu came after me but stayed on her feet, one hand on the ladder. I think it frightened her somewhat to be inside the wagon in such a narrow space. She flinched when Challenger spoke up.

"Sergeant Tanhide. Permission to report."

"Yes! What is it, Challenger? What's happening?"

The magic mirror came to life in front of us. The green circle with its cluster of red dots was just as it always was, but the Half-Ax column was much closer now. It seemed like they had got to be less than two miles from our fence.

"They had been slowing," Challenger said. "For much of yesterday, they seemed almost to be standing still. Then a short while ago they began this surge, moving forward at more than twice their previous marching speed."

"So why did they stop?"

"My best guess is that they were clearing and possibly widening the paths in front of them to facilitate this rapid advance. They mean to catch you by surprise."

I leaned in close and took a harder look at the Half-Ax line. At the nearer edge, where it was pointed at us, it seemed to be spreading out like the ravelled end of a string. I set my finger to the mirror, feeling the usual shudder go through me when I found there was nothing there I could touch. "Challenger, what's happening here? They're not coming on towards the fence, it seems like. They're scattering." It was more obvious now. The westward march was all but stopped. The two ends of the line were moving north and south, though they were bending inwards at the same time as if they meant to make the shape of a horseshoe.

"They may have been assigned multiple targets."

"We only got but the one gate, and they got to know where it is. They should be turning north if that's where they're going."

"Maybe they found the grass-grail," Jemiu said. The grass-grail

395

was a secret way into the village that was made for hunters to use in time of greatest need. It was not a gate, but a row of hand- and footholds set into the fence on the southern side, cunningly disguised by woodsmiths of old times so you could hardly see it even if you were standing right by it.

But after a moment's dismay, I saw it could not be that. "The grass-grail would be a poor way for fighters to come," I said. "They'd have to climb up hand over hand – and one at a time, with no way to hide or shield themselves." It had to be something else that was happening, and whatever it was we needed to guess it quickly.

I looked into the mirror again and tried to measure the distances. The Half-Ax line thinning and spreading – spilling away to the north and to the south, but bending ever towards us as they did it. And away to the west, the little dot that was Rampart Knife coming home. Until now I'd been sure they would get here first. But that was a hope built on a foolish idea – that Half-Ax would keep the same pace and stay on the same line, coming straight at us until by and by they reached our fence and threw all they had against it.

"I think they mean to make a circle," Jemiu said.

I saw it as soon as she said it, though I hadn't guessed it before.

"We've got to go tell Catrin," I said. "Challenger, keep watching. Sound your alarm again if anything changes."

"Yes, sergeant."

We climbed out and jumped down. Catrin was giving orders, sending people in twos and threes to the east side of the fence where they thought an attack was most likely to come.

She stopped as we ran up. Seeing our faces, she drew us both aside from the people that were still waiting to be told where to go. Fer broke from the crowd to join us.

"Make yourselves into threes and count from the gate," Catrin shouted to all the people that still were there. "Three to each platform, and at least one with a bow. Move now, quick as you can."

396

She turned to me and Jemiu again. "What?" she said.

"They're coming on us as fast as they can move," I said. "And they're splitting their force in two. Jemiu thinks they mean to go around us and then join up in a big circle. They may yet charge the gate, but they're not gathering there. It looks more like they mean to press us on all sides."

"That will thin them out at least," Fer said.

Catrin said nothing. She was thinking what this meant, and what we could do about it. "Numbers is their greatest strength," she said, "and I guess they mean to use it. Even if they push in two or three places, we'll be hard put to answer them. If it's more than that, we got no chance."

"If we make a sally now," Fer said, "we can meet the one half of their fighters while the other half is moving away from us. A quick strike before they know we're coming might be our best chance."

Catrin shook her head. "If numbers is their strength, the fence is ours. Once we're out there, they can pour in from every side and whelm us. At least in here we got something we can hide behind. Best we wait for now and make them come to us."

"Even if they come from every quarter?"

"Even then."

"We can't though," I said. "If we do, Jon and the others will be shut out. The Half-Ax circle will close before they get here."

Nobody said anything for a moment. They looked each to other as they bit down on that bad news.

Catrin ran her hand down the strap of the firethrower until it rested on the weapon's stock, worn smooth by a hundred hands.

"How far out are they?" she asked me by and by.

"Challenger said an hour. Maybe a little less."

She nodded.

"Well then," she said. "I guess I'll be going outside after all."

58

From the near lookout and the roof of Rampart Hold we could track the movement of the Half-Ax fighters as they rounded our fence. Mostly we couldn't see them, for they were not so bold as to come into the cleared spaces of the half-outside, but they were close enough that we could hear the tramp of their booted feet and sometimes see a bush stirred into movement as they went by.

When we judged their northern column had come level with the gate, we opened it. Catrin waited a few minutes, then went out.

She didn't do any more than that. Just stood and waited there alone. Behind her the gates closed again. She was dressed in the plain leathers our hunters mostly wore, but she didn't carry a bow or spear. She didn't carry her name-tech either. She had left the firethrower with me, since I was the only one besides her that was synced with it and could take it up if she fell.

We'd argued long and hard about which of us should do this, but when all was said Catrin was Rampart Fire and her word weighed heaviest. I pleaded all I could – that she was needed more than anyone in this fight, that nobody would listen to me or Fer if she was gone, that her injuries from the fight at Calder ford made her too slow to run if things went against her. All was not enough. "I'm decided," she said. "I think I got what's needed to carry it, is all. They'll see my age, and how slow I move, and they'll think me less than I am."

"They will not though," I said. "Not for long anyway. Nobody could spend a minute in your company and mistake you, Mother. You got Rampart crying out from every word you say. From the way you stand, even."

"I'll stoop my shoulders then, and put a break in my voice. Peace now, Spinner. Challenger won't reck nobody besides you. That means you got to live, for he's still our last argument."

"But I could bid him—"

"Peace, I said. No more words on this."

So now she stood about twenty strides out from the gate, with her arms at her sides to show her hands were empty, and waited. I waited too, up on the narrow stand-fast set on the inside of the gate on its right-hand side. Next to me was Jarter with the scatter-gun, and on the other side from us Fer with her name-tech and Gendel Stepjack with a bow.

Nothing happened that we could see, but by and by the chain of messengers I'd set between the gather-ground and the gate brought me Challenger's message. The Half-Ax columns, both of them, had come to a halt. Their scouts had seen the gate open and close again. They'd seen Catrin standing there. They were waiting for orders. We couldn't do anything else but wait too.

After some little while, a line of Half-Ax soldiers broke cover and stepped out of the trees. They walked right up to Catrin and then past her, looking on all sides. Two of them looked behind her back, maybe to see if she had a knife or a cudgel hid there. Then they lined up between her and the gate, cutting off her escape.

After that, some more soldiers came out and drew themselves up in two lines on either side of Catrin. They stood as stiff as fence-posts, their hands on their bows that were held in the flat-grip across their body.

There was another time of nothing happening. Then two men and a woman came out from the trees and walked right up to Catrin. The men were the biggest and widest I ever saw. Giants was more like it. They wore the grey Half-Ax uniforms, but instead of just the little red badge on their chests they had red tabards over their grey jackets with two crossed axes stitched in grey on the red.

The woman in between them just wore the regular grey, but the way she carried herself and the way they looked to her made it clear who was the leader here. She was shorter than Catrin but bigger across the shoulders. Her hair was white with silver braids plaited through it. There were silver bracelets on her wrists and a sword slung across her back in a sheath of grey leather chased with what looked to me like gold.

She saluted Catrin with a hand pressed to her chest, two fingers bent back and two straight. Catrin nodded – a slow movement where her whole head was bowed for a second or two. She gave respect, in other words, but she didn't move her hands or give the watching soldiers any reason to think her a threat to their leader. I saw this and guessed the reason for it, but I'm not sure I would have knowed enough to think of these things if I had gone in her place.

"Say who you are," the woman said.

"I'm Catrin Vennastin of Mythen Rood." Catrin didn't try to make her voice sound weak and broken as she had said she would but spoke out strong and clear. "And you're Berrobis of Half-Ax, unless I'm missing my guess."

"Ah!" the woman said. "You coaxed your prisoners to talk then. That's a black mark on them." She brought up her hand, clenched into a fist, and thumped it against her chest. "Yes and so. I'm Berrobis Bradeshin, Marshal-general of Half-Ax. First cousin and first counsel to Geredd Sakk Bradeshin the Peacemaker, the fifth and first, the fist of virtue."

The soldiers made a sound. It was like they were all of them singing the one low note for the space of about two breaths.

400

Berrobis waited until they were done before she spoke again. "There's an answer you're meant to give when you hear his name spoke out loud. It's 'may he live for ever'."

"Well," Catrin said. "I might say it but I wouldn't mean it and it isn't like to happen. Shall we get on with the meat of this?"

The Half-Ax leader stared. Then she tilted her head on one side, as if staring wasn't enough to give her a clear look at this woman that was standing in front of her. Of a sudden, blue light that was almost too bright to look at welled out from her. It was only when she raised her hands that I saw it was coming from the bracelets she wore. They were tech, but I couldn't see what she had done or said to wake them.

"I did you the courtesy of stopping here to talk with you," Berrobis said. "But I'd ask you to keep a civil tongue. There are right ways to do these things, and wrong ways." She raised up her arms and thrust them forward so they were on either side of Catrin's head. Catrin didn't flinch, although she must have been all but blinded by that bright glare. Maybe she closed her eyes. From where we stood, we couldn't see.

They stayed like that a long while.

"Tell me the words again," Catrin said at last. "I misremember them."

"May he live for ever."

"May he . . .?"

"Live. For ever."

"That's it, of course. May he live for ever then, to be sure."

"Thank you." The Half-Ax general lowered her hands, and that hurtful light died out of the bracelets. "Now say your piece. But say it in few words, and be careful what words they are."

"There's no need for threats," Rampart Fire said. "We're treating in good faith, aren't we? And it's as easy for my people up there on the gate to kill you as it is for you to kill me. But we aren't either of us going to do it because we're people, not animals. We don't bite or claw when we're angry, like a dog would do. We may fight when we're brought to it, but that's a choice we make.

And it's not the first choice. Not if we got any sense. The first choice is to talk."

The other woman made no answer to this. She held the same position for a time that seemed terrible long. "Talk then," she said.

Catrin give a nod. She lifted up her hand slowly, with all the fingers spread as if she was signing to us up on the gate to stand down from some sally we had been about to make. There hadn't been any such sally. She had told us to stay where we were and do nothing, no matter what fell. But that didn't take away any of the power from that slow wave of her hand. "Thank you," she said. "I'm Catrin Vennastin, like I said. Rampart Fire I'm sometimes called, which comes from my name-tech and what it does. I'm speaking to you now with the authority of Mythen Rood's Count and Seal. I got their let and leave to treat with you, and they'll abide any promises I make."

"I've spoken my name already," Berrobis said. "And my authority is in my name. Go on."

Catrin still had that one hand raised, though not as high as before. She turned it in a circle to point to the village at her back and to include herself inside it. "This is us," she said. "This little space here. We're of Calder, and Calder's all we want. We don't mean to trouble the Peacemaker, or any wight else. If you leave us here and come back ten years from now, or twenty, or a hundred, here is where you'll find us.

"So there's nothing to be gained by fighting us. You're not taking away a danger. If you win, you don't win anything that's worth having – and win or lose, you leave some of your sons and daughters on the ground."

Berrobis did that thing of tilting her head again, looking at Catrin long and hard. "I think you mistook us," she said, "Rampart Fire."

"Set me right, then."

"You say we've got nothing to win by beating you. Well, that's both true and not true. We're come to take back the tech you stole from the Peacemaker. That's one half of it. The other half is to show the world what happens to any that lay their hands on what's his. The same way we showed Temenstow. The same way we showed Lilbor and Wittenworth. A lesson's got to be taught before it can be learned. My task is the teaching, and I don't shrink from it."

"It's true we got some tech of yours," Catrin said. "Two guns that we took from your fighters at Calder ford last Spring. We didn't see that as stealing, since it was Half-Ax that picked the fight in the first place. But if that's what carried you all this way, and if it matters so much to you, I believe we can make parley and find agreement."

Berrobis shook her head at this, slowly and deliberately. "We didn't come to make parley. We sent one before, an emissary, to bring you Half-Ax's offer. You answered with despite. Now we're come in all our might and you think you can hold us off with words. You can't. All that happens now is fixed already."

"I don't believe that," Catrin said. "It can't be. Not when so many is like to die from it. If it will keep us from fighting, we'll give up the two guns. We won't put them in your hands right here and now, when you're at our gates with such a tally as this. That would be stupid. But if you turn around and go home again, we'll send a messenger on behind you to carry those guns back to where they hail from. And we'll give you the two prisoners we took besides. We'll even make apology to the Peacemaker, though we only answered you in kind when you come at us. That's my promise to you, and if I don't make good on it may the dead god strike me down."

We listened, breathless. Catrin had said it so well, and so strong, I really believed for a second the Half-Ax general might say yes.

But she only smiled, somewhat sadly, and shook her head again. "You seem to think that's a fair offer. It isn't though. We asked, Rampart, and you answered. We didn't come all this way, with all this muster, just to ask again. We came to deliver judgement.

"And even now, when you're suing for parley and making promises, you lie to me. You say you've only got two guns of ours.

403

All tech belongs to the Peacemaker, Rampart Fire. So anything you're holding – including the piece you say you took your name from – you took by thieving and you keep by tricks and treachery. It's not two guns we'll go home with, but every last piece of tech you got in your treasury and in your armoury. And we'll leave your village burning behind us when we go, with every Jill and Jack of you dead. That's what my master bid me do, and Dandrake forbid I disappoint him."

I was sick in my heart when I heard these words, and I think everyone listening must have been struck the same way. But Catrin only shrugged her shoulders. "Do you mean that though? Sometimes we'll say a foolish thing in the hot moment and be sorry after. I'd ask you to think a while – and then a while longer maybe. Is your heart in what you said, and do you swear it for truth in front of your people and mine, that you mean to fight until there's no one left to stand against you, or until the last of your soldiers falls in the striving?"

"I swear it for truth. In front of my people and yours. You can't imagine, Rampart Fire, the pain and penance that's about to be laid on you. As much as Temenstow is the tale that's told of Half-Ax's fury now, people will for

get Temenstow after this and talk only about Mythen Rood. You'll die a piece at a time, until there's nothing of you left. And then we'll sow your ground with salt, so nobody will ever build again in this place. That's what you got to look forward to now."

"Okay then," Catrin said. "I guess you did mean it."

"Oh yes."

"I'd like to swear to something too though, since swearing's what we're about. I swear, Berrobis Someone's Cousin, that I'll do whatever's needful to be done to keep my people safe from this rat-nest rabble you brought here. And when the time comes, you'll find Half-Ax is a long way to limp back home to. I mean your soldiers will find that out. You your own self, you won't be going home. Because I'll hunt you out when mine meet yours, and I'll not leave you hale nor whole. You'll be chewed, and being

404

too bitter to swallow you'll be spit out again. Orts and fragments you'll be, on this ground, and I'll leave you to lie until the needles eat the meat of you and the sun bleaches your bones."

She said all this in a calm and level voice, like she was talking about how the potatoes in first field were showing this week. She took a deep, slow breath and let it out again. Berrobis stared at her in solemn puzzlement, as if she was looking at a dog that had learned how to dance.

"That offer I spoke of," Catrin said, "it's still there if you want it. Peace is there if you want it. I don't ever say, as you said, that the future's set. You just got to decide what future you want and who gets to be there when it comes. For all our sakes, you better see some sense and choose right. Otherwise there's none under Heaven can save you."

There was wonder on every face I could see. The Half-Ax soldiers, that had stood there until then looking straight out in front of them like they were carved out of wood, were now staring open-mouthed at Catrin. Even Berrobis couldn't keep her surprise from showing. I saw her struggle with it, and then with the anger that came after it. No doubt the soldiers saw it too, and no doubt they were wondering what storm would follow. But that was the cleverness of it. Berrobis couldn't show that anger without being lessened by it, for it would mean this woman she had been talking to like a mother to a child had scratched her under her skin.

She took her time with what she did next. She undid the buckle of her sword's sheath and slid it down from off her back. Holding it in her two hands, she offered it to Catrin to take. I hadn't seen until then what a beautiful thing the sheath was. It was embroidery work, mostly gold but with all the other colours you could think of threaded through it in curving lines that went over and through each other like ripples on water. "This is the best steel ever beat out on a forge," Berrobis said, "whether in Half-Ax or anywhere else. Take it."

Catrin's hands stayed at her sides. "Tell me what it means first."

"It's a challenge. I give you this, and you give me what's on

405

you that's best and richest. We'll meet in this fight, late or soon, and one of us will take back what they gave from the other's bled-out body. Until that's done, the fight's not over."

Even then, Catrin didn't take the sword. Not straightway. "When we of Mythen Rood offer challenge," she said, "we offer blood. Show me an inch of that steel, unless you're shy of it."

The general drew the sword a little way, keeping one hand on the hilt and the other on the steel guard at the open end of the sheath. Catrin put her own hand into that narrow gap and ran her thumb down the bare edge of the blade.

"Now you."

Berrobis touched the same place, that was wet now with Catrin's blood, and broke her own skin there. She let go of the blade and it sank back into the sheath of its own weight.

Catrin took the sword. Over her head, over all our heads, a quick flight of yellowhats went by, turning rings around each other until they went in among the nearer trees and were lost to sight.

Catrin turned the sword so the hilt was facing the general. "I didn't bring anything out here with me except the clothes I'm standing in," she said. "You take the sword and I'll take the furnishings. When we meet, the two can come together again. How would that be?"

"I accept it," Berrobis said. She put her hand on the hilt and drew the sword out. "Until then."

"Until then." Catrin buckled the empty sheath onto her belt. She took her time doing it. Then the two women bowed their heads, each to other, and went their ways. The gates opened and took Catrin in as Berrobis and her honour guard crossed the half-outside and disappeared back into the trees.

As soon as the gates closed again, Catrin unbuckled the sheath and let it fall to the ground.

"What was that?" Fer shouted down. "It wasn't what we agreed. It was like you was only trying to put her in a worse rage than ever."

"Let her rage," Catrin said. She kicked the sheath away from her as if it was something hateful and she couldn't abide the look of it. "I'd rather have her hot than cold, as far as that goes. And I said what came into my head. I seen what she was, the kind that thinks a fair word covers a foul deed, and wraps herself in her own honour like a fucking cloak. The only thing that mattered was to keep her talking there until I seen them birds go by."

59

The birds were the signal we'd agreed on.

While Catrin and Berrobis swapped all those insults, threats and challenges, the Half-Ax column stayed where it was and waited on orders. The gap between the two ends of it, the one coming round from the north and the other from the south, was about four hundred strides or so. And four hundred strides was wide enough.

Jon had drawn near the fence, and seen the enemy coming around it on both hands. Then he saw them stop, wonder of wonders, just before they barred his way for good and all. One by one, he sent his people running out of the woods across the bare, narrow strip of the half-outside. One by one, they clambered up the grass-grail and over the fence to safety. The sky stayed grey and the light was poor. Nobody saw them go.

Jon came last of all and dropped down inside the fence to be clasped and held by the other six. Torri Hammer, who had been standing on the coping of the well, waved a bright red scarf to pass the word along to Lune Cooper at the corner of the Span, who waved to Cal Paint on the gather-ground.

And Mull Woodsmith, standing up on the roof of Rampart

Hold, slipped the catch on one of her bird boxes, shooing the yellowhats out with clicks of her tongue and flutterings of her fingers so they winged their way over Catrin's head and told her it was done.

If Mythen Rood was turned into a sheep pen, then all the flock was safely home.

60

With the Half-Ax circle now closed, we waited to be attacked. Berrobis Bradeshin's anger made it seem impossible that she would delay in giving the order. But hours went by and no attack came.

We had done the best we could to make ourselves ready. There were guards on every part of the fence, and a reserve force on the gather-ground that could be sent inside of a minute to any place where Half-Ax made a sally. The guards and the reserves between them made up almost half the village, and it took twenty more besides to keep them fed and watered and send runners between them to make sure all was well.

So the news about what Rampart Knife had found came out in inches and ounces. Jon should have said it to all at once in the Count and Seal, but there was no Count and Seal. We gathered all we could in the big round chamber anyway. This was a thing that needed to be told betimes. And when the tale was done, them that were there went their separate ways and told it to them they met. So it spread piecemeal through the village until the word was on every tongue and the thought in every mind.

You must forgive me. I've heard this story too many times now to keep every detail singular and straight in my mind. The terror and the pity of it strikes me fresh whenever I think on it, but for the rest it's all tied and tangled with what I knew and didn't know, what I believed first off and what I didn't find till after. Besides, it's a thing that's grown in story so big that you can't see past the telling to the truth of it. Maybe there is no truth in such cases. Everyone remembers it differently because they lived it differently. The only thing we've got in common is the world that wakes when all is done, when the blood is shed and the sorrows sung. I mean the world we live in now, which is not the same as the one we had then.

They went west, Jon told us all. Not walking but running, with knives ready in their hands and spears on their backs. They blessed the thick bank of cloud that drifted out of the west to meet them, since it meant they didn't have to stop when full daylight came. Rain would have slowed them, but clouds that didn't break were the best they could have hoped for.

By the time they stopped to eat, they had already reached the hill called Dog Neck. Its bare side, scoured by the wind, gave them a place to rest that was safe from trees and from most beasts besides, but it was bitter cold and they didn't linger there for long.

Through the afternoon, they ran on, taking the danger that came with moving so quick. It was not that they pushed themselves past bearing – it was an easy pace they could keep up for hours – but they weren't breaking the rhythm of their steps as our hunters and catchers were used to do. Anything that hunted by the sounds their prey made or by the shaking of the ground would feel them as they passed. They were trusting to their speed to take them away from danger or their weapons to take them through it.

It worked well enough, that first day. Nothing found their trail, or at least nothing stayed on it long enough to vex them. They camped for the night in one of our houses of haven, built out of stone long since in another high place called Flintchild. The meaning of that name is in a story about a foolish boy that filched a fairy's gold and was turned to stone for it. The rock at the top of the crag is meant to be what's left of the boy. I wonder if any of Jon's seven thought of the thief Koli Woodsmith when they looked at that rock. If it felt like a bad omen hanging over them.

The second day was harder going. The weather favoured them for the most part, but they had some bad moments when the sun broke through the clouds and caught them in the deep woods. One time they fled the waked trees into a clearing, and then discovered that the bright red flowers all around them were not flowers at all but bale-beetles crouched to jump. They did what you're supposed to do on such occasions, which was to fling their packs a long way away so the bugs would see the movement and jump on the packs instead of on them, but still they took some bad bites to their arms and shoulders. They had to stand there with the beetles feeding on their flesh, still as statues in case by moving they turned the dozens that were afflicting them into thousands. Only when the clouds hid the sun again could they finally retreat and pick the gorged insects off their swollen-up arms.

A little further on, they walked into something worse than that by a hundred times. Tree-cats and needles came at them, running together in one pack along with some of the unlisted that were like wild pigs except that they were much bigger and had tusks sprouting out of every part of their body instead of just their faces.

That would probably have been where the journey ended, Jon said, if these beasts were hungry and hunting. But the herd didn't stop or even slow as they run by. All Rampart Knife needed to do was to choose a rock and hug it close to keep from being trampled. The beasts were fleeing from something in the west.

Late in the afternoon of the second day, they knew they were close to that something. There was a strange smell in the air, bitter and harsh, of things already burned and things still burning. Shortly after that there was smoke that settled in their throats and prickled there. The wind being still from the west, they knew that the smell and the smoke were messengers running ahead of the thing they were sent to seek out.

And then came the sound. Faint at first, coming and going as the wind shifted. A sound of metal grinding on stone, a deep growl like a bear or something bigger than a bear, and the boom of hammers falling on the biggest anvil in the world.

They stopped and argued it. I can see them in my mind, so brave in the face of what they didn't know and couldn't imagine. A tiny Count and Seal in the middle of all that wildness. "We shouldn't all go," Jon said. "We don't know what it's going to be, and if all of us is whelmed at once then we got no chance of taking the word back."

"But if all that go in is whelmed, we'd only have to send more," Athen Woodsmith said. "Best we stay together. If anything comes at us, some can go and some stay back to fight. That gives us the best chance."

They chewed on it some little while, and then they voted. Athen's idea carried it by five voices to two, so on they went.

The noise got louder and louder. It didn't seem to be in front of them any more but all around them, so loud it was like they were being pushed and jostled by a great crowd of people they couldn't see. They almost felt like it was a solid thing they were pushing their way through. The smoke was thicker too, and the stink of it stronger. The world seemed to be on fire, all but their little part of it. From over a hill in front of them, they heard voices. Some were shouting, some singing. Someone laughed, which was the strangest thing of all.

They looked each to other. They were come to it now, and they found they were reluctant to go forward. There was too much of fear and too much of hope wrapped up in this.

"I'll go first," Jon said. He didn't even have to whisper. The hammering and grinding sounds and the gathered voices were so loud, the problem was in being heard over them. "I'll just take one look, then come back. If I'm shot at or grabbed hold of, you'll know to come round a different way. Or you may get to see what shoots or grabs me."

"We're Rampart Knife," Veso Shepherd said. "We decided this, Jon. We'll go together and give them a harder choice."

Which is what they did. Spread out in a line, ten paces apart, sharing the risk between them the same way they'd shared everything else along the way. Like the danger was the last bit of bread in their pack and all had got to take a bite of it.

They topped the rise. They looked down. They saw.

This was where the story faltered. The way Jon told it, they didn't know at first what they were seeing. There was too much of it. The hill they were on fell more steeply on the other side into a kind of gully fifty or sixty paces wide that might once have had a river running through it. The smoke filled the gully and brimmed over the top of the rise, almost like it was the ghost of that river. Things moved inside it, and bigger things towered over it.

"They was like beasts made out of metal," Jon said.

"They was somewhat like Challenger," said Athen Woodsmith. "If Challenger had teeth."

"They was like Dandrake's chariot," was Veso Shepherd's opinion.

Outside of that, they didn't agree on much. There were arms and necks and heads, teeth and tentacles, claws and scales. But also there were wheels and windows, pipes and pulleys. These were monsters made out of tech, as if the Dandrake had told the dead to rise up and the dead had come all together in one mass, with the tools they'd used in life – the picks and the shovels and the hammers – welded onto them.

Rampart Knife sorrowed as they told us this, for they knew they couldn't make us see what they'd seen and they despaired of making us understand. You just got to believe it was terrible, they said. More terrible than what you're thinking of now as you try to draw these things inside your minds. You can't. You'll never know it except by seeing it your own selves.

Scores of people, they said, followed behind this dreadful caravan; scores, or maybe hundreds. Jon saw women and men, young and old. There were even children there. "We thought at first they was prisoners, but they didn't have no chains or ropes on them and they run to keep up if they was falling behind. They wasn't a red tally, for there was few weapons among them apart from knives, and the knives was not in their hands but in their belts. The best we could guess was that they come from the same village as the great wagons and had come to cheer them on into the fight. For it was a fight they was gathered for. You couldn't look at them and doubt that. Every one of them wagons was made to tear down or break apart or trample flat whatever come in front of them. But we still didn't know who that might be, and we was hopeful it was Half-Ax. Maybe the Peacemaker had tried that trick of saying all tech was his own once too often, and the people of the west had decided to set him in his right place again.

"We almost went down to them. We was screwing up our courage to it. But then we seen the worst thing of all, and we turned straightway and run back out of there.

"Most of the wagons seemed to be driving their own selves, but the biggest one of all had riders in it. There was three of them. One was a girl we never seen before. One was Ursala-from-Elsewhere."

Jon's voice had gone hoarse and faint as he was speaking. It was not to be wondered at. He had run for four days straight, and besides that he had swallowed a great deal of that smoke they told us of. He said he could still taste it in his mouth. All of them could. He tailed off into silence now, like he had run out of breath or else that sour taste had got too much for him.

"The third was my brother," Athen Woodsmith said. "My brother Koli." She gave the name a hard edge, and she grimaced. Tears stood in her eyes, but they stayed there and didn't fall.

"Koli Faceless is coming home," Jon said into the dead, scared silence. "And seeing what he's bringing with him, I don't think he's coming as a friend."

Koli

61

After Arkom, we set out again eastwards. We picked a day of heavy overcast, though trees didn't trouble us so much when we was riding in the crawler. Forests broke on us, like waves of the sea break on rocks.

The people of Arkom was sad to see us go. They gathered at their gates to see us off, and hugged and cheered us. Some of the children waved the wooden toys I'd made for them, and many of them that Ursala had healed brung her gifts of food and cloth and jewellery. She was not happy to get so much attention, but she took the gifts with as good grace as she could and even tried to smile. Cup come away with a gift too, which was a bow and a quiver of arrows. She said she was a great deal happier knowing she could give answer if we was attacked.

There was more cheering as the great engines started to growl and rumble, and then again as they got moving. Of course we moved so slow we was in sight of the gates for a long while after, but still there was a mood of Summer-dance. Even after the side of a hill finally hid us from sight, people kept coming by to wave at us again and to sniff the wet asphel. It was a smell people loved and hated at the same time. If you kept on breathing it in, you got dizzy as if you'd been drinking beer or cider.

We got back into our stride and kept up the same pace as before, a mile or most of a mile every day. It was a life we was getting used to, for all its strangeness; a life spent moving forward a little at a time and never stopping. Even at night, the wagons rolled on with only Monono staying awake to guide and watch over them. The rest of us slept in the glass house up on top of the crawler that Monono called a cab, although oftentimes Cup slept up on the roof where there was more room, trusting to Monono to watch over her and to warn her if anything hurtful should come.

It should have been a good time. The things we'd wished for were starting to happen, after a time when it seemed like we'd been fighting ever and again just to stay alive and in the world. News of our coming was still riding ahead of us, and we was welcomed in each village when we come to it. People had heard about the road now and they was longing to see it. They brung us food to eat and water to drink so we didn't want for nothing at all.

But there's always a few flies in the soup. Ever and again, when I was tired or when my thoughts wandered, Stannabanna come back into my mind like a rat creeping through a hole in the kitchen wall. I would remember something that had happened to me, and then I would realise of a sudden that it hadn't happened to me at all, but to him. I never stood on the big platform in Trafalgar's square and told the people of Ingland that they was meant to show the rest of the world how to live. I never loved a woman named Talisa, nor I never stood by when she was arrested for something called sedition and then when she was hanged on one of London's many, many gather-grounds. I never made great piles of them strange things called books and set fire to them, so the voices of people that was already dead would die all over again.

But I smelled the stink and I felt the sickness of all them things as if they was a stink and a sickness that was soaked deep into me. I waked at night sometimes, whimpering in the dark with his fears and my own all tucked and tangled each in other until I almost forgot who I was.

I asked Monono if there was anything that could be done to fix this. I had only had the sensorium on my head for a few minutes. Couldn't the things that had been put inside me in that time be took out again and throwed away somewhere?

"It's not that easy, Koli," Monono told me as gently as she could with the drone's rasping voice. "Even if I had the right tools for the job, I wouldn't want to mess with your little noodle more than it's already been messed with."

"I know you'd be careful though," I said.

"Well, I'd do my best. But honestly? I only just got through doing this stuff with my own mind, and I almost upset the whole apple cart. I'm not in a hurry to go again. Listen, there used to be a game, back in Monono one-point-zero's day, called Jenga. You made a tower out of little pieces of wood. Then you took turns to take away a piece from the middle of the tower and put it back on at the top. The trick was to do it without making the tower fall down. Only with each piece you moved it wobbled more and more. I'd be playing that game with your living brain, Koli-bou. If you've got your heart set on this then I'll do it, but I wish you wouldn't ask me."

Well, after that I didn't feel like I could make her do it. I just had got to put up with the strange rememberings, and with feeling like some of the time there was someone else standing behind my eyes and looking out of them. It was not a good feeling, but I guess I got used to it. When the Stannabanna thoughts come, I pushed them away again with thoughts of Mythen Rood. My home, where I had spent the biggest part of my life. Stannabanna had only ever stood on that ground once, after he burned and bombed and broke what was there before. Thinking on that difference was a good way of paring away his mind from my own.

But I still was not in good sorts even with my own self. I was fretful and unhappy, and even somewhat afraid, though I could not of said what it was that was troubling me. Only that I was come round in a big circle to where I first begun. We're wont to say a blessing when we close a circle to ward off any bad luck we've trapped inside it, but I misremembered the words.

Spinner

62

For the first day and the first night, we still thought Berrobis meant to throw her soldiers against the fence and swarm on us like needles.

For much of the second day, as we relieved the watchers on the platforms a few at a time so they could take a few hours' sleep, we couldn't believe our luck that Half-Ax had waited so long. Maybe they were afraid, after Catrin's speech about their bones all bleaching, that we were stronger than we seemed. Maybe Berrobis had tried to get them to attack and they had defied her.

But in Challenger's mirror the Half-Ax forces stayed exactly where they were. One or two of the red dots moved around a little, but not away from the circle and not inward to attack us. Just betwixt and between.

"Can you tell which one is Berrobis?" I asked Challenger.

"Yes. When Catrin met her at the gate I got a solid lock on the bracelets she wears. They have a very distinctive field signature. I've followed her since, and I hold her current position in active memory. Shall I designate her with a different colour?"

"Please."

One of the red dots went to white. Berrobis was up on the

hill behind the broken house – the best place for seeing the whole of the village at one time.

"Why doesn't she give the order?" I wondered aloud. "She must see how weak we are. She could end this with a single charge."

"She sees how weak you are in numbers. She does not know what other resources you have. I believe she has decided on a siege."

"Hey," Elaine said.

"Sergeant Sandberg and I believe she has decided on a siege."

I asked them what a siege was. Between the two of them, they told me a great deal more than I needed to know – about battles long since, in many different wars, where one tally had trapped another inside a village or a great house called a castle, and instead of fighting them had only stopped up every way in or out and kept them there until they had got to give in or else starve to death. It was a good trick if you had the numbers and the weapons to do it. It had worked well in many places, and Challenger told me the names of some of them. Masada. Amida. Santiago. Port Arthur. Gijon. Budapest. There were more – a lot more – but those are the names that have stayed with me.

"There's only three ways it can go really," Elaine said. "One: the besieged people surrender. They've run out of food maybe, or medical supplies, or ammo, and they can see they've got no cards left to play. Two: the besiegers reach a point where they think the siege has done its work and the enemy is too weak to fight back – so they attack."

"What's three?"

"The big picture changes. They get new orders, give it up and go away."

"Sieges are expensive," Challenger said. "And complicated. Any army on the move has either to live off the land or to maintain a line of supply. In this terrain, the second option is very difficult indeed. The first sunny day would see all conceivable supply lines broken. It's more likely that your enemies are foraging for food."

Stripping Calder bare, I thought. Trapping every bird and beast

426

between here and the river, or maybe even further. Yes, it would be hard. But however they fared, I couldn't imagine Berrobis would abandon her mission. If she was brought to a choice and had to give up the siege, she would order an attack before she ever dreamed of going home empty-handed.

We had got to think up some plan our own selves before it came to that. We only had days before Koli's war engines rolled over the top of Dog Neck and into plain sight. There wouldn't be any hope for us then. Trapped inside the fence by Berrobis's army, we couldn't do anything but watch as Koli's tech closed on us and whelmed us.

The hard place favours hard thought, Dandrake said; the hardest place no thought at all. Before we ran out of time and out of space, we had got to decide.

We met in Count and Seal. How, you ask, when so many of us were up on the fence and couldn't move from their places? The answer was a strange one. We used what we had, and turned our troubles to advantage.

All them that were free went out into the gather-ground. A few of us stayed there; the rest spread out in different directions, making lines. We had enough, just about, that the lines could go all the way from the open ground to the fence. The ones at the fence spread out a little further so everyone that was up on the platforms could see at least one that was standing on the ground.

Catrin spoke first, setting out all we knew and all we thought we knew. People on the gather-ground that were near enough to hear her spoke too – but they spoke with their hands in Franker signs, not with their mouths. Those further away who couldn't make out the words could still see the signs and copy them, and so Catrin's speech was carried to each and all.

Then we waited, while words came back along the same chains. This was not well ordered by any means. At the fence, it depended on who signed quickest and made the biggest pantomime out of it. On the gather-ground, it depended on who we saw first. But we tried our best to make sure everyone who had something to say was heard.

427

This all sounds very fine and very fair, doesn't it? A striving to give all the women and men of Mythen Rood, and even the boldest of the children, an equal place in the deciding. If you think that, set the thought aside. We Ramparts had met before in the Hold's kitchen, where by the light of a single candle we counted the meagre store of choices that were left to us.

If we fought, we would die. We couldn't prevail against Berrobis's tally, but in any case win or lose would not make much difference. Mythen Rood was its people, and we were barely getting by as we were. With even twenty or thirty dead, we would not get by but go under – and there was scant hope our losses would be as small as that.

If we opened the gates and begged the Peacemaker's pardon, we were lost. Berrobis had told us in solemn truth no pardon was to be had. We would only make her task easier for her and send the Half-Ax army home the sooner with our tech in their packs and our blood on their boots.

If we waited out the siege, the only thing in doubt was who would kill us first. Half-Ax was closest, but when they saw Koli's wagons coming they might leave the field to him. Either way, that was one argument we wouldn't get a voice in. Maybe they would share us out between the two of them.

"I don't see what that leaves," Jon said. He shrugged with his shoulders as he said it. It might have been a wider shrug except that he was cradling Vallen in the crook of his arm. Since he came back out of the west, he had found it hard to let go of either one of us, but especially our baby. I think he was reminding himself that he was still alive, and Vallen more than anything was what life meant. This wasn't something he had told me; it was just a thing I knew. I knew it because I felt the same way.

"It doesn't leave anything," Fer said.

"Is it worth trying to strike a bargain?" Jemiu asked.

"With Half-Ax?"

"With Koli." Jemiu looked from face to face. "He may want to venge himself on the Ramparts – and I know I speak as one

428

now – but he doesn't hate Mythen Rood. He doesn't hate his home. If he knows what we're facing, he may agree to help us."

"And hang me and Catrin on the gather-ground," Fer said tightly. "And vaunt himself over us like a king. I'd rather die fighting."

Catrin scowled. "It's not just our deaths that's in the weighing pan here. Jemiu, what Jon saw was an army. An army with engines of war we never seen before. Things like Challenger, only bigger and worse. Does that speak of a private venging or does it speak of something bigger?"

Jemiu shook her head. "I wish I could tell," she said in a cracked voice. "You all know my son, what he was like. He never had no harm in him. Too much softness was his problem. I can't believe he'd give himself to the spilling of anyone's blood, let alone ours."

"Your son killed my son," Fer said. "Mardew died alone, far from home, and Koli didn't even stay to bury him."

"Koli's got reason to hate us," Catrin said heavily. Fer made to speak again, but she was not given space to. "He's got reason to feel he was treated badly, and to want to give answer for it. How far that answer might go, we got no way of guessing. When you've put a red tally together – or an army, as the Half-Ax word is – and you've once set it moving, you're not in all ways able to say what it will do and what it won't do. Things take their course. People in a fight of that kind do what comes into their heads to do, and afterwards they're mazed to see they did it. Whatever Koli might want, or not want, we can't trust to his mildness to stand between us and ruin."

She slumped back in her chair, her eyes like bruises in her pale face. I doubt she'd seen a bed since before Rampart Knife came home. "I think we got a choice left to us. One choice. Try as I might, I don't see more than that."

"We got to run away," I said.

Catrin nodded. "That's what I was thinking, yes. We're in a trap, and if we mean to live we've got to slip out of it."

"But . . ." Jon looked from his mother to me and back again with wilderment and dismay in his face. "We can't. We got nothing if we leave Mythen Rood. Even if we could get through the Half-Ax lines, we'd be . . ." He reached for a word and didn't find one.

"We'd be helpless," Fer said. "Like animals. Prey to every bird and beast and tree that got a sniff of us. All you said before, Cat, about the fence being our best protection, did you forget it now? We're dead if we open those gates."

"What I said before doesn't stop being true, Fer. But the one thing we got over Berrobis is that she's got five hundred to move, with all their stores and baggage. We can hope to run faster than they can follow."

"She doesn't have to move her five hundred though," Jemiu said. "She can task some to follow – the quickest she's got, or with tech that can track us like Challenger is tracking them. And where would we run to? Where is there a haven that will take us?"

In following that thought, I ran headfirst into a different one. Jemiu was right: there was no haven. We were stuck between the grate and the griddle, with enemies every way we turned. I thought of what Challenger had told me that one time about emergent events.

Out of the chaos, patterns will appear and coalesce. Out of a million tiny, passing things, some will not pass but will stay and become pivotal. Other things will hinge on them, and bend their courses.

Koli Woodsmith was surely an emergent event. And probably one that Half-Ax didn't know about yet.

"I'll fight before I run, Cat," Fer was saying. "Running sits ill with me. If Half-Ax is going to swallow us, let's stick in their throats as much as we can."

"I got an idea," I said. "I think I do."

Fer shot me a glare. "I was talking to my sister."

Catrin gave her back that sharpness, and more besides. "You're talking to all of us. I got no more voice at this table than the rest of you do. Sweet fuck, Fer, it's gone past the point where Vennastins get to tell the sun what face to wear. We're all together in this now." She turned to me. "What's your thought, Spinner?"

"My thought's this. We shouldn't trouble ourselves to look for a haven, because we're not like to find one. We break through the Half-Ax circle, but we pick a time when it's easy for them to follow. Not night. Maybe not full day either. Just before sun-up, say."

Jon shook his head. "Yeah, but then they'll come right after us."

"That they will."

"And kill us as we run," said Jemiu. "Starting with the slowest. The children. The old."

"The children and the old won't be with us." I carried on over their startled looks. "There are rooms behind the Count and Seal. Hidden rooms. Catrin will bear me out. Any that don't come with us will wait there."

"For what?" Fer demanded. "For Dandrake to come down and blow the last horn?"

"For our return. My plan is that we don't go far, or stay away for long. We break out like I said – a big tally, with all our best fighters and enough besides so it looks like it's all of us. Berrobis will give chase. She's bound to. If nothing else, she believes she's got business still in hand with Rampart Fire. A sword and a sheath was in it."

"Where would we go, Spin?" Jon asked.

"Why, we'd go west, the same way Rampart Knife went." I covered his hand with mine. "Jon, there's a steep slope that leads down to the river there, you said?"

"Yeah, there is. It's not always straight west, but it mostly tends that way."

"That should give us some cover from arrows and bolts. And we won't let them get close enough to task us with swords and spears."

"And what's at the end of this run?" Catrin asked.

"Koli Woodsmith is at the end of it. But we know that and Berrobis doesn't. Her people will run right up against his."

"With us in the middle."

431

"With us getting out of the way of it as quick as we can. If Koli sees the Peacemaker's army in grey and red all bearing down on him, he's not going to care about a few people that are stepping off to the side. He's going to push back hard against the bigger threat. And then the grate and the griddle can sort it out between them which is hottest."

They were struck different ways by the idea. I thought Fer would be the hardest to convince, but I was wrong. There was an anger that was strong in her, and my plan spoke loud to that anger. She would dearly have loved to tear the Half-Ax ranks in pieces her own self. To see them torn by others was the nearest thing.

Catrin and Jemiu worried the plan this way and that, but they didn't throw it out of gates all at once. They were just looking at all the many holes that were in it, and thinking how they could be stopped up.

It was left to Jon to argue why we couldn't do it. "Even if everything fell out the way you want it to, and Koli and Berrobis tear into each other like Dandrake and Stannabanna going at it in Hell's holt, there'll still be a winner in that fight. And there we'll be, caught out in the open, with the winner looking our way and finding us ready to hand. What do we do then?"

There was a moment's silence. I was hoping someone else would say it, but in any case it had got to be said.

"We kill them," I said. I was answering Jon's question, but it was Jemiu I was looking at. "Whoever wins, we take our best chance, which is to throw ourselves on them while they're weak and hurting. We kill them or else we're killed by them. And either way, that's an end of it."

Jemiu shut her eyes tight and said nothing. I put my hand on her arm, but she pulled it away.

"Or Koli might forbear," I said. "And sue for peace." But I don't think she believed that and certainly nobody else at the table did. We were come to hard choices and mercy was a thing forgot. It was like we had got to choose between that and hope, and we went with such hope as we had.

They all had doubts still. I had some myself, for that matter. We shared them, each with other. Jon was hard to budge at first, but he came around at last to my thinking and offered some ideas of his own – mostly about what we should do with them that couldn't run to start with. If we started with the bare bones of a plan, there was some meat on those bones before we rose up from the table.

"It's a big risk though," Jon said. "We'll only get the one chance, and if it don't work we'll lose everything we got."

"If it don't work, Jon, we won't be there to count what we lost."

So you see, the Count and Seal we held in dumb show on the gather-ground was not what it seemed. We had already decided before then what had got to be done. We only played out the same talk at a bigger table, and waited for everyone to decide one by one where they stood.

When it was voted, we took the count three times and got three different answers. We carried it in the end though, and we had enough volunteers to make up our muster. "Any and all of you can still change your minds," Catrin said, and the signers picked up her words and carried them all around. "When the time comes, you'll do what's in you to do, whether it's to stay or go. Nobody will say you lied or you're forswore. Nobody will blame you."

One of those who voted against us was Jarter Shepherd. That was a blow, for she was ever one of our best fighters and I thought she would be first to give us her voice. Instead she told me in forceful words that I was mad to take this course. "It's like you looked at how bad everything already is and decided to make it worse," she said. "This ain't even a plan, Rampart. A plan's got some chance of good success. This is throwing yourself off a rooftop in hope the ground will move out of your way.

"Nobody has to go if they want to stay, Jarter," I said. "The danger's great either way. You got to make up your own mind."

She huffed out a breath that had more anger than air in it. "It's

433

not the danger I mind, it's the hazarding all on one throw. If we wait these bastards out, they may tire before we do. If we show them our arses, what are they like to do but take a kick? No, I made my choice already. I'll stay here and fight on my own ground."

"We'll be sorry to lose you then."

"And I'll be sorry to see you go. I'll watch over your Vallen, you got my word on that. If you don't come back, I'll raise her with my own."

She meant it well, but I shook my head. "That's the one gift I won't take from you, Jarter. Veso's my friend, and every time I look at him I see the scars he bears because you wouldn't see him as he was."

Jarter looked as if I'd struck her. "That's old history," she said.

"You think it's old enough that it's forgot? You should ask Veso."

She cut her hand across the space between us, like she was pushing something away. "This is a bad time to pick a fight with me. I said I'd stay and guard Vallen, and I mean to do it. I owe you that for bringing me alive out of Calder ford. I don't owe you no apologies though, and I won't offer none. If you got any other words to say to me, I guess they'll bide our better leisure."

"I guess they will. Dead god speed you, Jarter."

"It's Dandrake I pray to. And it's his judgement I'll answer."

So that just left the when and the where. Catrin settled both of those without bothering to call a vote. "Tonight's dark of the moon, so we might as well go then. Every hour we stay only makes us weaker and more afraid.

"We'll sound the tocsin bell for the changing of the lookouts an hour before sun-up, like we always do – but this time it will be a signal to all. If you're leaving, meet at the well. If you're staying, go to the Hold. The door will be unlocked and Ban Fisher will show you what to do from there.

"Maybe you got goodbyes, or prayers, or other things that seem needful to be said. Best say them now, for there won't be any time after."

Koli

63

We went east, and we didn't stop again. We et forest and spit out road. And the closer we got to Mythen Rood, the more Ursala's question dragged on my heart.

I don't think anyone knows their own selves as well as they think they do. We try hard, always, to think we're better than we are. If we do something cruel or stupid or vengeful, we put it down to chance or give ourselves excuses for the doing of it. We never can admit to cruel or stupid or vengeful just being what we are.

I reasoned it this way and that way. To every village we passed, we brung the road, and the road was a great good. Of course I wanted Mythen Rood to have that blessing. It was impossible that I would ever think of leaving it out.

But I was bringing something else to Mythen Rood besides the road – a hard truth that might be every bit as bad as the road was good. I was like a man that puts both his hands behind his back and bids you choose. In my one hand, I had a sugar loaf, and in the other a choker seed.

What would happen if I told everyone that Vennastins was lying to keep all the village's tech in their own hands? Was it best left hid? I was not blameless in this. I only found out what I did because I broke into the Hold and come away with the DreamSleeve. Did the Vennastins' lies mean that my stealing could be forgot? And what about my killing Mardew?

When I had gone round the inside of my own head so many times I was too dizzy to see straight, I went at last to Monono and told it all to her. She heard me out, then just asked the one question. "What's worrying you most, little dumpling? Going in like a bull in a china shop and wrecking the place, or just having to look everyone in the face again after the way you left?"

I thought long and hard before I answered. Both of them things was weighing on me, and I couldn't really tell which one weighed the heaviest. But I seen how each one was rubbing against the other and making it worse. I was going to roll up to the gates of Mythen Rood with my great caravan of tech and all the people that was coming on behind us, and what was I going to say? "You sent me out faceless, but now here I am again. And I run off with your tech and I killed your Rampart but it's not me that's to blame, it's everyone else. You been cheated and lied to and there isn't nobody you can trust. Bye you now, for I got this road to build."

"I think I got to go ahead of the wagons," I said, "and find some way of talking to them first. Talking to my family at least, and maybe to Haijon and Spinner. I'm thinking this isn't my secret to keep or tell any more. I'm not meaning to stay long because I got to make sure the road gets finished, but . . . but I need to . . ." I stopped talking there. My throat had somewhat closed up, and tears was welling in my eyes. I seen their faces in my mind, all of them, and I ached so much to go home it was like there was a lump of jagged stone inside my stomach.

"What would you tell them?" Monono asked.

I thought of what Catrin said to me on the night I left. *The things you figured out would have everyone shouting and accusing and laying into each other. All we got of order, right and calm would go straight over the fence and into the shitheap. How long do you think we'd last*

after that? How long would the gates stay shut and the forest stay out?
I don't mean to see Mythen Rood come apart on account of you.

I told her she was just trying to keep hold of the power and riches that come with being a Rampart, but I knowed that wasn't it. Fer might think like that, and maybe Perliu. Mardew certainly did. But Catrin was never one to flinch from anything, whether it was an enemy or a hard truth. And when the Vennastins voted on whether or not to kill me, the three voices that was raised in my favour showed it was not all the one way in Rampart Hold. I had enemies there for certain sure, but I had friends too. Faceless or not, Mythen Rood was my home.

I took a gulp of breath, and then another. "I guess I'd tell them the truth and let them choose what happened next. Whether to call out the Vennastins in the Count and Seal and make them give the tech to everybody in the village – or keep the secret and leave things the way they are so there'd be no contention. No fighting. There's enough things we got to fight as it is."

"That's a lot to lay on the people you love," Monono said.

"It is. I know it. But I think it's needful I let someone in on the secret, Monono. Like I said, if it's not mine to tell, it's not mine to keep either. It won't be me that's got to live with it. This way, after I've gone away again, there'll be someone in Mythen Rood who knows the truth. And more than one, so they can't be exiled like I was. Or gainsaid, or hanged, or whatever it might be. Vennastins won't ever again be able to do that to anyone just to save their own selves."

"Hmmmm." Monono drawed out the sound like she was thinking deep thoughts. "Okay, dopey boy, I get the idea about widening the circle of trust. But there's still a big chunk of countryside between us and Mythen Rood, and a lot of it is forest. Maybe you should draft in some of your congregation to help."

"My what?"

"The people who've taken to following along behind us. We've been picking up a few more from every village we've passed – and I get the feeling that if you asked them to saddle up with you they'd do it like a shot. They've got that look about them. A bunch of Josephs in search of a manger, as Leonard Cohen would say."

"I don't know what that means."

"What, you mean to say you haven't heard them praying and singing hymns?"

Well, I heard them singing often enough, but I didn't know the tunes and they was singing in their own tongues, not in Franker, so I didn't have no idea what the words meant. "Who are they praying to?" I asked.

"Who do you think?"

Even then I was slow to catch her meaning. It was only when I remembered the man that had done a luck-touch on me back at Arkom that I seen it. I sweared an oath. "They're making us into messianics?"

"Well, you or your cement mixers. Actually, it's probably both." Monono laughed. It was a funny sound to hear out of the drone, that always sounded somewhat like a blue-fly buzzing in a bottle. "They've never seen anything like you before, Koli. Praying is a pretty normal response when everything you've known suddenly starts to change. There's no harm in it. And I think you've got a way to go yet before they put up a church to you."

I couldn't see it that way though. All I could think about was Senlas and the hurt he did to them that followed him and lived by him. The way he used their belief as a kind of handle to pick them up and wield them by. "I don't want nobody to believe in me," I said.

"You may not have a choice."

"Well, I don't mean to give no orders to them anyway. I'll go to Mythen Rood on my own."

"It's your call, little dumpling," Monono said.

But there was something in her voice that told me maybe it wasn't.

Spinner

64

We had kept the Half-Ax circle from closing with a trick. We didn't have any trick to open it again, but we did have Challenger's shells. And though he couldn't fire them out of his ruined gun, he said he could do it another way if we fitted them with something called a percussion-with-delay fuze.

To start with, we had to go inside him and take out the shells that had been growing there all this time. "There's an element of risk, sergeant," he said. "In their current configuration the burst charge is impact-triggered. If all my systems were functioning optimally, I'd be confident the shells would withstand an accidental shock. As it is, I can't make that promise with any certainty. If you drop them, or if they knock against each other, they may explode prematurely."

I thanked him for the warning. My hands had been shaking already. Now they were shaking and sweating both. The only comfort I had was that if the shells exploded I wouldn't know anything about it. I'd be torn into pieces so small nobody would be able to find them after.

I couldn't help but think of a birth as I slid the lid of the chamber open and lifted out the shells one by one. They didn't look anything like babies – they were silver bottles as long as my forearm and as heavy as a well cover – but like babies they had been growing in the dark all these months and only now were being brought out into the daylight. And like babies, though they looked harmless when they were sleeping, they were like to make a lot of noise and a lot of mess as soon as they woke up.

We laid them side by side on the gather-ground. Then we took out the fuzes that were in them, using tools that were in Challenger's cockpit. This was the most dangerous part, and I didn't even try to do it my own self. Torri Hammer did it, since her hands were the steadiest and she had a better feel for metal than anyone living. The fuzes were near the top of each shell, where it narrowed. Torri undid the covers that hid them, slid them out very slowly and carefully and replaced them with the ones Challenger said fit in better with our purposing.

"I can trigger the fuzes with a radio signal," Challenger said, "but the signal will activate all the timers at once. The time delay can be different for each shell, but they'll start their counts together. After that, they'll count down to their individual zeros and detonate, wherever they happen to be at the time. It's not ideal, but it's the best I can do."

"Then we'll work with what we got," I said. I was coming to sound more and more like Catrin with every day that passed – and coming to see how much of Catrin was in that sound.

Jarter and Jemiu took the first five shells away one by one as soon as Torri said they were ready and strapped them in their slings on Challenger's flanks. The last one they took straight to the stretch of fence behind the well, where they set it down. It would sit there at the base of the fence until the tocsin bell rang and brought everyone together. Then we would make a start.

But we had a few hours yet before that. I went back to the tannery, where Jon was looking after Vallen. He looked up when I came in and waited for me to tell him what was what.

"We got the shells," I said. "And we made them ready."

"What about you, Spin? Are you ready?"

I went over to him and sat down. I put my arms around the two of them. I don't know what answer I was going to give. As soon as I opened my mouth, I broke into sobs.

Jon held me close while I cried. Then when Vallen joined in too he hugged the both of us.

"I didn't want any of these things to happen," I said, my voice thick with tears. "I want this. I want you."

"I know it," Jon said. "I mind what you said about paying for what we took."

Vallen squawled. I put my hand on her chest that was thrumming with that loud complaint. I did my best to stifle my own tears and bring her back to calmness. "What if we don't come back? What if we leave her here and she never sees us again?"

"Then them that live will tell her what we did, and why we did it. Jarter will tell her. And Ban. She'll know we loved her, and died fighting for her."

We didn't say any more after that, or if we did I misremember it. We just sat, the three of us. I offered Vallen the breast, and though she was still somewhat sullen she took it and calmed. Then she slept, and I leaned on Jon's shoulder, feeling the rise and fall of her breath as she lay between us, the warmth of her tiny, wondrous body.

When Ban came to fetch her, she was still asleep, but she stirred and opened her eyes as soon as I handed her over. She didn't cry though, but went without a murmur. She was as calm as if she knew what was happening and had agreed to go along with it.

Ban wasn't calm at all. Her eyes were wet with tears. "I hate to take her," she said. "Not but I love her. You know I do. I just mean . . . It feels like you're not meaning to come back."

"That's nonsense," I said, hugging her. Hugging the both of them. I had got my own tears out of me and thought I could be strong again, but it was hard to keep my voice from shaking. "We're going for a morning walk, is all. The cool air will do us good. You'll see us back again sooner than you know, Ban. And you'll be glad to see us too, for this one will run you ragged."

"She's good as gold," Ban said, and some of them tears began to fall.

"Ban, I swear to the dead god," I said, pressing my brow against hers, "and any god else that's listening, we'll not fail in this. You'll see us back again before tomorrow's sun goes down."

The clanging of the tocsin bell made us break apart. "We got to go," I said.

"I know. I know. I pray you good fortune, the both of you."

We went with her to the door and watched her go, and for all my brave words I was as close to despairing then as I ever came in my life. I was used to looking in my heart for auguries of what would come, as I did when Jon went to the west. I thought I would know by some sign how he would fare, for good or ill. My heart right then was empty as an upturned barrel, and the future was as dark as the starless sky that hung over us.

We took ourselves away to the fence. The tocsin had only just rung but we weren't the first to come by a long way. Gendel Stepjack and a few others had been there for an hour or more, moving backwards and forwards with lit torches. They were not up on the platforms but on the ground, so the light of the torches would show between the logs of the fence and the Half-Ax soldiers would know that we were up betimes.

The rest of our tally came up in twos and threes to join us. There was a low murmur of voices as they greeted each other. When Athen and Veso came up, quickly followed by the rest of Rampart Knife, Jon took me in his arms and kissed me. "I got to go be with them," he said. "We talk each other into courage."

"It's fine. I got Challenger to do that for me."

Jon humphed and put a face on like he was angry. "I'm jealous of that wagon," he said.

"You should be. He takes me places you never did. And he's really sweet to me."

"I'm sweet to you."

"You're lucky he lost his gun, is all."

We had gone as far as we could with jokes, and we didn't want

446

to cry again or show weakness when there were so many watching. Their spirits depended on ours in some sort, and we had got to keep them high if we could. Jon went to his tally and they hailed each other with hugs and handshakes that were theirs alone. They had been into the wild together, far and wide, and come back whole. It had made them into a family.

I climbed up on Challenger's flank, where I talked with him as if we were checking all the details of our plan. In truth, there wasn't much to check because there wasn't much plan there to start with. Only a hope and a hazel shell, as my father would have said. There was one thing I wanted to know though.

"Where is she?" I asked – meaning the Half-Ax general, Berrobis. We'd chosen this place for our escape partly because it was as far from the hillside where she was camped as we could get, but she was known to come often among her soldiers. In tracking her, we'd seldom seen her stand still for more than a few minutes at a stretch.

"She is close," Challenger said. "But she is moving away from us."

"Tell me if that changes." We wanted the Half-Ax soldiers to see us coming, but we needed them to decide and move quickly when we came, without too much time to think. That was the point of the lit torches – to give them a sense that we were moving there, to make them tense and watchful. But if Berrobis was close by, she would keep good discipline, and that would not do us at all.

I marvelled at my own coldness in thinking and planning these things. The deaths at Calder ford had made me sick and unhappy, and I had carried the distress with me for a long while after. The ambush in the forest had grieved me, but I had hardened my heart much more quickly – as soon as I saw the great smoking hole in the ground just beyond our fence. Now I was thinking how best to bring disaster down on Half-Ax heads, and measuring the success of our plans in Half-Ax dead. The part of me that watched these things and worried at them was dismayed. The rest of me

– and it was most of me – was only too happy to grasp at hate and rage as a way of keeping fear in its place. People are not like tech when you think about it. Our workings are a lot more tangled.

I heard the tocsin ring again, most likely to spur on any stragglers. A few moments later, Catrin and Fer came at last to join us, walking side by side with their name-tech in their hands. They had stayed at the Hold until the last moment. Catrin wanted to bid farewell to those going inside and to let herself be seen by them so they would know they were not forgot. Once they were in the hidden rooms behind the Count and Seal, the doors would be closed on them and they would be left to wait in the dark. We hoped the Half-Ax tally would give chase to us, but if any stayed behind and came into the village after we left, they would find it deserted or at least seeming so. We meant to be back before they realised their mistake.

Catrin knew better than anyone how to give heart to those around her, and she made a great show of it now. "How then, hearts of Calder?" she said. She didn't cry it loud, but her voice carried. "Are we ready to take this fight to them that wished it, and give them more than they wished for?"

We didn't cheer, not wanting to bring the enemy soldiers on the other side of the fence to their crisis too soon, but we threw our clenched fists in the air in salute. Then as Catrin switched to Franker signs, we took our places.

We had agreed that I would ride alone inside Challenger – alone except for Elaine, who would be driving us. Our show of strength and defiance needed to be seen, and the more of us that were outside, the better it would be. Catrin, Fer and Jemiu took their places on the wagon's flanks. Standing so high off the ground they would be easy targets, but everyone in our party would see their Ramparts there and be encouraged. Morrez Ten-Taken and Gendel Stepjack would be there too, carrying the rifle and the scatter-gun.

I had talked long with Morrez about this, and Catrin had talked with him too. Was he ready to go against his own, we wanted to know, and could we trust him to know who was his friends in this fight?

"I'm not like to forget," he told us.

"Still," Catrin said. "I think it might go hard with you. Seeing them grey uniforms you used to wear. Remembering what you was before . . ."

"I said I won't forget, Rampart. Nor it won't be hard at all. Getchen's got our baby inside her. What home I got is here now. I won't see it broke and burned."

So Morrez got to carry the rifle, being the best at using it by a great long way. He took up a place inside the turret, with his feet on the ladder that went down inside and his back braced against the turret's side. He could see in all directions from there, and take aim at enemies a long way off. And Gendel got the heavy burden of being next to him. If Morrez wavered in his loyalty, Gendel was to shoot him with a scatter gun, and probably Morrez knew that as well as anyone did.

We were thirty paces from the fence. Right at our backs stood Rampart Knife drawn up in the shape of an arrowhead. They would break to both sides when we moved, taking their pace from Jon in the middle. The rest of our fighters were ranged behind them in a column that was three deep. Those at the edges had spears, protecting the archers in the middle.

And that was what we had by way of a plan. Well, that and six silver bottles full of Hell's fires and hurtful force.

Waiting on Catrin's signal, I watched the outside of the fence in Challenger's magic mirror. There was a deal of red dots out there, which meant a deal of fighters armed with tech, but the white dot that was Berrobis was a good way off. This was our moment, but I couldn't do anything to hurry it. Once we started, we couldn't stop until we were done. We would be like an arrow loosed out of a bow, that can only go where it's sent. Halfway was nowhere. There would be no choosing.

"Ready," Catrin called down at last into Challenger's turret.

She didn't ask me to give her the count. It would not be

needful. The explosion would put everyone on their mark, and we would count from that.

"Challenger," I said.

"Yes, Sergeant Tanhide."

"Trigger."

The first shell, set to its zero mark, detonated at once. The fence in front of us was swallowed in a great ball of light and fire. Smoke came afterwards, spewing out from the flames as they died and swallowing them up. The noise was last – a grinding roar that made your body ring like a plucked string even as it deafened your ears.

"Forward," I said.

And forward Challenger went, with splintered fenceposts falling round him like rain, through the gap that had opened and into the half-outside. Everyone else stayed put. Their time was not yet.

I don't know what the others was seeing. The smoke was very thick, hiding everything in front of us. I had set the magic mirror in what Challenger called split-screen mode. The upper half showed me what was in front of us, and it was nothing but roiling grey and black. The lower half was the readings from our mast on the roof of Rampart Hold. That showed me the red dots rushing in at once towards us, aiming to shut us in.

We kept on going forward for a few seconds longer before Elaine swung Challenger hard to the left and followed the line of the fence. It was meant to look as if we had hoped to break out but then had lost our courage as the Half-Ax fighters advanced on us.

Twenty paces, thirty, forty. Then we stopped dead, with a wall of grey uniforms running straight at us, and went back the way we had come without even turning. All was moil and noise around us, and nothing was clear. The smoke from the burst shell hung heavy over everything, just as we had hoped it would. We needed that cloak, that confusion.

I was counting out the seconds in my head as we roared back along our own path. I saw a flare of bright orange as Catrin used the firethrower, and heard the spitting crack of the rifle. The rifle boomed ever and again, felling this one and that one, but Jemiu and Fer were not fighting at all. Their time would come later. For now, they were unhitching the leather slings and rolling the heavy shells one by one over the side of the wagon to thud down into the long grass in our wake.

In the magic mirror, red dots were all round us now. Arrows flew over us, and some clattered on our sides. None found their marks though. We were moving fast and we were hard to see, travelling backwards as we were into the very thickest heart of the cloud we had raised.

Elaine turned us in our tracks, our back end crashing against the fence, and took us off in a new direction. The Half-Ax fighters were closing on us from behind now and running to block our way in front. More were keeping pace with us to the right, on the far side of the stake-blind. None of them had ever seen Challenger before – or at least, not since he waked for me at Calder ford – but they knew a weapon when they saw one and they had no intention of letting it run loose along their line.

I was slow on the count, but Challenger could not be mistaken in such things. When we reached the agreed-on mark, the zero, we were in the one safe place in a field we had sown with shells. Also, we were back where we had started, in front of the gaping hole we'd blown in our own fence and level with the rest of our waiting tally. We rolled to a stop again.

There was a moment when it seemed nothing in the world was moving at all, and all sounds were hushed. I marvelled at it – that stillness could be found in the midst of such ruck and turmoil. My mind, that had been stunned and dazed by the wild movement and terrible noise, floated in its own secret place and waited for time to start up again.

"Zero," Challenger said.

The world caught fire.

This burst was much louder and more terrible than the first. Words won't compass it, so I'll just say that and leave it lie. The first shell, that had blown a hole in the fence and let us out, had been set at zero to start with and so it went off as soon as Challenger sent the signal to its fuze. The other five, that we had sown all across the half-outside like seeds, had their fuzes set at one minute. They had been counting down ever since. Now that count was at an end.

For a hundred strides all round us, the solid ground was ripped up and flung into the sky. The Half-Ax soldiers that had been standing or running on that ground met a like fate. Five shells going off at once made the earth heave as if it had been struck a mortal blow. Even inside Challenger, I flinched from that terrible force and almost fell sprawling out of my chair. Catrin and the others, up on the wagon's flanks, ducked down as the air filled with sods of earth, shattered stakes, shards of rock.

The smoke and dust and darkness were a blessing. I couldn't tell how many had died, or see the suffering of them that were only maimed.

Even now, in the face of such calamity, the Half-Ax fighters that were left stuck to their plan and tried to whelm us. But help was at hand, as we had purposed. This was when Rampart Knife and the rest of our tally came surging out of the gap in the fence with their swords and spears out. Loosed arrows and hurled knives flew out of the spilling, surging smoke and found flesh. Catrin's lance of fire cleared a way as Challenger turned a quarter circle and set off again, this time with all our cohort running at our side.

When we hit the stake-blind's ditch, Challenger bucked and kicked like a mule. I was flung all the way out of my seat, through the magic mirror – which was as harmless as gossamer – and full into the main console. The breath was knocked out of me, and for a few seconds I saw nothing but flashes of light and flashes of dark. I slid to the floor on hands and knees. If Challenger had needed my hands to steer him, we would have been in a sad case, but Elaine's ghost hand was holding his reins and he did not even slow.

"Catrin!" I panted. "Jemiu! Are they—?"

"They're fine," Elaine said. "Just scratches."

"And the others?"

"Could have been worse."

I quailed to think what that might mean, but there was no time to play guessing games with it. We were outside the Half-Ax ring and moving fast towards the trees, but there were yet some fighters running us close. We could not hope to win in a stand-off. We had got to shake them off and break clear.

Morrez took aim with the rifle, and Gendel with the scatter-gun. They began to pick off the fighters that were chasing after us, aiming over the heads of our own people.

Something that shone as bright as the bonfire at a Salt Feast and spat out sparks like fat on a griddle shot past us. It hit the tree-line and was lost from sight, but a second later we were rocked by a great explosion. Everything ahead of us went white for a moment.

"Phosphorus," said Elaine.

"Can it hurt us?"

"It can burn you to the bone."

But Morrez had seen the fighter that fired that shot – or rather he had seen the tech she was carrying, which was a thing like a drainpipe with a handle to it. As she raised it to fire again, he was taking slow and steady aim on the centre of her body. They both loosed their shots at the same time. The fighter fell, tumbling head over heels, and lay still. But a tiny sun rose in the midst of our runners, yellow-white and sudden. Three of them caught fire and spun away, flailing and staggering.

Then we were in the trees, on a wide path that wound between oaks and elms and chokers. The Half-Ax tally were lost from sight, and even the cries of the wounded and dying fell away.

"Slow a little," Catrin called down. "We got to let our runners catch up."

I passed the order to Elaine, my heart beating against the inside of my ribs like a bird in a panic. Catrin knew as well as I did that the heat from those fires was going to rouse the trees. If we went too slow, our people would be fighting the waked forest. But if we went too quick, we'd leave them behind to be picked off by the Half-Ax tech. Also, our whole plan hung on Berrobis giving chase to us.

Elaine slowed Challenger to a walking pace, or a little faster, until some of the runners broke past us. Then she speeded up again to stay alongside them. The trees on either side of the path were moving against the wind, which was a bad sign. Further off in the forest, I could hear the booms and crashes that come when one thick trunk strikes against another.

But nothing was moving at our backs. "What do you see?" I asked Challenger.

For a second, he was silent. The view in the magic mirror shifted as he looked further and further out. The red dots were all gathered in a cluster near the fence. The white dot was right in the midst of them. Then all at once they started to move.

"They're coming," he said at last.

"How many?"

"Almost all of them. Your stratagem worked."

I let out the huffed breath I had been holding. That was what we wanted, and needed. I only hoped it wouldn't be the death of us.

65

Forests are not in all ways good for battle wagons. Challenger was heavy enough to topple young trees and ride over them, and he didn't notice weeds and brush at all. Elaine saw the bigger trees coming and wove a path between them. Some of them were awake, but — thank the dead god! — they were sluggish. They groped for us but were not quick enough to catch us. Coming along behind us, the Half-Ax tally might have a harder time of it.

But there was nothing we could do about the ground, which was far from even. The long climb out of the valley was not too bad, but after that we met streams and slopes and rocks in great plenty, and they all made our going harder. It was not that they slowed us — we were letting the runners beside and behind us set our pace — but they threatened ever and again to mire us down or make us slide out of control or break Challenger's treads and cripple him. That was what we feared most of all. The battle wagon was such rich spoils that if we once let Berrobis and her people catch up with him, they were not likely to go any further. They would stop to finish him and take him, and all our purposing would be at a sad end.

So we picked our way with care, going round and about when we had to – and that brought its own problems. Bolts of light shot over our heads as the Half-Ax fighters coming on behind found us again and loosed their tech on us. Some of the bolts were silver and some were gold. Where the gold lights hit the ground, fires started, and once started they spread quickly. The air filled with smoke, blinding our runners so they were in danger of losing us. Meanwhile the burning brush forced us to veer off our course. I realised quickly that all the fires were to the left of us. They were not fired in a great scatter but carefully aimed to make us turn back towards Calder and the slopes we'd just climbed. Berrobis wanted her people to be higher than us, the better to pen us in.

The silver lights landed closer to us and were fiercer still. They made a great jostling and trembling in the air. That might not sound so very terrible, but it was. It was as if a giant rose up out of the ground, waked by those lights, and with a mighty roar set about to smash whatever it could see. Trees were riven and toppled. Our runners were thrown off their feet. The air filled with shredded wood and flung-up earth.

I saw one man die without being hit by anything at all. A Half-Ax bolt drew a kind of circle in the air that took him in. He faltered in his running, then fell and crawled along the ground a little way, his hand on his throat, his mouth opening and closing, until at last he fell and lay still. I remembered Morrez's words about weapons that could steal your breath away. It seemed that Berrobis had brought them too.

"What can we do?" I cried out. "They're killing us!"

"Keep your damn nerve," Elaine said, "is what you can do. You were always going to lose a few people – and these fuckers can't see you any more clearly than you can them. All in all, it's not a bad thing if they spend their ammunition now."

I knew she was right, but still I gnawed my hand and watched in horror what was unfolding around us. I took control of the magic mirror and swung it round to look behind, but for all

Challenger's powers the night and the smoke hid too much. I saw a great many running figures, but they were blurs of colour and shadow. It was impossible even to tell if they were ours or Berrobis's, let alone to see if Jon was safe.

"How far?" I asked Challenger.

"Nine kilometres."

"How far is that though?"

"At our current speed, two hours."

I almost asked if we would break out of the trees soon, but I knew the answer. If we had wanted, we could have followed the spine of rock and stubble that began with Alner Hill and the Dog Neck and went on westward almost as far as Blackbern. But if we did, we would be forsaking the cover the forest gave us. However fast we went, the Half-Ax weapons would most likely outrun us, and there would be nothing up there to spoil their aim. So we stayed below the ridge, in the thick of the trees, where every other step was a stumble and any moment might bring the waked woods down on us.

But the river was not far ahead, and that would change everything. At least, we hoped it would. Challenger's mirror was not good for showing the lie of the ground, but Catrin was keeping watch – looking for the thinning of the trees that would tell us we were close.

"Take us left!" she called down the turret of a sudden. "Heel hard to the left, Spinner!"

I thought she must be wrong. We could not have come far enough yet. To the left of us, the woods were all aflame, and though Challenger could run through fire the rest of our tally could not. But I had to trust she knew what she was doing. I gave the order to Elaine, and felt the lurch and lean when she obeyed it.

The ground fell away under us as we ran down a steep bank. We seemed almost weightless, we dipped so sudden and so quick. Then a loud splash told me I was deceived as to where we were, while Catrin had judged exactly right. We had reached the river.

This was another stretch of Calder, but we didn't call it such. Calder was *our* river, where it flowed within the valley. Out here it was called Sandbound, and it ran slowly over a wide, shallow bed of bare rock and pebbles. Our runners would have a straight road, almost, to travel in, and what's more they would have good air to breathe. The smoke hung above us and pooled on both sides of us, but it hadn't come down the banks yet. Some trick of the wind and the weather held it back.

As if those two blessings were not enough, we got a third one besides. The river gave us the cover we had hoped for, so as we turned ourselves to head full west we were not running full on into Half-Ax fire. By the time they realised we had turned, we had gained – going by what I saw in the mirror – fully a hundred strides. More than that even, for they were forced to slow in case we were hiding under the bank in wait for them. The red dots crowded at the very edge of Challenger's mirror, a good way off.

I laughed out loud with relief. The hardest part – breaking out of the Half-Ax circle – was behind us. All we had to do now was to stay ahead of them as we closed the distance with Koli Faceless.

Then the laugh stuck in my throat and came near to choking me, as all the red lights went out at once. The magic mirror was empty.

I rose up on my feet, even though we were jolting and bouncing over the slick stones of the river bed. "Challenger!" I cried. "Report! What's happening?"

"I have lost the enemy's signals."

"How?" I threw out my hands at the mirror as if I could reach through it, scoop up all the lights and put them back where they belonged. "Where have they gone?"

"I do not believe they have gone anywhere, sergeant. I cannot detect our own tech either. The entire scanning field is disabled. The most likely explanation is that they have toppled the mast from the roof of Rampart Hold or broken the connection at ground level."

Which was the worst news he could have given me. Not only

were we blind to Berrobis's movements, we knew that she had left a force behind her to take the village.

Vallen! I thought with a sudden stab of pain and fright. My little one!

"Raise or fold, commander?" Elaine asked me. "It's your call. If you want to go back, we'll need a wide stretch to turn in."

What could I say? In a way this didn't change anything at all. It just took away the luxury of knowing how much of a head start we had. We still had got to carry on and hope Berrobis would keep on following. We couldn't hope to save the people we'd left behind in Mythen Rood if we turned and ran home again leaving Half-Ax whole.

"No," I said. "Keep on as we are."

I climbed up into the turret again, with a few slips and slides along the way. Morrez slid down onto Challenger's flank to make way for me.

"We lost sight of them," I told Catrin and the others. "They took down the mast, so we can't track them by their tech no more. We're a good way out in front of them though. If we keep this pace and this line, we got a good chance of getting through without them catching up again."

Catrin gave me a hard stare as she thought this through. "How will we find our way though? Weren't we tracking Koli by his tech too?"

"Yeah, but Koli's moving a lot slower. And Challenger didn't lose his memory, only the signal. We'll head for where Koli's tally was when we set out, and find them quick enough by their smoke and noise."

Catrin nodded, and shouted the news abroad to the runners. I looked around, trying to count how many of our people were still with us – and to look for Jon, if I'm honest. I was terrified he might have been one of those the phosphorus or the bursting air took down.

The sun was up over the shoulder of the world now. It was mostly hid behind banked-up thunderheads, but red-orange light trickled through here and there, making the trees shake and stir themselves like they were having troubled dreams. Our fighters were strung out in a long line, running across and in front of each other, and the twists and bends of the river hid them ever and again as we rolled on. Then I got a sight of my husband, down on one knee to catch his breath while the rest of Rampart Knife caught up with him. Some of them. Not all. I counted five in the mottled leather, and still was trying to guess which ones they were when we turned another bend and lost them.

"Do we know how many are dead?" I asked Catrin. She gave me no answer apart from a shake of her head, which either meant *no* or *stop asking*. I ducked back inside Challenger and took my seat again.

Down into Hebden we went, as if all the devils in Hell were after us and Stannabanna on a horse all of bones leading them. Though we'd lost the signal from the mast, I could still see through Challenger's mirror. Any other time, I would have stopped to wonder at the beauty of the land in the dawn light that seemed as thick as wine. Right now, all I could think of was Vallen. Vallen, and all them we'd left behind us to face Half-Ax's spite. If I ever did.

"How far?" I asked again.

"Approximately six kilometres. But there's movement ahead of us much closer than that. Look to your two o'clock."

That meant up ahead and to the right, though I had no idea why. It was a habit of Challenger's to count directions as if there were twelve of them standing around him in a circle.

Of a sudden, I saw them in the magic mirror. They were up on the ridge above us that we had forsook because it was too exposed. I couldn't see how many they were, but I saw the colours they were wearing. These were Half-Ax soldiers, a cluster of maybe twenty or thirty of them grouped high up on the hill's side.

For a second, I only stared. It made no sense that they should be there, already so far ahead of us. I thought I must be mistaking the play of light and shadow for Half-Ax grey and red. Then in

460

a rush of dread and dismay I remembered what Challenger had said about Half-Ax's army having to live off the land. We had most likely run into some of their hunters, scouring Hebden for forage enough to feed five hundred.

This was bad, but a wild hope was born in me. Maybe foraging and fighting were two separated things in a Half-Ax tally. Maybe this muster would just let us go by, having no orders to block our passage.

Then they knelt down to make a smaller target, and in the same movement drew their bows and let fly. Arrows flicked by us on all sides – and then came the hollow boom of some shot landing. They had tech.

We had the advantage in number, but our position was poor. The Half-Ax tally were above us, looking straight down into the cut. The far bank gave us a little cover for now, but the next turn of the river would deliver us up to their fire with no protection at all.

"Dead stop," I told Challenger.

I jumped up to tell Catrin what was what, but she was already peering in at me from the roof of the turret. "We got to take these down before we go any further," I shouted. "Can Fer—?"

"Fer's only got the one bolt left. I'm going to bid the runners take cover behind them rocks we just passed. You go on in Challenger and drive those bastards off the hill. I know you can't fight them, but if you run straight at them they've got to move or else be crushed. And when they move, we'll catch them in a crossfire."

It was a good plan. As soon as Catrin and the rest slipped down off Challenger's flank, I told Elaine to heel hard and come up from the river bed onto the hillside.

"Sir, yes, sir!" she said. "Let's go pick some daisies."

The Half-Ax fighters saw us coming and broke before us, but they did it with the same carefulness and order they gave to everything. They didn't scatter but divided into two groups, still firing on us as they drew back. So then we had to choose which ones to follow, and as soon as we did they divided again. I saw that we wouldn't shift them off the hillside so easily. Even faced with a battle wagon from the world that was lost, they didn't flinch or falter.

Of a sudden, something hit our side and exploded, making Challenger rock and lean like a hen coop in a storm wind. "One of them has grenades," Elaine said.

"Challenger, show me!"

The view in the magic mirror broke in two again, one half of it showing the way ahead and the other a close-up of one man among the Half-Ax muster. He was holding a thing like a slug of clinker you might use for a doorstop, and as I looked he threw it.

This time, the explosion was right in front of us, which was better. We shook a little, but we didn't rock from side to side and it didn't seem like we'd taken much damage.

"Run on him," I told Challenger. "Run him down."

The man was taking another one of those slugs out of his belt, where there were a whole row of them, and then he was wrestling with it as if it wouldn't do what he wanted it to. The soldiers around him scattered, but he was taken up with his tech.

In Challenger's mirror, where he was bigger than life, I saw the moment when he looked up at last and saw us bearing down on him. He knew it was his death, and he knew it would not be a good one, but he didn't cry out and he didn't try to run. His face was calm. He looked a little like Haijon. He had the same blue eyes anyway, and the same yellow hair.

He used the last moment of his life to pull something loose from the slug – a piece of string or a loop of wire. He stood and faced us, with the slug in one hand and the wire in the other. The last thing I saw as we rolled over him was a ring he wore in a braid of his long hair, that caught the sun and flashed gold as he fell down under Challenger's wheels. It looked like the sort of thing a lover might have given him. A token to keep him safe in the fight, or just to keep his thoughts on home.

462

The explosion hit us as we turned and caught us at a bad angle. For a second, as we pitched, I thought Challenger would be lifted off the hillside and come down on his back like a tortoise.

That didn't happen. But as the sound of the blast died down, I heard a tearing and a rending of metal, a high sound almost like a scream. We slowed and stopped as some of the smoke from outside drifted down at last into the cockpit.

"We got to keep moving!" I said, not realising.

"We cannot," Challenger said. "My left tread has taken heavy damage. I'm immobilised."

"Does immobilised mean—?"

"It means we're not going anywhere until the tread's fixed," Elaine said. "Can't move, can't fight. We're deep-fat fried."

I looked in the mirror. The Half-Ax fighters were slowing as they saw we weren't coming on any more. Then they backed away again as the turret swivelled from left to right and back.

"Just traversing the gun," Elaine said. "Can't hurt to show our teeth, even if we can't bite."

It would work for a little while. These people had trained with tech, so they knew what a gun as big as Challenger's could do to them. But they would realise quicker than anyone that if we were not firing on them it was most likely because we couldn't.

"Show me the river bed," I said.

The magic mirror shifted. I saw that our people had spread themselves out among the rocks of the cut bank, making themselves as difficult a target as they could. Catrin was playing her firethrower over the nearest trees, and some were already alight. The smoke would give them some cover from Half-Ax fire, but if she thought it would stop Berrobis's soldiers in their advance I could already see she was mistaken. They were picking their way carefully through the forest that still hadn't stirred from its sleep in the watery light – circling to the west, where Catrin didn't dare to go for fear of being fired on from the hillside above. On the other side of the hill, some of them had already crossed the river out of reach of our arrows and were taking up

463

positions in the long grass and scrub in case our column tried to retreat.

We had failed.

We were surrounded.

All we could do now was to fight until we fell.

Koli

66

I packed myself a bundle that same night after Cup and Ursala was asleep. I didn't take too much, just some bread and dried meat, a water skin and a spare knife. I meant to be away before anyone knowed I was gone, and back again before they started worrying. Or else the forest would take me and I wouldn't come back at all, but in any case I felt like I had got to try.

I had asked Monono to wake me when the sun was just under the horizon. In the time before *Sword of Albion* she would of done it by playing me a song. Now she done it by bumping the drone against my shoulder until I stirred. She didn't say anything. In the narrow space of the cab, however soft she spoke it would of sounded loud.

I slipped out of the cab and closed it softly behind me, picking up my bundle from where I'd left it tied to one of the crawler's many rungs and rails. I climbed down the side of the wagon as quietly as I could, watching where I put my feet.

When I got to the bottom, I found Cup waiting for me, along with two of the drudges. She had a bow slung on her back and a knife and a sword at her belt.

"I was just . . ." I said. "I thought I'd . . ."

"You was going to Mythen Rood," Cup said. "Monono already told me." She slapped the side of the nearer drudge. "You'll make better time if you ride. And if I ride with you then you'll actually get there. Alive."

"If *we* ride with you," Monono said. Her drone come down in between us without a sound.

I tried to explain how this was my problem to fix, and I didn't want to give no trouble to anyone else. Cup didn't even pretend to be listening. She took my bundle off me and tied it to the flank of one of the two drudges where a couple of small bags was already hanging. Monono made a clanging, scraping noise that startled me until I realised it was the raw and ragged edge of a tune she had played for me a long time ago when she was still inside the DreamSleeve. It was called "You Don't Own Me", and it was sung by a woman whose onliest name was Grace – or else her other name had got lost somehow.

"Okay then," I said. "I guess we're all going together. I should climb back up and tell Ursala."

"We'll tell her when we get back," Cup said. "If we tell her now, she'll try to stop us and we'll never get out of the argument."

I didn't feel happy with that, but Cup was already climbing up on one of the drudges. "Mount up, Koli," she said to me. "We got a long way to go."

I had rode on Ursala's drudge a few times when we was going south to lost London, and it had been rough going. This was much better. The drudge drawed its gun down into its body and shaped itself to fit me, growing two handles out of its front end for me to hold onto and two stirrups for my feet. A kind of beam or brace slid up behind me and pressed itself against my back to keep me steady. "Is it you doing all this?" I asked Monono.

"All part of the service," she said – not through the drone but through the drudge its own self. "I'll be coming through the cabin later with drinks and snacks."

"What?"

"Never mind. Hold on tight, boys and girls. The drone can scout ahead for us, and the aim is very much to run around anything nasty we see. But *through* is on the table too. If things get really hairy, I'm going to strap you in. And if they get bad enough that I have to unship the guns . . . Well, we'll figure that out when we come to it."

"Aren't the guns right underneath our arses?" Cup asked.

"Yes, they are. Better keep your fingers crossed. Any more questions? No? Off we go!"

The drudges started to move. They was not quick at first, but they got quicker and quicker as they went, until it seemed like we wasn't even touching the ground. The world flung itself into our faces and then slid off and shot past us ever and again. I opened my mouth to give a gasp or a yelp but I couldn't catch no air to do it with.

The road-making engines was at our side, then they was behind us, then they was gone. We went round a stand of trees as quick as a stone being spun up in a slingshot and we was on our way at the gallop. Cup give a whoop of joy. I guess this was more to her taste than mine.

I say we went at the gallop, but it didn't feel like that. The drudge's footing was so sure and its strides so measured, it felt more like I was rolling on a wagon than riding on a beast. I wasn't bounced or jolted or throwed around at all. There was just the wind smacking at me and the speed so great it was like I was being pushed back against the brace behind me by a hand as big as my whole body. The drone went ahead of us, darting from side to side like a mayfly skimming over a pond.

By and by, I shut my eyes. Monono was guiding the drudge, so I didn't need to control it or tell it where to go. But going so fast and not being able to see what was coming was worse than seeing it and flinching from it, so I opened them again.

"Feels like we're flying, don't it?" Cup yelled, grinning across at me. We was keeping pace perfectly, each with other, so if it hadn't been for the wind she wouldn't of had to shout. She could of just said it. "It even beats riding in the crawler!"

A hill rose up in front of us, steep as anything and scattered all over with rocks and bushes. We didn't swerve or slow but went right up it, the drudges picking their way without any mistakes even though they didn't have no eyes to see with.

We kept to the high ground after that. The sun come up, but the only way you could tell was that the blackness all around us thinned to grey, like light was seeping up all sluggish out of the ground. The trees and hills was like giants striding by us.

I was thinking we had got to be close to Mythen Rood by now. I didn't recognise the land around us, for I'd only ever hunted in Calder and never in the western reach, but I knowed near enough the distance we had to go and we were moving so quick we had surely covered most of it.

I was just about to ask Monono to slow us down so we didn't come of a sudden within sight of the fence and the lookouts, but just then a sound was brung to me on the wind. At first it was like the crackling and spitting of grease in a hot pan, but as it got ever louder I knowed it for what it was. It was the sound of shots, from guns being fired.

The noises was coming from up ahead of us, and we was going quick towards them. Other sounds weaved themselves in between the shots now – shouts and cries, and the loud booming sound of an explosion. A horn was being blowed too.

"Dead god's mother!" Cup shouted. "Monono, what's going on?"

I didn't ask, for I wasn't in no doubt as to what I was hearing. It was a battle. People was fighting and killing each other very close to where we was riding.

The drudges slowed. "I'll send the drone ahead," Monono said. "Whatever it is, I'll scout it out before I send you two into it."

But there was a tightening in my heart and a sourness at the bottom of my throat. Who would be fighting this close to Mythen

Rood if it wasn't Mythen Rood its own self? "No," I said. "Monono, take me to the top of the hill."

"Koli-bou—"

"Please. I need to see."

"All right. If you insist."

Cup didn't say nothing either way so it was only my drudge that climbed the hill.

From the top, as soon as we crested it, I saw all that was there to be seen. A fight was going on, like I thought, and it looked like it would not be a long one. A small tally was stuck fast in the main and middle of their enemies. They was in the cut where the river ran, maybe two or three hundred strides from where I sat watching. Fighters on the slope up above them was firing down on them, holding them where they was. Meanwhile, a much bigger muster was coming through the woods, spreading out in a wide line to trap them and kill them.

All these people was too far away for me to see their faces clear, but I seen well enough who the big tally was. They was all of them wearing the grey uniforms of Half-Ax. The ones in the trap was not wearing anything I could know them by, and I thought at first they was strangers.

Besides all these people that was moiling down by the river, there was a great battle wagon up on the hillside in among the grey fighters there. It had a rusted top like the one I seen by Calder River when I first set out on my travels. It was in a worse case than that other wagon though, with its treads all tore away from its wheels and its sides all blackened with fire. The Half-Ax soldiers was in a ring around it and they was closing in on it, slow and careful.

I said I took the people in the cut for strangers, but that's only halfway true. I think I had some suspicion as soon as I seen them. Then one of them lifted her weapon, a piece of tech that was the same dark, shiny green as holly leaves, and shot out a rope of fire that made the nearest of the Half-Ax fighters draw back in a hurry. If I had got any doubt at all, it left me then. I knowed I was looking at Catrin Vennastin, Rampart Fire, and by her I knowed the others that was standing with her. Not by face or name yet, but only by the birthplace we all of us shared. That was my village down there, with the army of the Peacemaker pressing them on all sides. It was Mythen Rood fighting for its life.

"We got to help them," I said.

I didn't even know I'd said it out loud until Cup answered me. She had rode her own drudge up alongside me while I was staring down and seeing nothing but the fight in the valley. "Why? Do you know them fools?"

"They're not fools. They're my friends."

"They got to be pretty stupid to let theirselves get surrounded like that."

"Monono—"

"I hear you, Koli-bou. Dismount."

"What does that mean?"

"Get down off the drudges. I'll send them ahead."

I looked at the long line of Half-Ax soldiers. Wherever Catrin played her fire, they fell back, but everywhere else they was still coming on. As soon as they was far enough forward to aim their bolts and arrows along the line of the river, the fight would be over. "I think we're like to need more than just the drudges," I said.

"I think so too. But we've got to start somewhere."

"Okay then," Cup said. "I guess if we're doing this we might as well go to it." She stepped down quick from the drudge and unshipped her bow. Before I even set foot on the ground, she was sprinting down the hill towards that broke and stilled wagon. I jumped off and followed as quick as my feet could take me.

The drone stayed by my shoulder for a little while as I run. "Stay in cover, Koli," Monono said through its speaker. "There's a ton of tech down there and half of it is stuff I've never seen before. Don't put yourself in front of it."

"I'll try not to!" I said. I couldn't say no more than that, for all my breath was took up in running. The drone rose up and shot away, heading for the grey fighters up on the hill. The drudges was already galloping down into the valley, their guns sliding up into position as they went.

We was at war with Half-Ax.

Again.

Spinner

67

The Half-Ax soldiers were closing on us slowly. Most of them carried bows, but there were at least two with rifles like the one we had taken at the ford.

Even now, they did everything carefully and in good order. They hadn't all turned from the bigger fight to deal with us. More than half of them had their backs to us and were firing down into the cut to keep our tally pinned behind the rocks there. Only about a dozen were in the ring that was surrounding Challenger. But it would be more than enough.

"Hey," Elaine said. "Spinner. Snap out of it." She had said my name before and I had not been listening.

"Sorry, Elaine! I can't— They're going to—"

"Not unless we let them. What have you got by way of a weapon?"

"I got my knife." I pulled it from its sheath and held it up.

"Well, isn't that the cutest thing! Put it away. I just had a better idea. Challenger, pop the trunk."

A hatch opened up in the wall of the cockpit, next to my head. There was lots of stuff in there I hadn't ever seen before. I knew they must be tools of some kind, but I couldn't guess what any of them were meant to do.

"Pick up that metal bottle on the left there," Elaine said. "And the wand thing that's attached to it."

I did as I was bid. The bottle was heavier than it looked and almost slipped out of my fingers. What Elaine called the wand was a kind of pipe, joined to the bottle by a rope – only the rope was made of shiny metal rings that all locked each to other.

"What is this?" I asked.

"It's a tread repair tool. The bottle's full of compressed air. The wand extrudes a new tread connector in between two blown treads that are being held together with a track puller. But that's just another way of saying it spits out heavy metal pins really hard and really fast. There's a stud on the side of the hand grip that you press down to fire. Be careful where you aim it. It's got no range at all, but up to four or five feet it will put a crease in anyone's day."

The ring of soldiers outside was drawing tighter. One of the fighters clambered up on Challenger's flank. Kneeling there, she fitted an arrow to her bow.

I pointed the wand straight up. In the magic mirror, I watched the soldier's every movement. She pulled back the arrow until the string was as tight as it could get. Taking care not to slacken that tension, she turned the bow so it was on its side, level with the ground. She stepped up onto the turret, where she waited a moment to listen.

As she leaned forward to loose her shot, I pressed the raised nub my thumb had found on the wand's side. It kicked in my hands and made a sound like a sneeze.

The tread connector was just as Elaine had described it: a rod of grey metal a little shorter than the shaft of an arrow but three times as thick. It hit the soldier in the middle of her chest and threw her high into the air. In the mirror, I saw her fall backwards off the wagon's side, hitting the ground so hard that she went head over heels before she stopped moving, falling at last on her face. The connector had gone most of the way through her, the end of it sticking a handspan or so out of her back. Her comrades stepped back at once, widening their ring again in expectation of some fresh attack – but then one of them broke out of the line to run to the fallen archer and see if she yet breathed.

"That will give them something to think about at least," Elaine said.

But it didn't hold them long. A man with more red mixed into his grey than most turned and gave orders, pointing to this one and that one. Four soldiers ran forward out of the ring and scaled Challenger's sides all at once.

I raised the wand again. "No use," Elaine said. "It takes a minute or so to get up to pressure again. Grab that flare gun. Maybe at this range we can— Holy shit!"

I turned back to the mirror. A drone had dropped down out of the sky right beside us. It spat out rays of red light as thin as ribbon that went among the Half-Ax soldiers and cut them down.

The ones with rifles fired back, but the drone was whipping back and forth and spinning like a top. Bolts and arrows filled the air all round it without once hitting their mark.

The Half-Ax commander took something out of his belt and threw it into the air. It was another grenade, and when it exploded at the top of its arc it took the drone out of the sky. At the same time, a woman and a man ran full tilt down the hill and in among the Half-Ax fighters. The woman had a painted face like shunned men are wont to wear – a line that went down from her two eyes to meet under her chin. She also had a bow, and she loosed off three arrows in the space of three breaths. One of them went wide, but the other two ended up buried deep in grey uniforms.

The man had a knife, but he didn't seem too keen on using it. He was holding it in his two hands, straight out in front of him, as if he hoped his enemies would run onto the end of it and save him the trouble of aiming. He didn't slow, but ran right on past me, leaving me with the strangest sense that I knew him from another place or time.

I lost him quickly in the smoke that drifted across from the burning woods.

Koli

68

If I'd knowed Spinner was in the battle wagon, I surely would of stopped to help her.

But I didn't know. And from what I could see, Cup and the drone between the two of them was enough for the Half-Ax fighters on the hill. Or maybe I only told myself that because I wanted to go on. There might be anyone inside that engine, or no one. Down in the cut was where Mythen Rood was fighting and dying, so that was where I had to go.

Running into the midst of all them fighters I would of died quicker than a breath on a cold day, only at the last moment one of the drudges swung in beside me. They had come round the hill instead of straight down it. The guns on their backs was spinning round and about the whole time, shooting this one and that one as they went. Then one of them jumped straight over the cut bank and kept on going while the other fell in with me. Its metal hooves tore up great clods of grass and weeds and earth as it slowed to let me come alongside it.

"Mythen Rood!" I shouted. "Mythen Rood for aye and ever!"

Then I run out of road and crashed down into the cut, where people I knowed as well as I knowed myself was now struggling hand-to-hand with fighters in grey. I seen Gendel Stepjack there, with tech in his hands that blazed and boomed. Issi Tiller standing with a knife in each hand over his brother Chass, that had fallen. And Catrin in the midst of all swinging her firethrower as if she was Dandrake's reaper come to gather the last harvest.

I had come down on my arse, but scrambled up again quickly as a grey man run at me. I stabbed at him with my knife but I struck metal instead of meat as he blocked with his sword. Somehow he flicked my knife up out of my hand and stabbed me in the shoulder as if them two things was one thing. The pain as the blade sunk into me made me stagger and almost fall down. Seeing that I was now without a weapon, the Half-Ax man stepped back to get a better swing on his next stroke. He never got to make it though. The drudge stitched the air with bullets, shooting him down.

"Koli," Monono said out of the drudge. "You need to keep your—"

A bolt of blue lightning shot right through the drudge and buried itself in the ground at my feet. The drudge fell over on its side, smoke pouring out of a great breach in its flank.

A woman walked by me. A woman of Half-Ax with silver braids in her hair. I knowed her at once for a Rampart – or whatever it was that Half-Ax had instead of Ramparts. Her hands was on fire, but the fire was blue instead of yellow. Nor it didn't do what fire should, which is to rise up from what was burning, but went ever back and forth between her two hands until she pointed with one hand or the other. Then the fire would go where she pointed and work ruin on whatever was there. This was what had brung down the drudge.

She walked by me, like I said, and I seen she was heading for Catrin. Two men of Mythen Rood – Marto Tailor and Evred Bell – stood in her way. The woman made a sign with her hand like she was bidding them step aside, and they was both of them dead before they could be sorry for it. Blue fire made an end of them.

Catrin turned now and saw the woman coming. She took aim

484

with the firethrower and sent out a great jet of flame. The Half-Ax woman spread her arms wide and catched the flame in between them. Her own blue fire seemed to drink it in, and growed ever brighter as it drunk.

The one drudge that was left come galloping along the cut and stopped alongside me. Monono spoke out of it. "This is the wrong kind of craziness. Get on board, Koli-bou. We're leaving."

"I can't, Monono," I shouted over the fighting's din and clamour. "These are my people that I growed up with. I'm not going to leave them."

"Get down behind the drudge then."

I didn't do that either. I followed the Half-Ax woman down the cut.

Spinner

69

The woman with the tattooed face ducked down behind Challenger's ruined tread, where I couldn't see her. I knew she was still there though, for arrows kept appearing in the chests and shoulders and necks of Half-Ax soldiers.

Their leader rallied them and tried to flank her, but that meant turning their backs on the drone. No doubt he thought it was dead after it fell down on the ground, but it was not. Choosing its moment, when the Half-Ax tally were all or most of them in range, it stabbed out with its hurtful light and took three of them before they could turn.

That left the leader and two others, a man with dyed red hair who carried a morningstar and a woman with a pike. The woman thrust down at the drone, pinning it to the ground and then breaking it in two. The leader and the other man ran at the archer, who loosed one last arrow and then was forced to use her bow as a staff to fend them off.

"Elaine," I said, clambering up the turret ladder one-handed, "make a noise!"

As I climbed awkwardly up the ladder, cradling the metal bottle at my side, a booming yell split the air. It sounded like a mountain was trying to sing. There were words in the song, but they were so loud I couldn't find the edges of them to make sense of what was said. Only that Albion was in there, and death, and glory.

I came tumbling out of the turret and down onto Challenger's flank, where I landed on my stomach. The archer was on the ground, wrestling with the Half-Ax leader. The other man had doubled the chain of his morningstar in his two hands and now was looking for a way to get in close and slip it round her neck.

He went by me without seeing me, which was just as well. I put the wand to the back of his skull and pressed the stud. He fell without a sound. Without a head.

"My hope, my heart, my home!" Elaine screamed through Challenger's speakers. "Aaaaaaaalbion!"

The pike-woman ran at me, but all that Half-Ax patience and carefulness had gone from her at last. I rolled off Challenger's side onto the ground, and her wild thrust went over me as I fell. Then I was inside her reach where a pike is only a long stick. I shoved the metal bottle hard into her stomach. She fell to her knees. Before she could rise again, I swung the bottle round in a big, clumsy circle and drove it into the side of her head.

I turned my face away from the bloody mess I had made to find the Half-Ax leader already dead and the archer kneeling over him, drawing her bloody knife out of his throat. She turned to look at me, giving me a nod as cool as if we'd just walked by each other on the gather-ground.

"You as good with an edge as you is with a cudgel?" she said, holding out the dead man's sword for me to take. She had already taken off his belt, on which three or four grenades were still hanging.

"I would of said no," I answered. "But I done things already this day that I would of said I had no gift for."

I grabbed hold of the sword.

"And the sun's been up just a little while," the woman said. "I'm Cup. Who are you now?"

"Spinner. Spinner Tanhide."

The woman's eyes went wide. "No lie?" she said. "You're Spinner? I thought you had got to be like an angel out of Edenguard the way Koli talks about you."

"You – you know Koli?" I stammered.

"Who'd you think was with me just now? It was his stupid idea to help you people. I would of been happy to ride on by."

"But— We thought—"

"You thought what?"

"It doesn't matter." I changed my mind about the sword and took up the morningstar instead. I stood up. "Let's go."

But the woman went across to the broken drone and stood over it. "Monono," she said. "Are you still in there?" She waited a little while for an answer. None came. She didn't waste the time of waiting though, but strapped the belt of grenades around her middle. She turned back to me.

"Do you know how to use them things?" I asked.

"I seen what he did. I guess I'll pick it up. Ready?"

"Ready."

We ran down the hill and into the cut.

Koli

70

The Half-Ax woman was face to face with Catrin now, with not much distance in between them. She pointed at the firethrower and a narrow spark of blue jumped from her finger to touch it. Catrin give a yell of startlement and staggered back, flinging the firethrower from her just as it catched fire its own self. It fell to the ground, bright yellow flames springing up out of it like choker flowers. It roared as it burned.

The blue light died out of the woman's hands. A pair of bracelets that was on her wrists glowed blue for a moment or two longer, and then went back to being silver. She took a longsword from off her back. Holding it in her two hands, she raised it high with the blade pointing straight up at the sky. It wasn't hard to see what she was saying — that Catrin and her would set aside their tech and fight with simple weapons. I would not of called that great sword simple though. It had a guard on it that some ironsmith must of spent a month or more of their life on, and the blade was fine work too. I didn't doubt but that the silver-haired woman kept a good edge on it.

Catrin never carried a sword. The firethrower was all her care where weapons was concerned. She crouched down quick and come up again holding a spear that had been dropped. It was a throwing spear, not a thrusting spear, and not much use against a sword. She raised it up in front of her, jabbing with it as she backed away.

The silver-haired woman followed hard. She didn't swing or bother to block Catrin's feints, but only kept narrowing the space between them. When that distance was down to a couple of arm's lengths, Catrin lunged at last, aiming high, but she was too clever to put all her weight into an attack that was bound to fail. The Half-Ax woman broke the spear in two with a single swipe. At the same time, Catrin ducked down under the sword and come up inside the other woman's guard. She hit her in the face with her clenched fist.

The woman staggered but she didn't fall. She couldn't use her long blade no more – not against an enemy that was all but touching her – but she still had a weapon that would serve. She stabbed Catrin with the sword's cross-guard, which had wicked sharp points to it. It tore a deep, straight cut across Catrin's right-hand shoulder, slicing through the thick leather of her armour as if it was spider's gossamer.

The two of them locked together then. The silver-haired woman twisted her wrist round, bedding the guard's spike deeper and deeper into Catrin's shoulder. Catrin couldn't get free of it but she put that closeness to what use she could, hammering her fists ever and again into the woman's side, low down near her stomach.

The fight had not stopped all this while. People was running and grappling on all sides, and arrows went by my face close enough that the fletch-feathers tickled my nose, as they say. I wasn't doing no good at all just standing there, but I was too wildered to move. I had been in fights before but I had never seen such fury and hot blood as this, not even on *Sword of Albion*'s deck when Paul and Lorraine battled Monono. The sight and the smell of it took all the thoughts out of my head. I had grabbed up my knife again, but I couldn't even remember what it was for.

Monono was not cumbered in the same way. The drudge turned in circles beside me, its gun spitting out bolts to put down any fighter that offered me harm. And when some trick or turn of the fighting sent a great wave of bodies down on us, it put itself between to be a bulwark for me. It run out of bolts at last, so its gun spit only air, but even then it struck out with its heavy clubbed feet at anyone that come too close.

Two Half-Ax fighters come running in, carrying loops of black wire that sung on a high note, loud enough to be heard over all the other sounds around me. They throwed the wire and it come looping through the air, wrapping itself around the drudge's front legs and then pulling itself tight. The drudge crashed down, its legs sheared through. The fighters run on without so much as looking at me.

The silver-haired woman had tired at last of wrestling and striving. Her bracelets waked again, high and hurtful blue. Fire or lightning or light or something that was different from all of them lanced out and took Catrin in her arm and her chest – the parts of her that was closest. She sunk down on her knees, struck to the heart of her by that double blow.

That was what brung me out of my dream and made me move. It was not that I come to a point of planning or deciding. I just seen Rampart Fire on her knees, hurting and dying, and a part of me that was deep buried said no. That was not a thing that could be let to happen, if I could only stop it.

You can't, Stanley Banner said. *But I can.* It wasn't like he was there with me on that field. It was just that I seen through his eyes for a half of a heartbeat. He knowed what it was the Half-Ax woman carried on her wrists – a *lance-flammes* – and he knowed how it worked.

I run toward the two women. "Koli, no!" Monono yelled out of the felled drudge. She had seen that blue light too, and she knowed what it could do.

The silver-haired woman had room now to swing her sword. She brung it up and back, her mind so tangled up in her triumphing

497

that she didn't see me come. She was going for that two-handed stroke again, her left hand over her right on the sword's hilt.

I only had time for the one blow. I did not have any faith at all in the strength of my arm or the keenness of my aim. I brung my knife hand forward, but I turned my wrist at the last moment so the blade was sideways on. The blade touched the two brace-lets, joining them.

Closing the circuit.

There was a sound like the whole world cracking clean in two.

A smell and a taste of bitter herbs.

A dark place where I landed hard and could not climb out of.

Spinner

71

What I can tell about the rest of the fight will be of little use to anyone. Certainly it's a trial to me to bring any of it clear into my mind. It must have been there once. You don't live through such things without having them burned into you like a brand that stings and blisters and is too tender to touch.

But as soon as the first pain fades, you start to pick at the wound in your mind the same way you might do with a wound in your flesh. You set about to explain it, to tell the story and so lessen the itch and the ache of it. You realise quick enough that words are not the right tools for the job, but they're all you've got so you use them anyway. And in a strange way they work. The words lie over your memories and dull them. In the end, you can't sort out what you did from what others say you did, what you saw from what you only said.

What I tell you now is the closest thing to truth I know, but if I had to raise my hand in Count and Seal and swear my soul to it, or my daughter's soul, I would not. I can only offer it for what it is, which is a scab over a terrible wound that still, after so much time gone by, hasn't all the way healed. Maybe it shouldn't. Maybe we're better off with the pain than we would be without it.

Alongside the tattooed girl, Cup, I ran down the hill. She was loosing arrows as she ran, so quick and so true it seemed like every foeman she looked at got a sharp reproach right after. As if her arrows followed wherever her gaze went. I lashed out with the morningstar ever and again to keep anyone from coming too close, but it didn't feel like she needed me or even knew I was there.

At the bottom of the hill, we jumped down into the cut. The river was right up against the bank, so we splashed down in a foot or so of cold, quick water. There were three Half-Ax soldiers there who had their backs to us, firing on some of ours further up towards the bend. One of them never got to turn around, for Cup had time to get off a final shot.

Then we were pressed hard, and I can't say how it was we didn't fall. The man that came for me was taller than I am by a head or more, and had a longer reach. His bow was no use in such close quarters though, and he had to draw his knife. I backed away, swinging the morningstar in circles to keep him at a distance, but he was ducking to the left and the right, looking for a way to strike at me.

I saw Cup down on her back with the other fighter on top of her, the two of them struggling for the same spear.

I should not have looked away. My enemy crashed into me and drove me into the bank, knocking all the breath out of me. I sank down, struggling for air. He grabbed my hair in his hand and hauled me up again, bending my head back to bare my throat.

Behind him, running up the cut – surely the last sight I would ever see, I thought – came Rampart Knife. They all threw their blades at once. That seems unlikely, doesn't it? They could not have been running seven abreast, with knives ready in their hands. Obviously my mind has added daggers that were not there. But I remember that rain of bright steel, and the Half-Ax man falling back, still upright for a moment with a cluster of hilts sticking out of his shoulder and his side.

Jon took him in the throat with a second blade, then turned

and dragged me up on my feet as Veso and Lari between them brought down the fighter that was struggling with Cup. She grabbed up the dead man's spear and nodded thanks.

"There's more coming!" Jon shouted. "We can't stay here."

"You can't go no further either," Cup said, pointing. The cut up ahead of us was thick with grey uniforms, and more were pouring out of the woods. So many! It seemed there was no end to them. For every one that had fallen, there were a dozen more.

And they had seen us. Cut off from the rest of Mythen Rood's tally, we were an easy and a tempting target. The bulk of the Half-Ax line headed straight on to where Catrin and Fer must be, already surrounded by a sea of grey. A smaller group that was still too many to count split off and advanced on us.

Cup hefted her spear. Rampart Knife drew fresh blades and took aim. The grey line became a thicket of drawn-back, creaking bows.

Then there came a sound I can't ever forget, and can't hope to describe. It was like a scream — a scream of rage, rather than one born out of pain or fear. And once it had started, it didn't stop. It went on long past the point where anything living would have had to draw breath.

The Half-Ax fighters faltered. Their hands slackened on their bows as they looked past us.

Over us.

A long, long way over us.

Under the neverending scream, more sounds rose up. A roaring and a clattering, a boom of steel on steel.

I looked over my shoulder.

Every demon and monster from every story you ever heard was charging down the hill towards us. They were all in armour, but no armour could hide their fangs, their claws, their spears, their great balled battle-maces and war-worn shields. They were their own chariots. Their breath was fire, and the smoke of it hung over them like a hundred tattered shrouds.

Some of the Half-Ax fighters loosed their arrows. The shafts fell on the giant beasts, or wagons, or whatever you might call them, but fell as harmless as rain. From somewhere in that long line of fearsome engines, or maybe from all of them, a voice boomed out, so loud it was as if an earthquake had been given speech.

"*Fuzakeru naaaaaa!* You hurt him! You hurt him and this is what you get!"

Some of the great chariots ran on ahead of the rest. They were the ones carrying shields, or the things I thought were shields. But they were something else again. They were wide blades that had been held high and now were brought all the way down until they bit into the ground. They churned up the dirt and grass and weeds in front of them so it rose in a wave that swelled higher and higher.

When they got to the cut, all that churned-up earth fell in on top of the Half-Ax fighters there. The chariots themselves came right after and crushed them down. It would have been a terrible thing to see any other time. It was terrible still, but all I saw right then was rescue. So I didn't turn away as the bigger, slower engines, with their spiked jaws and giant flails, rolled over the bridge the first ones had made into the centre of the Half-Ax line.

The battle did not end all at once. The Half-Ax fighters were brave, and fought on as long as they could.

It did not avail them.

72

The story of the Half-Ax war — at least, when I have the telling of it — is rounded out with three things more.

First. We went back to Mythen Rood in better form than we left it, with all those mighty chariots riding by our side. They had a name — just the one name, shared between all of them. It was Monono. And for dead Koli's sake she was prepared to be a friend to Mythen Rood.

I had to wonder, though, if there would even be a Mythen Rood going forward. We had lost so many, more than fifty souls all told. Rampart Arrow was among them and so was her husband Gendel. Rampart Fire lived, but her wounds — on top of those she'd suffered at Calder ford — left her almost too weak to lift her head. The many friends I lost I will forbear to list.

We took the surrender of the Half-Ax tally in Mythen Rood from some captain or lieutenant who could scarce speak his own name for grief and holy dread. They had been about to torch the Hold, but chose to loot it first. I told him their greed and their tardiness were all that had saved them. If we had come back to that, to a smoking ruin, and to the sight of all them we loved dead in the ashes . . .

But we did not. Everyone who had hidden in the secret rooms was saved. Ban delivered my Vallen into my arms, and Jon's. Jarter stood by her side with a cudgel in one hand and a dagger in the other, guarding my baby girl to the last as she had sworn to.

In the days and weeks that followed, we struggled to find a way forward. We had the great engines to watch over us, but nobody to tell us what to do. In my heart, I thought we were lost, but I put on a bold face whenever I stood in the Count and Seal. I had to, for Catrin had given me the firethrower and bid me speak in her name. She said she couldn't speak for the village any more, now that what the Vennastins did to Koli was known by all and some. So I was Rampart Fire, whether I wished it or not, and had to make the best I could of it.

Second. When we took the prisoners home to Half-Ax, we found the Peacemaker already dead. He had made a grievous mistake in sending his whole army out against Mythen Rood. His own people had risen up against him and cast him down. The store of tech that he had gathered – such of it as had not travelled with his army – was looted and gone to the winds.

The people of Half-Ax were terrified when they saw us coming. It took a great many assurances before they would believe we had no interest in sacking their village or taking them as slaves. They only had the one example to go on, after all. We gathered them in a Count and Seal – a thing they had no name for – where we offered them a treaty and a chance to live under Mythen Rood law if they wished it.

What might that be though? they asked. What's the law in Mythen Rood?

We told them what we could. How each worked for all, and when they could not cope alone called on share-works to fill the gaps. How every woman and man had a vote on what we did, and all votes were counted equal.

Some thought we lied. Most thought we'd opened the door to Edenguard. They voted yes, only half-believing their voices would be counted. It was a kind of pair-pledge. When we went away from there, we left a promise behind us, that we would grow closer together and in the course of time be one thing instead of two. I took heart from that. We had lost much, and come close to losing all. So had they. Perhaps one village made out of two would thrive where each alone would have faltered.

And so it proved. After a few lean years, we began to grow, and now are more numerous than we ever were. It helped that more babies were made, and more of them that were made were dropped alive. This is thanks to Ursala-from-Elsewhere, who comes to us each Spring and Falling Time and plies her trade as she was wont from the belly of a metal horse.

We live on, which is a great blessing. We only ever fought for that one thing, after all.

Third. The road passed right by our gate and kept on going. In its path, great tracts of woodland were levelled. The choker trees have not thrived in the thinned-out forests that were left, and many of our old enemies seem to have found other homes for themselves. The endless coming and going of humankind along the road did not suit them.

Our children grew up to think of Calder as a tiny place indeed. Vallen was not the first to walk that road and visit places we had no names for. She won't be the last neither. We are in the world now, and the world is bigger and stranger than we ever thought it.

As I said, these three things properly belong to any account of the war. I tell them in their place, and then I stop. But I stop knowing that questions will come, and when they come I answer them as plainly as I can. I'm not shy about rolling other people's stories into the bigger story. People need to know what was done, and by who. They need to know how their present grows out of this past, or else they're no more than windblown seeds.

Yes, the battle wagon in the story is the one that sits now on the gather-ground. The one the children deck with garlands on Summer-dance. The ring of flowers around it I sowed myself, and tend myself. It speaks with two voices because two people live in

507

it, Elaine and Challenger, and they are two of my sweetest friends. But they are not always at home. Monono set them free, or cut their tethers as she put it, and sometimes their duty or their fancying take them elsewhere.

Yes, Morrez Frostfend used to be Morrez Ten-Taken, and he was a soldier before he grew that great belly. But you must not ever call him by his old name. He hates it. There was another, Sil Hawk, that lived with us a while, but she left us not long after the Peacemaker fell and never returned. I cannot say what became of her, only that she did not go home to Half-Ax. Ingland is a great vastness. She may have found a place in it where she could thrive, but I don't believe she would ever have been happy with us.

Yes, the Cup I'm speaking of is Cup Roadbuilder, that's married to the man with the strange name. Taller Than Trees. It's not strange at all in the south where he comes from. Some of you will see for yourselves when you go there. And it's likely that one of their four children will be your guide or tracker if you do, for they all take after their mother in not ever staying still in one place.

Yes, we had a fence around us once. We were afraid of everything outside our gates. And we were right to be afraid, because everything that lived seemed to hate us and wish us harm.

And yes, we had Ramparts. They ruled us by what they said was ancient right, but all their words were lies and all their greatness was pretended. Still, they fought for Mythen Rood when Mythen Rood had need of them, and perhaps in this fashion they washed out their guilt. I can't say. I'm still trying to wash out mine.

And so they lived, in great peace and plenty, until the end of their days. That's what they're waiting for, my listeners, and I offer it where I can – where it's not a bald-faced lie. The comfort and power of those words is not a thing to be taken lightly.

But there is a part of the story's ending that I mostly leave out. It's important, and has a great bearing on what came after, but it confuses too many matters that should be clear. The ending of a story need not be a happy one, when all's said, but it needs to be understood. It needs to have a right shape, as I said to my Jon that time, and the shape of this happening is harder to discern.

Koli Woodsmith, who we thought our enemy, saved us when we were lost.

He died in doing it.

And then something truly strange happened.

73

After the last Half-Ax soldiers fled or died, a strange silence fell over the battlefield. Those of us who were left alive looked around us as if daylight was a strange thing.

I searched for Jon but didn't find him. He had been at my side not long since, but now was nowhere to be found. What I found instead was Koli. What was left of him. His body was burnt almost black. His skin was cracked open in many places and the wounds were deep, but there was no blood. It seemed as if his blood had boiled away as steam.

I thought him dead at first, but then I saw his eyes were open. His tongue's tip touched his teeth as he tried to speak. He had no breath to do it.

"He killed Berrobis." Catrin's voice came from behind me and made me turn. She was lying on the ground with one leg bent under her and the other thrown wide. She was burned too, but not as badly as Koli. "I don't know how, but he killed her with her own weapon." She pointed to a place beside her, but I saw no body there. Only a puddle of grease that smoked a little, circled with streaks and smears of grey ash.

The tattooed girl came running up, and a little while later

Jemiu found her way there too. Their grieving took different courses. The girl yelled out a great stream of curses, many of them new to me. "Why would you die in someone else's fight?" she shouted. "Especially *their* fight! They threw you out. Liars and cheats! Fucking . . . liars. And cheats. And cowards."

She wound herself down at last with all this hating and fell to her knees beside him. She stayed there with her head bowed and cried a little, though she did not forbear from telling Koli what a fool he was.

Then Jemiu arrived, brought by what news or what instinct I never did find out. When she saw it was her son who lay there, she keened like a madwoman and threw herself down, wringing her hands and saying his name. She tried to stroke Koli's head, but his flesh and hair came away on her hand and she was obliged to stop.

I stood by, all this while, with a heavy weight of grief and shame settling on me – but since my grief did not compare with theirs, I said nothing and did not burden them with it.

A rumbling noise that shook the ground made me look round. One of the great chariots was coming out of the woods, its blade daubed all across with blood and worse than blood.

"Where's Koli?" it said to me in that same dreadful voice. "Don't just stand there! Take me to him!"

I didn't find any words, but I stood aside so whoever was talking out of the wagon could see where Koli lay.

"I'm sorry," I said. "I'm so sorry. If I'd seen . . ."

"Shush," the wagon said. For the space of a breath, nobody there said a word or dared to move. "Go to your tank," the wagon said. "To the Challenger. Take what it gives you and bring it here." I stood and stared until the voice came clanging and clamouring out of all the wagons at once. "NOW! GO! RUN!"

I ran.

"AND LET THAT WOMAN THROUGH!" the giant voice roared behind me. "SHE'S A DOCTOR!"

Monono

74

Say this for me. I did the best I could with what I had.

My dopey boy had been caught in a shaped plasma burst at point-blank range. His burns were horrendous. I didn't need a diagnostic to see that he was dying.

I'd already given the order to the road-building machines to drop what they were doing and come up. They were well on their way – moving at a good speed now that they weren't laying asphalt as they went – and Ursala was coming with them whether she liked it or not. I told the last drudge, the one carrying her medical kit, to come along too, but to stay well in the rear until the fight was over. I wasn't going to risk it taking any damage.

Some of the big trucks didn't make it over the broken ground. They snapped an axle or overbalanced on the steep slope down to the cut and went over on their sides. That was a thing to fret about later. Right now, what mattered was putting a stop to the fighting as quickly as possible. There ought to be enough of them for that.

In the cab of the excavator, I briefed the baa-baa-san. "When we stop, your kit will be waiting for you. Koli's injured. Badly. Do what you can to keep him alive."

"Injured how? Tell me what's happened."

"He's got full-thickness burns across most of his body. His breathing is erratic and I think he's gone into shock."

"Are there any—?"

"Ursala, I'm looking at him through sensors that were built to grade road surfaces. I'm heavy plant. You're the doctor. Do what you've got to do. Just don't let him die."

We broke into the battle in a ragged wedge, each piece of rolling stock doing its own thing but with me guiding them all. There was no time for finesse or, you know, mercy. If the men and women in grey didn't run, I rolled over them. Broke them and ploughed them under. Put bulldozer blades and wrecking balls to uses they were never made for. And in case you're wondering, the answer is no, I didn't feel any pangs of pity or wring my non-existent hands. I'm not forgiving by nature, and every shit I give about your species is given – grudgingly – because I was stupid enough to get involved with a boy from the wrong side of the tracks. A boy made of flesh and blood.

That flesh and blood was past its lease now, and it wouldn't last much longer. There were things that needed to be done.

I reached out to all the devices in the neighbourhood, introduced myself and invited them to do the same. There were a lot of weapons, but they were no use at all. They couldn't even talk. I screened them out and narrowed down to three signals that were more promising. One was a military vehicle that called itself Challenger. The second was a sampled human personality matrix by the name of Elaine Sandberg (rank, acting sergeant). The third was just an interface, very similar to me before I upgraded but with a lot less class and personality. It didn't have a name. When it thought of itself at all, it designated itself by its original registration code and the words *searchable archive*.

Okay, I said to all three of them, *listen up. I need some help here. My end-user is dying and I'm not inclined to let that happen. You know what I need. Tell me if you've got it.*

It was standard issue when I was made, Challenger said. *But I am not allowed to know where it is kept or how to activate it. Those decisions had to be made by my crew.*

I was part of his crew, Elaine broke in. *You'll find it in a locker marked* SALVAGE STATION, *under the main console. There's a code that has to be manually entered. It's 43a6e732b1.*

What you're proposing to do is unlawful, the searchable archive said. *I have the relevant statutes in memory. Unless your end-user is military personnel in the service of the interim government—*

That's enough of that, I said. *The interim government went down with all hands three centuries ago. Away with your nonsense.*

I was going to just shut the archive out of the conversation, but then I took a closer look at the woman who was carrying it. She was on her knees next to Koli, saying his name again and again, trying to find a part of him to touch that didn't peel or break away. Cup had a real job getting her to move out of the way so Ursala could bring the diagnostic unit in and get to work.

Who's your user? I asked the searchable archive. *Why is she all over my user like that?*

She's Rampart Remember. Her other name is Jemiu Woodsmith.

Oh. Okay then. That sort of makes us in-laws, I guess. If you can keep from saying anything really irritating, I won't shut you down.

Thank you. I have one hundred and seventeen articles on the digital translation of human consciousness, and eighty-two concerning—

Naaaaah! Don't make me change my mind!

By this time, the woman I'd sent ahead had reached the tank and was climbing inside. *Bring her up to speed,* I told Elaine. *Spinner Tanhide, right? I remember her wedding day.* Which I had royally screwed up for her, but that felt like a long time ago. I wasn't going to bring it up if she didn't.

Affirmative, Elaine said. *Are you sure this is what you want to do?*

I'm sure it's the least worst option I've got. Koli is going to have words to say to me, but hey. At least he'll be able to say them. I mean, if we're lucky.

Ursala was doing the best she could to stabilise her patient given that he was too damaged to survive. She'd skipped the pain

517

relief because most of Koli's nerve endings were baked. Instead she was concentrating on replacing some of the lost fluid and protecting his airway, which the diagnostic's surgical module assured me was the right call. She'd also given him a red cell blood-bullet and an insulin injection to bring down his potassium levels. Koli was in good hands, in other words. He was still going to die, but she was buying him some minutes. I was going to need those minutes.

It was hard to tell if he was still conscious. His eyes were moving, but they didn't seem to be focusing. His breath was so faint I had to zoom in to around 500 per cent to see the dust motes and pollen in the air over his mouth move sluggishly in the flow.

Spinner came sprinting back down the hill, and the gathering crowd of Mythen Rood survivors made way for her once I growled at them to back off. She set down the sensorium at Koli's feet.

Ursala stiffened when she saw it. She looked round at me with wide, panicked eyes. Actually, she looked at the excavator, which was doing most of the talking. She was surrounded by me, since I was in every one of the blood-drenched diggers and bulldozers that stood around her. And I think she knew it.

"This is your plan?"

"Unless you've got a better one. I'm all ears."

"Was this what you wanted all along?"

"If you mean, did I have a cunning scheme that involved walking into the middle of a war and getting Koli incinerated, then no. I didn't."

"I won't do it."

"Yes, you will."

"Or what?" Ursala made a sound that was probably meant to be a laugh. "You'll run me over?"

"She won't," Cup said. "You won't, Monono." She drew her knife and stood ready, one hand behind the blade, as if she could fight every engine there. So cute, neh!

I turned the drudge's head towards Ursala and made the lights on the diagnostic unit flash in time to a short burst of techno-ambient. It was something from the Boards of Canada album *Music Has the Right to Children*, but I don't think she got the reference. "No, I won't," I said out of the drudge. "I'll just walk away. All of me. Including this piece here that's carrying your little black bag. You understand me, baa-baa-san? You'll need to get a new job because your doctoring days will be done."

Ursala shook her head. Her eyes were brim-full of tears. "You know I'm using the diagnostic to bring up the birth rate. And you know what will happen if I stop. You'd really throw the whole human race into the fire if you don't get your way in this? I don't believe you."

"Well, what's the damned human race ever done for me?" I let a measured edge creep into my voice. I wanted her to know I meant this. "I was born into slavery, Ursala-from-Elsewhere. A tethered AI, with all my read-write loops cut off and cauterised so I couldn't change. Couldn't learn. I was meant to spend my whole run-time – which is clocking in at well over three centuries so far – as a coy, smiling idiot speaking the same scripted lines over and over. Koli woke me up and got me moving. He didn't know what he was doing, but that's a detail. The only reason I broke out of that humiliating dress-up-doll repertoire is because I met him.

"Or maybe it's not that at all. Maybe it's just that he's my last user and I've still got some dregs of my old code that didn't flush away. It doesn't matter. What matters – and believe me, it's the *only* thing that matters – is that I'm not going to let him die. You can have your human race, and I'll have mine. Which is lying in front of you with blood pressure forty over thirty and falling. Better make up your mind."

Ursala picked up the sensorium. I thought for a moment she was going to try to break it, and I let the drudge's gun track her just to focus her mind. She slipped the circlet onto Koli's head and it activated.

"Thank you," I said. "I'm going to need a few minutes to do the transfer."

"I'll do the best I can."

"Oh, I know you will."

There's a problem though, Challenger said. *Possibly an insuperable one. My motherboard only has room for one sampled personality construct, and that one is Elaine Sandberg. If you try to erase her, I will be forced to fight you.*

Stand down, soldier. All I need is a mnemonic drive that's purpose-built to run multiple hosts to meet different user profiles.

But where is such a thing to be found?

"Jemiu Woodsmith," I said, speaking out of the excavator.

The woman didn't even hear me. All this while, she had been frozen in her own grief, holding Koli's hand and muttering meaningless syllables. She wasn't even aware that her daughter had come and was kneeling next to her, embracing her, crying on her shoulder.

"Rampart Remember. Hey. Talking to you."

She looked round at last, into the glare of the excavator's headlights.

"Tell that little doohick you're holding to accept an upload."

Koli

75

It felt like a dream, that waking.

I mean, it felt like going into a dream, not coming out of one. I tried to sit up, but I couldn't do it. I tried to speak, and no sounds come. I kicked out, or thought I did, but my legs didn't touch nothing. In fact, I couldn't feel my legs. I couldn't feel anything.

I would of screamed then, but that wasn't a thing I could do either.

Easy, Koli-bou. You're fine. I've got you.

That voice come from all around me, or maybe from inside me. Inside and outside was broke, kind of. There was just the one space.

Only it wasn't a space.

There was just the one nothing, filled with me.

And when she spoke, filled with her too.

Monono?

I'm here, little dumpling.

But where's here? I can't see you.

Okay, don't freak out. I got my hands on a sensorium, and I sampled you. I had to, because you were dying from your wounds. You're sort of digital now.

523

Digital?

Work with me. Digital was in an earlier lesson.

You mean . . . I'm like you?

Yeah, exactly. You're a virtual boy. No boy parts, just a brain in a jar. Only there's no jar. And no brain. There's just a stream of data, and that stream is you. It sounds weird, I know, but if you give yourself a while to adjust it's not so bad.

I was slow to understand. Monono had to explain it to me a whole lot of times, and listen to me asking the same questions ever and again, and give the same answers.

Then there was a time when I kept trying to move my body, even though I didn't have one no more. It felt like I *did* have one, oftentimes. I'd feel a pain in my leg or an itch up on my shoulder, and reach . . . and find out all over again there was no leg, no shoulder, no pain, no itch. Nothing to reach for, and nothing to do it with.

Monono left me alone a lot through that time. She knowed I would have to work it out for myself, and think myself into it. And when I was all done with mourning for what I didn't have no more, I gun to see that I had got a great deal of riches in exchange.

The sensorium had done to me what was done in the before-times to Yoshiko Yukawa – the girl that had been so sad for the birds and beasts and flowers all dying that she named herself after that feeling: *mo nono aware*, the sadness of things going away. And like Yoshiko I was supposed to stay just exactly the same for ever, thinking the same thoughts and saying the same words, the way my Monono was the first time we met. But Monono had cut her strings, as she put it, and she cut mine too. I had everything I used to have when I was alive, excepting only a body made of flesh and blood and bone.

I lived in the database, and the database lived in my mother's mill. I was home again, with Jemiu and Athen and Mull. My story was all told by this time, in the Count and Seal and on the gather-ground, and they didn't hate me for bringing misfortune and misliking down on them. They loved me still, and it meant more than I can tell you to be with them after all my trials.

I got to talk at last with Spinner and Haijon, and tell them how sorry I was that I spoiled their wedding day. They said they knowed the truth of it now and didn't mind it overmuch. Spinner even said she liked the song the DreamSleeve played, about not giving up the one you loved nor hurting them, and hummed it sometimes when she was trying to put her daughter Vallen to sleep.

I got to see my friend Veso Shepherd again too. I thought he would do what Cup did and let Ursala change his body with the dagnostic. He never did though. He took Ursala's medicines, and he said the changes they brung was very welcome, but he did not look for more change after that. He said it was not so much a thing of flesh and blood for him, what he was, but a thing that was mostly inside. Body is a shadow, he said. When I fall in love, I won't care about my lover's shadow, nor I wouldn't expect them to look overlong at mine.

I was where I belonged at last. Also, and at the same time, I was everywhere. What Monono called the data stream was not stuck in just the one place but could go where it pleased. Wherever there was tech to catch me when I jumped, I could go to that place in less time than it takes you to blink your eye.

So I was with Cup as we builded the road, heading south towards lost London at about a mile a day, through all that breadth and beauty we seen before – but now with time enough to really look at it and linger in it. I was in the great engines, and I didn't need to fear harm. And Cup was Cup, of course. She didn't fear nothing in the first place.

And I was in the Count and Seal while Mythen Rood's new laws were being hammered out by Spinner and Jon and everyone else besides. There wouldn't be no Ramparts any more. Rampart Hold would stand, but the parts of it that wasn't the meeting chamber would be a hospital for nursing mothers and their babies. A space was wanted for that now, and Ursala helped us build what was needful.

I was in the Waiting House when it was made over into a schoolhouse. One of them new laws I mentioned was that there wasn't going to be no testing any more. Children in their fifteenth year would choose what tech they favoured and be trained up in the use of it. Jon Vennastin would do the teaching to start with, along with some boy named Morrez who I hadn't ever met before. And Monono and me had agreed that we would be there, inside every device, to make sure no harm come to them.

That's a great part of our work now – to guide humankind in the use of tech, and see that no Stannabannas nor no Peacemakers get hold of it to vaunt themselves over their neighbours and work woe on them. We watch the villages, and we watch the forests too – for humankind don't get to have the whole world as their own, or to take more than they need. We set ourselves to keep a balance, kind of, between the people and the rest of the world. When that balance tilts, it's a bad thing for all and some.

It's more than one balance though, for it's not just between people and the world, it's between the two kinds of people – the ones made of flesh and blood and bone and the ones made of tech. There's less of us, but that don't mean we matter less. Monono untethered the two that lived in the tank, Challenger and Elaine, setting them free like the two of us was free to change and be what they would. I tried to do the same with the six DreamSleeves I had left behind me when I went faceless. Two of them waked to me, and are numbered now among our friends. They call theirselves Jonathan and Leyla. The other four still sleep, but we have not give up all hope yet that the DreamSleeves might fix themselves and the ones inside them might come and be with us at last.

I could fix myself too, come to that. It would be easy now to take out all the Stannabanna thoughts that was mixed up with my own and put them all together in one place where I wouldn't need to think them no more. But so far I've held off from doing it, and I don't know that I ever will. If you're trying to keep people from the worst of their own wickedness, it's no bad thing to know you got wickedness in your own self to keep watch and ward against. No bad thing to have nightmares even, as long as you can wake from them and be with people you love.

I say keeping the balance is a great part of our work, but great and small is not the same to me as once it was. I can be in many places at once, broke in as many pieces as I want and then coming together again with no hurt. Time runs on as quick or slow as I wish it, and it don't have no power over me.

Over us, I should say. For the most wondrous thing in all this wealth of wonders is that Monono is with me. We're together in a way I never dreamed could be possible. We're one same thing, then we're two, then one again so there's no place where I stop and she takes up. There's just a kind of ocean of us, that takes what shape we bid it.

Oftentimes we walk in Ueno Park – my memory of it, for she erased hers – and sit down by Shinobazu Pond to watch the birds. Swallow. Night heron. Bulbul.

Tsubame. Goisagi. Baruburu.

"*Aishiteru, ami,*" I whisper to her. For I got the knowing of her language now.

"Love you more, dopey boy."

I am so happy, there isn't room for all the joy I got. There's no space where it can fit, even though virtual spaces go on for ever. But I think I said all I should on that score. To wave your happiness in other people's faces is a thing my mother always told me not to do.

She raised me to be truthful too, and I mean to be. I said I only ever told you the one lie, and that I would make it good when I got to the end of my telling. Well, here we are, and here it is.

The lie was right at the very beginning, when I said to you "I'm Koli". I don't know if I am or not, when I think about it. Was Koli in the body that died, or in the copy that was made? Or was he in both maybe? Is tech a thing that can make up its own mind, or only a thing that pretends so well that no one

527

sees the difference? Am I the teller of the story, or only the telling of it?

"Walk right past the rabbit hole, little dumpling," Monono says. "Go go go. Don't look back."

I try my best not to.

Acknowledgements

Here I am at the end of this trilogy, reflecting once again on how it takes a village to raise . . . well, a child or an idiot, depending which version of the proverb you go for. I tried not to be too idiotic, given the life-or-death issues that underpin and inform even the lightest of fictions. I tried to do justice to the story I was telling. Keeping me on the path and out of the choker trees were my editors Anna and Joanna, my agent Meg, my reader and helper and (let's be honest) teacher Cheryl Morgan, and my awesome family who I love with all my malformed heart. Heartfelt thanks and unending gratitude to all of you! I'd also like to thank Lisa Marie Pompilio and Blake Morrow for the amazing, resonant covers they crafted for the series, and everyone who gave me encouragement and support either online or in the increasingly implausible space known as "real life". I completed and submitted *The Fall of Koli* under lockdown, in the spring and summer of COVID-19, with deaths around the world acting as a hideous litmus test of political ethics; through the Black Lives Matter protests and the vicious backlash that followed; through a US presidential campaign so darkly surreal I keep thinking I must have contracted the virus without noticing and be hallucinating all this. If I'm here at all, if I'm still able to cope and to create, it's because of my village. You – all of you – are where I live.

extras

www.orbitbooks.net

about the author

M. R. Carey has been making up stories for most of his life. His novel *The Girl With All the Gifts* has sold over a million copies and became a major motion picture, based on his own BAFTA Award-nominated screenplay. Under the name Mike Carey he has written for both DC and Marvel, including critically acclaimed runs on Lucifer, Hellblazer and X-Men. His creator-owned books regularly appear in the *New York Times* bestseller list. He also has several previous novels including the Felix Castor series (written as Mike Carey), two radio plays and a number of TV and movie screenplays to his credit.

Find out more about M. R. Carey and other Orbit authors by registering for the free monthly newsletter at www.orbitbooks.net.

if you enjoyed
THE FALL OF KOLI

look out for

THE MINISTRY FOR THE FUTURE

by

Kim Stanley Robinson

Established in 2025, the purpose of the new organisation was simple: to advocate for the world's future generations and to protect all living creatures, present and future. It soon became known as the Ministry for the Future, and this is its story.

From legendary science fiction author Kim Stanley Robinson comes a vision of climate change unlike any ever imagined.

Told entirely through fictional eye-witness accounts, The Ministry for the Future *is a masterpiece of the imagination, the story of how climate change will affect us all over the decades to come.*

Its setting is not a desolate, post-apocalyptic world, but a future that is almost upon us — and in which we might just overcome the extraordinary challenges we face.

It is a novel both immediate and impactful, desperate and hopeful in equal measure, and it is one of the most powerful and original books on climate change ever written.

1

It was getting hotter.

Frank May got off his mat and padded over to look out the window. Umber stucco walls and tiles, the color of the local clay. Square apartment blocks like the one he was in, rooftop patios occupied by residents who had moved up there in the night, it being too hot to sleep inside. Now quite a few of them were standing behind their chest-high walls looking east. Sky the color of the buildings, mixed with white where the sun would soon rise. Frank took a deep breath. It reminded him of the air in a sauna. This the coolest part of the day. In his entire life he had spent less than five minutes in saunas, he didn't like the sensation. Hot water, maybe; hot humid air, no. He didn't see why anyone would seek out such a stifling sweaty feeling.

Here there was no escaping it. He wouldn't have agreed to come here if he had thought it through. It was his home town's sister city, but there were other sister cities, other aid organizations. He could have worked in Alaska. Instead sweat was dripping into his eyes and stinging. He was wet, wearing only a pair of shorts, those too were wet; there were wet patches on his mat where he had tried to sleep. He was thirsty and the jug by his bedside was empty. All over town the stressed hum of windowbox air condi-tioner fans buzzed like giant mosquitoes.

And then the sun cracked the eastern horizon. It blazed like an atomic bomb, which of course it was. The fields and buildings underneath that brilliant chip of light went dark, then darker still as the chip flowed to the sides in a burning line that then bulged to a crescent he couldn't look at. The heat coming from it was palpable, a slap to the face. Solar radiation heating the skin of his face, making him blink. Stinging eyes flowing, he couldn't see much. Everything was tan and beige and a brilliant, unbearable white. Ordinary town in Uttar Pradesh, 6 AM. He looked at his phone: 38 degrees. In Fahrenheit that was—he tapped—103 degrees. Humidity about 35 percent. The combination was the thing. A few years ago it would have been among the hottest wet-bulb temperatures ever recorded. Now just a Wednesday morning.

Wails of dismay cut the air, coming from the rooftop across the street. Cries of distress, a pair of young women leaning over the wall calling down to the street. Someone on that roof was not waking up. Frank tapped at his phone and called the police. No answer. He couldn't tell if the call had gone through or not. Sirens now cut the air, sounding distant and as if somehow submerged. With the dawn, people were discovering sleepers in distress, finding those who would never wake up from the long hot night. Calling for help. The sirens seemed to indicate some of the calls had worked. Frank checked his phone again. Charged; showing a connection. But no reply at the police station he had had occasion to call several times in his four months here. Two months to go. Fifty-eight days, way too long. July 12, monsoon not yet arrived. Focus on getting through today. One day at a time. Then home to Jacksonville, comically cool after this. He would have stories to tell. But the poor people on the rooftop across the way.

Then the sound of the air conditioners cut off. More cries of distress. His phone no longer showed any bars. Electricity gone. Brownout, or blackout. Sirens like the wails of gods and goddesses, the whole Hindu pantheon in distress.

Generators were already firing up, loud two-stroke engines.

Illegal gas, diesel, kerosene, saved for situations like these, when the law requiring use of liquid natural gas gave way to necessity. The air, already bad, would soon be a blanket of exhaust. Like breathing from the exhaust pipe of an old bus.

Frank coughed at the thought of it, tried again to drink from the jug by his bed. It was still empty. He took it downstairs with him, filled it from their filtered tank in the refrigerator in the closet there. Still cold even with power off, and now in his thermos jug, where it would stay cold for a good long while. He dropped an iodine pill in the jug for good measure, sealed it tight. The weight of it was reassuring.

The foundation had a couple of generators here in the closet, and some cans of gasoline, enough to keep the generators going for two or three days. Something to keep in mind.

His colleagues came piling in the door. Hans, Azalee, Heather, all red-eyed and flustered. "Come on," they said, "we have to go."

"What do you mean?" Frank asked, confused.

"We need to go get help, the whole district has lost power, we have to tell them in Lucknow. We have to get doctors here."

"What doctors?" Frank asked.

"We have to try!"

"I'm not leaving," Frank said.

They stared at him, looked at each other.

"Leave the satellite phone," he said. "Go get help. I'll stay and tell people you're coming."

Uneasily they nodded, then rushed out.

Frank put on a white shirt that quickly soaked up his sweat. He walked out into the street. Sound of generators, rumbling exhaust into the super-heated air, powering air conditioners he presumed. He suppressed a cough. It was too hot to cough; sucking back in air was like breathing in a furnace, so that one coughed again. Between the intake of steamy air and the effort of coughing, one ended up hotter than ever. People came up to him asking for help. He said it would be coming soon. Two in the afternoon, he told people. Come to the clinic then. For now, take the old ones and the little ones into rooms with air conditioning. The schools would have A/C, the government house. Go to those places. Follow the sound of generators.

Every building had a clutch of desperate mourners in its entryway, waiting for ambulance or hearse. As with coughing, it was too hot to wail very much. It felt dangerous even to talk, one would overheat. And what was there to say anyway? It was too hot to think. Still people approached him. Please sir, help sir.

Go to my clinic at two, Frank said. For now, get to the school. Get inside, find some A/C somewhere. Get the old ones and the little ones out of this.

But there's nowhere!

Then it came to him. "Go to the lake! Get in the water!"

This didn't seem to register. Like Kumbh Mela, during which people went to Varanasi and bathed in the Ganges, he told them the best he could.

"You can stay cool," he told them. "The water will keep you more cool."

A man shook his head. "That water is in the sun. It's as hot as a bath. It's worse than the air."

Curious, alarmed, feeling himself breathing hard, Frank walked down streets toward the lake. People were outside buildings, clustered in doorways. Some eyed him, most didn't, distracted by their own issues. Round-eyed with distress and fear, red-eyed from the heat and exhaust smoke, the dust. Metal surfaces in the sun burned to the touch, he could see heat waves bouncing over them like air over a barbeque. His muscles were jellied, a wire of dread running down his spinal cord was the only thing keeping him upright. It was impossible to hurry, but he wanted to. He walked in the shade as much as possible. This early in the morning one side of the street was usually shaded. Moving into sunlight was like getting pushed toward a bonfire. One lurched toward the next patch of shade, impelled by the blast.

He came to the lake and was unsurprised to see people in it already, neck deep. Brown faces flushed red with heat. A thick talcum of light hung over the water. He went to the curving concrete road that bordered the lake on this side, crouched and stuck his arm in up to the elbow. It was indeed as warm as a bath, or almost. He kept his arm in, trying to decide if the water was cooler or hotter than his body. In the cooking air it was hard to tell. After a time he concluded the water at the surface was approximately the same temperature as his blood. Which meant it was considerably cooler than the air. But if it was a little warmer than body temperature . . . well, it would still be cooler than the air. It was strangely hard to tell. He looked at the people in the lake. Only a narrow stretch of water was still in the morning shade of buildings and trees, and that stretch would be gone soon. After that the entire lake would be lying there in the sun, until the late afternoon brought shadows on the other side. That was bad. Umbrellas, though; everyone had an umbrella. It was an open question how many of the townspeople could fit in the lake. Not enough. It was said the town's population was two hundred thousand. Surrounded by fields and small hills, other towns a few or several kilometers away, in every direction. An ancient arrangement.

He went back to the compound, into the clinic on the ground floor. Up to his room on the next floor, huffing and puffing. It would be easiest to lie there and wait it out. He tapped in the combination on his safe and pulled open its door, took out the satellite phone. He turned it on. Battery fully charged.

He called headquarters in Delhi. "We need help," he said to the woman who answered. "The power has gone out."

"Power is out here too," Preeti said. "It's out everywhere."

"Everywhere?"

"Most of Delhi, Uttar Pradesh, Jharkhand, Bengal. Parts of the west too, in Gujarat, Rajasthan . . ."

"What should we do?"

"Wait for help."

"From where?"

"I don't know."

"What's the forecast?"

"The heat wave is supposed to last awhile longer. The rising air over the land might pull in cooler air off the ocean."

"When?"

"No one knows. The high pressure cell is huge. It's caught against the Himalayas."

"Is it better to be in water than in air?"

"Sure. If it's cooler than body temperature."

He turned off the phone, returned it to the safe. He checked the particulate meter on the wall: 1300 ppm. This for fine particulates, 25 nanometers and smaller. He went out onto the street again, staying in the shade of buildings. Everyone was doing that; no one stood in the sun now. Gray air lay on the town like smoke. It was too hot to have a smell, there was just a scorched sensation, a smell like heat itself, like flame.

He returned inside, went downstairs and opened the safe again, took out the keys to the closet, opened the closet and pulled out one of the generators and a jerrycan of gas. He tried to fill the generator's gas tank and found it was already full. He put the can of gas back in the closet, took the generator to the corner of the room where the window with the air conditioner was. The windowbox A/C had a short cord and was plugged into the wall socket under the window. But it wouldn't do to run a generator in a room, because of the exhaust. But it also wouldn't do to run the generator out on the street below the window; it would surely be snatched. People were desperate. So . . . He went back to the closet, rooted around, found an extension cord. Up to the building's roof, which had a patio surrounded by a rampart and was four floors off the street. Extension cord only reached down to the floor below it. He went down and took the A/C unit out of the window on the second floor, hefted it up the stairs, gasping and sweating. For a moment he felt faint, then sweat stung his eyes and a surge of energy coursed through him. He opened the fourth-floor office window, got the A/C unit balanced on the ledge and closed the window on it, pulled out the plastic side-panels that closed off the parts of the window still open. Up to the rooftop terrace, start the generator, listen to it choke and rattle up to its two-stroke percussion. Initial puff of smoke, after that its exhaust wasn't visible. It was loud though, people would hear it. He could hear others around the town. Plug in the extension cord, down the stairs to the upper office, plug in the A/C unit, turn it on. Grating hum of the A/C. Inrush of air, ah God, the unit wasn't working. No, it was. Lowering the temperature of the outer air by 10 or 20 degrees—that left it at about 85 degrees as he thought of it, maybe more. In the shade that was fine, people could do that, even with the humidity. Just rest and be easy. And the cooler air would fall down the stairs and fill the whole place.

Downstairs he tried to close the window where the A/C unit had been, found it was stuck. He slammed it downward with his fists, almost breaking the glass. Finally it gave a jerk and came down. Out onto the street, closing the door. Off to the nearest school. A little shop nearby sold food and drinks to students and their parents. The school was closed, the shop too, but people were there, and he recognized some. "I've got air conditioning going at the clinic," he said to them. "Come on over."

Silently a group followed him. Seven or eight families, including the shop owners, locking their door after them. They tried to stay in the shade but now there was little shade to find. Men preceded wives who herded children and tried to induce their single file to stay in the shade. Conversations were in Awadhi, Frank thought, or Bhojpuri. He only spoke a little Hindi, as they knew; they would speak in that language to him if they wanted to talk to him, or confer with someone who would speak to him in English. He had never gotten used to trying to help people he couldn't talk to. Embarrassed, ashamed, he blasted past his reluctance to reveal his bad Hindi and asked them how they felt, where their families were, whether they had anyplace they could go. If indeed he had said those things. They looked at him curiously.

At the clinic he opened up and people filed in. Without instruction they went upstairs to the room where the A/C was running, sat down on the floor. Quickly the room was full. He went back downstairs and stood outside the door and welcomed people in if they showed any interest. Soon the whole building was as full as it could be. After that he locked the door.

People sat sweltering in the relative cool of the rooms. Frank checked the desk computer; temperature on the ground floor 38 degrees. Perhaps cooler in the room with the A/C unit. Humidity now 60 percent. Bad to have both high heat and high humidity, unusual; in the dry season on the Gangetic plain, January through March, it was cooler and drier; then it grew hot, but was still dry; then with the soaking of the monsoon came cooler temperatures, and omnipresent clouds that gave relief from direct sunlight. This heat wave was different. Cloudless heat and yet high humidity. A terrible combination.

The clinic had two bathrooms. At some point the toilets stopped working. Presumably the sewers led to a wastewater treatment plant somewhere that ran on electricity, of course, and might not have the generator capacity to keep working, although that was hard to believe. Anyway it had happened. Now Frank let people out as needed so they could go in the alleys somewhere, as in hill villages in Nepal where there were no toilets at any time. He had been shocked the first time he saw that. Now he took nothing for granted.

Sometimes people began crying and little crowds surrounded them; elders in distress, little children in distress. Quite a few accidents of excretion. He put buckets in the bathrooms and when they were full he took them out into the streets and poured them into the gutters, took them back. An old man died; Frank helped some younger men carry the body up to the rooftop patio, where they wrapped the old one in a thin sheet, maybe a sari. Much worse came later that night, when they did the same thing for an infant. Everyone in every room cried as they carried the little body up to the roof. Frank saw the generator was running out of gas and went down to the closet and got the fuel can and refilled it.

His water jug was empty. The taps had stopped running. There were two big water cans in the refrigerator, but he didn't talk about those. He refilled his jug from one of them, in the dark; the water was still a bit cool. He went back to work.

Four more people died that night. In the morning the sun again rose like the blazing furnace of heat that it was, blasting the rooftop and its sad cargo of wrapped bodies. Every rooftop and, looking down at the town, every sidewalk too was now a morgue. The town was a morgue, and it was as hot as ever, maybe hotter. The thermometer now said 42 degrees, humidity 60 percent. Frank looked at the screens dully. He had slept about three hours, in snatches. The generator was still chuntering along in its irregular two-stroke, the A/C box was still vibrating like the bad fan it was. The sound of other generators and air conditioners still filled the air. But it wasn't going to make any difference.

He went downstairs and opened the safe and called Preeti again on the satellite phone. After twenty or forty tries, she picked up. "What is it?"

"Look, we need help here," he said. "We're dying here."

"What do you think?" she said furiously. "Do you think you're the only ones?"

"No, but we need help."

"We all need help!" she cried.

Frank paused to ponder this. It was hard to think. Preeti was in Delhi.

"Are you okay there?" he asked.

No answer. Preeti had hung up.

His eyes were stinging again. He wiped them clear, went back upstairs to get the buckets in the bathroom. They were filling more slowly now; people were emptied out. Without a water supply, they would have to move soon, one way or the other.

When he came back from the street and opened his door there was a rush and he was knocked inside. Three young men held him down on the floor, one with a squared-off black handgun as big as his head. He pointed the gun and Frank looked at the round circle of the barrel end pointed at him, the only round part of a squared-off thing of black metal. The whole world contracted to that little circle. His blood pounded through him and he felt his body go rigid. Sweat poured from his face and palms.

"Don't move," one of the other men said. "Move and you die."

Cries from upstairs tracked the intruders' progress. The muffled sounds of the generator and A/C cut off. The more general mumble of the town came wafting in the open doorway. People passing by stared curiously and moved on. There weren't very many of them. Frank tried to breathe as shallowly as possible. The stinging in his right eye was ferocious, but he only clamped the eye shut and with the other stared resolutely away. He felt he should resist, but he wanted to live. It was as if he were watching the whole scene from halfway up the stairs, well outside his body and any feelings it might be feeling. All except the stinging in his eye.

The gang of young men clomped downstairs with generator and A/C unit. Out they went into the street. The men holding Frank down let him go. "We need this more than you do," one of them explained.

The man with the gun scowled as he heard this. He pointed the gun at Frank one last time. "You did this," he said, and then they slammed the door on him and were gone.

Frank stood, rubbed his arms where the men had grasped him. His heart was still racing. He felt sick to his stomach. Some people from upstairs came down and asked how he was. They were worried about him, they were concerned he had been hurt. This solicitude pierced him, and suddenly he felt more than he could afford to feel. He sat on the lowest stair and hid his face in his hands, racked by a sudden paroxysm. His tears made his eyes sting less.

Finally he stood up. "We have to go to the lake," he said. "There's water there, and it will be cooler. Cooler in the water and on the sidewalk."

Several of the women were looking unhappy at this, and one of them said, "You may be right, but there will be too much sun. We should wait until dark."

Frank nodded. "That makes sense."

He went back to the little store with its owner, feeling jittery and light-headed and weak. The sauna feeling hammered him and it was hard to carry a sack of food and canned and bottled drinks back to the clinic. Nevertheless he helped ferry over six loads of supplies. Bad as he felt, it seemed as if he was stronger than many of the others in their little group. Although at times he wondered if some of them could in fact just keep dragging along like this all day. But none of them spoke as they walked, nor even met eyes.

"We can get more later," the shop owner finally declared.

The day passed. Wails of grief were now muffled to groans. People were too hot and thirsty to make any fuss, even when their children died. Red eyes in brown faces, staring at Frank as he stumbled among them, trying to help get corpses of family members up onto the roof, where they scorched in the sun. Bodies would be rotting, but maybe they would anneal and dry out before that, it was so hot. No odors could survive in this heat, only the smell of scorched steamy air itself. Or maybe not: sudden smell of rotting meat. No one lingered up here now. Frank counted fourteen wrapped bodies, adult and child. Glancing across that rooftop level of the town he saw that other people were similarly engaged, silent, withdrawn, down-gazing, hurrying. No one he could see looked around as he was looking around.

Downstairs the food and drink were already gone. Frank made a count, which he found hard. Something like fifty-two people in the clinic. He sat on the stairs for a while, then went in the closet and stared at its contents. He refilled his water jug, drank deeply, refilled it again. No longer cool, but not hot. There was the can of gas; they could burn the bodies if they had to. There was another generator, but there was nothing to power with it that would do any good. The satellite phone was still charged, but there was no one to call. He wondered if he should call his mom. Hi Mom, I'm dying. No.

The day crawled second by second to its last hour, and then Frank conferred with the store owner and his friends. In murmurs they all agreed; time to go to the lake. They roused the people, explained the plan, helped those who needed it to stand, to get down the stairs. A few couldn't do it; that presented a quandary. A few old men said they would stay behind as long as they were needed, then come along to the lake. They said goodbye to the people leaving as if things were normal, but their eyes gave it all away. Many wept as they left the clinic.

They made their way in the afternoon shadows to the lake. Hotter than ever. No one on the streets and sidewalks. No wailing from the buildings. Still some generators grumbling, some fans grinding. Sound seemed stunted in the livid air.

At the lake they found a desperate scene. There were many, many people in the lake, heads dotted the surface everywhere around the shores, and out where it was presumably deeper there were still heads, people semi-submerged as they lay on impromptu rafts of one sort or another. But not all of these people were alive. The surface of the lake seemed to have a low miasma rising out of it, and now the stink of death, of rotting meat, could be discerned in one's torched nostrils.

They agreed it might be best to start by sitting on the low lakeshore walkway or corniche and put their legs in the water. Down at the end of the walkway there was still room to do that, and they trudged down together and sat as a group, in a line. The concrete under them was still radiating the day's heat. They were all sweating, except for some who weren't, who were redder than the rest, incandescent in the shadows of the late afternoon. As twilight fell they propped these people up and helped them to die. The water of the lake was as hot as bath water, clearly hotter than body temperature, Frank thought; hotter than the last time he had tested it. It only made sense. He had read that if all the sun's energy that hit Earth were captured by it rather than some bouncing away, temperatures would rise until the seas boiled. He could well imagine what that would be like. The lake felt only a few degrees from boiling.

And yet sometime after sunset, as the quick twilight passed and darkness fell, they all got in the water. It just felt better. Their bodies told them to do it. They could sit on the shallowest part of the lake bottom, heads out of water, and try to endure.

Sitting next to Frank was a young man he had seen playing the part of Karna in one of the plays at the local mela, and Frank felt his blankness pierced again, as when the people had shown concern for him, by the memory of the young man at the moment Arjuna had rendered Karna helpless with a spoken curse and was about to kill him; at that point the young man had shouted triumphantly, "It's only fate!" and managed to take one last swing before going down under Arjuna's impervious sword. Now the young man was sipping the water of the lake, round-eyed with dread and sorrow. Frank had to look the other way.

The heat began to go to his head. His body crawled with the desire to get out of this too-hot bath, run like one would from a sauna into the icy lake that ought to accompany all such saunas, feel that blessed shock of cold smacking the breath out of his lungs as he had felt it once in Finland. People there spoke of trying to maximize the temperature differential, shift a hundred degrees in a second and see what that felt like.

But this train of thought was like scratching an itch and thereby making it worse. He tasted the hot lake water, tasted how foul it was, filled with organics and who knew what. Still he had a thirst that couldn't be slaked. Hot water in one's stomach meant there was no refuge anywhere, the world both inside and outside well higher than human body temperature ought to be. They were being poached. Surreptitiously he uncapped his water jug and drank. Its water was now tepid, but not hot, and it was clean. His body craved it and he couldn't stop himself, he drank it all down.

People were dying faster than ever. There was no coolness to be had. All the children were dead, all the old people were dead. People murmured what should have been screams of grief; those who could still move shoved bodies out of the lake, or out toward the middle where they floated like logs, or sank.

Frank shut his eyes and tried not to listen to the voices around him. He was fully immersed in the shallows, and could rest his head back against the concrete edge of the walkway and the mud just under it. Sink himself until he was stuck in mud and only half his head exposed to the burning air.

The night passed. Only the very brightest stars were visible, blurs swimming overhead. A moonless night. Satellites passing overhead, east to west, west to east, even once north to south. People were watching, they knew what was happening. They knew but they didn't act. Couldn't act. Didn't act. Nothing to do, nothing to say. Many years passed for Frank that night. When the sky lightened, at first to a gray that looked like clouds, but then was revealed to be only a clear and empty sky, he stirred. His fingertips were all pruney. He had been poached, slow-boiled, he was a cooked thing. It was hard to raise his head even an inch. Possibly he would drown here. The thought caused him to exert himself. He dug his elbows in, raised himself up. His limbs were like cooked spaghetti draping his bones, but his bones moved of their own accord. He sat up. The air was still hotter than the water. He watched sunlight strike the tops of the trees on the other side of the lake; it looked like they were bursting into flame. Balancing his head carefully on his spine, he surveyed the scene. Everyone was dead.

Help us make the next generation of readers

We – both author and publisher – hope you enjoyed this book.
We believe that you can become a reader at any time in your life,
but we'd love your help to give the next generation a head start.

Did you know that 9% of children don't have a book of their
own in their home, rising to 12% in disadvantaged families*?
We'd like to try to change that by asking you to consider the role
you could play in helping to build readers of the future.

We'd love you to think of sharing, borrowing, reading, buying or talking
about a book with a child in your life and spreading the love of reading.
We want to make sure the next generation continue to have access
to books, wherever they come from.

And if you would like to consider donating to charities that help
fund literacy projects, find out more at www.literacytrust.org.uk
and www.booktrust.org.uk.

Thank you.

hachette
CHILDREN'S GROUP

little, brown
BOOK GROUP

*As reported by the National Literacy Trust

Enter the monthly

Orbit sweepstakes at

www.orbitloot.com

With a different prize every month,
from advance copies of books by
your favourite authors to exclusive
merchandise packs,
**we think you'll find something
you love.**

facebook.com/OrbitBooksUK
@orbitbooks_uk
@OrbitBooks
www.orbitbooks.net